I0668568

Scent of Love

A BILLIONAIRE, ENEMIES-TO-LOVERS, SWEET ROMANCE SET IN LISBON

MARINA PACHECO

MARINA PACHECO

Copyright © 2022 by Marina Pacheco

All rights reserved.

No portion of this book may be reproduced in any form without written permission
from the publisher or author, except as permitted by U.S. copyright law.

Get my short story collection Shorties for FREE!

Sign up for my no-spam newsletter that only goes out when there is a new book or freebie available and get my collection of short stories for free, at: https://substack.com/@marinapacheco

Find out more about me and all my books: www.marinapacheco.me

Contents

CHAPTER ONE

D iana waited at the entrance to the shopping mall as a burly
security guard took her temperature with a hand-held
scanner. He gave a satisfied nod and then showed her the reading,
37.1, safe, but an odd thing for him to do. Then he stood aside to
allow her in, waving a hand at the sanitiser.

She scanned the mall as she massaged the alcohol into her
hands. There was a hotel on her right with a modern mirror-bright
chrome edged double door. A deep blue carpet led to a seating area
populated by clusters of chairs and occupied by only a couple of
guests.

Slightly further into the mall to her left was the anchor shop, a
large department store that had given pride of place to the beauty
counters filled with rainbow displays of lipsticks and eyeshadow
and row upon row of boring, mass produced perfume. It made her
glad she had to wear a mask and could barely smell their cloying
fragrances.

Her duty done, Diana walked briskly towards the escalators.
Her every sense was heightened, topmost was anxiety. This was
her first trip away from home since the lockdown had eased.
Although there were only a few people in the mall, all wearing
masks, it still felt risky.

Fear number two was about seeing Fernando. She was surprised that he'd suggested they meet here. After six months of quarantining apart, she'd expected to either go to his place in Lisbon or for him to come to hers in Sintra. She didn't really care, just as long as she got to see him. They'd argued more often as the months passed on their regular Zoom calls and she needed to speak to him in person so that they could properly clear the air and get back to the way they'd been before.

Diana glance at a highly reflective shop window as she strode passed. She hadn't dressed this smartly in months. It felt strange and a bit uncomfortable. What she saw was reassuring. Her wrap skirt curved upwards to reveal a couple of layers of pretty frills below that looked feminine but not too princessy. Her legs, that had hooked more than one boyfriend, were tanned and satin smooth, and her peep toe sandals were adorable, not that she'd expect Fernando to notice that.

She reached up to her freshly styled and coloured hair. She loved the asymmetrical cut that left her with flowing wavy, locks on the right that graded to a pixie look on the left. It was quirky, especially with the addition of a couple of wedges of purple and blue. It was something that only somebody who worked for themselves could get away with.

Thought about work made her stomach tighten with fright again. She was running dangerously short of money to the point where she'd debated the wisdom of the cost of a haircut. But no, she couldn't appear before Fernando looking frumpy.

She breathed in to fortify herself as she stepped onto the escalator and inhaled the scent of her lipstick and face cream and a slight aroma of mint from her toothpaste. That was the thing about masks, you got way too much of yourself. She hoped the mask wouldn't mess up her lipstick. It was the first time she was wearing both, and she had grave misgivings about it.

Diana would have preferred an outdoors location and wondered again why Fernando had chosen this spot as the escalator delivered her to the top floor. Diana looked around the restaurant, searching for Fernando who'd spotted her arrival and stood up, waving to her from a table beside the floor to ceiling windows that offered a spectacular view of the city. Unusually for Lisbon, it was an overcast day and even the city lacked its usual sparkle.

There he is, Diana thought, and wondered, yet again, why she felt so anxious. True, they'd been apart for longer than they'd ever been before during the lockdown, but they'd stayed in touch. Their relationship could take something like that, couldn't it?

Fernando was a little on the short side and only a touch more handsome than average. His curly hair had a tendency to flop over one eye no matter how carefully his barber trimmed and no matter which products he used. He didn't have the luxury of quirky hair. He was a lawyer. Looking spick and span in his blue, pinstripe suit with his hair short and scraped back from his face was a requirement of the job.

'Sorry I'm late,' Diana said, hurrying between tables.

Fernando gave her a slight, resigned smile but made no move towards her. Diana hadn't expected a kiss in greeting. No one did that anymore. But Fernando's hand went up to ward her off, and he took a step back.

'Are you alright?' Diana asked, coming to a halt.

Maybe he was sick. As a perfumer, she dreaded that possibility. Or maybe he just didn't want to touch her. That was alarming for a whole other set of reasons.

'I'm fine,' Fernando said, and sat down.

Diana was even more surprised and barely noticed the waiter, who pulled her chair out for her to sit down.

'I ordered some wine,' Fernando said with a tilt of his chin at the already open bottle, the empty glass beside it and the face mask lying next to that.

Now he sat down and took a deep gulp. It wasn't like him to start without her, and it gave Diana another moment of anxiety.

'Oh dear, was I that late?'

'No later than usual,' Fernando said, and then he leaned back with a sigh. 'How's your shop doing?'

'You know how it's doing,' Diana said. 'It isn't like we haven't been chatting throughout the quarantine.'

Fernando leaned forward, poured a glass of wine for Diana and murmured, 'All the same, I worry.'

That was more like the Fernando she knew.

'I'll be okay now that people can go back to visiting shops.'

'So you still haven't gone on-line?'

This was a bone of contention between them.

'I've already told you, it's a personalised perfume shop. How on earth can I create a perfect perfume for somebody if I can't meet them, test their favourite scents and see how they interact with the client's personal scent? The internet is wonderful, but it isn't quite up to that yet. But once they're a client, and I have their personal blend, I send their refills through the mail.'

'But what about the rest?' Fernando asked and snatched the menu the waiter was holding out to him in an uncharacteristically tetchy manner. 'Why don't you just create some generic perfumes that anybody can wear? I mean, that's the way most people get their perfume. It's only the rich and the unusual who get personalised perfumes.'

'Why would I make a mass produced perfume? They lack soul. They mindlessly follow fashions. Every time a new scent pops up, half the women I pass on the street smell like variations of the same thing. What's worse, it doesn't even suit them. Why smell like everybody else when you can have something special? Something that subtly blends with your own body chemistry and is uniquely and beautifully you.'

'Because it doesn't make you enough money to live on,' Fernando snapped. 'At the very least have a website and a social media presence so that people can find you.'

'My grandmother didn't need either, and she left me a loyal following of customers who wouldn't dream of going anywhere else for their scents.'

'The problem is that your customer's daughters aren't doing the same. They're buying the mass produced junk that you're so dismissive of. Not to mention that one of your grandmother's perfumes was taken by the mass producing Zeller corporation and turned into their best seller. They made a fortune from it, there's no reason you can't too.'

That hurt, and Diana had to force herself not to shout back.

'You know my grandmother never forgave the Zellers. If I could only get a tenth of the money they made from Armour, I'd have no financial problems at all.'

Fernando snorted dismissively.

'We've talked this through to death. I've already told you, you can't copyright a perfume, for the same reason you can't copyright a food recipe. Courts around the world have ruled that perfume formulas, like recipes, are functional items. As long as it's just a list of ingredients, it is legally considered a statement of facts or a utilitarian product, not creative content.'

'But it is creative.'

Diana was practically shouting. Fortunately, it was still early and only two other tables were occupied. One by an elderly couple entirely absorbed in slurping their soup. The other by an older man with a young woman. The woman seemed momentarily distracted but then returned to her food.

'Let's not argue.' Diana put down the menu she hadn't even glanced at yet. 'I've missed you so much. Let's not do this today.'

'It isn't my fault it's taken so long to meet up,' Fernando muttered.

'You know why we couldn't get together earlier. One symptom of Covid is a loss of smell. I can't risk that. You know I can't. I wouldn't be able to make my perfumes if I couldn't smell anything.'

Fernando shrugged, apparently unwilling to concede.

'Yeah... well... being apart gave me a lot of time to think.'

This was going from bad to worse, and Diana found herself holding her breath. She forced herself to breathe out and was proud of how calm she managed to sound.

'To think about what?'

'Us.'

Sound faded about Diana, and time slowed down.

'What about us?'

'The thing is, my work keeps me really busy. It's difficult to meet up anyway. If we add staying away every time there are colds and flus going around and now with this virus. I mean... is there any point?'

'Any point?'

Diana stared in astonishment at the man she always called her soulmate. He couldn't meet her eyes. That was something for a patent lawyer who was used to dealing with corporate bullyboys.

'Is there somebody else?'

'Why would there be somebody else?'

'Because there usually is.' Diana took a bigger gulp of wine than she'd intended. 'Do you think the women who come to my shop are there just to buy perfume? Perfume is sometimes a weapon to be used in the battle to lure and keep men.'

'Not this time,' Fernando said. 'I just think we should call it a day. We've had a good run, but I need–'

His stop was so abrupt it made Diana blink.

'What do you need?'

'Somebody who can support me in my career. I'm pushing to be a senior partner. I need to focus on my work and not spend time worrying about other people's failing businesses.'

'Fernando, when did you grow so self-centred?' Diana was shocked by this man who was starting to feel like a stranger. 'After five years, why are you only saying this now?'

'I was more junior before. The work wasn't as demanding.' Fernando impatiently waved away the waiter who'd appeared to take their order. 'Things change. I need something different now.'

'Something different?'

Diana's mind was a blank. She didn't know what to add.

Fernando stood up and said, 'You stay, I'll pay for the lunch, order whatever you like,' and with that he pulled his mask on and walked away.

Diana watched him go. She wanted to jump up and scream at him to stay, to not end things in this heartless way. She wanted to fall on her knees and beg for a second chance, but she didn't move. The woman at the closest table gave her a pitying look that was almost more unbearable than watching Fernando leave. Diana turned away and gazed down the avenue towards the River Tagus. Today it was an iron grey and in no way consoling.

'Would madam like to order?' the waiter asked, bowing his head in something approaching sympathy.

Diana had never felt less like eating. She lifted the bottle of wine and examined the label.

'Tell me, is this wine expensive?'

She suspected it would be. Fernando had a thing for expensive wine.

'It is one of our more expensive labels, yes ma'am,' the waiter said.

'And the man who was just here said he'd pay for my lunch, didn't he?'

'He left us his credit card details,' the waiter said.

'Fine, then,' Diana said as she emptied her glass in a couple of gulps and inhaled the sharp acidic, fruity scent of the wine, 'bring me another bottle of the same.'

Armando sat back in the hotel sofa, one of a cluster of sofas dotted about in the lounge, all blue velvet chairs and glass tables. It looked fancy but was going to date rapidly. He had one elegant leg crossed over the other and examined the toes of a perfectly polished, handmade black shoe while his mother gave overly specific instruction to the waiter for her coffee and the one she'd ordered for him. He wouldn't be drinking it, they both knew that, but that fact didn't prevent her from making a fuss.

For the moment, he kept his mask on. The rest of the world might regret that they needed to be masked, but it suited Armando. He was hypersensitive to smells and the mask at least filtered the worst of them.

'Can you tell me now why you insisted that we meet?' Armando asked as the waiter hurried away.

'Can't a mother just want to spend some quality time with her son?' Odemira said.

Armando gazed at his mother as he considered the question. She looked well for someone in her sixties. The smoothness of her skin probably owed a lot to Botox and her raven black hair to the dye bottle. Her long black locks were pulled back into an ornate do designed to look like a casual, loose bun. She was still a handsome woman with strong features, large dark, almost black eyes, a hawklike nose and generous, curved lips, now painted with a deep red lipstick. Sometimes she reminded him of the stepmother from Disney's Cinderella but never in a good way.

'I'm sure some mothers would like to spend time with their sons,' Armando said and slid back the cuff of his suit to examine his watch. It was nearly three pm, later than he'd realised.

'Stop doing that!' Odemira snapped. 'And why do you always wear black? That suit looks so severe on you.'

'It simplifies my life.'

'Your life is hardly complex.'

Armando decided against a comparison of their two lives; it would only lead to an argument.

'All my suits are handmade in natural fibres to ensure a perfect fit and a minimum of smell.'

'You and your obsession with smell.'

'I'm a perfumer. My life and the future of the company depends upon my sense of smell. Why would I contaminate it with an ill fitting, off the rack, chemical impregnated suit?'

'All the same, some designer suits are very nice.'

Armando's heart sank to be reminded of his mother's ambition. If something was an expensive brand name, she would buy it, whether or not it looked good on her. She'd clearly been shopping in the surrounding mall because there were several bags, all with designer logos, stacked around her feet. It was the with for the hotel, expensive and famous, but not classy.

He, on the other hand, preferred measuring quality over price. His handmade suits fitted his athletic frame like a glove. They showed his powerful muscles rather than just covered them. The trousers fitted so well he didn't need a belt and no strain lines appeared across his broad shoulders. Off the peg suits, the last of which he'd had when he was still in high school, had always felt restrictive despite being from a top designer. There was no way he'd go back to that.

'I wish you'd take off your mask,' his mother said, tacit agreement not to enter into an argument about his clothes.

Armando reluctantly removed the mask, also made to fit perfectly by his tailor and with an additional filter insert which he could discard after each use. He crinkled his nose as the mask came away. The sofa gave off a faint whiff of cigarette smoke. Even though they had banned smoking in public spaces a long time ago, it still lingered. That smell combined with the fabric soap used to steam cleaned the sofa. It had a sharp acidic quality that tended to bring on a headache.

His mother's perfume, applied with a heavy hand, was the next scent to wash over him. It was from their range, called Desire. His father had created the blend especially for his mother and presented it to her on their wedding night. She never wore anything else. That scent was joined by the aroma of the two espressos the waiter placed with great ceremony on the table before he bowed and left.

Armando's mother gave him a knowing look, probably a result of his grimace, took a sip of her espresso and said vaguely, 'How's Albina?' in a pretence at indifference.

Albina was his father's second wife, a younger and if not prettier, then certainly blonder edition.

'She's fine,' Armando said without making a move to pick up the coffee.

The smell told him that the coffee had come through dirty pipes and would be unpalatable.

'And her children?'

'Helena and Eddy are both fine,' Armando said of his half brother and sister.

'You need to be careful of Helena. She has ambition, that one. And now with this competition–'

Odemira stopped so abruptly it made Armando look up. Was this why she wanted to meet?

'You heard about that, did you?'

'I did,' Odemira said with a put out sniff. 'Really, Armando, I should hear things like this from you, not via the grapevine.'

Armando wondered which of the people at the Zeller Corporation had gone running to his mother. No doubt there were quite a few. She was assiduous at maintaining her connections.

'My father has given notice that we three siblings will be given equal opportunities to see who is worthy of becoming the CEO. Is that what you wanted to hear?'

'It's outrageous. You're the eldest son and a perfumer. What more does Homero want?'

'The best person for the job.'

Armando wondered whether he could pull his facemask back up without further offending his mother. The smells were leading to a tightening sensation at the back of his eyes which, more often than not, led to a migraine.

'The best person for the job is you. At least we can dismiss Eduardo as a contender, but Helena is another matter. She's as devious a little snake as her mother.'

Armando knew for a fact that his younger half sister was trying to convince their father to leave the company to her. Why wouldn't she? But, although he wasn't particularly fond of his sister, he also couldn't bring himself to say anything against her to his mother.

'I won't allow her to take over the company.'

'How would you even know what she's up to? You're always locked away in your laboratory.'

'How do you know that I'm always locked in my lab?' Armando said, then followed his mother's guilty gaze across the hotel lounge to another cluster of chairs where his PA was sitting, working on his laptop.

Libero Rocha had been Armando's personal assistant from the day he'd gone to work for his father. Before that, he'd taken the role of tutor and staff. It was Libero who'd taken him to and from school, to all his sports practices and matches, his music lessons and even parties. It was Libero who'd sat in the audience for his school plays and his graduation from high school and university. His father had always been too busy at work and his mother had given up custody and not made much effort to remain in his life.

'What did you say to him to get him to reveal that information?' Armando asked.

It wasn't a big deal. Everybody knew he spent a lot of time in the lab. It just wasn't like Libero to spill the beans on him, especially not to his mother.

'Well...' Odemira said and shrugged. 'Maybe he's as worried about you as I am.'

'Worried? Why would you be worried about me?'

'You're getting older and you're not married. All my other friend's grown-up children have already given them grandchildren. But here you are, nearly forty, heir to the Zeller Corporation and you don't even have a girlfriend.'

'You're worried about the succession?'

Armando was genuinely taken aback. His mother had never been interested in grandchildren before.

'It's one way to make sure your father leaves the business to you. Think about it Armando, if Helena has a child and you remain single, your father might think the business would be better off in her hands with somebody to pass it down to.'

'Don't be ridiculous.'

The fate of the company after him had never bothered Armando. Even his mother's words didn't move him. After all, he'd be dead. What would it matter to him then?

'Besides, who says it has to remain a family business? We're down to the third generation in one family. That's not bad for any company. Invariably heirs run out of interest or ability and then it's right that the board remove them and put in a professional manager.'

'Armando, no!' his mother gasped and her hand supporting the espresso cup shook.

'Was that really all you had to say to me?' Armando asked, growing ever more exasperated.

Odemira gave him a less convincing smile and said, 'I was wondering whether you'd talk to your father about increasing my alimony.'

And there it was, the reason he found his mother so difficult to bear.

'That has nothing to do with me. That's between you, my father and your lawyers,' he said, stood and did up his two jacket buttons. 'Now I really must go.'

CHAPTER TWO

'Come on,' Armando said as he strode past the corner of sofas Libero had occupied.

'You're leaving already?'

Libero snapped the computer shut, pushed it into the leather bag he always carried with him and hurried after his boss.

'Have you ever known our conversations to last?'

Armando readjusted his mask for a tighter fit and stepped out into the mall.

'That's why I only scheduled half an hour in your diary for the meeting,' Libero said as he too pulled on his mask.

Armando looked down into the man's heavily lined face. His salt and pepper hair was more white than dark these days. His deep brown eyes reflected amusement as well as concern.

'Did you also conspire with my mother to find me a wife?'

It was a rare thing for Libero to show surprise, but now he did. 'A wife?'

'Quaintly old fashioned, don't you think? Apparently it will help to have an heir in the battle for succession.'

'Ah!'

Armando just shook his head to dispel the annoyance his mother always caused him. Not for the first time, he wished his father was more like Libero. Homero Zeller, patriarch of the Zeller family and current CEO, was obsessed with his father's legacy. Grandpa Zeller had built the company up from the ground. He was the son of a respectable, but hard up academic. He'd started his business with one perfume and had gradually expanded the range. By the time of his death, he'd created a company that was worth millions.

Armando's father had added aromatics and food flavourings to the company line. He'd turned the corporation into a multinational giant worth billions, all with the express purpose of showing himself to be worthy of Grandpa Zeller. Because of this, he'd worked late into the evenings and on weekends and had little time for any of his children or his two wives.

It was only once Armando was old enough to get involved in the company that he started seeing more of his father. It was also what had spurred Armando on to become a perfumer. He supposed, like his father before him, he wanted recognition too.

Libero cleared his throat respectfully as Armando stuck his hands into his trouser pockets and started strolling towards the exit.

'Actually, sir, as we were in the neighbourhood, I took the liberty of scheduling a meeting with the perfume counters manager, Mr Marinho.'

'Really? Must we speak to him?'

The counters manager looked after all perfume counters in all the major retail centres. He always smelled like he lived around the counters, too. Mr Marinho was a meaningless explosion of smells. For that reason, Armando tried to avoid him.

'You can't put it off forever, sir. But I've only given him fifteen minutes so it will keep the encounter as short as possible.'

'And I suppose if we're doing it here, I can at least keep my mask on, although nothing can block the overwhelming smell of an entire floor of perfume counters. It's like walking into an over loud nightclub with a dozen tracks playing all together.'

Libero gave him a sympathetic smile and indicated that Armando should go in ahead of him. Armando grimaced. Despite his mask, he was already getting whiffs of a multitude of perfumes. Once he stepped through the doors, he'd be in the thick of it.

He gathered his courage and walked inside. Every perfume company had a circular counter, all manned by over made up young women eagerly wielding spritzers filled with perfume. Wandering amongst them, applying sprays from each test bottle, were a handful of women of every age, class and level of attractiveness. They didn't seem to care that they'd already applied one or two puffs of scent to their pulses. They just did it again. On the back of their hand, one woman to the tip of her finger, another was spraying perfume into the air so it rained down on her.

Amid this madness, a woman stood in front of the Zeller counter, staring at an impressive, mountain like display of their best-selling perfume, Armour. With its elegant Art Deco bottle and its unusual lavender shade, the pyramid of bottles glittered with promise. The woman's purple and blue streaked hair match it and Armando gave her more than his usual glance. She was looking particularly belligerent as she swayed back and forth before the display.

'Mr Marinho,' Libero said to a small, slim, dark-skinned man with slicked back black hair.

'Ah!' The man hurried out from behind the counter, his arms spread wide as if welcoming a long-lost brother. 'Mr Rocha, Mr Zeller, how good it is to see you.'

Armando took a hurried step back.

'I think we'll keep to safe social distancing today.'

'Yes, of course, Mr Zeller.' Marinho wrung his hands as if the inability to shake caused him actual physical distress. 'I'm so happy you could fit me into your busy schedule.'

'Busy schedule of what?' the purple-haired woman muttered as she turned around and glared at them.

'Madam, please step away. This is a private meeting between me and Mr Zeller,' Marinho said as he indicated the direction to the exit with both arms.

'What you Zellers did to my grandmother is unforgivable!' The woman staggered forward, swerved around Marinho and bumped into Armando. 'Never trust a thieving Zeller, my grandmother always said.'

She thumped Armando's chest weakly with her right hand and groped at his face with her left. She dislodged the mask and Armando caught a whiff of warm honey, herbs and soil. It took him right back to a picnic Libero had treated him to as a child on the sunny side of a mountain amongst the olive trees. Then an overwhelming scent of red wine brought him right back, followed by a wave of all the surrounding perfumes.

'Madam, please!' Marinho grabbed the woman by the top of her arms and tried to turn her in an attempt to get her to leave. 'I don't know who this woman is,' he said frantically to Armando.

'But I know what he is,' the woman slurred and with surprising speed for one who was so unsteady on her feet she slipped out of Marinho's grip and thumped Armando on the chest again, 'Bastard man, bastard Zeller!'

Then she hiccupped, and wine spurted like a fountain from her mouth and splattered across Armando. Hot, vomit infused red wine soaked through his jacket and then his shirt.

The woman laughed, reached for one of the perfume bottles in the Armour display and with both Marinho and Libero lunging towards her, she wrenched the lid, spray and all, off the bottle and splashed the contents over the vomit.

'Here, this will cover it up,' she muttered, smiled beatifically and slowly crumpled to the floor.

Armando froze. The intensity of the smells overwhelmed his senses and brought on a sharp headache. His skin crawled, knowing what was soaking through his clothes and sticking to his skin. He didn't want to breathe because he knew what he'd be inhaling and he couldn't bear it.

'Get her away from Mr Zeller,' Marinho shouted to a pair of security guards who'd finally made an appearance walking cautiously towards them. 'And charge her with assault.'

'Are you alright?' Libero asked, stretching up to get a better view of Armando's eyes.

He nodded but still couldn't bring himself to breathe and wondered how long he could keep holding his breath. He wanted to rip the clothes off and fling them away, but that was impossible with all the watching people. There was a drumming in his ears. He'd have to breathe. He put his hands over the mask to further block the smell but still gasped in wine, vomit and perfume infused air.

'I'm so sorry, Mr Zeller,' Marinho said, rushing up to him and trying to take his hand.

Armando batted it away and took a step back while the security guards tried to wake the drunk woman.

'We'll prosecute her for criminal damage and assault, Mr Zeller. You don't have to worry about that.'

'Get me out of here,' Armando said through gritted teeth to Libero, who for no reason that he could see was talking on his mobile.

'Of course, sir, I've arranged for a room in the hotel. You can take a shower there and I'll bring you fresh clothes from home.'

'Yes, fine, good.' Armando backed away from everyone, desperate to get out of the reeking clothes. Then he stopped and examined the unconscious woman on the floor. 'Put that woman in a taxi. Make sure she gets home safely.'

Marinho looked surprised by the order and set to argue. Thankfully, Libero stepped in and Armando could leave him to arrange everything. He broke into a run. The sooner he was out of his stinking clothes, the better.

CHAPTER THREE

A thumping headache was the first thing Diana became aware of. The second was a vile taste wrapped around her tongue, too acidic and... God, she'd drunk far too much. She lurched out of bed, forcing her eyes open as she did, desperate to rinse her mouth.

She staggered across the room, bending to get through the doorway that led to the bathroom. She leaned over the cold water tap and turned it on full blast, gulping up sun warmed lukewarm water that slowly cooled as the water worked its way through the pipes.

Only as she closed the tap and exerted as much force as she could to reduce the rate of the permanent drip, did she realise she had no idea how she'd got home. She was still fully clothed in what she'd been wearing to see Fernando. A wave of sorrow so overwhelming it brought tears to her eyes washed over her.

'Oh God,' she muttered and plonked down on the closed lid of the toilet.

Tears ran down her face and she wiped frantically at them. She'd got so deeply, deeply drunk yesterday that she hadn't been able to think of the future. Now all she could think about was that Fernando had left her.

A familiar knock at her door prevented her from breaking into sobs, followed by Margarida's voice.

'Diana? Diana, are you awake?'

'I'm up,' Diana shouted as she hastily splashed water over her face to hide the signs that she'd been crying.

There was the sound of a key in the lock. Margarida was Diana's oldest friend. They'd gone to the same schools and inherited their parent's adjoining shops, so they also kept a spare key for each other.

'How are you?'

Margarida popped her head around the bathroom door and waggled a box of paracetamol at her.

'Better for seeing you.'

Diana lunged for the box, pushed out two capsules and swallowed them down with a swig of tap water.

'I'm relieved to see you looking better too,' Margarida said. 'I'll go make some coffee.'

Having somebody about was just the distraction she needed. Diana rushed through a shower, scrambled into a baggy t-shirt and old pair of 3/4 length leggings, all she could face today. Still towelling her hair, she made her way to her little kitchen.

Her home was on the floor above the shop and growing up, she'd slept on the sofa in the sitting room. After her grandmother died, she'd moved into the bedroom. She hadn't bothered to redecorate. Most of the furniture came from when her grandparents had first set up home. She sat down now at the simple square oak table in the kitchen and took a deep, appreciative sniff.

'Toast as well, nice.'

Margarida grinned at her as she set down the toasted bread rolls.

'They're the leftovers from yesterday.'

'Oh, those rolls.'

Diana had given Margarida the bread as she'd expected to be away for the weekend. They'd have been rock hard by Monday.

'I take it things didn't go as planned?'

Margarida placed a milky coffee in front of Diana and settled opposite with her own mug and a sympathetic, ready to listen expression.

Diana loved her for it and because she could always rely upon her.

'Ah, my beautiful friend, you are correct as always.'

Margarida flicked back her plait of thick black, slightly crinkly hair. She batted her long black eyelashes in mock seduction while her face tinged pink with genuine pleasure.

'So what happened?'

Diana sighed, then poured out the entire story, lingering on how angry she was at the coldness of the breakup.

'He didn't even look like he cared. I mean, would it have been so hard to at least look regretful?'

'Bastard,' Margarida said but not with as much heat as Diana would have liked.

'Yeah.'

Diana picked up a toasted half-roll, its edges slightly singed, and lathered on some butter before she bit into the dense, chewy interior. Toast and milky coffee was a treat, and she was feeling a lot better for it.

'At least he paid for your taxi home, though,' Margarida said.

'Did he?' Diana asked. 'Now that you mention it... I got home by taxi?'

'I'm not surprised you don't remember. The taxi driver came into my shop to ask if I knew you because you were passed out in the back of his car. He didn't want to just leave you on your doorstep. I had to give him a huge tip for helping me get you up the stairs, too. But he said it was a man who paid your fare. I just assumed it was Fernando.'

'I don't think so.' Diana searched her memory for any clue as to how she'd got in the taxi. 'He left me with half a bottle of wine. I doubt he came back for me later.'

'Well, that's a mystery. It's nice to know there are still good samaritans around.'

'Maybe.' Diana tilted her head as something vague popped up. 'There was a man, devilishly handsome, or maybe just the devil. I can't remember. And there was a lot of perfume.'

'It sounds to me more like a dream if it involved perfume.'

'Probably.' Diana breathed in a few wisps of steam from her coffee as she considered. 'Are you planning on opening today?'

'I will. This year so far has been dismal. The shutdown hit me badly and the tourists are only reappearing in drips and drabs. Sundays seem to be the busiest though, so I have to do what I can. I'll close tomorrow. What about you?'

'Since I wasn't planning on opening this weekend, and I feel like death warmed up today, I'm going to give it a miss. I'll probably curl up on the sofa and watch something mindless. I doubt I can concentrate on anything, really.'

'You do that. You're allowed to wallow once in a while.'

Margarida lingered to help clean up and only left once the dishes were done. Alone again, Diana staggered the short distance to the ancient, brown velvet sofa and dropped onto it, bouncing as she landed. She felt about under the cushions till her fingertips found the remote. With a click, she had the entertainment world at her disposal. She opted for a lightweight romantic comedy.

Halfway through the film she was crying again. Romance was the wrong genre for a heartbroken woman. So she quit the film and spent an hour surfing through show titles. Nothing really appealed. By this time she couldn't face another film so she turned the TV off.

Slumped on the sofa, she examined her little apartment. It wasn't much, but it was hers. Still, she thought, as her gaze drifted over to her desk and the pile of correspondence lying on it, she couldn't keep going the way she was.

Most of her mail came as bills, hardly any were refill orders from clients. Just as for Margarida, the quarantine had harmed her business. Even her regulars weren't bothering with perfume when most of them were stuck at home with nobody to tantalise. But she couldn't sell out and start mass producing perfumes. It would go against everything her grandmother had stood for.

Armando stepped out of the shower and reached for a pure white towel in his immaculate bathroom tiled in black slate. He still felt light-headed after the migraine the incident the day before had induced. He'd forced himself to go for a run on his treadmill followed by an hour of Tai Chi, both the slow, meditative form and the combat moves. He made sure that he'd worked up a sweat.

Even so, a day later, the scent of vomit and perfume lingered. After an hour long shower at the hotel, followed by another shower at home, rinsing his nostrils with distilled water, plus this shower, it was still there. He doubted he'd ever be able to tolerate the smell of Armour again.

It was impossible to have that smell in his hermetically sealed house with the state-of-the-art vacuum system that ensured the circulation of only clean, scentless air. He'd left the vomit soaked clothes at the hotel to be thrown away. So the only explanation was that it was the memory of a smell, not the smell itself. He had to get over it or it would throw everything off.

He walked through to his bedroom and glanced out of the row of windows that looked out across the terracotta rooftops of Lisbon and on down to the river and the red painted 25th of April bridge. The view was one reason he'd bought the house. Its nearly ruinous state meant it had been a bargain, and also reasonably easy to restyle into the modern fortress he wanted.

He'd just finished drying himself when his phone beeped with the ringtone he'd set for Helena. It was unusual for her to call him at the best of times, but to do so on a Sunday morning was unheard of. So he decided against getting dressed before calling her back. Instead he wrapped a towel around his waist and answered.

'What are you up to?' Helena asked with a mildly taken aback expression.

Armando examined his half sister with his usual critical gaze. She was beautiful, much like her mother. Her naturally light brown hair was artfully coloured to make her blond. The slight natural curl was straightened so that her hair fell in a perfect line to below her shoulders. Her skin was tanned a honey gold and her makeup was perfect, even on a Sunday morning. It was a pity she didn't stand out more, but in a room full of socialites, Helena looked pretty much the same as all the rest.

'What do you mean, what am I up to? You're the one calling me.'

'I mean the manly chest.'

Helena gave a downward wave of her hand that encompassed the lower half of her screen.

'I just got out of the shower.'

'Ah, I see. I should have known it wasn't because I'd interrupted you with a woman. Not if you're at home, anyway.'

Armando only allowed two people into his house. One was Libero. He made sure he never wore anything scented, didn't smoke, never ate garlic or onions or drank anything with powerful aromas. The other was his cleaning woman, who worked when Armando wasn't home. She used the scentless products he provided and then rinsed everything down with distilled water before leaving. With that and his ventilation system, he could happily live in his aroma less bubble.

'You know why I do it this way. I'm surprised at you, anyway. You've never expressed an interest in coming to visit.'

'And that's mutual, you've only visited my place once.'

'Where you'd smoked pot.'

Armando shuddered, recalling the intense headache the overly spicy cannabis scent had induced.

'The week before, Armando, a whole damn week before. It's not like I'm a pot head or anything. Honestly, the fuss you make leaves me grateful that I didn't inherit the genes to become a Nose.'

His ability was a mixed blessing to Armando, too, one he'd inherited from his grandfather. The old man had set up the business after an apprenticeship to a perfume house in Paris. Armando had inherited his grandfather's acute ability that enabled him to distinguish over a thousand individual smells and even whether those smells were synthetic or natural.

Although, his training had been different. He'd obtained a biochemistry degree first before attending the first postgraduate school in perfumery, ISIPCA, near Versailles. His half brother was just completing the same course and would shortly join the food division of the Zeller Corporation.

'Alright,' Armando said, tired of the conversation already. 'Why did you call?'

'Because, as Zeller Corporations Marketing and Media Director, I have to warn you we have a situation.'

'Then deal with it yourself. Why involve me?'

'Because it's about you,' Helena said at her most disdainful.

'About me?'

Armando searched his memory for anything he might have done to bring the company into disrepute and came up empty.

'Here, look,' Helena said, and an attached video pinged for Armando's attention in the chat box.

He'd have preferred to watch the video without his competitive half sister's eagle eye on him. As that wasn't possible, he schooled his face into his best version of unconcern and pressed play.

The whole damn scene with the drunk woman in the department store played out before him and brought back such an overwhelming sense of the smell that he had to suppress a gag reaction.

'What's the problem with it?' he managed to ask with tolerable composure.

'You running away wasn't helpful.'

'But the smell, Helena, I couldn't stand it.'

'The public neither knows nor cares about your sensitive nose. All they see is the heir to the Zeller Corporation fleeing the scene. But that isn't the worst. You ran after she accused you, and the company, of being thieves.'

'But that's nonsense. The ramblings of a drunk.'

'In vino veritas, it's precisely because she was drunk that she's getting traction. This video is all over social media. It started on YouTube, but it's already spread to Facebook and there's even a TikTok with some repulsive dance attached. Worse than that are the comments. They're all wondering what the company did.'

'She mentioned her grandmother, so whatever her problem, it's long gone and no concern of ours.'

Armando knew he'd have to do more. He couldn't look complacent and allow Helena to be the one who did everything to control this potentially harmful situation. Helena was obviously enjoying getting him on the spot too and sighed theatrically, like a long-suffering friend who was always pulling him out of shit.

'Please tell me you at least know who this woman is, and how we can contact her.'

'I can find out.'

Armando was relieved that at least he'd had the sense to get the woman home rather than abandoning her to security. Libero would have her address.

'Give me half an hour.'

'That's all you'll have. In the meantime, I'm trying to get the video clips taken down. Or at least balance the comments so we don't look quite so bad.'

'Okay,' Armando said and hung up.

He took a couple of deep breaths to consider the situation. The video was a problem. The current public opinion could affect their share price and his father and the shareholders would be furious about that.

He also worried about what Helena might do with the video afterwards. She'd keep a copy for herself and make sure all the senior staff, especially his father, the CEO, got a copy. She would couch it as being in the interests of keeping everyone informed, of course.

It was a golden opportunity to undermine him. She could point out that he was peculiar, a technician who shouldn't be running a company. Leave him in his lab, she'd say. He's a genius perfumer, no need for him to get involved in the money side of things.

Part of him might even agree. He was happiest in the lab, creating olfactory experiences that took people on a journey as one subtle fragrance unfolded after another.

But he was the eldest son and the rightful heir. He also cared about the company as much as his father did, although for different reasons. He wanted to maintain its integrity as a quality maker of fine scents. Scents that people felt comfortable using on the intimate closeness of their skin and which accompanied them during the most meaningful moments of their lives.

He had no confidence that Helena felt the same. Like her mother and his, all she cared about was money. If she could grow the bottom line by cutting corners, she'd do so without a second thought.

Armando sent Libero a message, apologising for disturbing his Sunday, but requesting the drunk woman's name and address. As expected, Libero had been efficient. He'd contacted Mr Marinho who'd gone through the woman's purse and photographed her ID card and a business card. He did this mainly so he could send her home, but also, Armando suspected, so she could be tracked down again if necessary. Libero now forwarded the photos to Armando.

It turned out her name was Diana Luna. Surprisingly, she was also a perfumer for a company called Perfumes da Luna. Neither her name nor that of her company rang a bell. Considering he knew all the big players, it meant she was either a nobody or too new to have been noticed by him so far.

A chill ran through him and he realised he was standing in the middle of his room still only covered in a towel. This was no time for hesitation. He got dressed, braced himself, and watched the video again.

He had his finger poised, ready to fast forward through the actual vomiting sequence, but his finger hit the pause a bit too early. It stopped at the moment the woman pulled down his face mask. For a second, his nostrils were filled with the scent of honey and herbs and warm soil again. He'd clean forgotten that with the shock of the rest.

That was a scent he wanted to return to. It wasn't a mass produced perfume. He was familiar with every major brand of perfume sold in the world. It wasn't the kind of thing most women would wear either. If the rest of that dreadful day hadn't happened, he might have pursued that scent further. Now though, all he had was a mission to conduct damage control.

He checked his text again, this time for the woman's address. It was in Sintra, so relatively easy to get to. The best thing to do would be to visit her. He was curious to see whether the interesting scent lingered on her and hoped to God that he could overcome the overwhelming memory of vomit and Armour that also hit him when he saw her face.

Given that it was a Sunday, the trip down the highway to Sintra only took Armando 40 minutes. He parked his Porsche Taycan, electric therefore no fumes, in the first space he found near his destination and looked about. It was a tree lined side street off the main tourist drag where the first leaves had yellowed in anticipation of autumn.

To his left was a steep woodland covered mountain that provided a deep shade. A high moss and fern encrusted wall topped with stone dogs screen off one of the many baroque palacetes, all towers, spindly balconies and stone lacework that Sintra was famous for. On his right was a short row of picturesque shops. They were a couple of hundred years old with small windows framed in wood. Only a handful of locals and tourists drifted along, gazing at the wares. This was unusual. Sintra was usually buzzing with tourists and the shops should have been full. The lack of passersby didn't bode well for the shopkeepers.

Armando checked his phone again for the number of the house he was after. Then he made his way, fully masked even though he was outside, along a narrow cobbled path. He passed a cafe, then an ironworker producing artisanal coat hooks, doorbells and other household furniture, a bakery, and a candle shop that specialised in beeswax candles and embroidered goods and finally stopped before a closed shop perfume shop.

The frontage looked ancient. A green sign with gold letters in an art nouveau style proclaimed: Perfumes da Luna. He peered into the dark interior that looked like it hadn't been remodelled since its inception. Inside, the walls were lined with wooden glass-fronted cases that appeared to be filled with small, dark brown vials.

He stepped back again and read the sign hanging on the door. Closed for the weekend. Hopefully, that didn't mean his trip had been in vain.

Below that, etched on the glass, was the information that the shop created personalised scents for its customers. The last time he'd seen something like that was when his lecturer had taken them on a tour of Paris. He'd said the shop was one of the last in the world making personalised perfume. Armando had no idea such a place still existed in Portugal.

He checked his phone again. The address he was after was a first-floor apartment. He looked up and noted that the shop had living quarters over it. Frilly curtains indicated it was somebody's home.

Further inspection led him to a stone staircase running up the left side of the building that stopped at a single door. All the way up the stairs and filling the landing was a collection of terracotta flowerpots containing scented geraniums covered in deep purple and lavender blooms. He wondered whether this woman extracted the scents from the leaves for her perfumes. Was she one of those hippy, all natural perfumes type?

Armando didn't want to go up. No, that wasn't quite right. Most of him didn't want to go up. But the fact that this woman was a perfumer, and he'd got that mysterious scent from her, was intriguing and needed further investigation.

More importantly, he had to make sure Helena didn't win an unassailable victory over him because of this outrageous and utterly unexpected event. Who knew that running into some random stranger could cause such upheaval? Armando gripped the banister and forced himself to go up the stairs.

Chapter Four

T he sound of her door knocker woke Diana. Margarida never used the knocker, so it wasn't her. Diana groaned as she straightened up and stretched, blinking vaguely and trying to decide whether she opened it or simply pretended not to be home.

The thought suddenly struck her it might be Fernando. Maybe he'd realised his mistake and was here to beg her to take him back. If it was him, she would not make it that easy. With that heartwarming thought, she hurried to the door and swung it open. Her expression was halfway between pleasure and an attempt to make herself look severe.

Only it wasn't Fernando.

A tall man dressed in the smartest black suit she'd ever seen, wearing a crisp white shirt and black mask, stood staring down at her. His deep brown hair was swept back, black perfectly shaped eyebrows curved above deep brown eyes, currently looking surprised as he took an involuntary step back. This was probably because she had wrenched the door open so violently.

Now she felt stupid, overly aware of her baggy clothes and the fact that she'd not bothered with a mask, so she also stepped back.

'Yes?'

Diana's mind seethed with questions while she groped towards the side table, feeling for her mask while keeping her eyes on the stranger.

Sunday wasn't a day for salesmen. Besides, salesmen couldn't afford the kind of suit this man was wearing.

'Please forgive the intrusion,' Armando said and pulled a business card out of his pocket. 'It's a matter of some urgency.'

Diana didn't make a move towards the card. She felt vulnerable with this strange masked man at her front door. She glanced down into the street and was relieved to see people wandering along. If she needed to scream for help, at least somebody would hear her.

'What do you want?'

The man leaned forward and stretched his arm out so that Diana could take the card.

'I'm Armando Zeller, we... ran into each other yesterday–'

Zeller was the only bit of the sentence Diana registered.

'No!' she snapped and tried to slam the door shut.

Only Zeller got his foot wedged in the door first, preventing her from closing it.

'I'm really sorry, but I need to talk to you about the video.'

'What video?' Diana asked, trying her best to squeeze his foot so hard he'd have no choice but to pull it away.

'The video of the two of us.'

Now Diana knew this was some weird ploy.

'There is no way I'd ever do anything with a Zeller, certainly nothing involving a video!' Diana shouted, jerking the door back and forth on his foot for added emphasis.

'I'll show you, look.'

Diana ignored the phone, held up at eye height till she realised it really was her on the screen. She let go of the door and barely noticed Zeller ease it open, still holding the phone as she watched herself throwing up on him in graphic technicolour.

'Oh God!'

Diana looked back up at Armando Zeller, felt her face go red and slammed the door shut. This time she was quick enough, but she locked and double locked just to be on the safe side.

'Ms Luna,' Armando said from the other side, 'I'm really sorry, but we do have to discuss this video.'

'Why?'

Diana felt so ashamed she couldn't even contemplate facing the man outside. Then she pulled herself together and took a deep breath. No, she wasn't wrong. It was embarrassing, but no more than what one of that terrible family deserved.

'Look,' Armando said, 'I'm not after an apology, but–'

'Apology? You'll never get an apology,' Diana snapped and slammed her hand hard against the door in emphasis. 'I don't know why you came and I don't care. Go away and leave me alone.'

'I'm sorry but I can't. What you said in the video about thievery and betrayal can cause reputational harm to my family's company. I was hoping we could discuss it and come to an arrangement.'

'An arrangement? Why would I come to an arrangement over the truth?'

'We don't actually know it's the truth.'

'Oh yes it is,' Diana shouted, getting angrier. 'Your grandfather stole my grandmother's formula and used it to create Armour. I can never forgive your family for that.'

There was such a long pause that Diana was about to check her peephole to see if Zeller had left when he said, 'What do you mean, my grandfather stole the formula for Armour?'

'Exactly what I said. You go and ask him.'

'I can't, he's dead.'

'Well then ask your father.'

Again there was a long silence before Armando said, 'Do you have any proof?'

'Oh proof, is it?' Diana laughed at the barefaced cheek of the Zellers. It was just as her grandmother had told her. 'I have her original book of formulas with the full list of scents for Armour.

But you don't need me to tell you that. If you know
anything about perfumes, you'll know that Armour differs from
everything else your grandfather ever produced. Every perfumer
works on a theme. They have favourite notes and combinations.
There is nothing in the other Zeller perfumes that's like Armour.
Because he didn't create it.'

Again the silence, but now Diana was expecting a comeback.
She wasn't disappointed.

'Look,' Zeller sounded infuriatingly calm, as if he was trying
to reason with a child. 'It's impossible to discuss this with a door
between us. Please let me in so we can clear things up.'

'Never. I will never allow a Zeller into this house.'

'How about neutral ground, then? We can go to the cafe.'

'I have nothing more to say to you.' Diana hoped her voice
held a sufficiently final tone to drive the man away. 'Please leave
before I call the police.'

'Alright, I'll go, but I'll leave my card here. If you change
your mind, you can contact me,' Armando said and slipped his
business card through her letterbox. 'I can make it worth your
while.'

Diana pressed her ear to the door, listening for the sound of
somebody walking down the stairs. It was hard to tell, but it
sounded like Armando Zeller had left. She double checked via
the peephole, which now just revealed the side of her neighbour's
house. So she leaned down and picked up the business card.

Aside from herself, she didn't know many people who still had
business cards. Fernando had always used that as an example of
how old-fashioned she was. Everyone shared e-cards these days
or just connected via phone.

Now this, she thought, feeling the satin smooth paper of the
card sliding under her fingers. It was a simple white rectangle
with bevelled edges. Armando Zeller's name written in an elegant
black curving script in the centre of the card, along with the
information that he was the head of the House of Zeller and
director of perfumes. His email and the company website address

were on the back of the card. Diana swore and threw the card into the recycling bin.

Then she fetched her laptop, sat cross-legged on her sofa and googled Armando Zeller. The first thing that came up was the video. It was too embarrassing to watch it again. It wasn't what she was after, anyway. Despite her grandmother's feud against the family, Diana had never expected to meet any of them. They were too high and mighty to meet the likes of her. She, therefore, had no idea what they looked like.

She clicked on the images tab and the page filled with photos of Armando Zeller in maskless pre-Covid days. Much as she hated to admit it, he was handsome. He had strong masculine features with a clear, angular jawline and a firm mouth. He didn't smile much if the photos were anything to go by. Was he always in the same black suit? Why not? He looked like a God in it. She assumed he had racks of them.

Zeller appeared to have a busy life, but most of the pictures were from business events and company announcements. He wasn't as prominent on the gossip pages. Since the Zeller family was one of the richest in Portugal, Diana had expected to see more about girlfriends. But there were no pictures of him with women. That was except for a black-haired woman who was, according to the captions, his mother.

Diana also discovered that he had a younger half sister and half brother, Helena and Eduardo Zeller. They did make a splash in the celebrity pages. There wasn't a single party the younger Zellers didn't attend. Helena Zeller was tall, slim and gorgeous and always accompanied by a handsome man. It was rarely the same man, although a certain prince from Lichtenstein was a regular. The younger brother appeared not just with one woman on his arms but at least two or three in every photo. He dressed more casually and his hair was sun bleached and tousled, unlike his immaculate brother.

Diana stared at the images, wondering what to do. She couldn't believe she'd actually run into a member of that family. Only she had run into him. More than that, Diana thought with a shudder.

She replayed the conversation over and over, trying to work out what it meant. Was it really so bad that the video had landed up on the web? That was embarrassing and needed further investigation.

So she forced herself to watch the video. Fortunately, none had her name. Diana prayed her clients wouldn't recognise her, as she'd been filmed from behind for most of it. Diana watched in horror as she sagged to the floor, passed out cold. Then she looked up at Zeller. He looked appalled.

What she didn't get was why he'd run off as if he was being chased. There was plenty of comment about that, too. Most of it called him a coward. Or a typical rich guy who just left the cleanup to his lackeys.

Then something else occurred to her.

'He said he can make it worth my while. What exactly did that mean?'

CHAPTER FIVE

A rmando, as usual, was one of the first to arrive at work. The Zeller Corporation headquarters was an immaculately preserved six story late 16th Century building that took up the entire block. Several high end shops occupied the ground floor, most prominent of which was the House of Zeller, the flagship for Zeller Perfumes. It was the shop his grandfather had opened when he started his company. Above that had been apartments. The company had kept the elegant wrought-iron balconies from those times. They'd gutted the inside and rebuilt to create their elegant headquarters.

Armando nodded to the security guard and headed for the lift that would take him to the top floor. Libero walked a pace behind him, as always.

'Were you able to resolve the issue with the video?' Libero asked as the lift doors closed and they were alone.

'I'll have to wait and speak to Helena. She managed to reduce the number of comments, so I suspect they have shunted the video to the backwaters of the internet.'

Armando wondered why he hadn't told Libero about his meeting with Ms Luna yet. It wasn't like him to keep such information from his PA.

The lift opened onto a wide hallway that oozed opulence with a mirror smooth white marble floor and gold patterned wallpaper. Armando thought it a bit over the top, but it seemed to impress their visitors. Since that was the intention, it achieved its goal and Armando therefore said nothing more.

If he turned left and walked all the way to the end of the corridor, he'd get to his father's office. It looked like something decorated for the king of Versailles with far too much golden furniture. His father, though, was as autocratic as an absolute monarch, so it suited his character.

Armando turned right toward his office. He thought it interesting that the two most powerful men in the building had their offices as far apart as possible.

'Armando,' came an all too familiar voice.

'Dad,' Armando said, turning back.

His father stood in the corridor, hands on his hips, a crushed newspaper clenched in his right fist. A deep scowl replaced his usual supercilious expression. His tall slim figure was clad in an impeccable dark grey suit. His black hair with the greying temples was slicked back with not a hair out of place.

'Why was I woken this morning by a call from the media?' Homero stalked forward and smacked the newspaper into Armando's chest. 'Who is this woman?'

'Nobody to be concerned about,' Armando said in his calmest voice.

'Then why has she got you into the newspapers and why are the trade magazines asking questions about our business practices? The moment the markets opened, our share price fell and you say it's nothing. Once negative rumours start, they're impossible to squash entirely.'

'I'm dealing with it.' Armando stepped away from his father whose Brill Cream was irritating his nose and would send him into a sneezing fit if he kept breathing it in.

'You didn't deal with it very well at the mall. What on earth possessed you to run away, on camera to boot?'

'Would you have preferred that I pass out on camera?'

Armando lowered his voice because heads had started appearing in doorways, peeking at him and his father.

'All the same, to get entangled with some drunken woman,' Homero said, shaking his head.

'She'd have done the same to you or Helena. It was the family name she reacted to. She has a grudge against our whole family. It was just coincidence that it was me.'

Armando regretted the words the moment they were out of his mouth. More so as his father's scowl deepened.

'A CEO deals with all problems and doesn't even think about deflecting blame. Helena did a great job of briefing me. I knew exactly what to say when the reporters started calling. You could learn a thing or two from her about keeping calm in a crisis.'

'I'm sure I could.' Armando pushed down his deepening irritation. His father was right and Helena had acted appropriately as the head of communications. He'd only make matters worse if he explained. 'I'd best get to work on damage limitation.'

His father sucked his teeth thoughtfully before he said so softly only Armando could hear him, 'Don't think because you're the eldest the CEO position is yours. You'll have to prove yourself to me, just like I did to my father.'

'Of course.'

Armando didn't bother pointing out that his father, unusually for the era, had been an only child. Armando remembered little about his grandfather. From what he'd seen and heard later, his grandfather had not been fond of his wife and had most likely married for money. His wife's father had owned the shop on the ground floor of what had become the Zeller corporation. Without siblings, his father, therefore, had no idea what it was like to have someone see themselves as an enemy practically since birth.

Homero examined Armando thoughtfully, perhaps waiting for more. Then he obviously decided his point had been well made, so he nodded while managing to convey that Armando had earned a black mark. Then he stalked back to his office and all the heads pulled back into theirs like so many alarmed tortoises.

Armando waited till his father was safely back in his office before he resumed the short walk to his own place. Libero set his briefcase down on his wide oak desk and loosened his coat buttons before giving Armando an expectant look.

'Any last-minute orders?'

Armando shook his head. He was too old to expect words of sympathy from Libero, but he felt like the man was on his side even if he said nothing.

'I don't see any reason to change the schedule for today, although I'm expecting Helena to come and see me before my first meeting.'

'Very good, sir,' Libero said with a brief nod.

This exchange was the same every morning, and the return to routine acted as a balm for Armando's nerves. He then made for the glass door that led to his office. It slid silently open and he stepped through a curtain of air into his laboratory come office.

It had been his grandfather's laboratory when he'd grown the business sufficiently to take over the whole building. The Zeller Corporation had grown so much since then that the main laboratories of the company now occupied a vast swath of an industrial estate outside of Lisbon.

Armando preferred to be in the city and had turned the laboratory into his office and lab. For that reason, he still had one long, marble topped lab bench. Marble because it had no smell of its own, unlike wood. Vents in the ceiling ran the length of that lab bench, drawing scents away so that they didn't linger.

On the other side of the office, he'd adapted another lab bench into a desk. So he had a wide, simple white marble topped desk. He'd gone paperless as soon as it was possible so that he didn't have the scent of slowly oxidising paper about him while he worked. He now removed his laptop from his bag and set it on his desk but didn't open it.

His mind wasn't focused enough for work. The encounter with Diana Luna had upset him more than he'd expected and not for the reason he'd expected. So he walked up to the French doors that gave a view out over a wrought-iron balcony and gazed into the street below, trying to organise his thoughts.

The Avenida da Liberdade was the pre-eminent street of Lisbon. It was a wide avenue leading down to the river, on either side of the road were broad pedestrian walkways paved in an intricate swirling black-and-white pattern of cobbles that he could barely see through the leaves of the tall plane trees that provided a pleasant shade.

He didn't open the doors because the smell of car fumes disturbed him. It wasn't just that it was a nasty smell; it was that it was poisonous. It boggled his mind that humanity thought nothing of driving around in vehicles that gave off a poisonous gas.

A light tap at his office door, followed by the swooshing sound as it opened, signalled Helena's arrival.

'Good morning,' she said, and her tone was crisp and businesslike. 'Have you checked the status of the video today?'

'I have.'

Armando made his way back to his desk and indicated for Helena to sit. He had two chairs for guests, specifically chosen not to be comfortable so that people didn't linger. He also had a couple of air vents above the chairs that looked like air conditioners, but that actually sucked air up and out so that the scent of his guests didn't remain after they'd left.

Helena waved her tablet at Armando for emphasis.

'It doesn't look like the woman in the video has responded. I looked her up on-line, and she barely has a presence at all.'

'You looked her up?'

Armando expected this. It was the least anyone would do. Helena wouldn't stop there, though. She'd keep digging till she knew everything about Diana Luna. Some of her methods skirted the edge of legality, but she often awed him with her efficiency.

She could find out anything because she was willing to go to any lengths to get it.

Helena crossed her legs, looking Armando up and down with disdain.

'I suspect, as she has such a small internet footprint, she may not have seen the video, but I wouldn't bet on it. Even if she hasn't, a well-meaning friend might tell her about it.'

'She has seen it,' Armando said and wished he didn't have to make this admission.

His sister arched a single eyebrow in query. Armando had heard that her employees found this an intimidating tactic as it usually signalled Helena getting angry.

'I visited Ms Luna yesterday and showed it to her.'

'You showed it to her?' Helena said in the tone of voice of one stunned by his level of stupidity.

'I wanted to talk to her, and I needed to explain why I was on her doorstep because she didn't recognise me.'

'For the Love of God, Armando, she was so drunk she didn't even remember the incident and you went and told her! How could you be so stupid?'

Armando actually squirmed under his sister's outraged gaze. They might be in competition over the CEO position, and she was no doubt doing all she could to undermine him. But when it came to the future of the company she would do what she could to protect it. He wouldn't expect anything less from her, either.

'The accusation that we are thieves bothered me.'

'This whole thing could have blown over with that woman completely unawares. Now you've made it worse by one, telling her about it and two, asking why we are thieves? Did you completely lose your mind?'

Armando had been aware of the risk, but there had been something about the woman's sincerity even when drunk that he couldn't let go of. Now, confronted by Helena's incredulous shock, he was regretting his trip. Especially as it had ended so badly and with a bruised foot to add injury to the insult.

Maybe because he wasn't saying much, Helena calmed down and sounded her own level self as she asked, 'What did she say we stole?'

'According to her, our grandfather stole a perfume formula from her grandmother.'

Helena gave a dismissive tut that indicated a loss of interest.

'That's ancient history. Nothing to get worked up about, after all. We've retired most of the perfumes grandfather developed because they fell out of fashion.'

'Mmm,' Armando murmured and wondered how his sister would take this further allegation. 'She said it was Armour.'

Helena let out a shocked gasp as if someone had punched her in the stomach.

'She has to be lying. That's the perfume that made grandfather his fortune. It's our flagship perfume. She's trying to cash in on our best seller. It has to be a lie.'

Helena had a point. If anyone was planning to blackmail them, then going for their best seller would be a good bet. Revealing that fact as a drunken outburst filmed by an accomplice and uploaded to the internet could be the beginning of putting on the screws that could be tightened at the swindler's leisure.

'Do you think there's any truth in what she said?' Helena asked, breaking in on Armando's new and worried musings.

Armando shrugged.

'You being vague is making me uncomfortable,' Helena said. 'I might not often agree with you, but I'd be a fool to ignore how much you know about perfume. Do you think she's telling the truth?'

Armando turned his hands over, palm up.

'I've always wondered about Armour. It differs from anything else our grandfather created. Ms Luna also claims to have her grandmother's notebook that contains the formula.'

'Can't she just have figured it out later? I mean, you can tell the components of a perfume just by smelling it. The rest of us can work it out by sending it through a machine that analyses all the molecules and their relative quantities. Could she have done something like that?'

'Maybe, but in our grandfather's day they didn't have the machines. It's possible grandfather reconstituted it from what he smelled, but that would still be theft.'

'This could be a disaster.'

Armando was beginning to fear the same. The company's reputation and stock price would suffer an even more severe blow if their flagship perfume turned out to have been stolen from its original creator. He was prevented from saying more by Bernardo, who stood in the doorway beaming at him. Helena wasn't fond of Bernardo, or any of Armando's friends.

So she stood and said, 'I'll do some further digging,' before she left, giving Bernardo a curt nod of acknowledgement as she passed him.

Bernardo grinned at her, then turned his still beaming face to Armando as he strolled over.

'Not interrupting anything important, am I?'

'Not at all,' Armando said as he watched his friend lower himself into the opposite seat to the one Helena had occupied.

Armando's oldest and closest friend was a big man in every sense. He was taller than most Portuguese, and chubby. He wore light coloured suits which emphasised his size even more. Today's was a mustard plaid which somehow worked well with his short cropped gingerish beard. One day, when he turned grey, he'd probably resemble Santa Claus, Armando thought.

He was wearing the perfume Armando had made for him. It had been an act of desperation on Armando's part because he couldn't get Bernardo to stop wearing a deodorant with marine notes combined with the most unpleasantly acidic aftershave redolent of cheap tobacco and pine. This, even when Armando had pointed out that a man with a beard didn't need to wear aftershave.

Now, although he insisted on wearing a scent, it was at least one Armando could tolerate and that also matched as Armando had turned it into an entire men's range, including deodorant. It had become one of their bestsellers. Armando had named it, Urso, bear in Portuguese, as a joke. Bernardo was rather proud of it, though, and lost no time informing everyone he met that he was the person Armando had made the perfume for.

'I came because I saw the video.'

Bernardo leaned forward and poured himself a glass of water from the cut crystal jug Armando kept on his desk. He didn't allow strong scented drinks in his office.

'Ah.'

Armando was resigned to the fact that everybody he knew would have seen the video by now.

'Are you alright?'

At least Bernardo understood the excruciating experience it would have been to have someone throw up on him. It was bad enough for a normal person but for Armando... He sniffed and shook his head dismissively.

'The smell still haunts me. But I was stupid to run.'

'Where did you go?' Bernardo asked, his face crinkling back into its habitual smile as he took a sip of water.

'To the nearest hotel for a shower and change.'

'Fair enough,' Bernardo said. 'I wish I was your size so I could take that expensive suit. I'm willing to bet you threw it away.'

'I wouldn't have been able to wear it again. No amount of washing would have obliterated the smell, or the stain.'

'No, I suppose not.'

'You don't wear black, anyway.'

'That is also true. I assume Helena was here to discuss damage control.'

Bernardo stated it as a fact. He was familiar enough with Armando's family that he knew what they all did. He also came from a wealthy family, descendants from port wine growers who'd moved down to Lisbon to become bankers a few generations before. So he was doubly aware of how wealthy families were managed.

'I don't understand why she was quite so flustered by a video though.'

'I think she's more focussed on how she can use it against me,' Armando said.

Bernardo would understand that too, he was always manoeuvring against his two brothers.

'Huh, the joys of wealth and power,' Bernardo said with a cynical laugh.

'Mmm,' Armando murmured in agreement. His mind was only half on the conversation. The rest was turning over his suspicion of Diana Luna and what she might really be up to. 'Do you think Maria would do something for me?'

Bernardo blinked at this change in the conversation's direction.

'My Maria?'

His surprise was understandable. Armando rarely met or spoke to Maria, even though she'd been Bernardo's girlfriend for the last seven years. She still dreamed of marriage, but Bernardo was commitment shy after a disastrous first marriage that had ended with a bruising divorce. Armando doubted he'd ever be willing to go through the same thing again.

'I want to find out more about the woman in the video, but she slammed the door in my face when I went to see her.'

'Wait!' Bernardo said so surprised he sat bolt upright, his eyes popping. 'You went to see this woman even after she threw up on you?'

'It wasn't that big a deal.'

'It wasn't? You say the memory of the smell is lingering, you live avoiding most smells and yet you were willing to visit a woman who spewed red wine vom–'

'Stop,' Armando said, throwing up his hand. 'Please, don't remind me.'

'That is precisely my point. You can't even bear to hear me talk about it, but you went to see this woman? Is she right about the theft?'

'Bernardo, don't make such a fuss, and whatever you do, don't spread it around.'

'You know me. I can keep my mouth shut if necessary. But what has this got to do with Maria?'

Armando trusted Bernardo completely, which was why he was willing to say as much as he did.

'I need her to do something for me and I can't use Helena.'

'Well, that's true. She'll never do anything that will advantage you.'

'And Diana Luna might recognise her as a Zeller.'

'Who?'

'The woman from the video.'

'Okay, but it isn't like Maria is a private detective. What is she supposed to discover?'

'This Diana Luna is a perfumer as well.'

'She is?'

'She owns a little shop in Sintra that makes personalised perfume.'

'Like you did for me,' Bernardo said, nodding his understanding. 'So you want Maria to get this woman to make her a perfume?'

'Exactly.' His friend's quick grasp of the situation pleased but didn't surprise Armando. 'And, if she can find out as much as possible about Ms Luna while she's there, that would be useful. I'm especially curious about her financial situation.'

'Can't Libero find that out for you? He's a genius when it comes to digging up financials.'

'I'll be asking him to get the actual figures, company records and the like. But I'm curious about perception. Diana Luna lives modestly, but how is she feeling? Has the current crisis affected her in a way that's making her feel more squeezed than usual? That's what I'm after, a state of mind.'

'Might she be desperate enough to do something drastic, you mean?'

'Precisely.'

Armando didn't know why, but he'd prefer it if Diana Luna was acting out of desperation rather than simply as a calculated ploy to squeeze money out of him.

CHAPTER SIX

D iana was sitting behind the counter of her shop, surrounded by bills and gripped by such a sense of panic that she barely noticed her surroundings. Usually, the shop brought her a tremendous sense of comfort. The shop itself was simple, a rectangular space with a floor to ceiling glass window that looked out onto the treelined street beyond.

It was disastrously short of people, though. Usually a pleasant hubbub of passers-by would drift in through her open door. Today, only a single couple had meandered by. They looked like tourists on their way to the world famous Quinta da Regaleira. Tourists rarely stopped at her shop, but a few had over the years and some had even become regular customers. A couple walking arm in arm was unlikely. They had thoughts other than getting a perfume.

This filled Diana with gloom because it reminded her of Fernando. At least when she'd had him, she could push her financial worries to the back of her mind. Partly as a distraction but also partly as an option, she'd considered selling the shop and moving in with him.

She'd never said anything to him because it wasn't really what she wanted. She'd feared that if she mentioned it, he'd try to get her to do exactly that. Maybe she'd been more aware of his wish for a more present, supportive girlfriend than she'd realised.

She couldn't even imagine losing the shop. It held so many memories of her grandmother, and her, and even a few of her mother. She'd never cared about perfume and had taken up smoking in open rebellion. That had been the start of the schism. Now all Diana got were postcards. They told her where her mother was and who she was with, but those had become fewer and fewer after grandmother's death.

Diana shook that thought away. She'd not needed her mother, and she'd be no help now. She was more likely to want to sell the shop and split the proceeds than offer any practical support.

Diana looked along the shelves of scents that lined the left and right walls. To her, they were miniature bottles of promise. All dark brown glass to protect the scents within from being degraded by the sun.

Not that much sun fell directly into the shop. It was north facing and the wall of the palacete opposite blocked what little direct sunshine she might get. Grandmother had also chosen Sintra as the best place for the shop because it was near Lisbon but considerably cooler. Most scents didn't like heat.

Today, at least, Diana did have a customer. She'd had a phone call from a very pleasant sounding woman, who'd booked an actual appointment. Maybe Fernando was right, and she needed to set up on-line bookings. But the thought of setting up and managing her own website brought her to the verge of panic. She didn't have the money to pay for somebody else to do it for her, either.

She was eternally optimistic though and hoped that this new client might bring in others. Usually her business grew by word of mouth and she'd get a flush of new customers after the first. So she gathered up the bills, put them into a neat stack in her drawer and closed it while trying not to shudder.

'Ms Luna?' a voice said from the doorway.

Diana jumped, even though she'd been expecting this client. The woman in the doorway was what she called the socialite class. She was impossibly slim and dressed in a timeless but expensive fashion. This one a light cream silk blouse with a subtle gold stripe and flowing palazzo trousers, beige designer shoes and a beige designer bag completed the ensemble. She was fitting what looked like a designer facemask on as she stood in the doorway.

'I'm Maria de Gouveia, I have an appointment for eleven.'

'Yes, of course, please come in.'

Diana pulled her own mask on, a serious looking, laboratory style mask she'd found most reassured her clients as well as herself.

'What a charming shop you have.' Maria de Gouveia stopped to admire the glass cases and leaned forward to read the cursive gold script etched into the glass that listed the contents of the case. 'Rose scents? I thought there was only one rose scent.'

'Oh no, there are many,' Diana said. 'Some that come from various varieties of roses and some that come from different plants altogether. Many of the rose scented perfumes are actually made using an extract from geraniums.'

'How fascinating,' Maria de Gouveia said, and her eyes crinkled up in a smile.

Diana pulled on a pair of disposable latex gloves from a cardboard box and said, 'Please come through to my laboratory. We can start on your perfume there.'

'I'm quite excited about this,' Maria de Gouveia said as she followed Diana through into the back room of the shop. 'Oh, it's quite different.'

Diana always enjoyed the reaction she got from clients when she first walked them into her lab. Her grandmother had fitted the shop out and Diana had never changed it. The back was her design.

She'd painted the walls a refreshing pale green. The two tall rear windows looked down across the tree filled valley below Sintra and added light and freshness to the scene. A white marble semi-circular desk with rings of levels filled with rows of brown glass vials dominated half the room, and a comfortable white cotton covered sofa occupied the other half.

'Please take a seat,' Diana said, indicating the sofa while she put down a tray with a jug of water and a glass. 'As we'll be going through your favourite scents, it's best not to add additional smells.'

'Yes, you also said not to wear anything scented,' Maria said.

'If you look up, you'll notice that you are sitting directly below what looks like a kitchen hood. That's my extractor fan. It draws all the air around you up and away. It was designed so you can smell each scent individually, without one lingering and changing the effect of the smell on the next one. But these days it will also protect you from Corona as the virus would also be sucked up and away.'

'That does reassure me. I was wondering how I was going to smell anything with a mask on.'

'You can remove your mask. I'll keep mine on.' Diana sat down at the circular desk and waved a hand at all the bottles. 'This is a perfume organ because it looks like the musical instrument. From here, I can compose your perfume. Are you ready?'

'Absolutely,' Maria said, smiling in anticipation as she removed her mask, folded it and put it in her bag.

'We will go through your favourite scents in a moment, but before we start, it's helpful to know what you want this perfume for.'

Diana was expecting the blank look of confusion she got, because her question usually puzzled all of her first time clients.

'Perfumes are used for many things. Do you want a scent that you wear to work, or something for a special occasion? You can go with something heavier for a grand night out that wouldn't work at the office. Or perhaps you need something for seduction.'

Diana said the last with a smile because, even if women might not admit it, perfume was a powerful tool in their arsenal.

'Seduction?' Maria asked and her face took on a considering look. 'To seduce a man to fall in love?'

'Or to keep him. I have lost track of the women who've come to this shop, first to my grandmother and then to me, either to beg for something to make a man fall in love with them, or to keep a man who was starting to lose interest.'

'Well then, I'd need a perfume to get a man who loves me to finally propose,' Maria said with a laugh that had a hint of sadness.

'You want to get married?'

'We've been together for seven years. I'm sure he loves me, but he's divorced and he lost a lot from the first marriage and not just money. People think he's bitter over the money, but she really did break his heart.'

'I see. That's a tricky situation.'

'Don't worry,' Maria said, flapping her hands as if to make Diana forget. 'I don't expect any perfume to perform such a miracle.'

'I would never promise to either. Even with my skills I couldn't keep my boyfriend.'

'You've had a recent breakup?'

Maria sounded so sympathetic that it made Diana blush.

'Last week. We'd been together for five years and I didn't even see it coming.'

'You poor thing.'

It was Diana's turn to laugh and wave her hand in dismissal.

'I drank a small fortune in wine to console myself. That helped. Now, let's see what we can do to find you something perfectly seductive.'

The two women began talking scents and Diana selected Maria's current favourites to start with before they broadened out the possible choices and started experimenting with combinations. The session lasted a couple of hours and Diana felt like she'd made a friend by the time Maria left.

It was lunchtime, and since she'd closed the shop for the consultation, she left it as it was and went upstairs to her apartment to make herself lunch. Then, with her sandwich balanced on one knee as she sat cross-legged on her sofa, she started going through emails on her phone. The first few emails were the usual collection of marketing and work related stuff.

Then her eyes lighted upon an email from the Zeller corporation. Just seeing the name made her stomach clench anxiously. The subject line said *Cease and Desist Notice*, which just made her angry.

She stabbed at the screen, and the email popped open. It informed her in legalese that her recent outburst, videotaped and put online, constituted a libellous action. If she didn't wish to be hauled through the courts, she would refrain from ever mentioning the Zeller Corporation again.

'Bastards!' Diana shouted and threw down the bread roll she was currently crushing between her suddenly clenched fist. 'How dare you!'

She noted that Helena Zeller had sent the email. So the bastard man who'd come to see her hadn't even bothered to write to her directly, but had used his sister as his messenger.

You're a coward, she wrote. *If you have something to say to me, do it in person. I will never, ever, stop telling the world that the Zellers stole my grandmother's perfume.*

You've made a fortune from it, but you didn't deserve to. What your grandfather did broke my grandmother's heart and you should pay for that, if nothing else. If you threaten me again, I'll never stay quiet. I have the proof of what you did, and no number of expensive lawyers will be able to erase that.

Diana was so furious she could hardly breathe as she wrote. She was determined that the man would hear from her directly. She wasn't going to hide behind a family member. Diana ran over to her paper recycling bin, emptied it out onto the floor and threw the papers around, looking for the business card.

She snatched it up with a triumphant, 'Aha!'

She rushed back to the phone, added his email address in the CC field with trembling fingers and then punched the send button. She was still standing in the centre of her living room, shaking from head to foot in combined terror at what she'd done and fury at the Zellers. Her grandmother, as always, was right, and never more so than when it came to the treachery of that dreadful family.

Armando signed as he looked over the client brief. Lately, the trend had been for pop stars to release perfumes. The Zeller Corporation had spearheaded the trend, which he regretted, but Helena had pushed for it. Now every pop singer, influencer and half famous starlet wanted their own perfume.

It was profitable for the company, as it seemed hordes of women and girls would rush out and buy their favourite idol's scent. Such was the magic of celebrity. It was as if the customer thought they'd gain some of that star quality by spraying the same scent on their bodies.

He wondered whether they'd be as keen if they knew that their stars seldom wore the perfume they endorsed. It would charm the star at first, of course, and they'd wear it to the launch party. They might even finish the bottle the perfume house gifted them, but after that they'd flitter off to another perfume and then the next.

Their briefs were ridiculous, too. This one, who went by the singular name of Céu, wanted a scent that reminded people of fresh air and gold. As if they were flying up to heaven with money beneath their pretty little feet. Ambition and freedom were the keywords. He'd leave it to Helena's marketing division to come up with a suitably pompous name for the scent.

He'd have to sit down with his top perfume composer, Pedro Martins, and try to decide what wind and gold would smell like. The shape and style of the bottle could encompass some of that. A few flecks of lighter than air gold leaf floating in the perfume would probably thrill the pop star.

'Sir, I think you should look at this,' Libero said as he walked straight to the desk, his tablet held out before him.

Libero vetted his email, so that Armando didn't have to deal with junk. If he was bringing something in, it had to be important.

He noted with surprise that the email came from Diana Luna. It was in reply to something from Helena, which caused a twinge of concern. Armando scanned the email, then scrolled down to see what Helena had sent. Then he sat back in his chair, staring at the ceiling to consider.

'I would say she wrote her reply in a rage,' Libero said. 'Hence the lack of coherence.'

'Mmm. I didn't think Helena could be quite this clumsy when dealing with a situation.'

'You went to talk to her. Does Ms Helena know that?'

'It's probably what precipitated the letter. Her coming down hard to nip whatever Ms Luna might have been planning next.'

'Ah, I see. Well, as you say, it seems to have backfired.'

'And complicated what I was trying to do.'

'You also had a plan?' Libero asked, at his most neutral.

He was still, days later, digesting the fact that his boss had taken the unusual step of going to see a woman who'd caused him distress. This from a man, Armando was acutely aware, who avoided people.

'I wanted to get at the truth. I'm not sure if Ms Luna is genuine, or if the whole thing is a fabrication designed to extort money. Looking at this email, she's either sincere, and deeply hurt, or she has never tried to extort money from anyone before and she's doing it badly.'

'Has she actually asked for money?'

'Not yet.' Armando tapped his finger meditatively on the email. 'Would you look into her financial situation, please? She owns a shop so the business must be registered with the Ministry of Finance.'

'I will do that immediately.'

Libero took back the tablet, clicked his heels and returned to his office.

Armando logged onto his computer and opened the email again. This time, he read Helena's email first. It was a form email that she sent out to any pretender who tried to get money out of the company, either by copying their fragrances or making too similar bottles and logos.

Those that tried to brazen it out landed up in court on the losing side. Helena had never lost to a scammer. But usually they were bigger or more organised fraudsters. It felt overly harsh to send something like this to a woman who appeared to live on her own.

Armando was so distracted by the email that he didn't realise an hour had passed till Libero came back to his office and he glanced at the clock.

'I've sent you the financial information about Ms Luna,' Libero said

'And?'

'Her shop makes very little. Her turnover most years scrapes €20,000. What with the Covid crisis, I doubt she'll make anywhere near that this year.'

'So she is under financial pressure.'

Armando said couldn't even conceive of how anyone could live on as little as €20,000 a year. He spent more than that in a month.

Someone tapped on the glass pane of Armando's door and Libero turned to see who it was.

'Ms Maria de Gouveia,' he murmured.

'I was expecting her,' Armando said and waved Maria in.

'Good afternoon, Armando' Maria said and also nodded a greeting to Libero, who took this as his sign to leave while giving Maria a nod of acknowledgement.

'I take it you've just got back from Sintra,' Armando said as he indicated for Maria to sit.

'I have.'

Maria settled in the chair, looking as uncomfortable as he intended for visitors but that they covered up. Maria was very attractive, with her long dark hair swept up into an elegant ponytail.

She also smelled different. Usually she wore a Zeller perfume. He sometimes wondered whether that was meant to flatter him or if it was a perfume she liked.

'Do you like the perfume Ms Luna made?'

'I do, very much.'

Maria smiled up at him. She had a rather fixed smile, something that looked determinedly friendly, rather than genuine. It was one of the things he found off-putting about her.

'I also liked Ms Luna,' Maria added. 'She's a very pleasant woman and we had a good chat.'

'Did you ask her about her financial situation?'

'Strangely enough, that didn't come up. You can't just come out and ask people if their business is going well. It would be rude.'

'Do you think she is struggling, though?'

Armando didn't want to offend Maria, but this was a serious situation. Maria appeared to relax a bit and shifted in her chair.

'This may be elegant, but it's very uncomfortable. You know, Armando, I can't help contrast you to Ms Luna. She was very welcoming. She made me feel comfortable in her laboratory and we had a delightful conversation. I felt quite dreadful spying on her. Is this really all about that video and trying to work out if she's some sort of con artist?'

'It is.'

'Well, I don't think she is a con artist. Anyone who meets her would know in seconds that she really knows about perfumes and she cares about them. On top of that, she cares about people. She put a great deal of effort into finding a scent that I liked and that works with my skin chemistry. I can't help feeling that a con artist wouldn't do such a thing.'

'Did she make the perfume there and then? Do you have it with you?'

'What you can smell on me is all I have so far. She said she will work up three slightly different formulas for me to try out and see how they wear on me across the day. Then I'll get back to her with the one I prefer, and she'll make me a larger bottle at that point.'

'How much does she charge?'

'Too little. €200 for the consultation and €150 for a bottle of scent. But I suppose that's all most of her customers are willing to pay. I'm tempted to tell all my friends to go and see her.'

'By all means. May I take a closer smell of the perfume?'

Maria looked reluctant for a moment, then held out her arm, pulse upwards. Armando stood up so that he could reach, and leaned down over her wrist, closed his eyes and took a quick, light sniff and then a deeper one as he opened his mouth. The scent was warm from Maria's body, musky, with a top note of freesia and a finish of just a hint of wood smoke. It was a surprising combination but one that worked on Maria.

'What do you think?' Maria asked as Armando sat back down. 'Is it enough to make you fall in love?'

Armando stared at Maria, trying to work out who was supposed to fall in love with whom.

Maria gave him her bright, fixed smile and said, 'Bernardo.'

'Ah... you know...'

Maria laughed and shook her head.

'Don't answer. It isn't fair to ask Bernardo's best friend. Besides, you aren't that keen on women anyway, so this probably wouldn't tempt you.'

Armando shook his head in apparent agreement, but his memory was filled with the scent of honey and herbs and soil as he did so.

'People smell overpowering sometimes.'

'Bernardo explained, don't worry. You don't have to tell me. I've also just worked out what that vent over my head is. I thought it was an air conditioner, but Ms Luna has one in her lab too. It sucks air and the fragrances they contain up and away, doesn't it?'

'Ms Luna has one too?'

'I assume it's a tool of the trade. Oh yes,' Maria said as something else occurred to her, 'I wasn't an entirely useless spy.

'Ms Luna has recently broken up with her longtime boyfriend. She told me she drank a lot of wine to get over him. I suspect you ran into her shortly after that.'

CHAPTER SEVEN

D iana was just finishing getting dressed when Margarida
started pounding on her door.

'Diana, Diana, get up. Your shop's been burgled!'

The news gave her such a fright that Diana was bereft of air and
ran over to open the door, her hands shaking.

'What's happened?'

'I was just about to go for my jog when I noticed your shop door
was forced,' Margarida said, bending over to catch her breath.

'Oh no!' Diana said and ran to look.

It was as Margarida had said, her shop door was shattered into
those tiny squares that safety glass broke into. It was still hanging
in the frame but bulging inwards, and there was a fist-sized hole
by the lock where they'd dismantled it. The thief hadn't bothered
to close the door, so now it stood half open to the street.

'I wonder what time this happened?'

'You should take photos.' Margarida already had her phone
out. 'And you should call the police.'

'Yes.'

Diana didn't move. She was too shocked to think clearly.
Thankfully, Margarida took things in hand and Diana was vaguely
aware of her calling the police.

'They said we should wait outside. Just in case the thieves are still here.'

'Alright.'

Diana didn't even look around. She wondered why she was in such a deep state of shock. It was only a break in, after all. It wasn't as though she'd been physically attacked. Whatever had happened could all be repaired. So why was she so upset?

The police station was nearby, Sintra being a small town, so that the police arrived a mere three minutes later. Two familiar officers got out of the car, a man and a woman. They patrolled the neighbourhood and would stop by at the Butterfly Cafe at the end of their rounds.

The female officer, Ramos, said, 'You waited outside, didn't you?'

'Yes.'

Diana didn't want to go in for fear of what she might see. Strangely enough, it wasn't in case the thieves were still inside.

'Please wait here, we will check the store first,' the male officer, Silva, said.

The two officers donned latex gloves, readjusted their face masks and eased themselves past the shattered door, being careful to move it as little as possible.

'What do you think they'll find?' Margarida asked, looking anxious.

'I can't imagine. I mean, it isn't like I have anything of value and I never keep money in the shop.'

'Yeah.'

Margarida glanced at her own shop and Diana realised she was worried this break-in might be the first of many. All the shopkeepers had grown more anxious lately, filled with the fear of what increasing unemployment might bring.

'Maybe as they left empty-handed from here, they'll not bother coming back,' Diana said in an attempt to reassure.

Margarida gave her an apologetic smile for worrying about herself at this moment but was prevented from saying anything as the police officers returned.

'It's all clear,' Officer Ramos said. 'We'll need the shop owner to come inside and tell us what's missing.'

Diana nodded, anxious to do a check and equally reluctant to go inside. It was an odd set of mixed emotions. So she followed in a daze. The main part of the shop looked fine. All the cabinets holding her scent bottles were thankfully intact. The drop down section of her counter was in the upright position. The thief had ripped the lab door open so forcefully he'd torn the locking mechanism out of the frame that was also shattered and splintered.

Diana took a moment to compose herself as she stepped into the lab. It was chaos. The rows of cupboards she had on the left and right walls had all been broken open. Fortunately, the latches were delicate little things, merely used to prevent the doors from swinging open, so there wasn't too much damage from that. But the room was filled with the contents of the cupboards. It was as if the thieves had tipped everything out in search of... What had they been looking for?

A sudden shock of realisation made her jump.

'Oh my God, my notebooks!'

'Your notebooks?' Officer Silva said.

'Yes, my black notebooks. They're filled with the formulas of all my perfumes, and the contact details of all my clients plus their orders. They're gone!'

Diana rushed to the cupboard that had held the notebooks and started pushing aside the drifts of paper on the floor, praying for all she was worth that the books were merely hidden.

'They're gone,' she said and tears sprang to her eyes, 'along with my grandmother's formula books.'

'Are these books valuable?' Officer Silva asked.

'They're vital for my work, and the formulas... I suppose they could be useful to other perfumers.'

The moment Diana spoke the words, a terrible suspicion sprang to her mind.

She was about to voice it when Officer Ramos said, 'We've written up the incident, and taken photos. Take some more photos for your insurance. Come to the station to get the case number and let us know if you find anything else that's missing.'

'Is that it?'

'We'll check the CCTV and see what else we can find. As this break-in doesn't seem to have resulted in major loss I'm afraid it's unlikely to be investigated further. But we will let you know what we discover.'

'Of course,' Diana said as a numb sense of futility settled on her.

She knew the police were doing what they could, but she felt let down all the same. She followed them out of the shop and watched as the two officers got back in their car and Margarida rejoined her.

'What did they say?'

'The usual when a shop gets broken into. But, you know, I don't think it was an ordinary robbery.'

'You don't? What did they take?'

'My notebooks and my grandmother's books.' Rage was building within Diana. 'I think it was the Zellers.'

'Industrial espionage?' Margarida said, giving Diana an astonished look. 'From you?'

'They're trying to remove all evidence of their thievery by committing even more theft. Well, I won't let them,' Diana said as she started back up her stairs. 'Margarida, will you do what you can to secure the shop, please? I have to go to Lisbon.'

'Now?'

'If I don't do it now, I won't be able to work up the courage again.' Diana pounded up the stairs, grabbed her travel pass and handbag, and ran back out again past an anxious-looking Margarida. 'You'll do that for me, won't you?'

'Of course,' Margarida shouted after her.

Diana barely noticed. She was running for the train station, her feet pounding on the cobbles.

She was so worked up that she stood for most of the journey into Lisbon, even though the train carriage was half empty. Every time she tried to calm down and sit, the outrageousness of what had happened would force an explosive swearword from her and she'd be back on her feet and stomping up and down the carriage.

She stood on the Metro too. This was fuller, but nowhere near the levels it had been at before the lockdown. Diana wondered whether it would ever fill up as it had before. She dismissed that thought. Now was not the time.

Diana didn't allow herself to stop and take a breath in case she chickened out, as she ran up the stairs out of the Metro and down the tree lined elegant avenue up to the headquarters of the Zeller Corporation. She knew where the building was because her grandmother had once taken her there to show her.

Diana stormed through the grand entrance into what looked like the lobby of an ancient and stately institution. One where a person should speak in hushed tones.

She slammed her fists down on the reception counter and said at the top of her voice, 'I demand to see Armando Zeller!'

The receptionist looked shaken by her vehemence, conveyed so forcefully even with a facemask obscuring half her face.

'Do you have an appointment?'

'An appointment? No, I don't. But if he knows what's good for him and his company, he'll see me right away. If he doesn't, then this fuss here in the lobby will not be the last thing he sees.'

'I'm sorry, ma'am, but if you don't have an appointment...'

The woman's voice faded, and now she was looking over Diana's shoulder. Diana turned around to see three security guards approaching.

'I'm warning you, if I don't see Armando Zeller right now, he will be so sorry and you will lose your job.'

'My dear lady, there's no point in making threats,' one of the guards said. 'It would be better if you just go quietly.'

'I'm not going anywhere.'

Diana gripped the edge of the reception desk to anchor herself. It would hardly prevent her from being dragged away, but she wouldn't give up without a fight.

'It's alright,' a calm voice said. 'I will take Ms Luna up to see Mr Zeller.'

Everyone in the lobby turned to see who'd spoken. It was a grey-haired man, dressed in an impeccable pin striped suit.

'Mr Rocha,' the receptionist said. 'I'm sorry, sir, I didn't realise she was with you.'

'Not at all.'

Libero smiled at Diana and indicated for her to go through the security barrier. She was so taken aback all she could do was follow him. She also said nothing as he called for an elevator and stepped inside, but she felt foolish now as she followed meekly along.

'I take it you have urgent business,' Libero said.

'Yes,' Diana managed to say. 'Is he here?'

'He's in his office.'

Diana stared at the man, nonplussed. He was being polite, even helpful. It was as if it was quite an ordinary thing to accompany a woman who only moments before had been shouting in the lobby and willing to resist so hard that they'd have to carry her from the building.

The doors of the lift opened with a discreet ping and Diana stared out into a broad corridor that she found tremendously intimidating. But no, she couldn't fail now, not when she'd come so far. She clenched her fists and followed the smiling Mr Rocha as he turned right and walked to the end of the corridor and into a simple-looking office.

'He's through here,' Libero said, pointing at a sliding glass door.

Diana took a deep breath, gave Mr Rocha a nod of thanks and stepped through the door. A curtain of air took her by surprise and then she was standing inside a sterile, scentless and chilly laboratory. Armando Zeller was typing away at a laptop and Diana realised it was the first time she'd seen him in the flesh without a mask.

The enormity of what she was about to do struck her and she took a step back, seconds from running. Armando looked up. An eyebrow rose in surprise and he tilted his head to the side, examining her in deepening curiosity.

'Ms Luna?'

She had to give him one thing; he knew how to keep his cool. She doubted she could do the same if she'd just gone off and robbed somebody. Armando stood. He was taller than she remembered and Diana took another step back.

'What brings you here?'

His tone was abrupt, impatient, and that was all it took to bring all Diana's rage back.

'I want my notebooks, and my grandmother's notebooks, you thief!' she snapped.

'Your notebooks?' Armando said, and a confused crease formed between his brows. 'I'm sorry, I don't understand.'

'You don't understand? That's rich coming from you. You broke into my shop and took all my notebooks and now you're acting all innocent? I mean, fine, I get why you'd want my grandmother's formula book, but to take everything else. All my formulas, my client's names and addresses and what I send them. Did you have to be that greedy? Are you so determined to ruin me?'

'I really don't know what you are referring to. Please, sit down. Have a glass of water, calm yourself and then explain. I'm sure we can clear everything up.'

'Clear everything up?' Diana said so angry that he was continuing this charade that she could feel tears welling up. Why did she always cry when she was enraged? 'I should have known better than to come here. I should have known you would never admit to it.'

She dashed her hand across her face, feeling so impotent now she might collapse if she stayed. This was too much. She turned away so that Zeller couldn't see her face, took a determined sniff and walked out with as much dignity as she could muster.

Armando stood, confused by what had just happened, and a wave of honey, herbs and sun-dried soil wafted towards him and was gone as his vents sucked it away. For the first time in his life, he wished they didn't do that. Then he went through to Libero's office.

'What the devil just happened?'

Libero was also standing, but facing his office door in the direction Diana Luna had gone. He turned to examine Armando.

'She looked distressed.'

'That is something of an understatement,' Armando said, his irritation building. 'How did she even get in?'

'I saw her in the lobby and decided to let her in.'

'For the love of God, why?'

Sometimes Libero acted like somebody who knew better, rather than somebody who was paid to make sure Armando suffered no inconvenience.

'It seemed something serious had happened. Was I mistaken?'

Libero spoke in his usual gentle way that most often got Armando to pay attention. Which it did again as his frown deepened.

'She said somebody broke into her shop and stole all her formula books.'

'Ah.' Libero sat down behind his desk and made a thoughtful steeple with his fingers. 'That does sound serious.'

'Yes.' Now that Armando considered it, Diana Luna was right; losing all her formula books and customer information would finish her. 'But I didn't do it. There's no point coming in here and creating a scene when it has nothing to do with me.'

'Are you sure?'

'Of course, I'm sure. I would know if I'd ordered a break in. For goodness' sake, man–' Armando stopped abruptly and glared at the wall for a few seconds, thinking. What had just occurred to him was so utterly outrageous as to be unbelievable. 'Helena?'

His sister was capable of taking stupid risks, but surely even she wouldn't do something like this to cover up a threat to the company. Armando felt a twinge of anger and suppressed it. He couldn't go off into a rage merely on a suspicion. On the other hand, if Helena had just blundered, this at least evened things out between them.

'Just a moment,' he said and stalked down the corridor to his sister's office.

Armando ignored her secretary, who tried her best to get him to tell her why he'd come, and threw open his sister's door. Helena's office looked and smelled like a boudoir. The room was decorated in shades of pink, a chaise lounge draped in something with tassels nestled in the corner and an elegant desk with legs so spindly they looked like they might snap stood before an open French window.

Helena seemed to glory in filling the office with the scent of her current favourite. At the moment, it appeared to be Flower Garden. Armando had created it but never intended for it to be used at such intensity.

There was much to object to in the room, but all else was swept from his mind by the sight of a large cardboard box sitting on Helena's desk. It was filled with black notebooks. Helena was seated at her desk, one shapely leg crossed and then wrapped behind the other, as she leafed through a book.

'Helena!' Armando snapped.

She gave a start, dropped the book and leaped to her feet. 'What?'

Helena did a good job at wide-eyed innocence, but she flushed guiltily too.

'Please tell me that box of books didn't come from Diana Luna's shop.'

'No, of course not.' Helena frowned and said more slowly, 'what do you mean by that question? Did somebody break into her shop?'

'You know damn well they did.' Armando flipped one of the books open and looked inside. The hard lined cover of the book bore a faded stamp with the words *Perfumes da Luna* with an attractive motif of flowers below. 'You were saying?'

'Alright, speak quieter.'

Helena jumped up, shot across the room and locked her door. Then she looked around as if checking for additional lurking people.

'This is ridiculous. Have you completely lost your mind?'

'No, I didn't,' Helena said, keeping her back pressed against the door. 'I hired somebody outside the company to investigate Diana Luna. He was just supposed to verify her story, at most slip into her lab and get photographic evidence. He's done similar work for me in the past. Instead, he brought me this,' she said, waving a suddenly limp hand in the direction of the cardboard boxes. 'Did he damage her property?'

'It sounds like it and Ms Luna has just left my office shouting that, not only am I a thief but I look like I'm determined to destroy her.'

'I'm not trying to do that.'

'So what happened? Why the break in? He was your employee after all.'

Armando was rather enjoying his bit of schadenfreude while simultaneously trying to come up with a solution.

'I'm afraid I might have overemphasised the need for him to act quickly.'

Helena hated ever admitting anything to Armando, so he realised, although she was working hard not to show it, that the outcome shocked her.

'I had to do something,' Helena said, going on the defensive. 'You didn't look like you would put a stop to Ms Luna.'

'Why would I, Helena, huh? I've been mulling over the video and the risk of Ms Luna popping back up and I was coming to the conclusion that we didn't really need to worry. After all, it's been over fifty years since grandfather started selling Armour and in all that time the Lunas have never approached us.'

'Well, maybe they were about to.'

'Then we should have dealt with it via our lawyers!' Armando shouted.

'And landed up with a hit to our reputation, and a potential payout sucking up our funds?'

'You mean as compared to us breaking into somebody's shop and stealing the evidence?'

'She has no proof it was us,' Helena muttered as she headed towards sulkiness.

'And why all the books, huh? Why not just the grandmother's notebook?'

'Because the man couldn't tell which book had the formula. So he brought them all.'

'Well, I'm giving them back.'

Armando took the book Helena had dropped on her desk, put it in the box, hoisted it and headed back to his office.

'You can't return them, then she'll know it was us for sure,' Helena said as she ran for him and grabbed the other side of the box.

'She already suspects it's us, and that's all she needs to take to the media,' Armando said, and shoved Helena away. 'So now we're going to have to come up with a way to not only stop the gossip over the incident at the perfume counter but also suspicions about the theft.'

'She'll never be able to prove it's us if we get rid of this box.'

Helena made a determined grab for it again and used all her strength to try to wrest it from Armando.

'Then you really will destroy her and prove that what she said is true. We're thieves and liars. No, I won't allow that. This whole bizarre mess began with me, so I'll resolve it. You stay out of it from now on.' Armando lifted the box so high that Helena could no longer hang on. 'And open the damn door.'

For once Helena obeyed, but she gave him a venomous look as he marched past her and her stunned secretary and out into the corridor.

The usual senior managers had emerged from their offices to see what the commotion was about. They stared at him and then whispered to each other after he'd passed. The silent battle over the inheritance had never broken out in public and Armando regretted it had become so visible today. But he was so angry with his sister that he was past caring. He also had an incipient headache brought on by the overpowering perfume in Helena's office, which didn't help.

Armando placed the box filled with books on Libero's desk.

'Make electronic copies of all of this for me, please. Let me know once you're done. In the meantime, send Pedro Martins in the moment he arrives.'

'She had them?' Libero said, considerably surprised. 'And you want copies?'

'Mmm,' Armando said with a nod.

His curiosity over Diana Luna had grown following Maria's visit. Ms Luna had a unique talent. She had made a blend for Maria that neither he nor any of his people would have conceived of, and it worked beautifully. It was probably because she wasn't traditionally trained. It was as if she had created jazz while they were all still playing classical music.

'Isn't that still just theft?' Libero said.

He was using his slightly disappointed tone of voice, which always worked to make Armando feel bad.

'It depends on what I use it for.'

Armando hurried to his office to find a solution that would work for both Ms Luna and the Zeller Corporation and also so that he no longer had to justify himself to Libero. His morning was not going to plan but, crazy as it had become, he still needed to keep to his schedule. So he popped a couple of painkillers and waited for Pedro Martins who arrived bang on time.

Pedro looked every inch the perfume composer of his job title, sporting trendy three day stubble and wavy hair that brushed his shoulders. He wore a suit that was draped rather than shaped, a silk scarf rather than a tie and a loose shirt, not tucked in. He was an excellent nose, which was why Armando had hired him.

'Morning Chief,' Pedro said as he sailed into the office and gave an over the top bow.

'What's this?'

'In lieu of a handshake,' Pedro said, grinning widely. 'I reckon those Asians are onto something with the bowing.'

'Fair enough,' Armando said and indicated for Pedro to sit down. 'Now, what are we going to do with our pop starlet's perfume brief?'

Pedro rolled his eyes.

'Wind and gold, the mind boggles.'

An hour later, the two men had come up with the beginnings of a profile for their new perfume and Pedro went away looking happy. Libero, on the other hand, came into the office still looking disappointed.

'I've done as you asked. All the copies of the notebooks are now in your personal cloud.'

'Thank you,' Armando said. 'Then I'll return the books to Ms Luna.'

'Now?'

'I imagine she'll be happy to see them.'

'But you'll be admitting that you stole them.'

'I'll go via our company lawyers, don't worry. I'll be led by what they recommend. But I believe if we return the books and pay for any necessary repairs we'll be alright. I doubt a judge would give us a hard time about it then, even if it ended up in court.'

'That all depends on whether the judge finds out about the copies,' Libero said back to looking disapproving.

'He better not.'

Armando hoisted the box of notebooks and headed downstairs to the legal department.

CHAPTER EIGHT

After a tedious meeting with the company lawyers, who always made everything more complicated, Armando was back on the highway to Sintra. It was ironic that Sintra, a world heritage site because of the beauty of its architecture and the unique Atlantic rainforest that surrounded it, was approached via one of the ugliest highways in the country. The stark, run down blocks of flats that lined the route were depressing. It was a relief, therefore, to finally leave the highway. The narrow, winding mountain road lined by gigantic plane trees casting a dappled shade along the road was far more pleasant. The sun flashed through the leaves like a strobe light, dazzling him every few seconds, and then he was out again and into the small town of Sintra.

One half of the central square, a flat space on the side of the mountain, was dominated by the massive white Palacio Nacional. The twin whitewashed beehive shaped chimneys that towered over everything gave the palace a unique look. The old kings of Portugal used to retreat to Sintra every summer, as it was always a good ten degrees cooler than the capital. Shops and restaurants clustered about the other side of the square, looking forlorn and empty with the lack of tourists.

Having grown up in Lisbon and visited Sintra umpteen times on school trips and with friends, Armando barely glanced at the palace as he kept to the left, following the road that went past the square and on down a narrow lane to Ms Luna's shop.

It was just after lunchtime when Armando arrived. As before, he found a parking space a little distance from the shop. Pre-Covid, there would have been so many parked cars that it would have been impossible to do so. He supposed the pandemic was being helpful in this one respect.

He paused for a moment as he undid his seatbelt, gazing at the cardboard box of notebooks on the driver's seat. This was going to be an awkward conversation. Why was it that he and Ms Luna kept crossing paths in such an unfortunate way? He couldn't help but feel that if they'd come across each other under different circumstances, they might have become friends.

As it was, he was more curious about Diana Luna than he'd ever been about any woman. With his family connections and money, he was a popular target with unmarried women. Some were blatant about why they wanted to go out with him, others were more subtle. None of them had survived first contact because Armando couldn't get over their various scents.

Armando left the box of books in the car, smoothed his suit and tie, double checked there were no gaps around his face mask and headed for the shop. The shattered door was being held together by sheets of plastic that had been spread tight and taped to the doorframe. Tiny squares of glass had fallen between the gaps of the square white cobblestones, showing that they had swept the area, but the break-in was recent. Armando pushed the door open and was relieved that the main part of the shop appeared to be undamaged.

'Hello?' He felt a fool now that he'd come. 'Ms Luna?'

'Through here. I'm sorry I'm not seeing customers today.' Diana emerged from the back room and her smile faded as she realised who it was. 'I have nothing to say to you.'

'Even if it relates to your books?' Armando said, regretting, once again, that they'd started out on such a bad footing.

'So you did steal them.'

Diana's expression hardened as her body tensed.

'I didn't.' Armando was aware that he was splitting hairs, but he also didn't want this woman to think of him as a thief. 'But I have a potential solution if you're willing to hear me out.'

'Why would I want to listen to a thing you have to say?'

'Because I'm in a position to help you, and you are in a position to help me.'

'What could I possibly do to help the all powerful Zeller corporation?' Diana said with a harsh laugh, staying well behind her counter.

'There is the minor matter of the hit to our reputation. I'm sure you don't care that the video of the two of us...'

Armando paused, so overwhelmed by the memory of it that the smell made his face curl up in disgust. It must have embarrassed Diana Luna too, because she flushed and looked away for a second, before her anger reasserted itself and she went back to glaring at him.

'That video,' Armando said diving in again, 'wiped millions off our share price.'

'You won't go hungry because of it. I doubt it will make much of a difference to your company, especially when your share price rises again. But losing my notebooks will finish me.'

'As I said, I can help you, too.'

It surprised Armando that Diana Luna wasn't leaping at the chance to save herself. It made him wonder what exactly had happened between his grandfather and her grandmother to engender such suspicion. At the moment, it looked like a mighty conflict was raging in her heart and reflected on her face as one thought followed the next.

Finally she said, 'What are you proposing?'

'Have you ever heard of a nondisclosure agreement?' Armando asked. This was the most delicate moment of the negotiation.

Diana mouthed the words, considering.

'Isn't that when disgusting male colleagues are protected by their organisations from allegations of sexual harassment by co-workers?'

'That's one of the ways an NDA is used, yes.' Armando wished it wasn't the one Ms Luna had homed in on. 'But we use them in business all the time. Many employees aren't allowed to talk about information relating to their work after they leave their company. They sign NDAs too.'

'So,' Diana said, looking thoughtful, 'you're offering to bribe me to keep my mouth shut. Is that it?'

'I'm offering to compensate you for past losses.'

The lawyers had warned Armando to be as non-committal as possible before any paperwork was signed. He hoped he was being sufficiently vague, but it was difficult to do that and be understood by Ms Luna at the same time.

'I don't believe you.' Diana crossed her arms and glared at Armando. 'Going on your family's reputation and what just happened to me, I don't believe you'll do anything for me. It's more likely you'll make promises but then renege on it the moment you get what you're after.'

'How about I tell you what I'm offering first, then you can decide how you want to proceed?'

'How about you give me my books back first?' Diana had issued a challenge and she was taut, like somebody ready for a firing gun. She might run off at any moment. 'After that I might be more willing to believe you.'

Armando had his doubts, but at least he'd come prepared.

'First, give me your phone.'

'My phone? Why?'

'So that I know we aren't being recorded.'

'Then you give me your phone,' Diana said, not one to be outdone.

'Of course.'

Armando took his phone out of his pocket and held it out to Diana Luna. She examined it closely, making sure it was off. Then she left it on the counter and went back into the lab. She re-emerged carrying a battered old phone and now also wearing a mask.

'Here,' she said, holding her phone as far away from herself as possible to keep Armando at arm's length.

Armando left his phone on the counter and put Diana's into his pocket and took a step back. After all, with Covid and their careers, it was best to be as cautious as possible. He noted that Diana Luna swiped his phone's screen again to see what was running before pocketing it.

'There's nothing, I assure you. Now, one minute, please.'

Armando headed outside to fetch the box of books. He felt like no hostage negotiation had ever been conducted more carefully. He came back in and put the box down on the counter.

'Your books.'

'So you did take them,' Diana said in a voice that would have chilled a polar bear.

'I'm sorry.' Armando was aware that no amount of apology would be enough. 'I didn't know what had happened when you came to see me. It turns out an overzealous employee–'

'I don't need to hear the excuse,' Diana snapped. 'Give me back my phone and leave.'

'But I wanted to discuss the rest, the NDA,' Armando said but did hand back her phone and accepted his in return.

'Get out,' Diana said, glaring at him.

'I really would like to make it up to you,' Armando said but felt like he was making no headway.

To his surprise, Diana said, 'Get out of my shop, but wait there. I need to check that you have actually returned everything.'

At least he had that. It wasn't much, but it would be better to do as he was told for now. Once Diana Luna was reassured, he hoped he'd be able to discuss the rest. So he gave an accepting nod and went to stand outside the shop.

It was a pleasant day. A cool breeze was blowing off
the mountain, bringing with it the damp smell of trees
and waterlogged soil. Armando wondered whether Ms Luna
actually wore perfume at all, or whether she simply smelled of
her environment.

That strangely bewitching scent of soil might have come
from the neighbourhood. He had smelled beeswax polish on
the furniture inside. Maybe the rest was a herbal shampoo.
Only it was so subtle and perfect, it couldn't be that. Could it?

A sharp squeal and hiss of air drew Armando's attention to
the far end of the road and his heart quickened. It was a rubbish
collection truck. Without thinking, he stepped back into the
shop for sanctuary.

'Ms Luna, I–'

'Out!' Diana said, pausing at the work of removing a book
from the box. A small pile already stood stacked neatly on the
counter.

'The thing is–'

'Out, out, out, out!' Diana said at her most implacable.

Armando took a couple of steps backwards, praying the
dustbin lorry had already passed. He hadn't heard it, though.
But one look at Ms Luna's face and he realised he had no choice.

So he stepped outside just as the truck barrelled past,
releasing a noisome stench of putrefaction. Armando clapped
his hand over his mask, pinching his nose shut through the
fabric and tried not to breathe, but he was too late. A piercing
pain hit him right between the eyes.

Diana glared after Armando Zeller, making sure he didn't come
back in till she was ready for him. She was still shaken and relieved
to see the notebooks again and taking her time to make sure he'd
returned everything. A rubbish truck roared past and a second

later there was a soft thud from outside. She looked up to discover that Zeller was lying on the ground, his legs out in the road.

'Wha–'

She waited a split second to see if he got back to his feet, but he didn't move. Oh God, what if he died on her doorstep? That would be dreadful, she though, and ran outside.

'Mr Zeller?'

Diana was reluctant to touch him. She'd always been bad at confronting death or serious injury.

'Mr Zeller!'

Diana gathered all her courage, grabbed his shoulder and gave him a firm shake. His eyes remained closed, and she wondered whether he'd had a heart attack. Diana had taken a first aid course years ago and come home with the certain knowledge that the best thing she could ever do for anyone was call an ambulance. She was hopeless at the rest.

Diana was about to run inside to fetch her phone when Zeller's pocket started ringing. She pulled his phone out, practically dropping it in the process and swiped once, and then again another couple of times, as it refused to connect.

'Come on, come on.'

'Armando?' A man's voice said when she finally succeeded.

'No, it's Diana Luna. Mr Zeller collapsed and I can't get him to wake up!'

'Ms Luna, it's Mr Rocha,' the voice on the phone said. 'We met this morning.'

'Yes?' Diana said, reassured by his calm voice. 'Should I call an ambulance?'

'Before you do, can you tell me whether anything strong smelling came near Mr Zeller?'

'Strong smelling?' Diana felt close to tears with the craziness of the day. 'No, I... there was a rubbish truck.'

'Ah, well then, there is no need to worry and no need to call an ambulance. If you can just make Mr Zeller comfortable, I'll come and fetch him.'

'Make him comfortable?' Diana asked, looking down at the unconscious man lying on the pavement.

'Will you do that for me?'

'Yes, alright, just hurry.'

'I will be there before you know it,' Mr Rocha said, and the phone went dead.

Diana put her hand on Zeller's chest and felt reassured that he was still breathing. Then she shouted, 'Margarida, Margarida, are you there?'

Margarida came flying out of her shop, then stopped and stared at the prone man at Diana's feet.

'My God, what happened?'

'I don't know, he passed out. Will you help me get him inside? Someone's coming to fetch him.'

'Shouldn't we call an ambulance instead?'

'I was told it isn't necessary.'

'What happened?' João, the man who owned the ironworks, said as he also ran over. 'I heard you shouting.'

Diana feared that at this rate they'd soon have the whole town leaning over Zeller. As it was, a couple of tourists had already stopped to watch.

'Just help me get him inside, please.'

Diana didn't like being the centre of attention and not for a situation like this. Heaven help her if this also got recorded and uploaded to the internet.

In the end, though, Diana was glad they had João to help. It turned out that an unconscious man was really difficult to carry. João had taken him under the arms and Diana and Margarida each took a leg, but there was still a lot of grunting and staggering before they had him lying lengthways on her sofa in her little lab.

'Thank you, I owe you both a coffee,' Diana said. 'I'll take care of him now. You need to get back to your shops.'

Margarida looked like she wanted to remain, but she accepted her dismissal in good part and followed João out.

Diana checked on Zeller again. He was frighteningly pale. She flicked on her air extractor, just in case, and then removed his mask. Maybe his pallor was due to lack of air.

She dropped into a chair and took a couple of deep breaths. What a hellish day it had been. Finding out her shop had been broken into, going all the way into Lisbon, creating a scene that had felt futile and back on the train again in floods of tears, convinced it was the end of her business.

Then having Zeller show up with her books and, just as she felt that maybe it wasn't a total disaster, the heir of a multi-million euro corporation passed out on her doorstep.

She checked on him again and realised that there was now a crease between his brows and his face looked drawn and tense.

'Mr Zeller?' Diana whispered. 'Can you hear me?'

He twisted his head and grimaced but otherwise didn't respond.

'Mr Rocha is on his way.'

Diana was uncertain if he would find that reassuring. It did make her feel better.

Zeller nodded but still kept his eyes closed. Diana gave a deep sigh and kept watching. It was difficult to reconcile herself to the fact that a Zeller was inside her shop. Her grandmother would have been outraged.

Then a second thought occurred. He was very good looking. She knew that, of course. She'd looked at his face on the internet, but it wasn't the same as seeing somebody in the flesh.

Photographs captured a moment. They produced an image, sometimes carefully crafted, sometimes just laden with the viewer's prejudices. But when you met somebody and saw them in three dimensions, it felt more real. The real Zeller was really handsome.

She also wondered why he'd returned the notebooks. It would have been better for him and the company to keep up the pretence that they knew nothing. Was it possible that he'd told the truth and hadn't known about the break-in?

He'd mentioned an over zealous employee. It must have been one he could home in on quickly though, wasn't it? Otherwise, how had he got everything back to her when she'd only just got back from Lisbon herself? Sure, he could get to her by car. That would speed things up, but, so fast?

'Ms Luna?' a quiet voice said from the doorway.

Diana looked up at the man who'd got her into the Zeller HQ.

'Mr Rocha,' she said, aware that her voice was filled with relief.

Mr Rocha gave her a kindly smile, then stepped up to Zeller.

'I've got your medicine, Mr Zeller. I'm sure Ms Luna will supply some water.'

'Of course,' Diana said and hurried to fetch a glass of water.

Libero pulled a box of painkillers out of his inside pocket, then supported Zeller's head and helped him swallow two pills.

'It will take a moment for the medicine to take effect,' he said, beaming at Diana as if she was a star pupil who'd done exceptionally well. 'If you have something else you need to do, please go right ahead. I'll watch over Armando now. We should be out of your hair in no time.'

'Um... before I do, and I'm sorry to ask at this moment, but, have the two of you been vaccinated against Covid?' Considering how close she'd come to Armando Zeller it was probably too late to worry about infection, but she did, all the same.

'Ah yes, we have both had all the shots quite early because of our jobs. I assume you are the same?'

Diana nodded as she glanced at Zeller, who'd pulled his mask back over his mouth and nose, but then had closed his eyes again, although the frown hadn't faded.

'I also made the case for getting vaccinated early because of my work. Heaven only knows when they'll get round to double jabbing the rest of the thirty-year-olds.'

'Indeed,' Libero said. 'Now I'm sure you have work to be getting on with so don't worry about us.'

'Yes, of course, thank you.' Diana supposed she might as well go back to checking over her notebooks. 'I'll be in the shop if you need me.'

She couldn't concentrate on what she was doing, but it was alright. She'd found her grandmother's notebook with the formula for Armour. Zeller had returned everything in the condition in which it had left.

Half an hour later, Diana heard the two men taking. Then Libero appeared, supporting the much taller Armando Zeller, who was now also wearing dark glasses.

'I'm sorry about everything, Ms Luna.' Zeller's voice sounded soft and tinged with pain. 'Please keep the bills for all the repairs. I'll be back to discuss the NDA.'

Diana was tempted to tell him she never wanted to see him again, but her sensible side made her bite her tongue and just nod.

'I hope you feel better soon,' she muttered.

Zeller didn't appear to notice as he was guided away, but she got an appreciative smile from Mr Rocha. Diana wondered what had happened to Zeller. Her grandmother had once told her about a Nose who suffered severe migraines brought on by certain smells. Was that Zeller's problem too? Mr Rocha had asked whether something strong smelling had gone past, after all. That was probably it.

Then a second guilty thought struck her. If he was that sensitive, getting thrown up on must have been particularly bad. Maybe that was why he'd run away in the video.

CHAPTER NINE

A rmando sat tapping his finger on his desk while glaring at his computer screen. He'd tracked down Diana Luna's grandmother's formula for Armour in the files Libero had scanned. Then he'd compared it to their version of Armour.

The current formula had been adjusted over the years. Sometimes it was just to bring it up to date. Once it was to switch to an artificial scent when the original organic scent price had increased a hundredfold because of a drought in Africa that wiped out the flowers the scent was made from. While customers were willing to pay a surprisingly high price for perfume, nobody would have accepted that kind of price hike.

So Armando had gone back to the archives. There, he'd gone through his grandfather's old notebooks and found the original formula. It disappointed him that the old man had taken the Luna formula item for item. He hadn't modified a single ingredient. He hadn't even bothered to write it out in a different format. There could be no doubt, with the images of the formulas side by side, that they were identical.

The only thing that was different was the date. The Luna formula was dated six months before his grandfather's. As there were formulas before and after in chronological order, Armando couldn't even make the case that the date had been added to the notebook later to make a fraudulent claim. The fact that the book had come to him due to a theft was another mark against them and in Ms Luna's favour. She hadn't brought the book to them when she or her grandmother could have at any time.

Armando wondered whether the grandmother had ever tried to get the compensation she deserved from being the original creator of the perfume. He suspected she had, otherwise she wouldn't have handed down such a powerful sense of a grudge to her granddaughter. Then he wondered whether there was any way he could win Ms Luna round. At the moment, she wasn't even willing to have him in her shop.

Well... that wasn't entirely true. He'd woken up in her lab. Waking up in an unfamiliar place wasn't new to him. But he'd grown more careful with age and it hadn't happened in a while.

Waking up with Ms Luna beside him was a first, although it had taken him a while to realise who it was. Usually, when he came round, it was with Libero nearby. Due to caution and the excruciating pain of the migraine, he'd only opened his eyes a crack to work out where he was.

She'd been more of a silhouette than anything else, surrounded by the dazzling fractured rainbows the headache brought on. He'd recognised her all the same. The migraine also affected his sense of smell, but not to the extent that he couldn't identify her scent. It had been strangely comforting lying in her lab with her sitting beside him. It was an unexpected experience.

His friends had worried when he'd moved out of his father's house into his own. They said it was unhealthy to live as alone as he was. Armando never bothered telling them it was a damn sight less lonely than living in a household where you weren't wanted. He'd thought he was fine in his solitary state, so it shook him to discover that he was hoping Ms Luna would stay by his side. Now he was even trying to find a way to see her again.

Armando tutted impatiently as he considered the problem. He believed in fair play and hard work. Industrial espionage was a fact of life in the perfume industry, just as in any other. He was meticulous when it came to protecting their secrets, but he was disinterested in trying to steal anybody else's.

His philosophy was that they should have the talent and skill in-house to produce the best. There was no need to steal. It hurt his sense of what was right, and his pride in the company, that its foundation had turned out to be built on a lie.

He had to make that right, whatever he thought of Ms Luna. Maybe meeting her properly might help with figuring that out, too. So he started composing an email, an invitation to meet. He kept it purposefully vague, as instructed by the lawyers. He also didn't mention the NDA because that had seemed to irritate her.

He could see why. It was a tacit acknowledgement that her version of events was the truth, and the Zeller Corporation was trying to cover it up. He wasn't sure about the facts yet, but he'd already verified one point where they were in the wrong. But it wouldn't do to make any promises that could be used against him later.

Armando was pretty sure that what he was actually considering would annoy his father anyway, so, for the moment, he had no intention of telling him. As the director of the House of Zeller, he had a substantial budget which he could and did spend at his discretion. He would use that for now if, that was, Ms Luna allowed him to.

That also meant he couldn't meet her at the office. It was better that nobody, especially Helena, knew what he was up to till it was a done deal. He figured a restaurant would be best, and he knew one he could rely upon to steam clean everything to perfection before he arrived.

He was halfway through composing his email, writing and rewriting it to make sure it didn't lead to misunderstandings and difficulties in the future when his door hissed open. He wasn't expecting anyone and looked up, irritated at being disturbed.

'Eddy!' Armando said as he took in the tall, athletic frame of his half brother. 'I thought you were only due back on Friday.'

'I got bored with Paris,' Eddy said with a grin and a vague wave as he dropped into the chair on the other side of Armando's desk.

He knew better than to come closer for a hug or even a handshake.

'You've been to the sea.'

Armando said it as a matter of fact, picking up the scent of salt water as well as noting the pinkish tinge of sunburn to his brother's cheekbones, chin and the bridge of his nose.

'There's no hiding anything from you, is there?' Eddy said with a laugh. 'I got in first thing this morning, dropped my bags off at the house, said hello to Mom and then went straight to Guincho for some surfing. Now I'm doing the rounds at the office, Dad, Helena and now you. I don't suppose you'll come by for a welcome home supper tonight?'

Armando shook his head as he looked his brother up and down. He'd grown in his two years away in France. His already broad shoulders looked broader, maybe because of the tight fitting surfer t-shirt he was wearing. His face looked more adult too, despite the boyish style cut that was more appropriate to a beach bum than an executive. He didn't bother saying anything about it, no doubt their father already had.

'I don't think Albina or Helena would be happy to see me tonight.'

'Mom, I was expecting, but have things really got so bad between you and Helena?'

'It's the succession thing.'

Armando accompanied his words with a shrug to show nothing could be done.

'The bloody succession,' Eddy said, shaking his head.

'It would be remiss of me not to ask, even though I'm pretty sure of the answer. Would you consider going for the CEO position?'

Eddy was so surprised by the question that he just blinked in amazement at Armando, as if trying to make sense of what he'd just said.

'Are you joking?'

'One should never make assumptions.'

'There is no way in hell I'd take the CEO position,' Eddy said, waving his hands for emphasis. 'If it was given to me, I'd sell the company and spend the rest of my days as a surfing beach bum.'

'Best not tell dad that,' Armando said with a laugh.

'Well... I guess you're taking it seriously.'

'I am.'

'Same as Helena.' Eddy grinned slyly at Armando. 'She also interrogated me on my ambitions.'

'So you told her you'd sell the company too?'

'You bet. I know how you keep your mouth shut, and I wanted to make sure Dad knows my intentions too.'

'You could just tell him yourself.'

'Are you kidding? Then I'd have to endure a half-hour lecture on being lazy and entitled? No, thank you. I had quite enough of that from Helena, who also lobbied me to support her claim. She gave me quite the run down of complaints about you.'

'Did she?'

Of all of his family, Armando liked Eddy the best. But Helena was Eddy's full sister while he was merely a half brother that their mother didn't like. Armando feared that if things came to an all out war between him and Helena, Eddy would take Helena's side.

'She said you're infatuated by that woman who threw up on you.' Eddy leaned forward, his eyes sparkling as if he was imparting a juicy piece of gossip. 'I mean you, Armando, have you really seen that woman again?'

He said, that woman, with emphasis, as well he might. Eddy knew that part of the reason Armando wanted to skip supper with the family was because of the smells at the house. Yet, as Bernardo had already pointed out, Armando had been willing to see Ms Luna again.

'Yes,' Armando said, being careful to maintain a neutral tone of voice, 'three times.'

'Good Lord!' Eddy sat back in his chair, blinking in surprise. 'Really?'

'Helena didn't tell you why?'

'Oh no,' Eddy said and his expressive face showed instant disappointment. 'There's a reason other than a crush?'

'A crush? Did you really believe Helena about that?'

'So what is the reason?'

'Damage control. Not something I'll bore you with.'

Armando refrained from mentioning the break in. He didn't want to be the one to make Helena look bad to her little brother. He would leave it to her to either confess or keep it buried.

'Well, that is disappointing.' Eddy attempted to lie back in his seat. Since the chairs had been designed to prevent that, he nearly slipped onto the floor. He was forced to pull himself more upright again and then gazed at his flip-flop clad, sunburned toes peeping out from the bottom of his ragged jeans. 'I'm not sure I want to start on Monday.'

Armando wasn't surprised. Eddy was a happy-go-lucky soul who enjoyed parties and socialising and surfing. His vision of hell was probably being stuck in a lab all day. What did surprise Armando was that Eddy had actually stuck with the ISIPCA course all the way to the end. Now, his father's plan to ease him into the company was for Eddy to take over the food flavours department.

'Do you think you can live without the money our father gives you?' Armando asked, genuinely curious whether his brother could.

'Are you saying that's the only way I can carry on without working here?'

'The agreement was he'd give you a generous allowance until you finished your training. After that you have to work at the company and live off your pay cheque.'

'And be like you, sober and dedicated to all things to do with the Zeller Corporation. But I'm not like you Armando. I want to take full advantage of what life offers and being stuck in an office,'

Eddy said, encompassing Armando's clean white space with a wide gesture of his arms. 'It doesn't do it for me.'

'Maybe you should try it and see what it's really like before you decide.'

Eddy looked disappointed to hear something he'd been hoping not to be told. So he shrugged and gave a deep sigh.

'Sensible as always, Armando. I suppose I'll have to do as you say.'

Armando was aware that his brother felt let down, but there was nothing he could do about it. He'd grown up a bit in France, but he still had a way to go. He looked back at his computer, and the half written email to Diana Luna. What would Eddy make of that? He suppressed a cynical laugh. He didn't know himself what he thought of the whole situation.

He turned back to Eddy, who appeared to be brooding, and said, 'I have work to do. Why don't you enjoy your little break and we can catch up properly one evening soon.'

Diana was so surprised by the email she got from Armando Zeller that she made straight for Margarida's shop. Margarida was alone, sitting in her comfortable wicker chair at the entrance to the shop, embroidering a cute, pink edged baby's bib. Similar embroidered bibs, hand towels and aprons, as well as her honeycomb candles, surrounded her. The stitch work was exquisite, but the sales were way down and Diana feared she'd soon be running out of space to store everything she made. Although Margarida had taken her shop on-line and that seemed to be doing well.

'Look at this!' Diana said, holding her phone out for inspection.

'An email from Armando Zeller?' Margarida said, scanning the from field.

'That's not important, read the rest.'

Diana leaned against the doorframe from which vantage point she could keep an eye on her shop and dash off if anybody went inside.

'He wants to meet you?'

'To discuss the Armour situation. What does that even mean? He couldn't be more vague if he tried.'

'What I think is stranger is that he's suggesting you meet at a restaurant,' Margarida said, her eyes narrowing thoughtfully. 'Why isn't he inviting you to his office, or even coming to see you at your shop?'

'Well… I won't let him into my shop and considering what happened at his office, I wouldn't want to go back there either.'

'No, but why would he worry about your feelings? If he was going to come down hard on you, he'd want to see you on his home territory. And he's also asked whether you prefer lunchtime or evening. He's being very considerate.'

'That's because he knows he's in the wrong,' Diana said, buoyed by a feeling of righteousness.

'Honestly, sometimes you are so naïve,' Margarida said as she handed the phone back. 'All the same, it's good that he's willing to talk, but maybe you should speak to Fernando first.'

'Fernando? Why would I speak to him?'

'I know you're angry with him,' Margarida said, and she bowed her head over her work as if in deep concentration.

It did not fool Diana. Her friend had a soft spot for Fernando and would do what she could to get the two of them back together again. Diana, on the other hand, felt like something had broken in the restaurant that could never come back. Margarida wouldn't understand if she told her, though.

'I am angry with Fernando, furious, and hurt and cursing myself for having given him five years of my life with nothing to show for it.'

'All the same. He's a lawyer. Whatever Armando Zeller suggests, don't accept a single thing until you've run it past a lawyer.'

'I can't afford a lawyer.' Diana picked up a small candle shaped like a smiling cat from Margarida's display and gave it a sniff. 'Do you know how much Fernando charges?'

'I have no idea.'

'€300 an hour!' Diana said and was satisfied by the gasp that elicited from Margarida. 'Considering how he left me, I doubt he'd waive the fee just for old times' sake.'

'All the same, you should try. I'm sure Fernando is already feeling bad about the way he ended things with you.'

The way Margarida spoke gave Diana pause and made her examine her friend's face more closely.

'Have you spoken to him?'

The way Margarida blushed and went back to focusing on her stitchwork was confirmation enough. She was a good friend, though, and honest, too.

'I emailed him to tell him how sorry I was and how disappointed I was in him.'

'Did he reply?'

Diana immediately regretted the question. She wanted to forget all about Fernando. Right now, it still hurt to talk about him.

'He hasn't got back to me yet. But I'm sure he's very busy.'

'You've always made excuses for him.'

Margarida gave her a guilty smile and Diana decided against saying more. Mainly because she didn't want to talk about her ex, but also, based on her increasingly guilty expression, because she had a growing suspicion that Margarida's soft spot for Fernando might be something else.

'Let's talk about more important things. What do you think I should do about the Zeller invitation?'

'Aside from discussing it with a lawyer? This email, vague as it is, sounds like it could be important. So you should go. Heaven knows you need the money.'

Diana nodded, and the panic she lived with daily over her finances reared its head again. She'd just been going through her bank balance and all her bills and was sickeningly aware that she didn't have the money to cover everything. Not with the additional shop repairs after the break in. It was astonishing how expensive it was to replace a shop door.

Because of that, she'd already spent the better part of the morning looking into government loans for shops affected by Covid. But even if she was successful, she doubted she'd get the money in time.

'This email probably means nothing. I shouldn't get my hopes up.'

'Have you at least sent them the bill for the repairs?'

'I will.' Diana was guiltily aware that the email with the attached bills was still sitting in her out tray. She felt humiliated asking for the money even though it was the Zellers who'd caused her to suffer the loss. 'It's just hard to work out how to phrase the request. I mean, Armando Zeller gave back the books, but he was very cagy about the entire business.'

'Maybe you should just ask for the money when you meet.'

'That might be the best way after all.'

Diana was surprised by how easily she was agreeing to meet Zeller considering their fraught family history.

'In the meantime, think about how to bring in extra money,' Margarida said. 'My online shop is going well. Just the other day I got an order for a dozen of my hand stitched napkins from Germany.'

'It's easier to sell candles and crafts online than personalised perfume,' Diana said, stifling the urge to run away. Margarida was only trying to be helpful after all.

'I know it goes against your principles, but maybe you should make some scented hand creams or lip balms that you can sell to passersby, at least. Or let me put them online for you in my store.'

Her conversation with Fernando about diversifying her offer and going online still made Diana smart, not least because she knew he had a point. It made it worse that Margarida was saying the same. It was as if the two of them were ganging up on her.

She nodded as she watched a yellow leaf detach itself from the tree overhead and spiral to the ground.

'I've emailed and written to my regular clients to find out if anyone needs a refill and suggested that I can add their personalised scent to hand creams and other toiletries. I'll wait and see how that pans out.'

Margarida gave her a look that clearly told her she was running out of time, but thankfully she said nothing more.

Chapter Ten

A rmando Zeller was quick to respond to Diana's reply and willingness to meet. Which meant that three nights later, having been picked up by a taxi sent by Zeller, Diana was standing outside the Sea and Sun restaurant that overlooked Guincho beach.

She'd decided on an evening meeting. She didn't want Zeller to assume that she had nothing better to do with her days than meet with him. Which was true, she had a shop to run after all.

Now she stood, almost frozen by indecision, as a strong Atlantic wind blew off the ocean, making her wish for something warmer than the cardigan she'd opted for. Since it was a weeknight, and earlier than usual for the trendy Lisbonites to hop in their car for the hourlong drive up the coast, the car park was still empty. As it was getting late, most of the surfers had also packed up and left. It gave her a dismal sensation of being far from home and all alone.

Which was strange because Guincho was an unusually wild and beautiful landscape. It had mountains and cliffs to one side, dunes behind and a wide beach below. It was probably just a reflection of her anxiety over the impending meeting.

Because of its beauty and proximity to Lisbon, the road leading to the beach had a sprinkling of restaurants on either side. They were all large and on the expensive side. With her constrained budget Diana had only eaten around here a handful of times and usually at some friend's event. A wedding reception and christening were the two that first came to mind. She's never been on a date here, and certainly not for a business dinner. Business lunches and dinners were what rich people and corporations did.

The sun was just setting now and the clouds that streaked the blue sky were lit up in bright yellow. She could delay no longer, although she was shaky with fear.

I have nothing to be sorry for, she thought and clenched her fists. All the same, it felt like false bravado as she stepped inside the Sea and Sun. For a moment, she thought she'd come to the wrong place, as it looked empty. Then a waiter hurried over.

'I'm sorry, I...' Diana said, her eyes darting about the restaurant.

That was when she spotted the silhouetted figure of a man standing at the floor to ceiling windows, his hands behind his back, gazing out to sea. He was dressed in a suit and looked taller than she'd remembered. The waiter was still looking at her expectantly.

'I'm here to meet with Armando Zeller?' Diana's voice rose at the end and made it sound like a question.

'Of course, madam, this way, please.'

The waiter gestured towards the silhouetted figure that turned to face them. Diana was guided to a table with a fantastic view of the wild Atlantic coast and the waves pounding on the rocks below.

It was odd to Diana that this was the only table with a tablecloth and setting. The few additional tables, all spread out carefully to ensure social distancing, were bare.

'Ms Luna,' Armando said, giving her a slight bow.

'I didn't think business would be so bad out here,' Diana murmured as she stood uncertainly opposite Zeller.

'I booked out the restaurant.'

'What? The whole thing?'

Diana was so surprised that she ignored the waiter who had pulled her chair out for her.

'Mmm.'

Armando indicated she should sit and sat down himself. Diana blinked at him, lost for words. He'd opened the menu and was giving it his full attention, which gave her a chance to examine him again. This evening he was maskless. Since there were just the two of them sitting at opposite ends of a large table, Diana decided it was safe to remove her mask as well.

Then she glanced back at Zeller. Damn, but he was handsome, dressed in his plain black suit, the crisp white shirt and simple black tie. He must have sensed the inspection, because he looked up again and gave her a slight smile.

She couldn't understand that. It had no warmth, but it didn't look cynical either. Possibly just a reflex at having been stared at.

Diana look down hastily and gasped at the prices. She'd been worrying about the bill when she arrived. Now it looked like her fears had been underestimated.

'Please, choose whatever you want from the menu. Since I've invited you, I'll pay for the meal,' Armando said, as if reading her mind.

Diana wondered whether she should punish him by ordering the most expensive dish. Unsurprisingly, it was the lobster. She glanced back at the tank in the entrance hall filled with the beasts floating about inside and decided against it.

She didn't like to eat something that had been alive only moments before. It would be better to just go for something she liked. Then another thought occurred to her.

'Is there anything you'd rather I didn't eat? I mean... the smell...'

He looked surprised by her consideration and tilted his head to the side, apparently weighing up his options.

'If you could avoid the fish, I'd be grateful.'

Diana nodded acceptance and wondered why Zeller had decided on a seaside restaurant if he didn't like the smell of fish. Then she went back to perusing the menu. She opted for a steak. It was also on the expensive side, but she was determined to enjoy herself as much as she could while sitting opposite a member of a family her grandmother had a feud against.

Zeller ordered the steak as well. This partly relieved Diana, but also made her wonder why. Then she dismissed the thought. There was no point trying to read anything into whatever Zeller did.

'And to drink, madam?' the waiter asked.

Diana looked back down at the menu and then at Armando.

'Ah... if you wouldn't mind avoiding the red wine...'

She looked up at him, surprised by the request and then was filled with embarrassment because she'd just remembered the video and what she'd done at their first meeting.

'I'll have a sparkling water with a slice of lemon.' Diana handed the menu back to the waiter and noted Zeller's relieved expression. Since she didn't want to dwell on the humiliation of the video, and she couldn't bite her tongue any longer, Diana asked, 'Why did you want to meet?'

To her surprise, Zeller took a deep breath and silently puffed it out. It was an unexpected gesture of discomfort that made Diana feel better. At least he wasn't being all calm and superior.

'I um...' Armando paused and looked like he was trying to work out how best to phrase his next words. 'I compared your grandmother's formula for Armour with my grandfather's.'

So, that was why they were here. It had been her best guess, and she supposed she should have been pleased that he was bringing it up. What worried her was what he might say next.

'And?'

'They're exactly the same.'

'I know that.'

Diana was pleased that she could keep her voice calm and level. She could have jeered an I told you so, but there would have been no point, at least not till she knew where Zeller was going with this.

'I didn't know,' Armando said. 'My grandfather never mentioned it to me. As far as I'm aware, my father doesn't even know that his father didn't create Armour.'

'Haven't you asked him?'

'Not yet.'

'Why not?'

'Because I don't need to. It's obvious enough that the formula was stolen. The question now is what we do about it.'

'What we do?'

Diana wondered who the we was supposed to be. Was he referring to the Zeller Corporation?

'You and me,' Armando said.

'You and me?'

Diana was utterly confused now.

'Your grandmother developed the formula and you, I have ascertained, are her sole living relative.'

'There's my mother.'

'I could find no trace of her. Is she still alive?'

'Most probably.'

Diana was enjoying being cryptic. She was damned if she was going to make things easy for Zeller.

Armando nodded and apparently thought about it for a moment.

'Let's assume she has no say in this matter, either. So there's just you. I'm the director of the perfumes division of the Zeller Corporation. It is up to me whether we acknowledge your claim and whether we pay out compensation.'

'So you and me,' Diana said.

'I have taken legal advice and been informed that as the perfume was developed over 50 years ago and that there is no copyright on perfumes anyway, you have no legal claim over it or the profits it has made.'

For an instant Diana wished she had actually spoken to Fernando about the perfume. But she supposed he'd told her the same more than once. She also found it difficult to believe that Zeller had invited her to this expensive restaurant just to tell her this when he could have said the same in an email.

'So?'

'You may not believe it, but I want to be fair. I will pay you the compensation your grandmother should have received. I'll only consider the years when the perfume was exactly the same as your grandmother's formula. After we updated it, I feel it's sufficiently different to no longer owe you for it.'

Considering her finances, Diana would have jumped at any small offer of money, but she wasn't sure where Zeller was headed and she didn't trust him. Especially after he said he would limit the time over which they owed the payment.

'How much are we talking, exactly?'

'According to my lawyers, based on the earnings of the perfume in the early years of the House of Zeller, and taking into consideration similar payments for loss and injury sustained from the break in, they have suggested one million euros,' Armando said. 'Would that be acceptable?'

'One million euros?'

Diana repeated the words because she couldn't believe that's what Zeller had actually said.

'Mmm,' Armando said with a nod, 'but you would have to sign a nondisclosure agreement at the same time.'

'A nondisclosure agreement?'

Diana's eyes narrowed. This was more like it.

'Rumours that have hurt the company and already knocked several million euros off our share prices have been circulating ever since the video of you and I went viral.'

Zeller's his lips curled with distaste as he spoke and Diana felt simultaneously embarrassed again as well as offended.

'I am not the person in the wrong here.'

'But our company can't afford any further damaging revelations either,' Armando said back to his calm neutrality.

'So actually you're paying me to keep my mouth shut,' Diana said, and it made her angry.

How dare this man think he can just wave money at her and make his problem go away? She was about to launch herself to her feet and tell him to go to hell when her sensible side forcibly intervened and kept her bottom firmly fixed to the chair. One million euros would save her crumbling business and home.

Just then, the waiter arrived and placed her steak down before her. It broke the tension and Diana could look back up at Zeller, who was watching her, one eyebrow raised as if he was halfway through thinking of a question. Then he too leaned back so that the waiter could put his steak in front of him.

He waited till the waiter had left before he said, 'if my offer is acceptable I'll have the contract drawn up. You can have your lawyers look it over and decide whether or not you'll sign.'

'My lawyers?' Diana said with a hollow laugh, ignoring the food. 'I can't afford one lawyer, let alone a team. Now I'm thinking you might be offering me way less than you should and trying to rush me into a decision when I'm in no position to double check. That would certainly ensure that you get the best deal possible.'

'Ms Luna,' Armando said as he cut into his steak with a wicked looking serrated steak knife. 'My best deal would be to pay you absolutely nothing. There is no advantage for my company to pay out, in fact it looks like us admitting fault.'

'Hence the NDA,' Diana snapped.

'If you would like an advance so you can commission a lawyer to give the contract the once over, I will be happy to do that.'

'You would?' Diana stared at Zeller, trying to understand what was really going on. The rich were rich precisely because they didn't give their money away. 'Well... then I will consider it.'

'Good,' Armando said and gave her a slight smile. 'Now please, do try the steak. It's excellent.'

Diana was so stunned by the turn of events that she hardly tasted the steak. She kept rolling the concept of a million euros around and around her mind. It was such a massive sum of money it was hard to comprehend. It felt like she'd just won the lottery at the moment she needed it most. A wave of panic washed over her at the thought that she might lose it all and that it was a mirage and nothing would come of it.

'So,' Armando said and cleared his throat. 'Have you always lived in Sintra?'

Diana looked up at him in surprise, but he had kept his head down, apparently absorbed in cutting his steak.

'Yes.' After a moment of silence Diana felt she should reciprocate and asked, 'have you always lived in Lisbon?'

'Pretty much. I studied for a while in England and France, but aside from that, I've been in Lisbon.'

'What did you study?'

'Biochemistry in London, and perfumes at ISIPCA.'

'Ah, I would have liked to have studied at ISIPCA.'

'It would have been a waste of your time.'

That made Diana bristle as she said tightly, 'There's no need to be so blunt about it, even if you don't think I have any talent as a perfumer. I would still have liked to have taken the course.'

Armando looked surprised and said, 'I didn't mean it as an insult. You have a natural talent and the perfumes you produce are unique. It would be a shame if you'd turned into another perfumer clone.'

'Like you?'

Armando's face twitched at the direct assault.

'I like to think I have some creativity at least.'

'Some perfumes the House of Zeller produces aren't bad,' Diana conceded.

'Thank you,' Armando said and gave a slight, ironic bow. 'I was not aware that you are familiar with our work.'

'Did you formulate any of them yourself?'

'We have a team that works on most of our fragrances. But there are a few that I created on my own.'

'Which ones?'

Diana was now curious to see what she thought of Zeller's actual ability.

'Flower Garden is one of mine. I also created Urso for men.'

'They're not bad. Both are very light, almost not there at all, but in a good way,' Diana added hurriedly.

'That is my weakness as a perfumer.' Armando gave her a slight smile in apparent appreciation for the fact that she'd tried to soften the blow of her words. 'For me, they are at the right intensity, but my formulations always need to be strengthened to get them to market.'

'It's your sensitive nose, isn't it?'

Diana wondered how Zeller would feel to have it pointed out. Then she wondered why she cared about his feelings. He was so rich he could hire an entire restaurant for the night and offer to pay her compensation. He hardly needed pity from her.

'There are advantages and disadvantages to being as sensitive to smell as I am. I suppose you could say I'm a consequence of over breeding. My grandfather was a Nose, as was my grandmother. They produced a son with high sensitivity and he, in turn, married a perfumer. They stayed together long enough to produce me. It was bound to happen that we'd hit an excessively sensitive level of breeding.'

'You'd best not marry a perfumer yourself then,' Diana murmured.

Armando looked up at her as if surprised by the comment. Diana blushed and suspected that Zeller had too but in the dim light of the restaurant it was hard to tell. Diana realised no candles were present. Was that also by Zeller's request? Instead, they had an attractive table lamp now providing the light as night had fallen.

Then another thought struck her.

'How do you know what my perfumes smell like?'

'I was wondering when you'd realise I'd said that.' Armando dabbed his lips with the tip of the napkin. 'I looked at your notebooks before I gave them back and I've tried one or two of your formulas. I liked them.'

'You tested my formulas?'

Diana was offended and frightened in equal measure.

'I won't steal them,' Armando said, correctly reading her expression. 'I'm nothing like my grandfather. I was just curious.'

'You would have been missing the most important component of each of my formulas anyway,' Diana snapped, still shaken by his admission.

'What did I leave out?'

'The person I made it for. They best suit just one person. It's something you mass production perfumers will never understand.'

'There is an art to producing a scent that works for a vast swath of the population too.'

'But it's always a compromise. Once you've made a perfume for just one person, you'll see how much of a compromise it is.'

'I am actually aware of that.'

'You've done that? Made a perfume for just one person?'

'I made Urso for a friend. I had no intention of commercialising it. But he just blended what I made with an off-the-shelf deodorant and an off-the-shelf shampoo and his fabric softener and God only knows what else, so I had to turn it into a range he could buy. As it happens, it's become popular with a lot of men, but it smells best on my friend.'

'So you do know.'

Armando nodded and said, 'Your service isn't expensive, Ms Luna, but even so, you know most women would not spend what you charge on perfume. Wouldn't it be worth your while to produce a couple of ranges people could simply buy from you?'

Diana shrugged, tired of a conversation she'd had with people she liked better than Zeller.

'The joy of my job is the transformation I see in the women who come to my shop. It's the fun of creating something special for one individual that has the power to lift her up and make her feel special. I would be sad if I never met the women who bought my fragrances. If it was just the scent itself that I enjoyed creating, I could get a job in any one of the many perfume houses around the world.'

They spent the rest of the evening talking shop. Armando enjoyed talking about scents, but it was usually with employees who were deferential, even though he recruited free thinkers and encouraged them to voice their opinions. It was different to talk to someone who didn't owe him anything.

Ms Luna had also relaxed a bit. She'd arrived at the restaurant all prickly with suspicion. She hadn't let her guard down, and now and then he saw her seesaw between anger and, more confusingly, something approaching panic. But she could dismiss that most of the time and appeared to be enjoying herself.

He wished he could remove the doubt she still harboured over his intentions but he'd have to give her time for that. Hopefully, when the first sum of money landed in her bank account, she'd relax. He'd tried to sound her out about the state of her business, but that she'd not been willing to talk about.

It was her business, after all, and they were far from being friends. A small part of him still worried Helena might be right and Diana Luna had approached him to extort money. The only reason that didn't ring true was her reluctance to sign the NDA. If money was the aim, she should have agreed to keep quiet about everything. Or maybe she was playing a long game to get even more money out of him.

'That was a lovely meal, thank you,' Diana said as she laid her fork down on the now empty plate.

It surprised Armando that, despite his lingering doubts, he'd enjoyed himself too.

'Would you like desserts or coffee?' the waiter asked.

Diana looked over at Armando with a question on her expressive face.

'Please have whatever you'd like,' Armando said, assuming she fancied a coffee. 'I'll have a lemon tea.'

'I'll have the same,' Diana said, and gave the waiter a far friendlier smile that she'd managed with Armando.

Armando felt a twinge of regret blended with a touch of jealousy.

'I'm really okay with you having a coffee.'

'A lemon tea suits me fine.'

Diana spoke in a calm, firm way that Armando found he liked. She didn't fuss or make a show that she was doing things for him. Maybe it was because she did prefer a cup of tea. He wasn't sure. He wished he could understand her better.

That thought pulled him up short. He'd never felt that way about any other women before. Well, that wasn't strictly true. He tried to understand his mother and Albina and even Helena, but they were all part of his family. No woman beyond that till now.

He watched as Diana thanked the waiter when he arrived with her tea, blew on the steam and then held it up to her nose and inhaled. A smile of pleasure spread across her face at the lemon scent that wafted towards her. She was so absorbed in what she was doing that Armando felt it was safe to give her a closer examination.

She was on the short side, but slim and with great legs. Her face was attractive without being a great beauty, and her hair was quirky. She was very different from the kinds of women he usually came across.

All the women he met at the parties he was dragged to looked like clones of Helena. They were all exquisite but bland. The business women he met were always in tight fitting suits with their long hair swept up off their faces and precision applied makeup. Ms Luna was a novelty.

But in what mattered most, how she smelled, she was impossibly seductive. He'd expected the same scent of honey and herbs that she'd worn all the other times he'd met her. But this evening she'd surprised him with a delicate scent of spices with a hint of black chocolate. It was blended to leave the impression of warmth and luxury without a trace of sweetness.

For the first time in his life, he wanted to get closer to someone so that he could get a better smell. He nearly laughed out loud as that realisation hit him, but he suppressed it and just grinned.

Ms Luna noticed the smile and raised an eyebrow in query.

'It's nothing,' Armando said as he finished his drink. 'I'll take you home.'

'A taxi will be fine.'

'It's late and it's a long way for a taxi to come. There's no need for you to wait around when I can take you. It isn't much of a detour from my home, anyway.'

Armando stood and walked to the door as he spoke to prevent Ms Luna from insisting on the taxi.

'Shouldn't you pay?' Diana asked as she hurried after him, pulling her handbag onto her shoulder.

'I paid up front,' Armando said as he stopped to thank the chef who'd just emerged from the kitchen. 'Delicious as always, Stella.'

Stella wasn't only the chef but also the owner of the restaurant. She was tall, slim and rather elegant for somebody who was engaged in hard and boiling work every single day. She'd made a success of it and people flocked to her restaurant. At least they had before Covid. Armando hoped they would again soon.

'It's always a pleasure, Armando,' Stella said in her husky voice.

Aside from her delicious cooking, that was always a draw, Armando found her voice sexy. He had done since high school, where he'd asked her out and been rebuffed. He'd considered it again after he came back from France, but the scents of the kitchen, gas and fish most prominently, and a slight whiff of sweat had stopped him only seconds before he'd made his second attempt.

'How's business?' he asked, hoping to hear it was going well.

'I've been surviving on takeaways, difficult when the restaurant is so far from any built-up areas. But things are looking better now that the lockdown has eased.'

'I'm glad to hear it.'

'You are always welcome, you know that, don't you?' Stella said, sliding a hand down his arm.

Since Stella had made double this evening what she would make on a normal night, her pleasure was understandable. She was also a friend and one he didn't mind lending his support to.

'I'll come back soon and remind everyone else you're still around.'

'Thank you,' Stella said as she waved Armando and Diana away.

'I've known her a long time,' Armando said as he realised Diana had been watching the exchange with a curious tilt of her head.

'It's unusual to find a female chef.'

'It's very hard work.'

Armando walked up to his electric blue Porche, opened the passenger door and looked expectantly at Ms Luna.

She looked torn and tried a last ditch, 'Honestly, I don't mind calling a taxi.'

For a moment Armando was tempted to call a taxi after all. His car was a two-seater. That meant he'd be closer to Ms Luna than he had ever been before, and it might be too much.

He'd avoided women so far because of the smell. Men smelled worse, far more intense, but all people had a particular aroma that intensified in an enclosed space. Would he be able to cope in such a tight vehicle all the way back to Sintra?

'Get in,' he said, before he could change his mind.

Diana gave him a dubious look but got into the car. Armando felt a surge of triumph as he closed the door and then hurried to his side. He tried not to make it obvious that he sniffed the air as he got inside. To his relief, all he got was a stronger whiff of Ms Luna's delectable perfume.

She, on the other hand, rolled her window down as he started the car. Since there was a stiff wind blowing off the ocean, a surprising and horrifying new thought occurred to him.

'Ms Luna, do I... do I smell bad to you?'

'What?' Diana asked as she swivelled around to look at Armando.

'I'm sorry, that must seem like a strange question. It's just that I find most people's personal smell rather intense. Not you. But I suddenly realised that you might also be sensitive to a similar thing.'

'Not really. I notice people's personal scent. I've been trained to do so, and to work with it to make my perfumes, but the smell rarely bothers me. It's been that way my whole life so, why would I object?'

Armando raised a reflective eyebrow. He wished he could simply accept how everybody smelled.

'Then... I'm not the reason you opened the window?'

'Well, you are a bit.' Diana's smile broadened in a way Armando found incredibly seductive. 'I worried I might smell too intense.'

'You don't.'

For once, Armando was telling the truth. He'd reassured other women in the past but never meant it.

'I did once meet a man whose personal scent I couldn't tolerate,' Diana said as she slid the car window shut. 'Not that he didn't bother to bathe. In fact, he was fastidious about cleanliness, but I couldn't stand to be in the same room with him. Once, when I visited his house, I had to make an excuse and leave because it was making me feel ill.'

That was a feeling Armando was all too familiar with, from both men and women.

'The funny thing was, when I mentioned his smell to my friend, Margarida, she was surprised. He didn't smell odd to her at all.'

'It probably means you were a dangerous genetic match.'

'A what?'

'There's research showing that, especially amongst women, an off-putting scent from a man is a warning sign that your offspring could be affected by a genetic disease. You're incompatible.'

'How do you know that?'

'I learned about it in my biochemistry degree. But I also experienced it firsthand. One of my female employees put in a complaint about one of the male staff. She asked if someone could discreetly tell him to bathe, because he stank. But when I asked around, nobody else had the same problem. It turned out he cycled to work and showered when he got to the office, so the smell wasn't down to him not bathing. I had to conclude they were genetically incompatible.'

'How fascinating,' Diana said and lapsed into silence.

Armando was content to end it there. He could concentrate on the dark road and mull over how it felt to have somebody in his car whose scent he actually liked.

CHAPTER ELEVEN

D iana slept well. It was the first time in a long time that she didn't wake at three am worrying about whether she could pay the bills or have enough money to feed herself for the month. The relief that brought combined with the bright blue sky and warm sunshine that felt like summer might linger for a week or two more meant she bounded down her stairs to the shop with more enthusiasm than she had in a long time.

As her foot landed on the pavement, though, she stopped in astonishment. Fernando was standing at her door, examining the newly installed glass. He hadn't noticed her yet.

'Fernando?'

'Diana,' Fernando said as he turned around with an enormous smile on his face.

It threw Diana because he was behaving as if nothing had happened between them, as if he hadn't dumped her within minutes of her arriving at the restaurant.

'What are you doing here?'

'I came to see if you are okay.'

'If I'm okay? What do you mean?'

'Well... at first I was annoyed at you for spending so much on wine,' Fernando said, giving a great impression of somebody who was amused at his own foibles. 'But then I saw the video, and I realised you must have been really upset.'

Diana couldn't believe it. The last thing she'd wanted was for Fernando to see what a wreck she'd become because of him.

'You saw that, did you?'

'José sent me the link.'

José had been Fernando's friend who had become a mutual friend. Diana was now consigning José back to being Fernando's friend alone.

'Ah, he sent you the link.'

Diana didn't want to discuss the matter further.

'I can't believe you actually threw up on a Zeller,' Fernando said, his apparent amusement deepening. 'After everything you've told me about them, it couldn't have worked out better, could it?'

Diana was about to send Fernando away with a sharp instruction never to show up at her place again when her meeting with Armando Zeller made her pause. Maybe she could use Fernando for legal advice after all. It was definitely what he deserved, she thought, ignoring the twinge of guilt she felt at using anyone.

'I'm about to have breakfast. Do you want to join me? You'll be paying.'

Fernando smiled fondly at her, apparently convinced that all was forgiven.

'Of course, I always pay.'

'Come on then,' Diana said and headed for the Butterfly Cafe.

She sailed past Margarida's shop and noted that a shelf in the window was now filled with jars of honey. Apparently, her parents had sent her some more from the farm they'd retired to. Margarida was sitting where she usually sat, but she wasn't focused on her embroidery, she had clearly been waiting for Diana to come in for a gossip.

Her jaw dropped at the sight of Fernando, and she mouthed, 'What's going on?'

Diana shrugged and mouthed, 'I'll tell you later,' without slowing down.

The Butterfly Cafe was tucked into a small space between Margarida's shop and what had once been a shop that sold souvenirs, mainly made from cork. Since its lifeblood was tourists, it had closed down and a for sale sign was slowly gathering dust in the window. Maria da Conceição and her husband, the owners of the cafe, complained every day that the empty shop would ruin the street.

Which was a shame because they worked hard to make their cafe inviting. They'd painted the walls a cheerful lemon yellow, hand painted pottery plates with traditional Portuguese village scenes adorned the walls and Margarida's embroidered table cloths covered the plain wooden tables. Ever since restaurants and cafes had been allowed to re-open, they'd also been given permission to expand their area of business into the street.

The pavement on this street was so narrow that most tourists just ambled down the middle of the road. But now, to either side of The Butterfly Cafe's door, the white cobbled pavement was occupied by a table and pair of chairs to either side of the front door. Diana now selected the table that got the most sun and left Fernando to settle opposite.

Diana had known Maria da Conceição her whole life. She therefore didn't need to relay an order. Within seconds of their arrival, Maria brought Diana a cup of milky coffee, a freshly baked croissant and a small pot of honey.

'From Margarida's parent's farm,' she said with a smile. 'I'll bring your order next,' she said to Fernando, bustled back to her counter and returned with an espresso and toast.

It was what they always ate, and it gave Diana a pang that this little ritual of hers and Fernando at the cafe was over, even if he didn't know it yet. He wasn't her first boyfriend to change his mind, but Diana found she had no wish to return to what they'd had before. She wondered why not. Maybe the possibility of absolute financial freedom had made her reassess her needs.

'I hope you haven't had any fallout from the video,' Fernando said as he took a sip of his coffee.

Diana wondered why he'd gone back to the video. Was he trying to make a point about how she needed him because she was a mess without him?

'There was a consequence from that meeting, actually,' Diana said. 'But it wasn't what you might expect.'

'It wasn't?'

'Well... at first I guess it was. I got a nasty letter from the Zeller Corporation telling me to cease and desist. So I went to confront the Zeller I thought wrote the email, the one I threw up on. Long story short, he's offered to pay me compensation.'

Diana decided against mentioning the break in. For some reason, she didn't want to show Armando Zeller in a bad light. She could almost feel her grandmother staring disapprovingly down at her from heaven because of that, but she shrugged the guilty feeling away. Hopefully grandma would approve of a Zeller actually, finally, paying up.

'He offered you compensation?' Fernando said, and he looked astonished. 'No big corporation would willingly pay out if they don't have to. Are you telling me your story about Armour is true?'

Diana stopped midway through spreading honey over the edge of her croissant to stare at Fernando.

'Are you telling me you never believed me?'

Fernando shrugged expressively and said, 'I thought maybe your grandmother had been exaggerating.'

'Well, she wasn't. Armando Zeller is offering me a million euros.'

'One million?' Fernando said faintly as his hand holding the tiny coffee cup froze halfway to his mouth.

'Do you think that's reasonable?'

'I've never heard of anything like it. If he's willing to pay you that much, there's something really weird going on.'

'Is there?' Diana said, and her anxiety shot up. 'Do you think he's lying to me?'

Fernando shrugged, but also tilted his head. Then he put his espresso down as he considered.

'If he's willing to make such a big payout, then I'm willing to bet it would cost the company more if the story got out. If you play your cards right, I'm sure you could get Zeller to increase the offer.'

'Do you think I should? He mentioned an NDA.'

'Ah, then it definitely is about damage limitation. You should see if their stocks have been affected, and if they have, how much they lost. That's the kind of figure you could ask for then.'

'But I don't need more. I'd rather have a fair payment and have the Zellers acknowledge my grandmother created Armour.'

'You're wasting your time if you try that.' Fernando snorted, picked up his coffee and swallowed the lot in a single gulp, as if putting the final period to his case. 'That's the whole point of the NDA.'

'I don't know,' Diana murmured, nibbling on the end of her croissant. 'Much as I hate to say it about a Zeller. He seemed to have a sense of fairness.'

Fernando's immediate loud laugh made it clear that, in his mind at least, there was no such thing as fairness in the business world.

'Don't be naïve. Zeller is the head of a massive arm of an even bigger corporation. He knows how to close deals. He'll have made sure to give you the bare minimum and shut you up into the bargain. I know you're still angry with me,' Fernando said, which surprised Diana, as she'd been trying to look like she was fine having coffee with him. 'But, whatever he sends you to sign, make sure you have it properly scrutinised before you do anything. If you like, I can look it over for you with a couple of my partners at the law firm.'

'I'll think about it.'

Diana realised Margarida was peeping through her shop window, watching the two of them and mouthing something Diana couldn't understand. She shoved the remains of the sticky croissant into her mouth and was about to tell Fernando she had to go so that she could have her deferred gossip with Margarida. But as Fernando was paying for breakfast, a tourist stopped at Diana's shop and peered interestedly through the window.

'I've got to go,' Diana said, hurrying away.

'Don't forget about what I said,' Fernando shouted after her.

Diana barely noticed as she hurried up to the potential new client, her key at the ready to let them in. As she did so, she noticed that Fernando, rather than leaving, stepped into Margarida's shop.

Damn, now he was going to give her the gossip about her evening with Armando Zeller. How infuriating.

CHAPTER TWELVE

Armando drove up to Sintra with the same feeling he'd had as a schoolboy in the weeks leading up to the summer holidays. He was filled with delicious anticipation. Sure, he'd had crushes on girls before and, once he'd left school, with his looks and family name, he'd been able to meet any woman his fancy fell upon. But none of those meeting survived first contact. Now here he was really looking forward to seeing Diana Luna again.

How was it possible to be so excited to see a woman who had...? He flicked that memory away and focused on the restaurant instead. She'd smelled great to him. He hoped they could conclude their agreement swiftly so that he could move on from business and ask her out on an actual date.

He'd spent the days since their meal together running over everything that Diana Luna had said and done. He'd realised that she had two more advantages over any other woman he'd met. First, she knew about perfumes, so she could understand his work and the skill it took. In fact, she was as skilled as him and maybe more creative.

Second, she knew all about people's smells and didn't think he was a freak for being sensitive about it. She'd actually considered his difficulties in such a non-judgemental way that it had come as a positive relief.

So he was feeling cheerful as he got out of his car and crossed the road to Perfume da Luna. He stopped at the front door. It was standing open, but he had no intention of crossing a threshold beyond which he wasn't welcome.

'Ms Luna?' he said from the doorway.

'Just a minute,' Diana's voice came from her lab and she stepped out into her shop. 'Oh, Mr Zeller.'

It relieved Armando that she merely looked surprised rather than put out. He waved the manilla envelope he was carrying and said, 'I've brought the legal documents. I'm afraid it took longer than I'd hoped. Lawyers are such a careful breed.'

'You didn't need to deliver them by hand,' Diana said and stopped halfway through her shop so that there were a good two meters between them.

'I've also sent it by email, but since I was in the vicinity, I thought it might speed things up if you gave it a once over while I'm here. That way we can agree on any major changes straight away, and you can give me your bank details so that I can transfer the necessary funds.'

'Oh, yes.'

Diana looked thrown by him and, at the mention of money, more wary, which hadn't been Armando's intention.

'Would you care to check the contract over lunch?' Armando glanced at his watch as if just realising the time when actually he'd planned to be there exactly at this time. 'I'll buy.'

Diana tilted her head, apparently considering his offer, then gave an accepting nod.

'Just let me fetch my bag,' she said and vanished back into her laboratory.

Armando wanted to give a whoop of joy to have succeeded so far, but he restrained himself and kept his triumph merely to a satisfied smile.

'Did you have somewhere you particularly wanted to go?' Diana asked as she first fitted her face mask, flipped over the sign that said "gone to lunch" and locked her shop door.

'I don't know Sintra very well, so you choose.' Armando felt yet another thrill of anticipation shoot through him. Never in his adult life had he allowed another person to pick a venue, but he trusted Diana Luna to find something he could tolerate.

'Then I'll take you to my favourite. We can walk. It isn't far.'

As the pavement was too narrow to walk side by side, Armando followed happily along behind Ms Luna as she led him to the main square, which was dominated by the massive Sintra National Palace. In pre-Covid times, the square would have been packed with tourists visiting this world heritage site. The palace still had the rope barriers that organised the queues of tourists, but there was only one family currently heading for the entrance and, aside from having to zigzag their way to the door, they had no waiting to do.

'Here,' Diana said as she stepped up onto the wooden deck of a restaurant on the edge of the square and selected the table closest to the street.

It was shaded by a white umbrella that was still necessary for the heat of the autumn sun. Especially for someone wearing a black suit. Since traffic was next to non-existent, Armando was happy to comply and sat down opposite.

'Alright, let me see the contract,' Diana said, and held out her hand.

'Of course.'

Armando was confident that the contract was fair and hoped that it would please Ms Luna. If it didn't, he'd have to rethink her motive for first running into him, and he didn't want to do that.

The waiter, who'd kept his distance till now, descended, all smiles with a menu. Armando would have preferred that he merely hand it over and leave, but he evidently knew Ms Luna, so stayed to chat. From their conversation, Armando gathered Diana hadn't been to visit for a while. Looking at the prices, he assumed it was because they were on the expensive side.

'Try the beef baked in salt,' Diana said. 'I think you'll like it.'

Armando ordered the beef and was surprised when Diana asked for chicken. He'd rather hoped they'd be eating the same thing again. He also wished she'd give him a bit more attention, but she was working her way through the contract in meticulous detail. Since that had been his ostensible reason for his visit, he couldn't really object.

So he waited, taking in the scenery beyond the square where the forested mountain rose around them dotted with ornate, wedding cake style palacios in pale blues, yellows and pinks. Ms Luna picked absently at her lunch while still going through the contract.

'I'm afraid it's rather dense legalese,' Armando murmured.

'It's alright. My last boyfriend was a lawyer, so I've got some experience with this kind of thing,' Diana said without looking up.

Armando wondered whether this was the man who'd left Ms Luna to drown her sorrow in wine and shook away that thought before the memory of the smell could come back. At least she was drinking sparkling water again today.

He had started to wonder when lunch would appear when Diana finally reached the last page, closed the stapled contract and looked up at him

'There are two things that bother me about this contract.'

'Only two?'

Armando hoped they were minor, although Ms Luna's serious expression made him doubt that.

'The first is that I really don't like the NDA. I mean, if your family was in the wrong, you should admit it. Why do you want to keep denying the truth?'

Her first caveat relieved Armando. At least it wasn't about the money.

'Ms Luna, if it was just down to a conversation between the representatives of two families, I'd be happy to–' he cut himself off. The lawyers had been crystal clear on this front. Never admit liability. 'The thing is, the business world is different. Companies rise and fall upon their reputation. Would you really want your story to come out if it results in the loss of thousands of jobs? Jobs of most people, I might add, who weren't even born yet when Armour was created and who can ill afford to be without a pay cheque.'

Ms Luna blinked at him.

'I wouldn't want anyone to lose their job.'

'What is your second concern?'

'It's the amount of money,' Diana said.

Armando wished she hadn't said that. So here it was now, the true reason for their meeting. At least she had the grace to look embarrassed.

'It's a very generous settlement, believe me.'

'My boyfriend said that it's your opening offer and I have room to ask for more.'

'Your boyfriend? The lawyer?'

Armando was beginning to wonder whether they'd actually broken up at all.

Diana flushed deep red and said, 'My ex-boyfriend. Who else could I ask about something like this?'

'So you are still on speaking terms?'

'He came by unexpectedly a couple of days ago,' Diana said and then looked up defiantly. 'I don't see why I should explain this to you, anyway. Besides, you told me to get legal advice.'

She made a point he couldn't argue with, so Armando just nodded.

'Are your two objections insurmountable?'

'What?'

'Which would you prefer, no NDA and no money, or the NDA and a sum of money still to be agreed?'

Armando had already decided, disappointingly, that Diana Luna would opt for the money, so it took him by surprise when she hesitated.

'Can I think about it?'

'Are you really going to forgo the sizeable sum I'm offering for the sake of your family pride? I mean, you could go public and tell the world all about us, and go bust in the process. Is it really worth it?'

'Don't you care that your entire company is built on a lie?' Diana snapped.

'A bit,' Armando said and then paused as the waiter finally brought their food.

His beef looked like an oblong crystal, so encased in salt you couldn't tell what was inside at all. The scent of the salt also obscured the smell of the beef, and he wondered why he'd opted for this dish. Especially as he'd lost his appetite after the argument.

'Only a little?' Diana was also ignoring her chicken in a creamy mushroom sauce that snuggled around a dome of herb flecked rice that was steaming gently on the table before her. 'Millionnaires obviously have very different ethics.'

'If we only made money from Armour, it would bother me more. But my grandfather, father and I have all produced many more perfumes and grown the business in different directions. My grandfather also got a leg up from his father-in-law, so it wasn't all down to one product. That's why I don't feel overwhelming guilt about this. But it is why I'd like to end the rumour mill before it causes more difficulties for the company and its employees.'

Diana blinked at him, then looked down at her food, and poked a piece of chicken with the tip of her knife. It left Armando in the same position as at the start of their meeting, uncertain of what Ms Luna was actually after.

'How much time do you need?'

'I don't know... a couple of days? Maybe a week.'

'Okay, a week.' Armando made a first assault on the beef, putting a crack through the salt crust and then peeling off a centimetre thick layer that he shoved to the side of the plate. 'If you give me your bank account details now, I can transfer the necessary funds for the lawyers to you straight away.'

'You're still willing to do that?'

'I wouldn't want you to think I go back on my word, Ms Lima,' Armando said and smiled so that she wasn't overly offended by his words.

Diana gazed at him for a moment, probably trying to decide what she did next. Then she shrugged, took out her phone and gave Armando her bank details.

'Would €10,000 be sufficient?' Armando asked.

'€10,000? Really?' Diana said and surprise flickered across her face. 'Are you sure? That sounds like a lot.'

'Not really.'

'Is that what it cost you to draw up the contract?'

'Not at all. I used our company's lawyers,' Armando said as he went into his banking app and made the transfer. 'It's part of their job.'

'I suppose so.'

Armando nodded and said, 'It's done. Once you've had a chance to consult and think things through, you can get back to me.'

'I'm sorry I'm dragging this out,' Diana said. Which did surprise Armando. 'I just really need to think about... everything.'

'It's alright. Most of the contracts I negotiate have a similar amount of back and forth.'

It was the truth, but he'd hoped that he'd be able to get this thing between him and Ms Luna over with quicker. The sooner the better when it came to the battle for succession. A quick resolution would also mean a change in the relation between himself and Ms Luna. Wanted that, especially to clear up why she'd approached him in the first place. This constant swing between believing it was a coincidence, to thinking it was deliberate was exhausting.

Diana Luna was picking at her lunch, apparently as distracted over the negotiation as he was. But it gave Armando a chance to examine her more closely.

After their last meeting, he'd felt like they'd become easier in each other's company. But today her guard was up again, and she seemed wary and uncomfortable.

He had to do something about that, but it was with some trepidation that he said, 'May I ask you a question? You can tell me to mind my own business, but I am just curious.'

'Good heaven's, that's quite a preamble,' Diana said, looking up. 'Ask away.'

'The perfume you're wearing at the moment... how did you get the scent of soil?'

'Ah, you can smell that, huh? I suppose I shouldn't be surprised.'

'Other people don't smell it?'

'It's probably more accurate to say that they don't notice it but it's part of the perfume and it doesn't work as well without it.'

'It's an unusual addition to an unusual perfume.'

'A trip to Margarida's family farm in the Alentejo inspired me.'

'Does Margarida own the shop next to yours?' Armando said, putting the honeycomb candles together with the display of honey in the window.

'She does indeed. We've been friends forever and in the summer we'd spend a lot of time at their family farm. One of the things I loved about it was the smell of the place. It's very different from misty Sintra. It's hot and dry and filled with herbs. So I created a perfume with the scent of herbs and honey, but it wasn't quite right. It felt incomplete.'

'Until you added the soil element,' Armando said. 'Yes, I see. But how did you isolate the correct scent? I can see how you could distil the smells from the herbs and the honey, but soil?'

'Well, you probably know that the smell of soil mainly comes from the living organisms within it, don't you? The bacteria and the fungi.'

'Yes. It's the smell coming from the bacteria that gives soil its aromatic smell when it rains.'

'Exactly. So I found out what the chemicals were that those organisms give off, and experimented with those till I got the right smell.'

'Clever.' Armando sat back in his chair and admired Ms Luna, not just for her ingenuity, but for the way her face lit up when she talked about her work. 'I really like your perfumes.'

'Why?'

'They're unique, which I think I mentioned before. But your current scent also brings back a happy memory, so I suppose that makes me like it even more.'

'Does it?' Diana said, and she coloured slightly.

That encouraged Armando.

'I was on my way from high school to Évora to meet up with my father for a business seminar. I was tired and probably being a royal teenaged pain when Libero stopped the car on the side of the road and made me walk halfway up the hill. As a typical teenager, I grumbled all the way.

'Then he sat me down under the shade of an olive tree and we had the packed sandwiches I was just going to eat on route in the car. It was a hot day, and the shade wasn't particularly deep, but all around us were wildflowers and the scent of herbs and dry soil. Somehow it was very relaxing. After that I was okay to carry on to meet with my father.'

'You were going to business seminars even as a kid?'

'My dad's form of training me to take over the business. I didn't mind that, really. It was the only way I got to spend time with him.'

'That sounds a little sad.'

'It's the life of a corporate heir,' Armando said with a laugh. 'It isn't all glamour.'

'Poor little rich kid,' Diana said sarcastically, but her voice held a note of sympathy. 'At least my grandmother was always around.'

'But not your mother?' Armando said and regretted the remark as he remembered what Ms Luna had said about her mother before. It was too late to take it back, though.

'My mother is the definition of a free spirit. She was never interested in the shop or in perfume making. Her idea of fun is travelling the world. The last time I heard from her she was in Turkey.'

'Don't you need money to do that kind of thing?'

'It depends on how you do it. She doesn't have much. Everything she owns fits into a backpack and she's great at making friends, sleeping on their sofas and working as a bartender.'

'A bartender?'

'They make more money than waitresses.'

'I see.' To Armando, it sounded quite exotic. 'I think my brother would like her.'

'Your brother, why?'

'He'd like nothing better than to become a surfing beach bum.'

'We should introduce them to each other,' Diana said and gave Armando a first, genuinely warm smile.

He liked it.

'Does your mother not hate the Zeller family too, then? That might make it tricky.'

It was a stupid thing to say because Diana's smile faltered. She took a deep breath, though, and made the effort to smile again.

'I think she'd say it was all in the past and we should learn to love each other. She's a gigantic hippy.'

'Maybe I should negotiate with her after all,' Armando murmured.

To his surprise, Diana actually laughed at that.

'Feel free to try. I'm sure she'd love to get her hands on a million euros.'

CHAPTER THIRTEEN

Diana paused outside the depressing concrete facade of a nineteen-seventies office block on a narrow Lisbon street. A few straggly trees that would have looked better on the African planes formed a sad, yellowing parade down the length of the pavement. Cars were parked tightly between them, their noses pushed so close to the buildings that you had to walk in the road to get past them.

She hadn't really wanted to come here, but it was Fernando's office and he'd suggested they meet officially to discuss the Zeller contract. Since he'd set up the meeting for noon, she had the sinking feeling that he was going to invite her for lunch afterwards.

Oddly enough, she'd had a similar suspicion over her meeting with Armando Zeller earlier in the week. She'd felt less reluctant about going to lunch with him, though, which made her wonder why. Maybe it was because he was also a perfumer. Since her grandmother had died, she had nobody else to talk to about the art of composing perfumes. She found it exhilarating to have somebody who not only understood the skill required in her craft, but apparently thought she was good at it.

Fernando had always been rather dismissive of what she did and treated it like an amusing hobby. In his mind, it in no way equated to the years he'd spent at university. People didn't respect craftsmen much in Portugal. To gain real social status, you needed a degree. Maybe that was why Fernando had broken up with her. He wanted a more prestigious girlfriend and, ultimately, wife.

But even law degrees didn't net you a million euros in a single year. With that invigorating thought, Diana stepped into the building and took the narrow lift, that could barely squeeze in four people, to the third floor. The office was nondescript. The glass door had the name of the firm lettered on it and opened out to a moderate sized reception where a middle-aged woman intercepted all visitors. She was very good at putting you exactly in your place and making you aware of how lowly that place was.

'Hello Ms Teresa,' Diana said.

'Ah Ms Diana, it's so nice to see you again,' the receptionist said and her face broke into an unaccustomed smile.

It was so unusual that Diana was immediately suspicious that Ms Teresa had seen the video. It was either that or she knew about the settlement. Diana dismissed the second suspicion. Fernando might have turned out to be a cad, but he was a lawyer through and through and he would never reveal anything about his client's business.

'Mr Raposo is waiting for you,' Ms Teresa said, 'please go straight through.'

That was also unusual, Ms Teresa usually insisted on accompanying all visitors to the person they were coming to see. So Fernando had said something, but what it was she didn't know. It wasn't worth bothering about though and Diana just made her way down the green-tiled corridor, her heels clicking with every step and knocked at Fernando's office door.

'Come in,' Fernando shouted, and Diana heard his chair being scraped backward.

She stepped inside as he was still coming out from behind his desk, his arms open wide in welcome. Diana couldn't help compare that to his greeting when he was about to dump her. She smiled but didn't come in for a hug, instead looking around the room.

It was a generic office with a boring office desk and a separate circular table in the other half of the room, with five chairs around it for client meetings. Perhaps it was more proper to call it generic legal office because law books filled the shelves that took up two walls, while stacks of folders and loose papers occupied every other available surface. They were piled so high on Fernando's desk that he'd have trouble seeing over the top of them if a client sat opposite him. That was probably why he waved her to the circular table that only had a modest stack of paper in its centre.

'You're looking well,' Fernando said as he pulled out a chair for Diana.

'Thank you,' Diana said at her most neutral. 'Now tell me about the contract.'

'Ah yes, the contract.'

Fernando spoke as though he'd clean forgotten why she'd come. He hurried back to his desk, lifted a couple of files from three of his piles before tracking down the manilla envelope Diana had given him. Then he sat down opposite Diana, beaming at her.

'It's a surprising contract.'

'Is it?'

Diana worried that surprising might be a prelude to something bad.

'It appears to be entirely to your benefit. I can find nothing that a legal expert might object to, although I have suggested a few minor changes.'

'Really?'

This news was even more astonishing. Diana had expected at least a few major alterations and, at worst, to be told that the whole thing was a sham.

'Amalia thinks it's because Zeller likes you.'

'What?' Diana said, wondering why one of Fernando's legal partners had made such a comment.

'I was so surprised by the contract that I asked Amalia to look at it as well. Our conclusion is unanimous. The contract is extremely beneficial towards you. The only reason we could come up with for that fact is that Mr Zeller likes you.'

'That's ridiculous.'

'Is it?'

'Of course!' Diana said although she was now forced to look at the two meals she'd had with Armando Zeller in a new light.

Fernando looked relieved by her reaction.

'Amalia tells me that aside from being super wealthy, Armando Zeller is good looking. It's not something I would have noticed, but still.'

Diana gave a cynical laugh at that comment. It was ridiculous that men pretended not to notice the looks of other men when any woman could easily tell a pretty woman from a plain one. Now wasn't the time to bring that up, though.

'So I can go ahead with the contract?'

'Send Zeller the suggested changes. I doubt his legal team will quibble over them, and if they do, I recommend you just accept whatever proposals they make as alternatives. It won't impact the final outcome. It will make you a rich woman, however.'

'Okay, well, thank you,' Diana said as she shoved the contract into her bag and rose to leave. 'Send me your bill when it's ready.'

Fernando looked surprised by her abruptness.

'I thought we could have lunch.'

'Why?' Diana asked looking down at him. 'Do you usually take clients out to lunch?'

'Clients? Diana, I'm asking you on a date.'

'But we broke up.'

'I thought we'd made up again.'

'It's going to take more than buying me breakfast to make up.' Diana realised that wasn't the message she was aiming for and added, 'for me, Fernando, our relationship is over.'

'You mean now that you have money!'

That was unexpected and painful comeback.

'When did I ever ask you for money?'

Diana couldn't keep the anger from her voice. How dare he accuse her of something like that?

'I'm sorry, I shouldn't have said that,' Fernando said and had the good grace to look ashamed. 'But at least, you know, I went back to you before I knew about this contract.'

'That is one thing in your favour. But since then, you have surely been reevaluating how useful it will be to have a wealthy girlfriend now that you're more senior. I can't even say I blame you for doing that, but I'm afraid I no longer feel the same way I used to about you. So I think it's best we stop here.'

'You think you've got a chance with Zeller!' Fernando said as if struck by sudden insight. 'Well, dream on. People like him don't date people like us, even if he has just made you a millionaire.'

'I have no intention of ever dating a Zeller,' Diana snapped. 'I'm just telling you, I saw you in a whole new light when you dumped me and I can't get over. You finished it, and I can't see a way back for us. So, thank you for your speedy turn around on this contract and I hope everything goes well for you in the future.'

Diana rushed for the door, praying Fernando didn't follow her. She managed to get through it and hear the firm click before a faint, 'Diana...' came from Fernando.

By that time it was too late and she made it out of the building trembling, but unhindered and with her resolve intact.

Chapter Fourteen

Armando checked his email for the third time that morning. It was a bad habit and one he had developed ever since he'd received the email from Diana informing him of the very minor changes her lawyers had suggested. His legal team was going over the amendments, but it looked like there would be no disagreement and he would soon have a final version that he could print out and take to Ms Luna to sign. He intended to make an event out of it and had already picked out an excellent champagne they could share.

The shrill ring of his mobile jerked him out of his pleasant daydream. It was the tone he'd chosen for any calls from his father, and it was never a good sign if he called.

'Yes, Dad?'

'What the devil are you playing at?' Homero bellowed down the phone. 'Come to my office immediately!'

Armando looked at the phone in surprise. His father was famous for his bad temper but even so, being shouted at was unusual. Having him hang up so abruptly was less out of character. Either way, it was best not to keep him waiting.

Armando had no intention of looking flustered, though. So he made sure he looked impeccable before he took the walk from his end of the building to the other. He was being watched by the staff. That also wasn't unusual, but if something big was brewing, they didn't look like they were aware of it.

His father's secretary didn't look flustered, either. Then again, Clarisse Alma, unlike her glamorous name, was an extraordinarily plain looking woman who was built like an Olympic shot-putter and had the emotional range of a stone. His stepmother had selected her for her obvious lack of charm, which she made up for with frightening efficiency.

'He's expecting me,' Armando said, sailing past her.

'Yes,' she said without moving from her desk.

'What is the meaning of this?' Homero bellowed and threw a stapled stack of papers into Armando's face the moment he stepped into the room.

He ducked, which meant he only got a glancing blow from the document. Then he leaned down to pick up the offending item. It alarmed him to see that it was his contract with Diana Luna.

He was even more dismayed when he realised Helena was seated in the section of the office that was laid out like a sitting room with an elegant collection of gilt chairs covered in a stripped gold silk. At least she didn't look smug. It seemed that even she was surprised by the rage his father had flown into.

The fact that she was sitting here, though, probably meant that she'd come running to her father with the contract. There was no reason the legal team would bring it to his father's attention.

Armando took his time straightening up, although he doubted it would give his father time to calm down.

'What is the problem?' Armando said, keeping his voice calm and his body relaxed.

'What's the problem? You've got this woman, this libellous opportunist to sign a non-disclosure agreement?'

For a moment, Armando was thrown. He'd expected his father to be angry about the money.

'It's damage limitation.' Armando glanced at Helena, but she offered no clue and looked equally surprised. 'Our stocks went down on this rumour. I was simply making sure it didn't blow up even more.'

'An NDA is admitting that we were at fault.'

'Not necessarily.' Armando was surprised that his father was baulking at the same point that Diana Luna had. If he wasn't so furious, Armando might have found some humour in the situation. 'It the quickest way to shut down the gossip. That's all.'

'It's a legal document admitting we're at fault.'

'The lawyers actually went to great lengths to make sure we don't admit fault.'

'The lawyers be damned,' Homero roared. 'I know what it means, and anyone else seeing this document will know it too.'

'But nobody will see this document.'

'I've seen it,' Homero said, banging his fist against his chest. 'It's a bloody pack of lies. My father was no thief. He was ambitious, yes, but not a thief. You're giving that... that woman a million euros based on a lie. It's outrageous.'

'Father, I've looked at the two formulas. They're identical. Diana Lima has a valid claim.'

'Rubbish, if she's shown you the formula, you can bet she's built up a good story for her con. She will not blackmail me like this. How dare that woman drag our family name through the mud?'

Armando looked across at Helena again, certain she wouldn't own up to stealing Diana Luna's note books. His father was also in no mood to be reasoned with. His rage surprised and shook Armando. He knew his father had always looked up to his grandfather. He'd put him on a pedestal, and always told the story of the founder of the Zeller corporation at the annual staff bash. Armando had just not realised how invested his father was in the story.

'The lawyers suggested this was the best way,' Armando said, trying to calm his father.

'You're giving away a million euros of the company's money to some nobody with a bogus claim and now you're hiding behind the lawyers?' Homero roared. 'You should own your mistakes.'

'It isn't a bogus claim. I verified it, as did Helena,' Armando said, looking towards his half sister again.

'What rubbish.' Homero stalked up to Armando and poked him in the chest. 'What is all of this really about?'

'I've already said it's damage control, and,' Armando paused. Now wasn't the best time, but he had to add, 'it's partly paying off a debt.'

'And more than a bit of trying to get into Ms Luna's pants,' Helena said.

'It's a fucking immoral and expensive way of doing it,' Homero ground out, emphasising each word with another jab at Armando's chest.

Armando felt his own anger rising. He hated being shouted at, but he was used to that from his father. No, he was angry at Helena for being so crude.

'The House of Zeller's budget is mine to spend as I please. The amount I have allocated to Ms Luna is a very minor payment when you consider how much more we could lose and,' he said, his own mulishness coming into play even when he knew it was stupid to provoke his father, 'when you consider what we have made from Armour over the decades.'

'It makes us look guilty, and it's an entirely unnecessary spend. We could just crush that woman.'

Thus proving our ruthless immorality, Armando wanted to say, but decided damage limitation would be better after all. He couldn't let his temper get the better of him, too. Helena would just love it if he did.

'Our profits from last year were over a hundred million euros, our turnover was five times that. We can afford this payment.'

'It is unacceptable. Just because you've suddenly got the hots for somebody doesn't mean the company gets to pay out for your lust.'

'I wish you would stop making something of this that it isn't. We owe the Luna family for this.'

'Never!' Homero roared. 'Never will I acknowledge that my father was a thief. Never will I sanction a payout to some drunken opportunist.'

'Well, you're going to have to.' Armando gave his sister an exasperated stare. He expected her to do something like this, so he didn't know why it annoyed him. 'I am using my budget to do it.'

'It's my company,' Homero said, coming so close his forehead was nearly touching Armando's.

When he was younger and lighter than his father, Armando would have backed down at this moment because he knew a beating was a possibility. But he wasn't willing to do that now. Not when there was a matter of principle at stake.

'Both parties have agreed the contract.'

It was a lie, a stupid one at that, but he couldn't give up without a fight.

'It hasn't been signed yet.'

'So you want me to break it, and have a breach of contract?'

'It isn't a breach if it isn't signed,' Helena chipped in unhelpfully.

'The signatures are beside the point. Ms Luna has all the emails with the copy of this contract. She is just waiting to finalise everything.'

'Well, she will never get a cent from us,' Homero said. 'Not while I am alive.'

'I don't see how you can stop me,' Armando said.

'You're fired.'

The words hung in the air of the suddenly silent office. Helena looked shocked, her mouth making a little oh of surprise, but her eyes were sparkling with delight. Armando could barely comprehend the words.

'What?'

'You heard me.'

Homero stood stock still, his jaw clenched in the way it did when he'd made a pronouncement that couldn't be overturned.

'You're going to fire me over a tiny expenditure that won't impact on our bottom line, simply because it hurts your pride?'

'Nobody calls my father a thief. He was the genius who built up our company. I won't have you or that Luna woman or anyone else sully his name. Get out of my building.'

Armando took a breath, ready to argue, and then realised that his father was in no state of mind to be reasoned with. His face was red and his breath was coming in fast gasps.

'Let's have this conversation again when you've calmed down,' Armando said and walked away.

'Don't bother,' his father shouted after him, 'and don't show your face to me ever again.'

Armando took a deep breath to calm himself as he walked in what he hoped looked like an unconcerned way back to his office.

'Is everything alright?' Libero asked.

'I've just been fired,' Armando said, and forced a smile. 'You may as well go home. That's what I'll be doing. I'll think about the rest later.'

'Fired?' Even though Libero was usually good at hiding his surprise, he couldn't do it this time. 'Why?'

'The contract with Ms Luna. I suspect Helena got wind of it. She's been cultivating people all around the company and she would have been remiss to not get herself a pet lawyer. She must have taken the contract to my father.'

'Maybe it would have been better to tell him about it ahead of time?'

'Maybe, but I don't discuss any of my other spending decision with him so I don't see why I needed to talk to him about this either.'

He'd behaved as he always had with any contract negotiation. His father would have brushed him off and questioned his ability to be a CEO if he had tried to discuss any of his other contracts with him. But maybe, with this one, he should have been more sensitive.

He should have known his father would react badly to any criticism of his grandfather. He'd always treated the old man like an infallible being. Now this... he wasn't even sure what he should do next.

'Are you sure you want me to go home?' Libero said.

'I don't see what else you can do at the moment,'

Now that he was calming down, Armando felt the need to get away and not have to deal with other people's surprise.

'Alright, then I'll go,' Libero said, 'but in a little while. There are a few things I'll have to reschedule given... current events.'

'Fine.'

A sense of numbness was settling about Armando from the shock of the confrontation, but he was careful to maintain his calm demeanour as he collected his jacket and bag and made his way down to the underground garage.

It surprised him to see a couple of security guards standing in front of his car.

'I'm sorry Mr Zeller, but the boss, that is, your father said he was impounding the car.'

'It's my car.' Armando had bought it with his own money, but clearly his father was in such a rage that simply firing him wasn't sufficient. 'What if I just take it?'

The guard shifted uncomfortably and said, 'We've been ordered to use bug spray on you if you try. I'm sorry, sir.'

Armando was astonished. His father knew bug spray would bring on a severe migraine or even knock him out. His stepmother had used it liberally around the house whenever she was feeling particularly vindictive.

The fact that his father had gone to such lengths surprised and angered him. Especially because now their massive falling out would become known across the company. There was no way the security guards would keep their mouths shut about that.

Armando gazed at them for a moment, thinking, then gave a resigned nod and walked away. There was no point in making a scene in front of them. He fitted his face mask on as he took the stairs up to the street level and walked outside.

He was shaking now, shocked by how this day had turned out. His mind kept running through the argument with his father. He pushed those thoughts away. They were unhelpful. For now, he just had to figure out how to get home.

If memory served him right, there was a tram that ran from this area to his house. He'd never taken it, so it would be a novelty.

The tram was one of the old yellow varieties with the wooden roof and the slatted wooden seats. It was small, a vehicle from a distant era, although probably the only size that could make it through the narrow winding roads of Lisbon. At this time of the day, there were only three other commuters and a pale-skinned couple who were probably tourists. It appeared that some people were still willing to travel despite the risks of the virus.

Thankfully, the windows of the tram were all wide open, but Armando pressed the mask more tightly around his mouth all the same. His hands were still shaking, and he barely noticed the scenery as the tram screeched its way slowly up the hill.

Armando got off at the park at the top. It was small, one half was lawn and trees, with a romantic marble statue in the middle of a nymph. The other half was a stone paved balcony that gave spectacular views over the city and on down to the wide Tagus river far below. Armando tended to avoid the park, as it was usually full of tourists. Funny that he hadn't even noticed that they'd been absent for months.

He headed for the road on the right that descended steeply downwards to his house. The retaining wall of the park soon loomed high overhead to his left, and tightly packed houses blocked the view of the city. It was a miss mash of facades, some freshly renovated and painted, the area was gentrifying, some tiled in blues and greens, with a floral, Art Deco trim under the terracotta eves.

One or two houses were abandoned and slowly falling apart. Here the paint had flaked off to reveal bare tan of sandy plaster and stone walls beneath that held together with mud. One particularly dilapidated house no longer even had a roof, just some bare timbers poking into the sky. Armando usually drove past it so quickly he'd seldom taken in the ugliness of it, and the way it made the rest of the street look desolate.

No, that was just his bad mood today. It was fine. Somebody would buy the land any day now and either restore the building or knock it down and infill the space with something modern. Just like he'd done with his house.

He'd reached the end of the road. Lisbon was like that, all meandering roads that curved around the many hills and sometimes led somewhere but often just ended, like this one. This was home. The clipped box hedges indicated the beginning of his property.

He stepped through a modern metal gate and into a plain white space. Simple rectangular stepping stones led to the front door. The rest of the small garden was filled with white gravel. He'd planted tall, thin, almost black cypress trees along the white walls that enclosed the space. A square of sparkling water led the eye to the front door. Seated on the simple marble bench at the door were another pair of security guards.

'What the devil are you doing here?' Armando asked as he hurried over, although he already had his suspicions.

These two looked as uncomfortable as the men guarding his car as they leaped to their feet. It must have been strange for them to be doing this to the eldest son of the company. At the moment, though, Armando couldn't care less about their feelings.

'I'm sorry, sir, we've been told not to let you in.'

'Are you also armed with bug spray?'

'Yes, sir, sorry, sir.'

Armando felt as though he'd received an actual slap. He was tempted to roar at the men to get the hell off his property. He doubted they'd actually dare to use the spray. But what if they did?

Fine, if that was the way his father was going to do things, he'd take matters into his own hands. He'd fetch the police and force the men obstructing access to his own home to leave. He nodded at the men, who looked like they might melt under his fiery gaze, then turned around and walked off.

The house was his, bought and paid for with his own money. It was ridiculous that his father was doing this. He reached for his phone, determined to call the police and a lawyer after that. That made him pause. Which lawyer? He couldn't use the company lawyers now.

But he'd started walking, phone still in hand. The steep road was what he needed. He realised he was getting winded as he pounded uphill, cursing under his breath so furiously that an elderly woman coming the other way crossed the street to avoid him.

But as his fingers hovered over the phone, he stopped. He was furious, so angry he could barely think straight. But if he did this, it would mean an all out war with his father. The old man was remote and domineering, but he was his father. He didn't want to land up like so many of his friends who'd fallen out so badly with family that they were no longer on speaking terms.

He had to do something to get back to work as well. The company was probably Helena's now. She'd played her cards pretty well. But he couldn't just hand it over without a fight.

Armando walked back up to the park and sat sideways on the deckchair like benches that had been laid out under a copse of ancient stone pines. He ignored the spectacular view and kicked at the ground where the grass had turned brown and bare patches of earth showed. He had to calm down and think, but right now he was at a loss to know what he did next.

CHAPTER FIFTEEN

Diana was humming to herself as she brushed her teeth. It was amazing what having some money and the promise of more could do for a person. The NDA clause still bothered her, but Margarida had helped her to finally make up her mind about it last night.

They'd been sipping an evening coffee at the Butterfly Cafe, outside, just in case anyone showed an interest in their shops. It was past closing time, but both would have been willing to open if a potential customer showed up.

They didn't, and that finally prompted Margarita to say, 'You should take the money.'

'Really? What about the clause?'

'Forget the clause,' Margarida said with an impatient wave of her hand. 'Who would you be telling, anyway? I know, Fernando knows–'

'Not that he believed me,' Diana muttered into her coffee cup.

'Your grandmother knew,' Margarida said, giving her a stern stare, 'and that's it. Nobody cares anyway, so just take the money. You could retire with that kind of money. Imagine that, retired at thirty.'

'Fernando thinks I should ask for more,' Diana said, but with less strong feelings than she had over the NDA.

'I know, but in this instance I disagree with him.'

'How do you know about that? I hadn't got round to telling you.'

Diana suspected Margarida blushed, but it was difficult to tell in the dim light. She did look away, gazing down the empty street, dotted about with fallen yellow leaves.

'Fernando told me last night. He called to get me to convince you to take the money.'

Diana got the distinct impression there had been more to the call than that. But as it had grown considerably colder as the sun went down and the street lights pinged on, she decided against pursuing that line of questioning. It could wait. Instead, she finished the last of her coffee and the two of them hurried back to their respective homes.

Now here she was bopping away over the bathroom sink. She'd decided not to ask for more than the million. She honestly didn't need it. With a million, she could make all the repairs she needed and run the perfume shop exactly as she pleased. No need to go on-line if she didn't want to.

All that left her to do was contact Fernando and ask him to send the finalised agreement back to Armando Zeller.

Thankfully, the contract had required little legal work, even though Fernando had quoted an extortionate sum for what he had done. So she still had most of the ten thousand euros to spend as she wanted and she'd been able to pay all her overdue bills. The sense of relief it gave her to not have those things hanging over her was tremendous.

The knowledge that she would have more soon led her to consider what else she might spend the money on. There were a multitude of repairs needed to the shop and her apartment. The constantly dripping sink tap being a case in point, Diana thought, as she spat out the toothpaste and rinsed her mouth.

After that, she could look at fixing the roof. She was sure there were a few broken tiles, but she'd not had the courage to find out. Every time they had strong winds or heavy rains, Diana worried the house would spring a leak. That too would soon be a thing of the past.

Diana grinned at herself in the mirror, gave a happy nod and went back to the bedroom to get dressed. With more money, she'd also be able to buy herself some new clothes. She hadn't done that in years and everything was getting threadbare.

She had just finished dressing and was in the process of brushing her hair when her phone rang. It was from an unknown mobile number and Diana was tempted to just ignore it. Then she thought it might be a new potential client, so she swiped the screen.

'Ms Luna?'

It was Armando Zeller and Diana felt a thrill of excitement go through her. This had to be about the contract.

'Yes, Mr Zeller?'

'I um... I'm sorry, Ms Luna, but I'm afraid I've hit a snag with your contract.'

He sounded so serious Diana's cheerful mood evaporated, and her stomach constricted with fright. She mustn't overreact, though, in case it was nothing.

'What do you mean?'

'Things just got a bit more complicated. I will get back to you as soon as I have more information. I'm sorry, Ms Luna,' Armando said and hung up.

Diana gasped and stared at the now dead phone in her hand.

'Things just got more complicated? What does that even mean?'

Diana stabbed her phone back to life, put Zeller's number into her contacts and sent a text message.

I'd appreciate a bit more information.

She felt more strongly about it than that, but it was best not to escalate things. She was stunned by how upset it made her. It wasn't about the loss of money either; it was how betrayed she felt by Zeller.

I will explain as soon as I have something to tell you. Please give me some time.

The reply felt utterly inadequate. It was exactly the kind of thing you would say if you intended to fob somebody off. It made Diana's disappointment almost overwhelming.

She dropped onto her sofa, trying to think, and decided that there might be more information from Zeller in her emails. She called them up and scrolled through all the useless marketing stuff and then stopped. There was an email from the Zeller Corporation. Only it didn't come from Armando Zeller but from Homero Zeller, CEO.

Diana had a horrible feeling that was Armando's father. Her hand trembled as she held it over the button that would open the attachment. She felt that the moment she read it, her wonderful dream would be over.

It didn't take long to get through the document, but by the end Diana was having difficulty seeing through her tears. The letter filled her with so much rage and hurt that she nearly hurled her phone clean across the room. Fortunately, sense prevailed, and she merely flung it at the sofa. It bounced and flew off to land on her rug.

Diana was tempted to give into the rage and howl her frustrations into a tightly clutched pillow, but that would do her no good. She had to take action. So she retrieved her phone, called up Armando Zeller's number and pressed connect. The phone went straight to voicemail. It was so instantaneous that Diana guessed he'd switched his phone off. The coward.

That left her with only one option. Cursing under her breath, she hurried downstairs to Margarida's shop. Fortunately, she checked whether she was free, so didn't barge in already proclaiming her woes. Instead she stood around, pretending to be a customer looking at the wares while Margarida sold a set of prettily embroidered dishcloths to a French tourist.

The woman didn't linger to chat. The moment she'd stepped out of the shop, Margarida turned an alarmed face to Diana

'What's wrong? Your face is all red and puffy.'

Diana couldn't explain so just held out her phone with the offending letter from the CEO of the Zeller Corporation.

'Look.'

It took Margarida a while to get through the document and her expression turned to one of horror as she read.

'No, how can this be?'

'I know, right? I mean, I wasn't the one who suggested the contract, but the CEO is saying that if I ever approach any of his family again or make any accusations against the Zeller corporation, he'll crush me.' The actual words Homero Zeller had used was that he would bring the full weight of the law down upon her, but she knew exactly what it meant. 'What's worse is that Armando Zeller called me right before. He said there was a problem, but he sounded like he'd try to fix it. Then I saw this and now...'

'What did he say exactly?'

'Check his text,' Diana said, waving at her phone that Margarida was still holding. 'He phoned first and said pretty much the same thing.'

'He said he'll explain, but he needs time?'

'Exactly, and that was vague enough, but coupled with this email, I don't know what to think. My grandmother always warned me not to trust a Zeller. She said they draw you in with their charm and then they turn around and bite you and their bite is filled with poison.'

Margarida tutted dismayed agreement and sat Diana down in a chair.

'This is so wrong, especially after that Armando Zeller looked like he was doing the right thing.'

'He's just undone the lot. I never want to see him or any of his deceitful family again,' Diana said, and tears dripped unchecked down her face.

'Oh no,' Margarida said and grabbed one of her embroidered hankies from the display stand and handed it to Diana. 'Maybe he will be able to fix things, you never know. Have some faith.'

'In a Zeller?' Diana gave a bitter laugh as she dabbed at her eyes. 'He made me think my problems were on the way to being resolved. Now I'm back to square one, worrying about the bills that are just going to pile up all over again. I will never, ever trust a Zeller again.'

Chapter Sixteen

A rmando meandered down the boardwalk that was built to go over and between the dunes, heading towards Guincho beach. He hardly noticed their elegant half moon sweeps, although he was dazzled by the sun that bounced off the light coloured sand. It had been a week and his sense of frustration at his inability to help Diana Luna had only intensified over that time. The hurt in her voice during the phone call haunted him and he wished he could do something about it.

His anger towards his father hadn't subsided. Every time he thought of Diana Luna, it also reminded him of the final bruising confrontation and everything that followed. This included calling Ms Luna the following morning. He'd had to leave it till the next day because he'd been far too angry to contact her there and then. He'd also hoped that his father might relent, but he hadn't.

Armando reached the end of the boardwalk and stepped out onto the broad sweep of the beach. The gigantic waves of the Atlantic carved the beach away so that it dropped from quite a height down to the water's edge. Since it was morning on a weekday, there were only a few surfers about and a handful of people walking on the firmer sand at the water's edge.

Armando didn't want to get too close to the water. The smell from a distance was fine, but up close it was too salty. It also still carried a trace of sewage smell, despite the fact that they no longer pumped raw sewage into the sea.

So he turned left along the dune line and went to settle in his favourite place. It was within an alcove of dunes where he was shielded from the almost permanent wind. He sat down on the loose sand, leaned back and luxuriated in the warmth that permeated through him from the sun. The sky was a beautiful blue without a single cloud to break it up. Overhead, almost out of his vision, lanky dune grass fluttered and waved.

'Another glorious day,' Armando murmured.

It was turning out to be a pleasantly warm autumn in general.

'Armando!' somebody shouted.

For a moment Armando wondered who it could be. Then Eddy appeared, ploughing his way through the soft sand.

'Hah, I knew I'd find you here.'

Eddy gave a triumphant grin and dropped to the ground beside Armando so that his back was also to the dunes and he could admire the sea view.

'How did you know to look here?'

It surprised Armando to see Eddy at all, but more so because he was wearing a suit.

'That was easy, don't go giving me credit for intelligence. I asked Libero who, of course, had called Bernardo the moment he couldn't get hold of you. Bernardo told Libero he'd lent you his beach house.'

'Ah.'

Armando felt strangely touched that his brother had made this effort.

'Have you even switched your phone on over the last week?'

'Not once. I can't tell you how nice it's been.'

'Have you checked the internet then?'

'Why would I?'

'Because I got promoted, you bastard!' Eddy shouted in mock outrage. 'I haven't even figured out the food flavouring department yet and Dad called me in and made me the bloody Director of Perfumes.'

'I see.' Armando wasn't sure how he felt about hearing the news. He'd been waiting for his father to calm down and call him back to work. 'Congratulations.'

'Congratulations?' Eddy stared at his brother like he was a fool. 'Do you think I actually wanted the job? I don't have a clue what I'm doing. Thank God for Libero; without him I'd be making a total mess of it. I mean... I have made a mess of it. That pop star, Céu, gave me such a hard time that I told her to leave if she didn't stop bugging me, so she did. That made me unpopular, I can tell you.'

'Mmm, it would have. We were expecting great things from the sales of her perfume.'

Armando noted he didn't really care about the loss. If he'd still been at the company, he'd be moving heaven and earth to get the pop starlet back. Now it felt entirely unimportant.

'On top of that,' Eddy carried on, 'Helena's being a total bitch. She threw a fit when I was promoted. She thinks I am actually after the CEO role, no matter how many times I tell her I'm not interested.'

'She has two disadvantages when it comes to being a CEO and she's very aware of both of them. That's why she's over reacting now. Don't worry about it.'

'She has disadvantages?' Eddy said with a snort. 'She's got spies in every department. She knows everything before dad. What disadvantages could she possibly have?'

'She's done all of that because she is aware of her disadvantages, even if you aren't.'

Armando closed his eyes and went back to leaning against the dunes. It was funny how Helena's actions and insecurities were obvious to him, but not to Eddy. It made it clear that Eddy really wasn't interested in the company.

'Hey, Bro', what are the disadvantages?' Eddy asked as he grabbed Armando's shoulder and gave him a shake.

'She isn't a nose,' Armando said, opening one eye to squint at his brother, 'and she's a woman. Those are two points against her with our father.'

'Really?' Eddy said and stopped to consider. 'Well, that explains her bad mood, I suppose. And you want to know why Dad blew up the way he did?'

'Because I accused our grandfather of being a thief. I knew he'd be sensitive about that. I just didn't realise how sensitive.'

'Yeah, okay, he always looked up to the old man, but it's not only that. Mom asked him for a divorce the night before Helena showed him your contract.'

'A divorce?'

This news surprise Armando so much he sat up again and gave Eddy a closer look.

'Can you believe she's found herself a toy boy? She's apparently infatuated by her tennis coach.'

Although Eddy was making light of the situation, Armando realised he was hurt and embarrassed by what his mother was doing.

'Maybe she'll change her mind.'

Eddy shrugged.

'I don't know why the news came as a shock to me. I mean, it isn't like Dad hasn't had a few mistresses since he married Mom. I half expected him to divorce Mom and marry an even younger model. But instead, Mom turned the tables and I'm weirded out over it.'

'It's never easy when parents get divorced,' Armando said and pulled at a brown knob sticking out of the sand to discover that it was a short stick.

'Anyway, the divorce is their problem to sort out. I came here to find out what you are going to do.'

'Me?' Armando said and set to drawing a couple of wavy lines in the sand with his stick.

'You can't leave me to look after the perfumes department. That will never do.'

'Resign then. It wasn't what you wanted to do, anyway.'

'But it is what you want to do. I might not want the job, but I don't want the company to fail. If you stay away, things will go downhill. I mean, they groomed you to the role and, more importantly, you care about what you were doing. I know the hours you put in. I'm having to do the same myself now and it's hell. You can't just leave.'

'It isn't down to me,' Armando said, examining Eddy, who looked and sounded desperate. 'If that's how you feel, you need to bring it up with Dad.'

'He doesn't listen to me, but he listens to you.'

'Not at the moment he doesn't,' Armando said and went back to drawing in the sand. 'And not where it really matters to me.'

'You mean the Luna contract?'

'We did that family wrong. We should set it to rights and try as I might, I can't find a way to make that clear to our father.'

'He sent her a vicious email warning her off.'

Armando swore under his breath.

'Well, I suppose that's destroyed any chance I had to make it up to Ms Luna.'

'You like her, don't you?'

Armando looked back up at Eddy, remembering what Helena had said about the reason for his contract. Maybe he'd been more generous that he might have with anybody else because of Ms Luna, but he didn't like the way Helena had phrased it.

'It was a fair contract.'

'You had to like her,' Eddy said with his goofy, sympathetic smile. 'You saw her more often than you've ever seen any other woman.'

'Mmm, that's true.'

'What if I patch things up between you? Will you help me out then?'

'You're making an impossible bet. You can't patch things up with Ms Luna. You have no idea how much she distrusts our family and no doubt she feels fully justified now. And I currently have no leverage with our father, so I can't help you.'

'You're my big brother,' Eddy said with a broad grin. 'There isn't a thing you can't do.'

Armando laughed, but he was touched that Eddy felt that way.

'Ah well,' Eddy said, stood up and gave his trousers an energetic brushing off. 'I have to get back to the office even though I'd much rather stay here with you.'

'Or be out on the waves,' Armando said, tilting his head towards the sea.

Eddy groaned like a man in pain. 'Don't even remind me,' he said, grinned and strolled away.

Armando watched him till he vanished around the edge of a dune. He wanted to go back to just lounging and soaking in the sun, but Eddy had brought him back to unpleasant reality.

It wasn't like Armando to switch off and cut all connections, but that was what he'd done. He'd needed time to think, but time had passed. He hadn't come up with a plan yet, and now he'd discovered that Eddy had been promoted into his job.

If he was being optimistic, he might think that his father had done that to keep the position available for him so that he could return. It would have been more final if they'd gone for an open recruitment. All the same, he was probably out of the running for the CEO post.

He regretted that he'd let the opportunity slip through his fingers. It surprised him that he was even willing to do that. And why had he taken this stand now, at this critical time? Was it really because of a woman? It was crazy to have done so for someone who had never particularly liked him and who now probably hated his guts.

CHAPTER SEVENTEEN

It took a while, but Diana finally accepted the latest twist of fate. She didn't really have a choice. She sighed as she looked about her laboratory. She'd had such grand plans for a refurbishment. She'd even started making a list in her notebook of some of the latest perfume making kit she'd wanted to buy in the past but had dismissed as impossibly expensive. So many possibilities had opened up to her with the promise of a payout, and now they had come to nothing.

She flung the notebook away from herself impatiently. It slid more violently than expected and bumped into a glass beaker half filled with her latest creation. It wobbled dangerously, teetering on the edge.

'No!' Diana cried and launched herself towards the beaker.

In her haste she jolted the desk and the beaker tipped over, felt to the floor and shattered, sending glass shards flying and perfume splattering everywhere. Diana stared at it in dismay, sat back down with a bump and wiped away the tears that came welling up.

Lately she was bursting into tears at the littlest things. She was behaving like she'd broken up with a beloved boyfriend. Well, she had, Fernando. She'd shed tears over him, but nothing like she was doing now.

Fortunately, Margarida was around to mop up the tears and distract her when possible. Also fortunate was the trickle of new clients she'd got from Maria de Gouveia. She'd got back pretty speedily with her favourite of the three scents Diana had made for her to test. She'd then also recommended Diana to her friends.

Diana was actually just getting ready for another of those friends. Maria de Gouveia had booked the appointment for her, one Eddi Z. It was a quirky name and Diana liked those kinds of clients. Usually they were willing to create a more interesting than usual perfume.

She'd just finished cleaning up the broken beaker and scrubbing away the scent when the bell rang over her door and she hurried through to her shop. She stopped in surprise when she saw a tall scruffy young man in faded jeans, rather than the socialite woman she'd been expecting. He was wearing a mask, but there was something familiar about his face.

'I'm sorry, sir, I'm expecting a client. Unless you're after something I can deal with quickly, you'll have to come back. Were you looking for a perfume for your girlfriend?'

'No, I am your next appointment.' The young man approached her, his hand outstretched. Then he remembered they no longer shook hands, stopped and lowered it. 'I'm Eddy Zeller.'

'What?' Diana said, shocked first and then her anger grew. 'Get out of my shop,' she snapped. 'I won't have a Zeller in here.'

'Please, I just need to explain–'

'Out!' Diana said at her firmest, not budging from behind her counter but hoping her anger was getting through to the man. 'Wait, do you know Maria de Gouveia?'

'Yeah,' Eddy said as though that was a given. 'She'd my brother's best friend's girlfriend.'

Diana felt as if she'd suffered yet another blow from the Zeller clan.

'That good for nothing, sneaky, dishonest, thieving–'

'Please, Ms Luna,' Eddy put his hands out in an attempt to stop her. 'Let me explain.'

'I don't need an explanation from you.'

Diana couldn't contain herself. She lifted her countertop, rushed through and pushed Eddy as hard as she could.

He staggered backwards but said in a rush, 'Ms Luna, I have to tell you something my brother never would. He doesn't make excuses for himself, so he won't have told you this, but he got fired over your contract.'

'What?' Diana said, pulled up short by the revelation.

'Yeah. And even so, I'm pretty sure he's still trying to figure out a way to fix things and get you the money you're owed.'

This was such astonishing news that it quenched Diana's anger, if not her suspicion.

'So what?'

'Please, just give me a chance to explain everything and then, after that, if you still don't believe me, I'll go and never bother you again.'

'I don't know,' Diana murmured.

Her grandmother would warn her against this, but her curiosity couldn't just shove this new Zeller out.

'I do have an appointment,' Eddy said and his eyes crinkled into a smile.

Diana had the feeling it was a smile he used to win people over. Even with the face mask on, he had an easy charm his more serious brother lacked.

'Alright, come inside. But I'll expect full payment up front.'

'Fair enough,' Eddy said as he followed Diana into her lab, settled on her white sofa, and fished the required fee out of his wallet.

'You can remove your mask now,' Diana said as she flicked on her air extractor.

Eddy did as instructed and looked expectantly up at Diana, still smiling. It was hard for Diana to maintain her anger, but she reminded herself that the best thieves could get you to give up your most precious possessions with a smile.

'Are you also a nose?' Diana asked.

'Yeah, I've just come back from training at ISIPCA. I was supposed to head up the food flavouring department, but now I've been put in Armando's job instead.'

'Really? At your age?'

'It's where Armando started too,' Eddy said as he leaned back on the sofa, his legs stretched out before him. 'Of course he was better prepared for it.'

'Was he?'

'He went to everything my father did when he was still growing up. Even in high school, he got dragged out to business meetings and spent evenings with our dad in his office learning the ropes.'

'It doesn't sound like fun,' Diana said, although she supposed she'd also learned everything from her grandmother in the same way and from an early age. 'Do you actually want a perfume?'

'Since it's a consultation, we may as well,' Eddy said, turning from staring at the ceiling so he could grin at her.

'How do I know you won't just take what I've made and turn it into a Zeller product?'

'I give you my word as a Zeller that I won't pinch your perfume,' Eddy said, placing his right hand over his heart.

'Well, that doesn't count for much.'

'I'm afraid it's all I can give you. But I am curious about what you produce. It must be pretty spectacular to have attracted Armando's attention.'

'Really?'

'Oh yeah, he's the best. We have a whole handful of noses at our laboratory and they're all excellent, including our chief perfume composer, but none of them can produce a real winner. Armando has tweaked all of our best sellers. He's something else.'

'He never mentioned that.'

'He wouldn't.'

'Why not?'

'He's not a boastful person. You probably won't believe me, but Armando has a strong moral code. He doesn't make excuses when things go wrong, he just fixes it. He doesn't steal other people's work, and he believes in fair pay for a product. It's one reason he and my sister Helena don't get on. She's always passing the buck, cutting corners and trying to drive expenses down. For her, success is all about growing the bottom line.'

'I see,' Diana said, although she wasn't sure she did, really.

What was all this about? Why had Eddy Zeller come? She supposed there was only one way to find out, and that was to continue with the consultation.

'Since you're also a perfumer, I think we should go about making your perfume differently.'

'Why?'

Eddie leaned back onto the sofa, looking so relaxed Diana wouldn't have been surprised if he nodded off. It was the complete opposite of how she felt.

'I'm sure you already know which scents you like,' Diana said, waving her hand to encompass her scent organ and its rows upon rows of brown glass scent bottles.

'Well,' Eddy said and gave her a conspiratorial wink. 'I wasn't a great student. I'm not that into perfumes, which was why I was originally given the food division. And while I had to produce a scent for men as part of my final graduation product, it was... I guess Armando would call it pedestrian. I didn't even bother to keep the formula. I barely got a passing grade on it.'

'I see.'

'Just do what you normally do for a client. I have a feeling it might make me a better perfumer into the bargain.'

Despite her suspicion, Diana couldn't help but be charmed by Eddy. Easy-going people could rub along well with anybody. But, she decided, she preferred people who took life more seriously. Her mother was one of the easygoing crew and she was fun to be around, but utterly unreliable.

'Alright, what do you want from the perfume we're making today? Something to wear during the day, or something for special events?'

'Mmm, let's go for something I can wear every day.'

'And you work in an office?'

Eddy actually shuddered.

'You don't like being in an office,' Diana said, and wondered whether her beach bum first impression had been correct.

'Honestly, I love surfing.'

'I see. Did the perfume you make for your graduation feature floralozone?'

Eddy blinked at her as if she was speaking in riddles.

'What?'

So Eddy was correct. He hadn't been a great student.

'The scent that smells like sea air.'

'My scent was an old-fashioned, tobacco and musk scented horror that nobody would wear, even nose blind grandfathers would steer clear. I told you I have no talent for this.'

'Okay, well then, I will start at the beginning. I usually ask my clients about what they love doing and eating. The activities they favour give me an idea of lifestyle. Their favourite foods tell me whether they're more attracted to sweetness, florals, fruitiness, animalistic notes or savoury scents. Since you're keen on surfing, I thought you might like the sea, fresh air and some sandy or grassy notes.'

'That's very good!' Eddy swung his feet back to the floor and leaned forward intently. 'Why did I never think of doing that?'

Diana looked up, checking that he was still sufficiently below the hood of the air extractor.

'Let's start with the fresh air, oceanic and maybe some grassy and earthy scents, then. After that we can experiment with some of the animalic notes and some woody tones.'

Diana dripped the scents from three bottles onto three individual strips of blotting paper for Eddy to smell. 'Put these in your order of preference.'

Eddy smelled each strip, naming the scents as he did.

'Adoxcal, a clean linen scent, one of the Aldehydes isn't it, with quite a grassy smell and Aldehyde Supra, the best for a clean citrus fragrance. I like the grassy smell best here.'

Diana got the impression this was Eddy testing himself, rather than showing off. Then he gave the strips back in order of preference.

Diana attached his favourite to a string with a crocodile clip and handed over another three strips. All the while, she was wondering why he'd come to see her. He must have realised she wouldn't be happy to see him and had thus done his preparatory work.

'Does Armando know you're here?'

'I didn't tell him I was coming.'

'So why are you doing this?'

'For two reasons,' Eddy said, smelling the scents on the new paper strips and taking his time as he sniffed each one and considered the aroma. 'One selfish reason and one not.'

'What's the selfish reason?'

'As I said, my father promoted me into Armando's job, but I really don't want it. If I can get Armando back into his post, then I can return to a job I'm better suited to.'

'And the other reason?'

'I want to help Armando. He's helped me his whole life and for once I get a chance to help him.'

'For once?' Diana asked as she hung Eddy's preferred choice and prepared another three strips.

It was helpful to be doing something she didn't need to concentrate on, because the conversation had her brain seething with questions.

'I sound self indulgent, don't I? I need to explain a bit more though, so you can understand Armando better and see why I trust him and want to help.'

'Go ahead.'

Diana wanted to sound like she wasn't really interested, but actually, now that Eddy was talking, she wanted to know more.

'Armando was eight years old when our father divorced his mother and brought my mother home,' Eddy said. 'My mom didn't like the fact that he existed. She always wanted me and

Helena to be the sole heirs. He also suffered from terrible migraines that kept him in bed for days at a time.

'My mother said he was a burden, and she went out of her way to be nasty to him. One of the ways she did that was by filling the house with strong smells, like cooking fish and garlic, intense room fresheners and the most perfumed of fabric softeners. She knew how sensitive he was to them, and that they brought on even more migraines.'

Diana was tempted to label the woman a bitch, but thought it best not to since she was actually Eddy's mother.

'She should have taken him in properly. She was his new mom.'

'She's just very ambitious,' Eddy said. 'But you see, despite the way he was treated at home, Armando was always very kind to me. Even though he was ten years older than me, he'd play with me for hours at a time. I especially liked it when he'd put me on his back and we'd run around the garden.

'And when he went off to university, I was eight years old and heartbroken by the idea. So my teenage brother, who surely had way more interesting things to do, called me every Monday night without fail for a chat. And when he got back, and I was a bumptious thirteen-year-old, he convinced my father to let me take up surfing.

'I'd been trying to get Dad to let me do it for months without success. I don't know what kind of deal they made, but it was Armando who came to Carcavelos beach with me every Saturday and spent his time working at a cafe while I got my surf lessons.'

'He sounds like a good brother,' Diana said and she was impressed despite herself. 'What about your sister? Is he as good to her?'

'Helena sided with my mother from the beginning. My mother was also determined to make Helena the CEO at Zeller, so they've always been at war. But Armando never says a word against Helena. Certainly never to me, and I also think not to anyone else. While Helena does her best to spread as much muck about Armando as she can. That video of him and you,' Eddy said and gave an apologetic smile to have brought it up. 'Helena spread it all around the company. I'm also pretty sure she told our father about your contract.'

'Was she doing all of that to undermine your brother?'

It annoyed Diana that she'd become a pawn in somebody else's game.

'I think so. And that's pretty messed up. It's another reason I don't want to be the Director of Perfumes. I don't want to get involved in company politics.'

Diana nodded. She had some sympathy for Eddy's predicament. She was glad she'd never had to work in an office and deal with all the backbiting.

'So what is Armando doing now? Since he's been fired.'

Eddy sighed and said, 'He's staying at a friend's beach house, since my father also confiscated his car and his house.'

'He did what?' This revelation shocked Diana. 'In this day and age? How angry was your father over this contract?'

'Very angry.'

'Is there nothing Armando can do about it? I mean, that's just theft. Can't he take it up with the police?'

'I'm sure he could. But at the moment he's turned off his phone and seems to spend every day at the beach. I've never seen him like this before. It's as if he's lost interest in the company. It just isn't like him.'

'Why do you think he's behaving in that way?'

'Because he lost you,' Eddy said and gave Diana his biggest grin yet.

'What?' Diana gasped, staring at Eddy. Was he right? It didn't seem likely.

'I've never heard of Armando seeing a woman more than once. The smell you know.'

'So?'

'How many times have you two met?'

'Five... no six times if you count the time I threw up on him,' Diana said, and felt her face flushing in embarrassment.

'Evidence for the prosecution, if it's needed. After throwing up on him, you should surely have been the last woman on earth he'd ever want to see again. So the next five meetings are a miracle.'

As a test Diana said, 'He even gave me a ride in his car.'

'What? No way! He never lets anyone in his car, not even me.'

Diana did not know what to say about that or the beaming, knowing smile Eddy was giving her. She felt as if her entire world had turned on its head yet again.

CHAPTER EIGHTEEN

L ong after Eddy had left, Diana was still turning his words round and round in her mind. The moment closing time came, she shot straight over to Margarida's to discuss and dissect everything he'd said and what it could mean.

Uncharacteristically, Margarida was less than her usual supportive self.

'Don't get involved in their power games. You're the only one that will suffer from it.'

'But Armando Zeller is also in trouble because he tried to set things right.'

'Says his brother. You'd be much better off and safer with Fernando.'

'If you like Fernando so much, you take him,' Diana snapped and instantly regretted it. 'I'm sorry, I didn't mean—'

'It's alright. I suppose, if you really want to know how you feel, you need to go and see Armando Zeller yourself.'

The idea was simultaneously tantalising and terrifying. Diana had realised, after Eddy left, that one reason she'd been feeling so low was because she felt betrayed by someone she'd started to trust and that she thought she'd never see again. It was preposterous, clearly, and yet, so it seemed.

Was he a nice man? She didn't know. What he'd done for her and for his brother seemed to point to the fact that he was. He was certainly handsome. That was a given. He was rich, although maybe less so now. Would that matter? He was good at his job and did the same things she did, so he understood her. These were all things in his favour.

He was a little aloof, though. She liked people who were more friendly. And he kept his thoughts to himself. They wouldn't have had such a severe falling out if he'd only told her what had happened. Then, at least, they could have been outraged together. But that, apparently, wasn't Armando Zeller's style.

'I think you're right. I have to do something about it.'

Diana gave Margarida a kiss on the top of her head and ran home. She grabbed her handbag and the little square of paper where Eddy had written his brother's current address. Then she headed for the town square, where there was always a queue of taxis waiting for tourists. She gave one the Guincho Beach address. Fortunately, it was less than a half hour drive, so it wouldn't cost her too much.

The sun was just beginning to set when the taxi dropped her off at the entrance to a modern, single-story house that nestled amongst the dunes. The grey exterior was clad with driftwood that blended in well with the surroundings. Diana stepped onto the wide verandah that ran around the house and made her way to the double width front door.

With her heart bobbing in her throat from anxiety, she rang the doorbell. She waited for what felt like an age, but nobody appeared. She tried peering through the orange tinted knobby glass pane that ran the length of the door, but couldn't make out any light or movement.

Had he gone out? Now, when Eddy said he never went anywhere? Maybe he was still at the beach? Before she headed in that direction, Diana decided to check the front of the house, just in case.

She walked as quietly as she could, but the wooden boards still squeaked under her weight. She rounded the bend to the front of the house where the verandah opened out onto a broad deck. The view over the dunes to the sea was spectacular and made even more so by the slowly setting sun that was turning the sky yellow and pink.

Standing at the end of the deck, his arms resting on the railings, was Armando Zeller. He was dressed casually in sun bleached black trousers and a grey t-shirt that made her realise he was more muscular than she'd expect from a desk-bound executive. It filled Diana with a burst of pleasure to see him that immediately answered some of her questions.

'Hello Mr Zeller.'

He spun round, looking surprised.

'Ms Luna?'

'Yes.' Diana was pleased to note that he looked happy to see her. 'Your brother told me you were here,' she added by way of explanation.

'I see.'

'He also told me they fired you because of me.'

'Not because of you, Ms Luna. Because of what I attempted to do.'

'Do you know, I think being fired on my behalf makes you a friend. I would really like it if you called me Diana.'

'Then you should call me Armando,' he said with a slight, appreciative laugh.

'I'm glad we've settled that.'

Now Diana didn't know what else to add. She'd confirmed her feelings. She was growing to like Armando. That was all she'd really needed to know. She had given little thought as to what else they might say to each other.

Armando watched her from his position, the safe distance of two meters apart, with the strong and slightly chilly ocean breeze blowing past them.

'I don't know if you remember, but your Personal Assistant, Mr Rocha, confirmed that I have been vaccinated. And I always take precautions,' Diana said and held up the little bottle of hand sanitiser she carried in her bag. 'And we've safely met before.'

It felt stupid to say this, and the least romantic thing possible, but it was all she could come up with. Armando gave her an appreciative smile.

'In that case, would you like a drink?'

'I would.'

'Make yourself comfortable,' Armando said, waving at the couple of deckchairs, placed to admire the view, with a coffee table between them.

Diana watched Armando head inside through the wide open floor to ceiling bifold doors and her happiness continued to grow. He'd been glad to see her, and she'd been glad to see him. She hardly knew him at all, but she supposed that was where most relationships started.

All the same, knowing her own feelings didn't amount to knowing his. Maybe Eddy was right about his brother, but maybe not. Maybe Armando merely liked her as a fellow perfumer. She had to be careful she didn't jump to the wrong conclusions.

Armando returned with a tray laden not only with a jug of water, but a bottle of white wine, some bread and a selection of cheeses and cured meats.

'Just in case you're hungry,' he murmured as he put the tray down on the coffee table.

'Doesn't all of that smell a bit intense?' Diana asked as she sat side on to the deck chair.

Armando pointed enquiringly at the wine, so she nodded and he poured her a glass and then poured a glass for himself.

'It is a bit intense, which is why I prefer to eat outside. Having said that, maybe I enjoy it more because I get the full impact of all the flavours and smells.'

'So you can cope with powerful smells.'

'Most of the time. It's just the extremely acidic, chemical or rotten smells that affect me badly.'

'I see.'

Diana noted that none of the cheeses he'd brought out had a particularly strong smell or were the class that sometimes let off the odour of ammonia. She spread some cream cheese onto a slice of bread and bit into it appreciatively. She'd been so thrown by Eddy and what he'd said that she hadn't even noticed skipping lunch.

'So,' Armando said as he took a sip of wine, 'how have you been?'

'Fine. Are you okay?'

'Why wouldn't I be?' Armando said with a slight smile.

'Losing your job, for one. Having your car and house taken away for another.'

'Eddy was very chatty, wasn't he?'

Armando looked less happy about the further revelations.

'I suspected he thought a full confession was the only way he would convince me. I wasn't that interested in hearing him out.'

'Not with a thieving, lying Zeller, huh?'

'Exactly.' Diana was glad that he'd relaxed again. 'What will you do now? Is there no way you can get your home and car back? I mean, that's astonishing. How can your father confiscate everything? Are they company property?'

'They are not. I bought and paid for it all with my salary but my father is old and often behaves like an emperor to his family. His every word is law.' Armando's face conveyed a blend of exasperation and tiredness. 'His iron clad conviction will be that he has every right to do what he has done.'

'But is there nothing you can do about it? Can't the police intervene?'

'If I wanted that, then yes, I could get back my car and banish the guards he's set up at my house,' Armando said as he raised his wineglass and held it up to the light of the setting sun so that it took on a rosy hue. 'But if I did that, I would ruin my relationship with my father. So I decided to wait, give him time to calm down, and eventually reason with him.'

'But Eddy told me he's already been given your job.'

'Exactly,' Armando said and took a sip of wine.

'What do you mean?'

Diana was so focused on trying to understand that she put her bread and cheese down on the edge of the plate.

'Eddy is a terrible choice for the House of Zeller. He lacks the interest in the post and my father is well aware of that. Which means it's a temporary position. My father expects me to feel humiliated by the ousting and go crawling back to him with an apology.'

'Will you do that?'

Diana wondered whether she could apologise for something that wasn't her fault. It would be difficult, but maybe, if it was better for all concerned, she might do it. She wasn't sure it was a good strategy to give in to a tyrant, though.

'My father is very hurt. He can't believe his father was a thief,' Armando said. 'So I need to deal with the situation with some tact. But in answer to your question, no, I won't apologise. I won't go back to the company if they don't honour the contract we were working on either.'

'That sounds tricky.'

Diana was astonished to hear about the offence her claim had caused in the Zeller family. She'd always assumed her grandmother was in the right, and Grandpa Zeller in the wrong. But it seemed he'd kept it from his family, and now there was this unexpected backlash.

'What will you do about it?'

Armando tilted his head thoughtfully, then he stood up and wandered off into the house.

'Did I say something wrong?' Diana said to the empty space and shivered.

It was getting cold. Autumn days were warm but when the sun set it got cold, especially out on a deck unprotected from the ocean wind.

Armando reappeared with a fleecy blanket that he draped around her shoulders before returning to his lounger. He'd also put on a thick grey woollen jumper.

'So what will you do?'

'I honestly don't know,' Armando said as he cut himself a wafer thin slice of cheese and speared it on the tip of his blade. 'I thought I was going to inherit the company. It came as a shock to see that expectation vanish. It looks likely that my sister will take over Zeller now.'

'Even if you apologise?'

'Even then. She played her cards better. She was underhanded and ruthless. I don't think she'll be great for the company, but she won't be terrible either. She's competent enough to take over.'

'You can't just let her win like this, though, can you? I mean, that isn't right either.'

'That's business.'

'So fight back. Show them what you can do too.'

'Oh, so now you think I should be the head of a multinational company, do you?' Armando said, beaming at her.

Diana laughed. It was ridiculous. She believed small was beautiful and yet, here she was urging Armando to fight for the big ugly company she'd always despised.

'What else could you do?'

Armando shrugged.

'I don't suppose you know of any perfume houses who are looking for a perfumer?'

'Considering who you are, and the list of perfumes you have to your name, I wouldn't be surprised if you were headhunted by any number of companies the moment they find out you're available. Especially with all your connections.'

'That makes me sound very important.'

'Am I wrong?'

'Not necessarily.' Armando bit into his slice of cheese and chewed thoughtfully. 'You're right about the connections and the power of the name.'

Diana like his lack of false modesty. She guessed Armando kept his mouth shut for a similar reason. He would not lie, but he wouldn't pretend he had no skills either, so it was best to keep his thoughts to himself. She decided it was a good trait. Now, despite how important it was for Armando to sort out his future, she wanted to know something else.

'Eddy thinks you like me.'

Armando swore under his breath, apparently taken by surprise and shaking his head.

'Was he mistaken?' Diana asked, taken aback by the strength of Armando's reaction.

'Sometimes brothers can be a little too helpful,' Armando said with a wry smile. 'He probably suspects so because he hasn't seen me with many women.'

'He said the smell puts you off.'

'You, on the other hand, Diana, smell really nice to me,' Armando said and swung his legs off the deckchair so that he could face her.

Diana felt a tingle of pleasure shoot through her at his words and the way he was watching her, measuring the impact of what he'd said.

'My grandmother would probably kill me for saying this, but I think I like you too.'

'You only think?'

'I've been so focussed on your family name and the history between us, and the contract, aside from recently breaking up with my long-term boyfriend, that I didn't realise I was developing feelings for you. It's one reason I came today, to figure it out.'

'I was only waiting for the contract to go through. Then I was planning on asking you out on a proper date.'

Armando dropped his knife and reached towards Diana's hand. Their fingertips touched and Diana turned her hand over, sliding her fingers under his, revelling in this first contact.

'It's a shame things didn't work out the way you were planning,' Diana said, but her focus was on Armando's hand that had moved upwards, his thumb brushing gently against her pulse.

'That's quite an understatement,' Armando said as his fingers curled about her wrist and tightened. 'Do you think you'd be interested in me now that I've become a beach bum?'

'Well, you're no lawyer,' Diana said, but didn't resist as Armando stood, still holding onto her wrist, and she rose to match him. 'I was aiming to improve on that rather than going down the social ladder, but–'

Armando stepped around the table and stood so close that all Diana could see was his chest and all she could feel was the grip on her wrist and the warmth of his body.

'But?' Armando murmured as he came in for a kiss.

Diana breathed in the cool crisp linen scent of him mingling with the wine on his breath. She thought about stepping back, but only for a second before she leaned up to meet him and felt his soft, warm lips against hers. They kissed once and then again. Armando wrapped his arms around her and lowered the two of them onto the sun lounger, Diana on his lap. Diana, holding the edges of her blanket, wrapped the two of them in it as he kissed her again, gently at first and then a whole lot more passionately.

CHAPTER NINETEEN

Armando woke to the warm scent of Diana and her honey like perfume. He opened his eyes a crack to find he was nestling right against her. His face was millimetres from the nape of her neck. Normally such closeness would repulse him, but this morning he just wanted to wrap his arms around Diana and pull her even closer.

This was truly astonishing. With every other woman he'd ever had sex with, he'd either left immediately afterwards or, if he could stand it, waited till they'd fallen asleep before leaving. His reactions were hurtful towards the women and was why he'd hardly slept with anyone over the years. To wake up with a woman and to want to stay with her was an entirely new experience.

'Mmm,' Diana murmured and rolled her shoulders in a stretch.

'Are you awake?' Armando asked running the tips of his fingers along her bare arm.

'Uh-hu.'

'Are you going to turn around then?'

Diana shook her head and pulled away, dragging the sheet with her, which she wrapped around her body. Her petite, marvellously curvy body.

'Not till I've brushed my teeth,' she said as she hurried for the door. 'There's no way I'm exposing you to morning breath.'

Armando laughed at that, but was grateful that Diana considered such things.

'I'll make breakfast,' he shouted after her. 'What do you like?'

'Milky coffee and toast,' Diana said from the bathroom. 'But make whatever works for you and take your time, I'm going to shower.'

Her consideration was cute. Armando's family had never worried about how painful intense smells were for him. But, at the same time, he wondered whether they could get on if she was always worrying about him and his sensitivities. This was going to take a bit of work, he realised as he headed for the guest bathroom for a quick shower of his own.

Then, in record time, he was done and in the kitchen, pulling together a simple breakfast. He started humming and cut it short, unwilling to be caught sounding so ridiculously happy. But he was. He was filled with teenage like excitement. The last time he'd felt this way had been over a high school crush, Stella, his friend and the owner of the Sea and Sun restaurant. He wondered how Diana would feel knowing about this long ago infatuation.

He'd just assumed, as a boy, Stella would be keen on him too. Plenty of other girls were. But she had rejected him and broken his young heart. Fortunately, not for too long as he was popular and always followed around by a bevvy of girls, some hyper excited to be near him, others painfully shy. So he'd had no trouble looking like he hadn't minded the rejection, although that was far from the truth. His only consolation at that point was that Stella never seemed to like any other boy, either.

At least the same couldn't be said for Diana. She liked him. Despite their family differences, she'd come to see him and last night...

Armando realised he was grinning just thinking about the two of them again. He glanced towards the bedroom and the closed door, wondering what was taking Diana so long. At this rate, breakfast would get cold.

Since it was a pleasantly warm morning, Armando pulled the kitchen table and two chairs outside under the slatted awning. It extended halfway across the deck and provided a bright striped pattern of sun and shade that provided just enough protection from the autumn sun.

He was setting the finishing touches to breakfast when Diana emerged, still towelling down her hair and wrapped in one of the white waffle robes Bernardo provided for his guests. She looked happy and relaxed, which was what he'd hoped for.

'Oh, you've made exactly what I asked for. Does that work for you?' Diana said as she wandered over.

'I'll be fine as long as I have the same.'

'So our breaths take on the same scent, just like last night.'

'I knew you'd understand,' Armando said and sat down, inviting Diana to do the same with a wave of his hand.

He'd spent a stupid amount of time trying to decide where to place the chairs. Opposite each other meant he could watch Dian's expressive face, but it was a bit far away. Right next to her seemed clingy, so he'd opted for the quarter mark.

Diana, oblivious to all of this, settled contentedly and looked over the spread. Armando had put out a linen lined basket filled with rolls cut in two and toasted. A silver butter dish held a log of butter and there was an array of jams and honey. Since he wasn't sure exactly what Diana meant by milky coffee, Armando had made a pot of coffee and filled a jug with steamed milk so she could mix the coffee exactly as she liked it.

'It looks perfect,' Diana said, smiling at him.

'So do you,' he said with a wide grin, cringing at his stupid boyish comment, and then was relieved when Diana coloured at the compliment.

It took some self-control to not carry on staring at Diana as she picked out a piece of toast and spread it with butter and then a thin coating of raspberry jam. Armando poured himself a black coffee, took a sip, leaned back in his chair with a satisfied sigh and looked out at the view. A couple of seagulls called to each other as they wheeled overhead, their feathers looking impossibly white against the bright blue of the sky.

He heard a crisp crunch as Diana bit into her toast and he glanced back at her. She appeared to be totally absorbed. So he buttered himself a piece of toast and enjoyed the scent of warm bread and slightly salted butter before he took a bite.

'Have you thought about what you're going to do now?' Diana asked.

'Not really. I was more focused on solving the issue over your contract to give the rest much thought, although...'

'Although?'

Diana tilted her head as she examined him, the toast balance in one hand.

'I haven't had a break like this in a long time. Before, even when I was supposed to be on holiday, I was constantly interrupted by calls and emails. Or I was just worrying about one thing or another to do with the business so, mentally, I never stopped. But being fired removed it all. I could finally let it all go and think of nothing at all.'

'Your brother said you even turned your phone off.'

'For the first time in my life. Maybe that was to make sure my father couldn't change his mind and call me back. Although it also meant I didn't know when he gave Eddy my job.'

'I know you think it's reversible but, are you angry about that?' Diana asked as she took a sip of coffee.

'A bit. But I have learned, as a manager myself, that nobody is indispensable. You might think so. You might wish your key member of staff wouldn't quit, but I've always found a replacement. They would have different strengths, but after a couple of months, I was no longer missing the former employee. So I keep telling myself I am no different and even if Eddy doesn't cope, somebody more experienced can easily replace him.'

'The thing is,' Diana said, her voice taking on a cautious note lest she cause offence, 'you didn't resign.'

'No, I suppose that's what angers me the most. I was booted out for doing what I thought was right and my brother replaced me in under a week.'

'Did you even get severance pay?'

'I doubt it.'

'So that would be something else you could take your father to court over.'

'Sure, and drag the company's name through the mud with another lawsuit.' Armando poured himself a second coffee and swirled it around in his cup. 'When I'm at my angriest, I have actually considered doing that.'

'Do you not have the money to hire a lawyer?'

Armando looked up into Diana's face because her voice sounded so astonished that he wondered how it looked.

'I have plenty of money. You may not think it, but I wasn't a big spender, so my bank account is pretty flush.'

'It sounds to me like you were overpaid. No person on a normal salary can build up a lot of money in the bank.'

'But then I was the Director of Perfumes at a major corporation and the head of the House of Zeller,' Armando said with an amused smile.

'That is also true.'

Diana looked like she wanted to say more, but was holding back. Armando assumed because she thought it was his business and he should take care of it in his own way. That was his opinion anyway.

'I suppose, now that I've had a bit of a break, I should put a few things in motion. Especially as I owe Eddy.'

'You do? The way he tells it, he's the one who owes you.'

Armando just laughed at that and waved the suggestion away.

'We had a deal. I agreed to get him out of being the Director of Perfumes if he could patch things up with you.'

'Good grief,' Diana said.

'Yeah.' Armando gave Diana a warm smile, his gaze lingering on her face that looked more beautiful to him every minute that passed. 'I only agreed because I thought he'd never pull it off so there was no danger of me having to keep my end of the bargain.'

'You didn't think he could explain things to me?'

'He must be a lot more charming than I am. It's an adult part of him I'm not familiar with. However, I'm pretty sure, if I'd turned up at your shop, that you wouldn't have heard me out.'

Diana blushed and suddenly looked away as she shook her head.

'You're probably right.'

'So I owe him.'

'Can you do it though?'

'According to Eddy, I can do anything.' Armando laughed as he remembered his brother's cast iron conviction. 'So I'd best not let him down.'

'I feel like you have the beginning of a plan.'

'Maybe I do. Would you be willing to help me?'

Since Diana had finished eating, Armando took her hand in both of his, as if adding weight to his request, but really just because he liked touching her.

'Me? Well, yes, anything in my power. I feel like I owe Eddy, too. But what on earth can I do to help?'

'To start with... can I rent some space in your lab?'

'My lab? It's tiny and not very sophisticated.'

Diana's eyes were wide with surprise, and she swivelled around in her chair so that she was facing Armando, her knees touching his leg, which he found surprisingly distracting.

'It's more than adequate for my needs. I'm also going to try and lure in a client for you if you're willing to collaborate on a mass produced perfume?'

'Now you're dragging me into an area I don't want to go,' Diana said, and tried to pull her hand away.

'No wait,' Armando said, hanging on. 'If we can do something for this one woman, a pop star, it will bring hoards of clients in for you too.'

'A pop star? This sounds less and less ideal.'

'I need something big and painful to get my father to the negotiating table,' Armando said, as he also turned in his chair so that now they were face to face. He took hold of her other hand and drew both towards him. 'The possibility of losing the pop star should do it. Will you trust me with this project, Diana, please?'

'Are you sure legal action wouldn't be a better option?'

'He's liable to just dig his heels in and spend far more money than I was going to spend on you in a legal battle against me. Besides, as I said last night, I don't want to become estranged from my father. Tipping him into a legal battle would make everything worse.'

'Well...' Diana had at least lost her worried look and the tension that had made her shoulders rise eased as well, 'in that case, I will help where I can. My sole proviso is that you have to keep me informed about the plan. Eddy told me you don't make excuses or explain but I need somebody who will share his thoughts with me.'

'I will do my best,' Armando said, and leaned forward to give Diana a kiss.

Kissing a new boyfriend is just wonderful, Diana thought. Who'd have believed this would ever happen. Only a few weeks ago, she was convinced she was going to marry Fernando, so kissing somebody new was strange. Kissing a Zeller took it to a whole other level of weird.

'Wait!'

Diana pushed Armando away, suddenly flushed and uncomfortable.

'Is something wrong?'

'I just thought about my grandmother,' Diana said, between embarrassment and wry amusement at herself. 'And I couldn't.'

'Your grandmother? Would she disapprove?'

'And then some,' Diana said, and slipped sideways out of the chair, avoiding Armando's questing grasp. 'I'd better get changed.'

'Are you going home?' Armando asked, lounging over the side of the chair rather than chasing after her.

That was a relief.

'I probably should. I hadn't intended to stay, and I don't have a change of clothes.'

'I can lend you a t-shirt. Please stay a while longer.'

Diana wanted to stay. She'd be happy to spend the rest of her life in this house, tucked amongst the dunes. She loved the beginnings of romance, the way her heart soared in almost painful elation just thinking about her new man.

'Well then... okay, till tonight.'

'Excellent,' Armando said back to beaming at her as he leapt to his feet and went in search of something for her to wear.

'Now what?' Diana said as she emerged dressed and filled with anticipation and tingly nerves.

'Do you fancy a walk down to the beach?'

'That sounds perfect. We may as well take full advantage of these last sunny days. It turns so suddenly from summer into winter.'

'At least it's warmer down here, then it is up in Sintra,' Armando said as he put his arm around Diana's waist and pulled her closer.

She sighed with pleasure as she leaned against him and they made their way down the road and then along the long boardwalk that had turned grey through years of exposure to sunshine and sea spray. Their footsteps sounded loud and hollow as they strolled along, being careful not to trip over any warped or loose planks. It was a good 500m walk through the dunes before they reached the beach and, since it was still early, they were among the first to arrive.

'What with all the travel restrictions and the time of year, it looks like we'll practically have the beach to ourselves,' Diana said. 'Just as though we're millionaires with our own private space.'

'Yeah, just like that,' Armando said as he stepped down onto the sand and then held his hand out to help Diana down.

Under normal circumstances, she'd have told whoever she was with that she was more than capable of dealing with steps, thank you very much. But today she just took his hand and thanked him, aware that it had caused her to blush. Armando kept hold of her hand and guided her downwards, their feet sinking almost to their ankles in the sand which poured into Diana's shoes as if they'd been designed for the express purpose of sand collection.

'Wait, I need to take them off.'

Diana hung onto Armando now for balance as she pulled her trainers and socks off. She shoved the socks into the trainers, tied the laces to each other and swung the lot over her shoulder. Armando had come more prepared, she noted. He was wearing flip-flops.

'Where to now?'

'Let's go to the water's edge. The sand is firmer there. Unless you're after a proper workout.'

'I may die of exhaustion just wading my way through this soft sand to get to the water. Running a shop isn't exactly great for keeping in shape.'

'Oh, I don't know, you seem pretty shapely to me,' Armando said with a provocative smile.

It made Diana blush and she gave Armando a push. He ran off down the beach, looking back to see if she was coming, and she chased after him and finally caught up where the waterlogged soil became harder and easier to walk on.

'Oh my lord,' Diana said, bending over to catch her breath. 'I don't think I'm a teenager anymore.'

'Do you want me to carry you then?' Armando said, pulling her near.

She leaned against him, laughing, but grateful for his support as well as he turned and started walking towards the western most cliffs. It was by far the most attractive view because the olive grey scrub and emerald green pine forest covered peninsula beyond loomed above and jutted far out into the ocean. If you took the road that went past Guincho, it would eventually wind its way to Cabo da Roca, the westernmost tip of Europe. Beyond that was the Atlantic Ocean, a sprinkling of islands and then America.

Diana took a deep contented breath of air laden with the tangy scent of sea water, and gazed out at the waves that produced a continuous roar as they broke, one after the other, on the beach and then washed back. Summer or winter, the ocean was icy cold so, tempting as the crystal clear turquoise water looked, Diana decided against wading through it, and pulled Armando away as a particularly large wave surged towards them. They barely got up the slope in time to prevent their feet from getting wet.

'That was close,' Diana said and then realised Armando wasn't listening anymore.

A pair of gorgeous long haired golden retrievers were sprinting their way, the wind blowing their fur about. Their owner was throwing a ball out into the shallow waves and the pair would charge after it. Then emerge triumphant, the ball in one or the other's mouths. There followed a brief tussle with their owner to release the ball, and off they'd charge again.

To Diana, it was a sight of unalloyed joy. Armando, though, tensed. His grip on Diana tightened, and he turned them upwards, back into the soft sand.

'Don't you like dogs?'

'The smell you know,' Armando muttered, 'especially when they're wet.'

'Ah, I see. Wet dog smell can be pretty intense.'

'Mmm,' Armando murmured and, apparently deciding they were a safe distance away, he guided them back to the wet sand.

Diana looked up at his face to guess what he was thinking, and he gave her an awkward smile. She smiled back, confidently, trying to let him know it was okay, but aware that the two of them were a little more on edge than she'd been with a new boyfriend.

Sure, all relationships started off awkward as you tried to get to know the new person, understand their likes and dislikes, the things they really cared about and what didn't bother them. But here there was more. In part, it was their awkward family relationship. Diana felt like a traitor towards her grandmother and she wondered what Armando's father would think too.

The rest was Armando's sensitivity to smell. Every now and then, his face would twitch with discomfort. Once, as they were heading towards the boardwalk, it was because an ancient camper van sputtered along the road, spewing black smoke. Then there were the dogs and now he was detouring around a coconut scented suntan lotion that a bronzed, bikini wearing woman was slapping on enthusiastically.

Diana didn't mention it. She didn't want to spoil the day, but it made her worry about herself. She was wearing a borrowed t-shirt, one of Armando's, and her trousers from the day before. Did she smell offensive too? Since he was not only willing but apparently eager to kiss her, she hoped not. But she wondered what it would mean for the future. Would she become intolerable to him one day too?

'You're deep in thought,' Armando murmured as he leaned down and gave her a peck on the lips.

'It's nothing important.'

'Are you sure?'

'Nothing that can't wait till Monday. Today feels like the last day of a perfect holiday. I don't want to ruin it by talking about work.'

'I feel the same. It's the end of my holiday, and it couldn't have been more perfect. I'm so glad you came to see me.'

Diana loved every minute of their Sunday. After strolling up and down the beach a couple more times, they headed back into the dunes and a semi-circular sun trap where they'd lounged about kissing and chatting about nothing in particular. Then they walked to a restaurant tucked in a gap halfway up the cliffs for an immense toasted ham and cheese on pão de soloio, a thick dark, chewy bread. Afterwards, more walking, chatting and finally just sitting in silence, Diana wrapped in Armando's arms as they gazed out to sea.

Now, as they made their way home in the twilight, Diana's mind, that could never stay still, turned to considering what came next. Especially as they rounded a bend in the road and the house came into view.

'So... what are we going to do tomorrow?'

'Ah, I see the holiday is over.'

'Not quite, but I was wondering, especially as you asked to rent space in my laboratory, and you were talking about that pop star. But I suppose you'll also have a few things to do before all that, so I was just trying to work out what would happen next.'

'I'll need to spend tomorrow coming up with my detailed plan, and working out how I capture the pop star.'

'So you won't be coming over tomorrow?'

'Probably not,' Armando said, but gave her hand a gentle squeeze. 'Although I could do all my plotting and planning with you at your shop.'

'Which may smell a bit more than you're used to.' Diana was finally voicing to her true concern. 'You might not like the smells although I have extractor fans in the lab.'

Armando stopped walking to turn to examine her face, which was harder to do in the darkening gloom.

'This whole smell sensitivity thing is difficult for you, isn't it?'

'I've seen firsthand what can happen to you if a smell is too intense,' Diana said with the memory of Armando passing out when the dustbin lorry went past still vivid in her mind.

'It's awkward for me too,' Armando said as he started walking, taking Diana with him. 'I moved into my own house as soon as I was able so that I could control things. But before that I lived at home where my stepmother did her best to drive me up the wall with smells. So I can cope.'

'I don't want to drive you away, though,' Diana said as they stepped up onto the deck of the house.

'I've been thinking about that, too. I honestly don't know how this whole thing between us will work out in the end, but I'd really like to try it.'

'Have you ever lived with anyone aside from your family?'

'Never. Even when I was at university, I had my own place. I doubt I would have survived in the halls of residence.'

'So this could be quite hard.'

Diana was disappointed and worried in equal measure about whether they could make things work.

'We won't know unless we try.'

Armando gave her an encouraging smile and Diana hoped it wasn't false bravado. But since he'd made the request, and he was apparently willing to go along with it, she wasn't going to be the one to back down.

'Okay, I'm sure we can make it work,' Diana said. 'Now I should get my bag and go.'

'Must you?' Armando asked, tightening his grip on her hand. 'Why don't you stay over again tonight?'

It was at moments like this that Diana wondered whether it wouldn't be better to say she had a pet she absolutely had to return to. On the other hand, she didn't have anyone waiting for her, so she could do as she pleased and she didn't want to leave Armando's side just yet, either. She realised Armando was watching her face rather closely, and she hoped she didn't look too reluctant.

'Why not?' she said, grinning like a fool.

Chapter Twenty

S o they spent their second night together and woke after a too short sleep, to an autumn dawn that was more dark than light.

'We'd best get going if I'm going to open my shop on time,' Diana said, scrambling for the shower.

She still worried about smells putting Armando off and wondered how long it would take for her to relax and no longer care.

Armando got dressed and then picked up a leather briefcase that had been leaning against the wall by the door.

'I brought it from work, and haven't looked at it since.'

Then they'd hurried out in answer to the taxi's summons.

It was the usual black taxi with the green accents and the light on the roof. Diana favoured Ubers because they were cheaper, but Armando had called for this car. The taxi driver was the usual maniac who roared at high speed up the narrow, meandering road through the hills to Sintra.

Diana and Armando sat with their masks on, staring out of opposite windows, watching the sun come up. Diana wondered what she was doing. She'd gone from treating Armando as an enemy, to a lover, and now into a business partner, albeit an arm's length one at the moment. Would this work out? Either way, would her grandmother understand.

'Well... here we are,' Diana said, as the taxi roared away. 'Come on in.'

It was going to be weird having Armando with her throughout her working day. On the other hand, they had a common passion for perfume. She'd loved that she could talk to her grandmother about scents all the time. She hoped she and Armando would have the same thing.

'This is it,' Diana said, pushing opening the door into the lab. 'It's probably shabbier than any lab you've ever worked in before. Although you may not have noticed last time you were here. You were a bit...'

Diana didn't know how to continue. Last time Armando had been carried in by her and her friends and had staggered out, supported by his personal assistant.

Armando looked around, taking in the extractor fans and the scent organ as well as the cupboards, holding all her records. The repairs had been done so well that you could no longer tell they'd been broken open.

'It's fine. I won't have any difficulty working here.'

'Good.' Diana took hold of Armando's arms and walked him backwards till his legs hit the sofa and he was forced to sit down. 'You may as well get some clean air while you tell me what you're planning.'

With that, she flicked the switch that set the extractor running.

Armando smiled affectionately at her and said, 'Thank you,' as he patted the space beside himself invitingly.

Diana, out of habit, was about to take up position in the office chair that was pulled up in front of the scent organ. But she loved that he wanted her closer, so she happily joined him, her back against the armrest so that she could face him.

Armando took her hand and sighed thoughtfully as he examined her.

'I have a plan and a potential back up for resolving my brother's problem and fixing the mess over the contract.'

'Wow, two plans, an A and a B, that's good.'

'Wait till you hear them first. They may not be that great.'

'I'm all ears.'

'As I said, I want to convince the pop star, Céu, to come here to get a perfume made. I'll need to act quickly before the other perfume houses realise she's back on the market.'

'Why do you need to get her before everyone else?'

'Because, if she goes to another perfume house, Zeller has lost her for good. But if I can get her, then there is a way for us to ease her back to Zeller.'

'Which would make your father grateful, huh?'

Armando laughed.

'My father is never grateful. What it will do is give me leverage. He'll believe he can negotiate with me to hand Céu over.'

'Which is when you'll make it a condition to take you back and pay me?'

'That's plan A. Knowing my father, it won't be that easy.'

'So what's plan B?'

'We just go ahead and make a perfume on our own. I have the contacts, so we'll have no difficulty finding someone who can mass produce things for us. I know a talented bottle designer and great distribution people. I can convince a whole host of stockists to take the perfume as well. It won't be as slick as if the House of Zeller was doing the promotion, but it would be good enough.'

Armando looked more enthused by his second plan than his first, which interested Diana. She was hesitant to go against his wishes, but she wasn't willing to compromise her principles either.

'You know I don't want to be a mass marketer, don't you? Why do you want to include me in this? You can just create a perfume for Céu yourself.'

'I could,' Armando said, and it seemed to Diana that he was examining her even more closely now. 'The thing is, I really like what you do with perfumes. I want to work with you. We could make this annoying pop star something really great, not just a perfume that sells for a season and then vanishes, but something as enduring as Armour.'

'Ha, Armour, the perfume that was stolen. I'm not sure you should bring that fragrance up right now.'

'But if we do something together, wouldn't that make up for some of that? We can show the world, and your grandmother, how well we work together. You said Armour differed from everything else the House of Zeller has produced and in part you were right,' Armando said, leaning forward and speaking quickly as if that would convince Diana. 'But I've realised that there are homages to Armour in everything we produce. It's like a strand of DNA infused into everything that came afterwards. Your grandmother's talent has been responsible for much more than just Armour. The company could not and never would pay for that. But what if we started again and made something acknowledging both of our talents?'

Armando looked so enthusiastic that Diana just had to laugh.

'I'm glad you think we can work together. It's very flattering.'

'I don't flatter. I am telling you my heart's desire,' Armando said, flushing in embarrassment at being so open.

Diana sighed. The vision Armando held out to her, and his passion for it, was very persuasive, and she had to admit it tempted her.

'The thing is, I believe strongly in what I do, the right perfume for every woman.'

'Why can't you do both? We can have a mass produced perfume for Céu, that will kick everything off nicely for us. At the same time, we can make a big deal of her coming to see you. That will bring hordes more women to your shop. They'll all want to get what Céu got.'

'Wait, so, you want me to be the composer of Céu's perfume?'

'Yes, that's what I've been saying. The pop starlet can get a personalised scent. I can then take what you create for her and tweak it for the mass market.'

'Will she go with that?'

'You were the one who said women feel special to have their own personalised perfume. I doubt Céu will be any different. We can manage the marketing so that all the pop starlet wannabes feel like they are getting close enough to the same thing.'

'Well then,' Diana said and realised that she'd also leaned forward, listening to Armando with gathering enthusiasm. 'Maybe it is doable.'

'Excellent, then I will contact Céu. Once I set a date, I'll spend some time getting a website up and running for you.'

'A website for me? Now you're sounding like Fernando.'

'Mmm,' Armando said, looking less pleased to be compared to an ex. 'Why don't you have a website?'

'I suppose because I felt I didn't need one.'

'But you were struggling financially.'

'True, but also, therefore, not in a position to hire somebody to do my website and I'm not techy enough to do it myself.'

'You can leave that to me.'

Diana felt like she'd jumped onto a rollercoaster over which she had no control and she didn't like that.

'Wait, don't get carried away too soon. Let me think about it. There's still so much that's uncertain. What happens after everything, assuming you get this perfume made? What will you do then? Will we still be working together at that point?'

Armando laughed and pulled her in for a hug.

'I have no idea. Let's try these first few steps and see where they lead us. I have more than enough money to keep myself going for a couple of years so there's no need to worry.'

'A couple of years?'

Diana wondered what it was like to have such financial security that having no work at all didn't bother Armando. She was moving swiftly on to her worry phase, as every possible disaster rose to be considered.

'But... what happens if this Céu turns you down? Have you already met with her? What's she like?'

'I haven't met her, although I've received her brief. She wanted something that represented flying up to heaven with gold beneath her feet.'

'Ah,' Diana said, 'so that's where she's coming from.'

Armando sat bolt upright at her words.

'Wait... that actually makes sense to you?'

'I've been listening to women describing what they want from a perfume for most of my life. They hardly ever come in saying, "I love the smell of jasmine, make me something like that."'

'A scent to make someone propose,' Armando murmured, as if recalling something.

'Yes,' Diana said, surprised he'd brought that up. 'A lot of women are actually after a love potion. As for marriage, that was Maria de Gouveia's starting point.'

'Did she tell you I sent her?' Armando asked, suddenly wary.

'Eddy did. I should be furious about you sending a spy.'

'I'm sorry.' At least Armando had the grace to look embarrassed. 'I was trying to understand what was going on and you wouldn't speak to me.'

'Did you... order the break in?'

'I honestly didn't. But I did take this and have been meaning to give it back only I've never found the right moment,' Armando said, holding out a flash drive.

'What is this?'

'Electronic copies of all of your notebooks. I made them so that I could find the evidence I needed while getting your books back to you as quickly as possible. This is everything. I don't have these files stashed anywhere else, and you should probably have a backup.'

Diana snatched the drive out of Armando's hand and stared at it in shocked surprise. 'I can't believe you did that.'

'I'm sorry, but it did lead me to the truth, that my grandfather copied your grandmother's formula word for word. And I discovered what a talented perfume composer you are.'

Diana gave a gasp of surprise, jumped up and took a couple of turns about the room.

'Are you always this high handed? Doing exactly what you want whenever you want it?'

'I suppose I am,' Armando said apologetically. 'I did it with the best of intentions though.'

'That's not good enough,' Diana said, on the verge of losing her temper.

'I'm sorry,' Armando said as he stood and took her hands. 'But I don't regret it, because my underhanded methods brought me to you. If I had just let you push me away and left it at that, we wouldn't be standing here today.'

Diana tried to pull her hands out of Armando's firm grip and couldn't.

'You're hurting me.'

'I'm sorry,' Armando said, but didn't let go. 'I was selfish, and I am still being selfish, but I don't want to lose what I've just found in you.'

'You're an idiot,' Diana said, shaking her head, but also calming down.

'I will happily agree. Will you please also explain to this idiot what Céu's perfume brief really means?'

'So you're trying to distract me with work, are you?'

'If I can.'

'Fine,' Diana said, and pulled Armando back to the sofa. 'What your pop star says is a starting point. I use that to guide me to their scent. From what Céu said, I'm guessing she's strongly Catholic, or had a Catholic upbringing. She's probably got a picture of the Madonna being taken bodily up to heaven in her mind, surrounded by a golden halo.'

'So?' Armando said, tilting his head as he considered.

'I'd probably start with Frankincense and Myrrh, as I did with Maria. The smoke from church incense is supposed to take prayers up to heaven.'

'Just like floating on air. Funny, my perfume composer and I were thinking of some sort of ephemeral, nearly non-existent scent, whereas church incense is really intense.'

'I wouldn't use it as one of the stronger notes in the perfume, as it is rather overpowering. But scent, as you know, taps straight into our emotions. It can transport you to a place and time more powerfully than almost anything else. So even a virtually subliminal level of scent will evoke memory, and speak to the client.'

'What about the rest?' Armando said, leaning forward enthusiastically again.

Diana laughed. He was just like her grandmother.

'I would have to wait and meet this Céu first. I need to see what she looks like and how she dresses, and then I need to find out which fragrances appeal to her the most. Once she has something she loves, the brief will hardly matter.'

Diana knew she might sound arrogant, but actually it was experience talking. She suspected that the pop star knew nothing about perfume and had probably produced a brief after talking over this new perfume making experience with her friends. No doubt it had been a lot of fun, but she would have had no clue about what she really wanted. It was going to be Diana's job to work that out.

It was funny that Armando's absolute faith in her made her swell with confidence and, more than was safe, affection for him. She'd never met someone who believed in her abilities so absolutely. Her grandmother had always treated her as a student. One she was proud of, but still a junior. It was exhilarating to meet somebody at the top of the profession who saw her as a worthy equal.

After reviewing his options with Diana, Armando took his laptop out of his briefcase and spent some time on the sofa under the extractor fan, writing everything up. It was much the same as pulling together a project plan at work, but it was all still annoyingly vague. Then again, it was good to have got back a sense of purpose. Lazing around on the beach had been pleasant. But he liked his job, and it was good to get back to a semblance of it.

The moment he'd finished his project plans, with the two headings of A and B, he went through all the correspondence he'd had with Céu and her agent. As was expected, most of the communication had been via her manager.

Armando felt a momentary twinge of guilt as he read through the agreements that had been signed between the House of Zeller and Céu. He wasn't officially one of them anymore. Legally, he shouldn't even have access to all of this.

Fortunately, he backed things up to his personal cloud. So, even if the office had shut down his official email, he could get hold of the old documents. He wasn't looking at any developments post his ousting either. As for Céu, she'd left the House of Zeller and was therefore fair game.

Armando paused for a moment, looked up from his screen and watched Diana as she used a pipette to put the exact quantity of each scent into somebody's personalised perfume. An attractive green cardboard box with Perfumes da Luna written on it in a gold curly Arte Nouveau font sat on the bench beside her, along with a fluted perfume bottle with a bulbous circular bottom and a stack of pale green tissue paper.

Diana finished adding the last ingredient. She then held the beaker against a machine that spun everything together with a gentle whirr. The floral scent whose top note was honeysuckle wafted across to Armando before the extractor fan whipped it away.

Diana gently decanted the scent into the bottle, filled the box with artfully crumpled tissue paper, pressed the bottle into the centre, added a handwritten card, topped the lot with more tissue paper, put the lid on and sealed the box with a gold ribbon.

It mesmerised Armando to watch this process that surely hadn't changed in a hundred years. It was so different to the Zeller factory where everything was done by robots and never touched by human hands. The bottles trundled down an assembly line, clinking against one another as they were filled via a jet propelled nozzle, sealed, boxed and shipped.

'I'm just going to take this to the post office,' Diana said, looking up. 'If anyone comes into the shop, can you tell them I'll be back in twenty minutes?'

'Sure.'

Armando was pleased to be given this task, minor as it was. It reflected a profound change in Diana, that she trusted him enough to not only leave him alone in her shop, but even to help out where necessary.

Since he was alone, it was now an opportune moment to call the pop star. Fortunately, he'd had the foresight, when he was still in the Zeller Corporation, to get her direct line. If he'd had to go via her manager, he doubted he'd reach her at all. He called with more than his usual trepidation. It was one thing being the Head of the House of Zeller. It was something else calling as freshly fired Joe Nobody.

But he'd prepared what he wanted to say. He just wished he knew what Eddy had done to make her to storm off in the first place. Some stars were notoriously difficult to please, so it may have been something minor. Either way, it gave him somewhere to start.

'Hello, is this Céu?' Armando said when the phone was picked up after a nerve-wracking six rings. 'This is Armando Zeller.'

The female voice on the other end was petulant and abrupt.

'What do you want?'

'I understand you've parted ways with the House of Zeller. So have I,' Armando said before she could hang up.

'You have? Why?'

So at least he'd piqued Céu's curiosity.

'My reason is utterly boring.' Armando doubted the starlet cared, and he wanted to get to what would interest her. 'I'm much more curious to know why you've left them.'

Doubly so because, in his experience, Eddy was great at winning women over.

'That awful Eddy Zeller said I was wasting his time with my brief. He said what I was asking for was impossible.'

'Did he really?' Armando tutted sympathetically. 'I'm afraid he's new to the job and inexperienced.' Armando felt only a twinge of guilt about sacrificing his brother in this way. 'What you want is entirely possible. Would you give me a chance to prove it to you?'

Since Céu didn't object, Armando went ahead and explained about Diana and a personalised perfume.

'I thought you were just going to make something based on my brief,' Céu said back to sounding cross. 'I'm very busy, you know?'

'Wouldn't you like something even more special. Something that other pop stars don't get?' The pause on the other end of the line told Armando he'd recaptured Céu's interest. 'Something utterly exclusive.'

'Well… since you put it that way. I guess I can get my manager to find me a free couple of hours.'

So after that, all Armando had to do was call a few key people in the media to give them advanced notice that Céu would be coming to Diana's. He promised to follow up with a date and time as soon as he had it. He'd also encouraged the pop starlet to tell the world in general and her fans via social media what she was up to. Which she wasted no time in doing.

'You're looking smug,' Diana said upon her return.

'I've just got over the first hurdle. Soon your shop will become famous for hosting a pop star.'

'Oh my God, did she say yes!?'

'No need to look quite so astonished. One would think you didn't believe I could do it.'

Diana flushed guiltily and muttered, 'No, um, yes, I mean–'
Armando laughed and planted a kiss on her lips.
'It's okay. I had my doubts too.'

CHAPTER TWENTY-ONE

Even though she had refused to go on-line when Fernando and Margarida had suggested it, Diana found herself considering the proposal now. At first she'd said that as her grandmother hadn't needed a website, she didn't either. Her ex and her friend had both mercilessly pointed out her ever decreasing income, which had made her dig her feet in even more.

'But Diana,' Margarida had said months ago. 'The internet is ideal for small business people like us. I mean, I can now sell my things around the world. I don't have to wait for somebody to walk past me shop window to be drawn in.'

'That's fine for your stuff,' Diana countered, 'but what use is it when I still have to actually meet the client.'

'But what about a few things just to help the shop along, like scented hand creams or lip balms? You can even use the beeswax from my parent's farm.'

But no, Diana had remained firm, even when Margarida had pointed out that the lockdown provided her with the ideal moment to learn new skills such as website design.

Now, though, even Armando had said she needed a website and had offered to make one for her. So how could she refuse?

Especially when he'd said the magic words, 'Online appointment booking form.'

'A what?'

'People can book appointments to see you on-line. You advertise the uniqueness of what you provide, tell people where you are, and they can book themselves in to see you.'

'How do I prevent double booking? Or decide when I can go on holiday.'

'You block those out. Once a booking is made, nobody else can book the same time slot and you can book yourself out whenever you need to.'

'Oh.' Diana was thinking of the large, double width black covered book that lived by the phone and in which she and her grandmother before her had used to take all their client bookings. 'I suppose that is a good idea.'

So now, here she was browsing the internet looking at perfume websites to get an idea of what she should have on hers. At least it helped her look busy. She wondered what Armando was doing because he had his head bowed over his computer for hours without taking a break or even looking up. He made her feel like a slacker.

Now evening was falling, and she had to turn on the lights so they could continue working. Armando barely noticed. The deep frown of concentration didn't even flicker as the lights came on. So Diana slunk back to the stool she'd brought in from the shop and started flipping through her pile of Scent in Time, the perfume industry's trade magazine, looking for articles about on-line selling. An hour passed in silence and finally Diana couldn't take it anymore.

'Are you ever going to stop?' she asked so loudly that Armando jerked up and stared at her in surprise. 'It's six thirty. Have you not had enough?'

'It's half-past six? That's still early, plenty of time to do more and–' Armando stopped, apparently halted by Diana's outraged stare. 'Do you want to stop?'

Now Diana felt like a complete slacker. The last thing she wanted from Armando was an observation that it was no wonder she wasn't doing well if she didn't put in the hours.

'Well... I don't really have anything else to do today. But if you need to carry on working, don't let me stop you.'

'I'll stop.' Armando closing his laptop, stretched, reaching far above his head and yawned as he did so. 'We haven't had much sleep the last couple of nights, have we?'

Diana felt her face grow hot but decided against encouraging Armando's thoughts down that road.

'Would you like to come up to my house before you go? We could get a takeaway or something. If you're okay with that. If the smell would be off-putting, I'd understand.'

Diana tailed off. Maybe she was expecting too much. Three days and nights in a row with a new lover might be over the top. Much to her surprise, Diana wanted Armando to stay. She'd been imagining taking her home for much of the day. But now that she'd made the suggestion, she was losing confidence.

Armando gave Diana a smile she couldn't read. Was it amusement or rueful apology?

'I'd like to see your place.'

'Okay, let's go,' Diana said, delighted and anxious in equal measure.

She kept looking back at Armando, who followed her through the shop, waited as she locked up, then followed her again to the steps up the side of the building that led to her apartment. At this point, she was already regretting her invitation, as she imagined every smell he might encounter in her home. Even the slight peppery rose scent of her geraniums made her worry as she brushed past them on the way up.

Diana swung the door open and took a deep sniff. She was trying, for the first time, to smell what a new visitor might smell. She was horrified by how pungent everything was.

She was assailed by the smell of wood and beeswax polish, coffee and toast and...

'My God, I didn't realise the mildew smell was so strong. I'm sorry. It's Sintra, you know, it's very humid here.'

'It's fine,' Armando said as he stepped inside.

Diana flicked on the light so that she could better see his reaction. He looked studiedly unperturbed. Then she put her keys down in the little terracotta bowl that sat on the narrow table beside the door and her eye caught her favourite photograph. It was of her and her grandmother arm in arm in front of the shop.

'Oh dear, sorry Grandma!' she said as she hastily flipped the photograph so that it was face down on the table that also held the TV.

'Is that your grandmother?' Armando said and made to pick the photo up.

'Yes.' Diana put her hand on the frame, holding it down so that he couldn't lift it. 'It's too soon for me to introduce the two of you. I hate to think what she'd make of this whole situation.'

'Hopefully, if she had it explained, she'd understand.'

'She might,' Diana said as she stepped deeper into her living room. It looked small, frumpy and far too full of furniture after the minimalist beach house.

'You got on very well with her, didn't you?' Armando said, looking around as he put his bag down.

'We were pretty much each other's only family.' Diana looked up, marvelling at how a tall person could make her sitting room look even more tiny than it usually felt. 'Now then...' Diana riffled through the drawers of the table by the door and pulled out a wedge of pamphlets. 'Here, what do you fancy eating? The one thing the Coronavirus taught me was the wonderful convenience of takeaways. Sintra might be small, but we've got all the cuisines of the world. There's Portuguese, of course, but also Chinese, Italian, Indian. Oh, I suppose the Indian might be a bit intense.'

'Actually, I like curries,' Armando said, much to Diana's surprise. 'The spices are intense, but when blended together well, it can be excellent. Just as long as everything is cleared away, right out of the house afterwards and all the dishes are washed. I'm fine.'

'You are?'

Diana beaming up at Armando, relieved that she wouldn't have to give up curries.

'I do prefer eating that at a restaurant, though. I never take them to my house.'

'Oh no, I can see why not. How about a pizza then? We have an excellent local place with a wood-fired oven.'

'Sounds good.'

'I'll order a bottle of wine as well,' Diana said, hastily adding, 'white, of course.'

Armando laughed, then sat down on the sofa and gazed up at Diana.

'Horrible as our first meeting was, I have a lot to be thankful for towards the red wine. After all, if you hadn't got totally wasted and then...' he waved his hand to indicate throwing up. 'We might never have met.'

Diana found herself laughing, too.

'I'm relieved you can see it that way. I've never been more embarrassed than when you showed me that awful video. Who films stuff like that and then to upload it onto YouTube, really?!'

'Something else to be thankful for,' Armando said as he leaned forward to catch hold of Diana's hand and pulled her to the sofa.

'Here,' she said, handing him the menu. That way she could see what he was having and get something similar, probably avoiding anything garlicky. So much for her usual garlic bread. She decided against asking Armando about that. Time enough to ask him some other day.

While they waited for the food they talked shop, Armando was interested in how Diana had been taught by her grandmother.

'Mostly it was just by watching her with the clients. She also made me smell each individual scent and memorise them and she'd test me every Monday morning.'

'We had to do a similar thing at ISIPCA.'

The conversation continued over the pizza and the wine. Diana pulled a cushion off the sofa and sat cross-legged on it, on the opposite side of the coffee table, while Armando remained on the sofa. They talked and ate and talked some more, each fascinated by the other's experience.

'Oh my God, it's past midnight,' Diana said when a huge yawn interrupted her story of a pigeon that had got into the shop and flown about in a panic knocking the scent bottle onto the floor, so she'd grabbed her phone for the time. 'You can't go home now. The taxi drivers won't be keen. How do you feel about sleeping over? And I really mean sleep.'

'Not a bad idea,' Armando said, mirroring Diana's yawn. 'If that's okay with you?'

'Of course it's okay.'

Diana was feeling warm affection for this man, who was smiling sleepily up at her.

'You stay here for a minute, I'm going to change the bed sheets.'

'So... we're sharing a bed?'

'We did at your place.' Diana felt stupid and like she was rushing everything again. 'But I can turn this into a bed too,' she said, pointing at the ancient brown sofa.

'If you don't mind sharing, then I don't either. I'm afraid I have no experience of this type of thing.'

'So you've only had girlfriends round to visit?' Diana said without thinking, remembering too late what Eddy had said about Armando's lack of girlfriends.

'To my house? Never,' Armando said and looked around again.

'But... not their place either?'

'Usually a hotel.'

Now Armando had the look of a man who wasn't entirely sure what he was supposed to do, but was willing to try his best.

'Stay there,' Diana said, feeling like she was making things worse every time she opened her mouth. 'I'll fix the bed. It isn't dirty or anything, but I would prefer if you have clean sheets.'

'Don't you want help?'

'No,' Diana said firmly.

CHAPTER TWENTY-TWO

A rmando lay in bed watching the gradually lightening dawn
via the frilly curtains. He'd hardly slept. The combination
of being in a strange house and a host of unfamiliar smells had kept
him up. He now had a dull ache at the back of his head that was
threatening to grow more painful. Fortunately, he always carried
his painkillers with him.

Armando glanced down at Diana. She was still fast asleep. Her
hair had slipped down across her face, half obscuring it. Why he
found this ridiculous woman so appealing, he did not know, but
he did. Waking up beside her for the third morning in a row made
everything else bearable.

Still, it was best to nip any oncoming headache in the bud or
else he'd land up with a full grown migraine. He also didn't want
Diana to think it was her fault, blame herself or worse, decide
they weren't compatible. So Armando eased himself out of the
bed, being careful not to disturb Diana. He slipped out of the
bedroom, closing the door carefully behind himself, and went in
search of his briefcase.

Once he was in the kitchen, he felt it was safe to make more
noise and dug through his bag to find his painkillers. He was
running low, so he'd have to find the local chemist sooner rather

than later. The kitchen was simple and old-fashioned and he'd got to know most of it last night as he'd helped set the table for their takeaway. Now he opened the cupboard that held the glasses and poured himself some water from the tap. Without his usual water filters, the smell of chlorine was intense, so he pinched his nose shut as he gulped down his medicine.

Then he sat down at the kitchen table to consider his next move. He'd been wallowing in self-pity but pretending he was taking a holiday so that he didn't feel entirely inadequate. Fortunately, Diana had turned up and put an end to that, and now he'd even taken the first steps of his new plan.

He tapped his phone to get the time. It was just past seven. That made him wonder what time Diana usually woke up. He was feeling lonely.

He laughed at that. He'd lived alone for most of his life. How could he be lonely now?

Because she was still asleep, obviously.

To distract himself, he sent a text to Libero. He'd been trying to decide how he approached Libero. He was the person he trusted most in the world. There wasn't a time he could remember when Libero wasn't around. But after he'd got fired, he'd realised something awful; Libero was a Zeller employee. He'd looked after Armando because it was his job. Since they had booted Armando out, he had no official connection with Libero, and he didn't know what that meant.

He knew Libero well enough to realise that the man was fond of him. But how fond he wasn't sure. He'd always been polite and attentive, kind when Armando had needed it as a boy and strict when called for.

But would his loyalty to the company trump his possibly only vague friendship with Armando? He was working for Eddy now, after all. But Eddy had said that Libero had contacted Bernardo to find him, so he'd at least cared that much.

In the end, Armando kept the text short: *Are you up? Can we talk?*

The phone rang almost immediately.

'Good morning, sir,' Libero's calm voice said.

'Libero!' Armando said with a relieved laugh. 'I'm sorry I just vanished.'

'It was understandable, sir. Master Eddy told me he'd been to see you and that you were looking well. He thought, perhaps, a little too well.'

'Is he doing alright in the job?'

Armando wished he didn't care about that, but he worried about both Eddy and the firm.

'He will get the hang of it eventually. Reluctant as he is.'

Armando realised that as a loyal employee, Libero couldn't really say more. Besides, the troubles of the Zeller corporation and its Director of Perfumes were no longer Armando's concern. Or at least, so he would keep telling himself for the time being.

'I know I have no right to ask this of you, but could you do me a favour?'

Armando realised as he spoke that this was something he should have been asking of Eddy. But he'd always relied upon Libero and that was who he'd thought of first.

'Of course, sir, anything within my power.'

Armando wondered whether Libero knew what a comfort his words were.

'I haven't been able to get back into my house. Although, to be fair I haven't tried but, could you pack some things and bring them to me, please?'

'I will do it this morning. Shall I bring everything to the beach house?'

'No.' Armando laughed to himself as he wondered what Libero's reaction would be as he said, 'I'm at Ms Luna's house.'

There was a moment of what Armando decided was stunned silence.

Then Libero said in his usual calm voice, 'At the perfume shop?'

'Above it.'

'I see. Well, I should be there shortly.'

'Thank you.'

Armando felt better now that he knew Libero was still an ally.

'Did you sleep alright?' Diana said from the doorway.

She was still in her pyjamas, a string vest and pair of shorts. He could smell her minty breath, so she'd already brushed her teeth, which was more than he'd done.

'I slept fine. I'm just used to getting up early.'

'I see.' Diana's gaze glanced over the box of painkillers still on the table. Then she went to the kettle and filled it with water. 'Do you fancy a coffee?'

'I do,' Armando said as he shoved the meds back into his bag, cursing himself for having been so careless.

Diana opened what was once a biscuit tin covered in a pattern of flowers and then tutted.

'It seems I'm out of coffee. My bread will be rock hard by now too. There's nothing for it. We're going to have to go out for breakfast. I'll get changed first, you can go afterwards,' Diana said, hurried back to the bedroom and closed the door firmly.

Armando looked after her in surprise. He'd already seen her naked, so why was she suddenly shy? Was she worried about him again? Not for the first time over the last few days, he wished he had more experience of dating. Or that he had Bernardo around to explain. He would know what was going on.

He wasn't sure whether he should say anything and decided silence was the best option when Diana emerged, showered and dressed, drying off her hair.

'It's all yours,' she said with a smile.

Despite the coolness of the autumn morning, she'd left the bathroom window open. Armando peered through the small square out into a foggy morning where the trees below were only just visible as ghostly shapes emerging through the gloom. He debated whether he should shut it to keep the warmth in. He left it open. It was best to leave things as he found them.

It was just going on 8am when he was done and dressed.

'I'm ready.'

'Alright,' Diana said and held the front door open for him, 'What will you be doing today?'

'Working on how to market Céu's visit. I need to make a splash so that my father sees what I'm doing. To get maximum attention, I'm going to offer to do an interview for the Scent in Time on the blending of modern techniques with old when creating celebrity fragrances.'

'Wow, you're really going all out, aren't you?' Diana said as she locked her front door and made her way downstairs.

Armando followed breathing in the smell of the rose scented geraniums mingled with the early dawn air that was redolent of wood smoke. No doubt half the houses around here had wood burners going. It was the most popular way of heating a home in Portugal.

Armando stopped at the bottom of the stairs and looked enquiringly at Diana.

'We'll go to my regular cafe,' Diana said, tilting her head in the direction of the Butterfly Cafe.

The cafe had just opened, ready for the trickle of commuters that stopped by on their way to work. Armando wondered how many that was nowadays.

Diana pointed at the two tables on either side of the cafe door. 'Inside or out?'

Armando glanced inside through the misted windows. A man and woman were waiting behind the counter, watching them hopefully. There were only a pair of unoccupied tables inside. It would smell the same way most cafes did, a warm, humid, coffee and pastry kind of smell.

'Let's sit outside,' Armando said, despite the chill.

Diana pulled her thick woolly cardigan more tightly about herself.

'Okay, I prefer that, too. It gets stuffy inside.'

A middle-aged woman came out to greet them, wreathed in smiles.

'Diana, I'll get your usual. What can I get for you, sir?'

Although she was speaking to Armando, she was giving Diana an enquiring look.

Diana coloured and said, 'This is Armando, my new boyfriend.'

Armando was surprised but not displeased at being described as a boyfriend. It was also a first.

'Boyfriend?' Maria da Conceição gasped. 'What happened to Fernando? You were only with him last week.'

'Two weeks ago,' Diana corrected her, wincing at her indiscretion. But that was Maria. She just blurted everything out, 'and we'd already broken up,' she said, staring pointedly at Armando.

He'd just experienced a sudden and unexpected sensation of intense jealousy.

'You broke up?' Maria da Conceição said, 'but he looked so happy to be with you.'

'He was the one who broke up with me. Then he came crawling back, but what he'd done, and how he did it... I couldn't forgive him.'

'I see,' Maria da Conceição said, eyeing Armando up and down. 'So what would you like for breakfast?'

'Coffee,' Armando said and forced a smile. 'And toast with butter, please.'

'I'm sorry,' Diana said as Maria da Conceição went back into her shop where her husband was watching and obviously waiting to be told all about the conversation. 'Our street is just like a village. Everybody knows everybody else's business.'

'I gathered as much. I suppose it isn't that different to my office. There's always a lot of gossip.'

'And I really have broken up with Fernando, although I used him for his legal advice.'

'That's fair enough.' Armando found himself wishing that Diana had used a different lawyer. 'Can I ask you something unrelated?'

'Of course, anything.'

'I was curious about your mother. You said you hadn't seen her for a while and that she went off travelling. Do you really not know where she is?'

'Oh,' Diana said, and waved her hand dismissively. 'I have her phone number if I really need to get hold of her. As I said, she's probably in Turkey, that's where she was last.'

'But she didn't bring you up.'

'Having a kid was too much responsibility for her,' Diana said and stopped as Maria arrived with a tray of coffees, croissant, and toast. She waited till she had left before she continued.

'When my mother fell pregnant with me, she was going to have an abortion, but my grandmother persuaded her not to. The deal was that my grandmother would look after me. So that's what happened. When I was younger, my mom would drop in occasionally and we'd go out for a meal or a day trip. But then she'd go off again, travelling or living with one man or another.

'As I grew older, her visits became less frequent. Then one day, my grandmother and I realised it had been two years, and she hadn't shown up. I think my grandmother called her then, just to make sure she was still okay, and my mother phoned that Christmas to speak to me. I think because she'd been told to.'

'Doesn't that upset you?'

'Sometimes. But she was never very reliable, and I had my grandmother, so it mattered less. I'm okay with it now.'

'I see,' Armando said and realised he had similar lukewarm feelings towards his own mother.

'It's my turn,' Diana said as she picked up her croissant and started to nibble on the pointy end. 'I've been wondering why you didn't live with your mother when you were growing up. Isn't it usual for the children to stay with their mother after a divorce?'

'Yeah, that is the usual. But my father would never allow the eldest Zeller son to be brought up away from his household. My mother only married him for his money though, so she was willing enough to let go of me for a hefty alimony payment.'

'Really, she only married him for his money? I thought you said she was a perfumer as well.'

'She met my father when they were both students at a perfume shop in Paris. I suspect she used every trick in the book to hook him the moment she discovered who he was.'

'What makes you think that?'

'Some of the things she's let slip over the years. But also the fact that she never went back to work after the divorce. She spends all of her time shopping.'

'She must have got quite a payout.'

'Yeah, but let me ask you this,' Armando said and waited as Maria da Conceição appeared, ostensibly to provide them with paper napkins. He sensed she just wanted another look at him. 'Would you have shut up shop and devoted your life to shopping once you got your million?'

'The million you promised but I never got?' Diana said and took the sting out of her words with the impish smile she gave him. 'I honestly hadn't thought that far. I might have done things differently, but I wouldn't have given up making scents.'

'There you are, then. That's the difference between you and my mother.'

Diana watched Armando closely all the way through breakfast, trying to work out how he was feeling. She'd been worried to see the painkillers in the kitchen but, now he looked perfectly relaxed as he sipped his coffee. She wished there was somebody she could ask about warning signs that told her when Armando was struggling.

She also wished he would be more open with her about what harmed him and what didn't. So far, he'd acted as if he was relaxed about the surrounding smells. But the precautions he took in his life, the way he'd veered away from unpleasant smells at the beach, and the fact that he was taking painkillers worried Diana.

It made her wonder whether their initial flush of excitement to be together would last. She loved the honeymoon period, but she'd never had a boyfriend with such complicated needs.

It was just as well that breakfast was brief, because the cold has started to creep in under her cardigan and Diana was relieved to get to her shop. A night of proper sleep had left her refreshed and ready to kick start her website. She even had a few ideas on the design and the information she wanted to have on the site. She was going to start off with the philosophy of a personalised perfume and why, even in the modern age of industrialised production, anybody, woman or man, should consider a personal scent, or two.

She had just finished opening up and was considering working in the shop so that passersby could see her when the tinkle of her shop bell drew her attention. Diana looked up, hoping for a customer. Instead, she found Mr Rocha looking about the shop with interest, a wheelie suitcase by his side. For a stunned moment Diana wondered whether he was planning on moving in.

'Libero!' Armando said as he swept past Diana and took the suitcase. 'Thank you for bringing my stuff. I hope it wasn't difficult.'

'Not at all, sir.' Libero removed his mask to reveal a wide grin as he nodded a greeting to Diana, while still keeping his distance.

'I asked him to bring me some clothes,' Armando said in explanation. 'I need some of my work suits.'

'I see. I thought you might have done that before.'

'I was too depressed before.'

Armando's sunny smile made Diana's heart flutter. Did she have such a profound effect on him?

'How is everything going at work, Libero? Is Eddy doing alright?'

'Everything is fine, sir. I can see that you are doing well now too.'

'I am. You can leave me in Ms Luna's capable hands.'

'I believe I can,' Libero said and his eyes crinkled into a deep crease as he put his mask back on, waved and took his leave.

'That was quick,' Diana said.

'He has to go to work and the less time he spends with me, the better. That way I can't try to pump him for information he isn't allowed to give.'

'I see.'

Diana had just realised that Armando was putting on a front of being okay. Seeing the man who had raised him as merely an employee of his father's company was one of the many things he was struggling with now that he'd been thrown out of his life. A life he could never have dreamed he'd be tipped out of.

'There's one other thing we need to do,' Armando said as he pushed his suitcase out of the way.

'Oh yes, what is that?' Diana said, heading back to the lab.

'We should draw up a contract.'

Diana was so surprised by the suggestion that she stopped in her tracks and turned around to examine Armando.

'I don't want us to land up in a similar situation to your grandmother and my grandfather.'

'I really don't want to spend any more time and money on lawyers. And it's not like you've got a whole legal team to fall back on now either.'

'No. But it doesn't have to be anything fancy. We can just write up an agreement, sign it and keep a copy each.'

'Don't you trust me?' Diana felt a knot of anger growing in her chest. 'I mean, it wasn't my family who tried to rip you off. It's the other way around, actually.'

'Exactly. And look what happened. I want to make sure that this time you get your fair share. You're going to develop the perfume for Céu and I'm just going to tweak it. That means you should get paid as the perfume composer and get a fair share of the earnings.'

Diana didn't like the suggestion. She had always believed that there shouldn't be contracts between people who were in love. She'd always thought prenups were appalling. Now Armando was suggesting a contract, as if there was no trust between them. She supposed, if she was being charitable, that coming from his background, it was understandable.

'I'm doing this for you,' Armando said as he leaned down to look at her face and gave her a wry smile. 'This is business, not personal and I think your grandmother would agree.'

'That is a low blow,' Diana said. 'Alright, but I don't want any contracts to get in the way of our personal lives.'

CHAPTER TWENTY-THREE

A rmando was pleased both with the speed at which Céu had set up a meeting and with the press turnout for Céu's arrival at Perfumes da Luna. By the evening before she was due to arrive, they already had a mini encampment of fans and paparazzi in the street in front of the shop in eager anticipation of the big day.

As a result, Armando spent another night at Diana's rather than go back to the beach house. He was rarely at Barnardo's place anyway, as they always seemed to find one excuse or another for Armando to sleep over. His growing collection of clothes at Diana's house attested to that fact.

He was glad he had slept over come morning because there was now such a crowd, swelled by fans, that it needed the police to keep the street open for traffic. He'd have struggled to get through it and be at the shop to welcome their celebrity.

'I've never seen anything like it,' Diana said, peering through her net curtains at the crowd below.

'It's exactly what we need,' Armando said coming up behind her and wrapping his arms around her waist. 'I'm also hopeful Céu will say something good about you and the shop on her way in and her way out.'

'Even if she doesn't, I'm already fully booked for the rest of the month. I've never had as much interest in my perfumes.'

'At this rate you may have to take on an assistant.'

Diana laughed, turned around in his arms and pointed at him. 'Who do you think that would be?'

'Mmm, that all depends on what my father does next. So, are you ready?'

Diana gave a twirl to show of her sparkling white lab coat that Armando had insisted she wear.

'I suppose so.'

'Let's go to the shop then.'

At least the work Armando had put in so far was paying dividends for Diana, he thought, as he accompanied her down the stairs. He had to push a few over eager fans out of the way who'd slipped under the cordon and ran towards her as they emerged.

'You'd better lock it,' he said as the two of them rushed into the shop and slammed the door shut. 'I thought the police would do a better job of keeping everyone back.'

'They aren't used to this kind of event,' Diana said, looking through the glass shop frontage at the four police officers who were working on keeping the crowd behind a cordon they'd set up on the opposite pavement.

Officer Silva was shouting at one fan whose mask had slipped to below his nose.

'At least the other shops here will also get some business, especially the cafe. So it's working out for everyone.'

'Good.'

Armando looked around and rubbed his hands together. It was a gesture of anxiety from his youth that he quickly suppressed. A lot was riding on today, but at least he had an alternative if his father proved too stubborn.

'I'm going to check my lab,' Diana said and vanished into her back room.

Since she'd checked and rechecked the lab yesterday, Armando realised she was nervous too. He had more experience of being in the limelight. He'd been to hundreds of high-profile events with heavy press presences. But he'd never had to manage the lot before. It gave him a newfound respect for Helena, who made sure such events ran smoothly for the media and the guests.

His heightening anxiety spiked as a cheer rose from the waiting crowd and a white Rolls-Royce pulled up outside the shop. Armando was astonished to see it. He was expecting a plain limo.

'She's here,' Diana said.

It made Armando jump because he'd not realised she'd come back out.

'In her vintage car with its curving lines that look very much like a cloud,' Diana said with a nod as she took in the vehicle.

Armando laughed and said, 'I think she's somewhat obsessed. That model is called the Silver Cloud.'

'Good.'

Diana watched as a short man dressed in a skintight white suit helped Céu out of the Rolls. The pop star was statuesque and had long wavy white hair styled like a fifties film star but with blue dyed tips. She was wearing a figure hugging deep blue velvet dress with a glittery silver swirling pattern and a fishtail train, with a matching face mask and the highest heeled shoes Armando had ever seen in his life.

With her already substantial height, she dwarfed her assistant. It was just as well he kept a hold of her hand as she walked the short distance to the shop or she might have toppled over.

Armando swung the door open and executed a bow.

'Welcome to Perfumes da Luna, Céu. We are happy to have you here. Let me introduce you to Diana Luna, the most talented perfumer I have ever met.'

Armando enjoyed the blush that brought to Diana's cheeks.

'It's a much smaller place than I expected,' Céu said, looking around.

'It's a boutique,' Armando said. 'Where the most exclusive scents are produced for only the most discerning women. Every perfume produced here has a client of exactly one, herself.'

'But how will I make money from this perfume then?'

'We will take what Ms Luna produces and tweak it for the mass market. Your scent will be unique, just like you. But you will be able to share it with the people who love you in a slightly modified form.'

Armando felt like a fraud laying on the praise as he was, but it had to be done.

'Why does it have to be changed if it's going to be so perfect?' Céu said, looking at Diana.

Armando was going to leap in so that Diana didn't have to come up with anything to say.

But before he could intervene she said, 'No perfume smells the same once it's on the body. We each have a unique chemistry that changes how it smells. That's why your friend's favourite perfume smells great on her but might not work on you.

'When I create a perfume specifically for somebody, there is a higher chance that it will smell absolutely fabulous on you. But there is also a higher chance it will smell less good on everybody else. That's where Mr Zeller's expertise will come in. He knows how to tweak a scent so that it will work on the most people possible, and thus, ensure the highest possible sales.'

She sounded less than approving of the last bit, but at least she convinced Céu, who nodded in a worldly wise way.

'Alright then, let's see what you can do.'

'Please come through to the lab,' Diana said and waved them in.

Armando was about to follow Diana, Céu and her manager when his phone went off with his father's ring tone. He gave Diana an encouraging wave and waited only till the lab door was shut before he answered the phone.

'What the devil do you think you are doing?' Homero shouted down the line.

Armando had expected him to be angry, but he sounded incandescent. His greater rage came as a surprise. It seemed his father's divorce would be making Armando's life more difficult, too.

'What do you mean, what am I doing?'

'You know exactly what I mean. I'm watching a live stream of Céu visiting your girlfriend's shop.'

'And?'

'And!?' Homero exploded. 'She's ours. How dare you poach her? You're using insider information to draw away one of our clients.'

'I am not. The news that Céu left Zeller was prominent in three trade magazines and also made it into the entertainment pages of Diário de Notícias. I also discussed what we'd be doing for Céu in Scent in Time, in an article that appeared a week ago. If Helena didn't tell you about that, then she's slipping.'

'Céu is our star, and you'll stay away from her.'

'I will do as I please.' Armando's anger growing. He pushed it down. He had to stay calm if he was going to get anything from his father. 'But I am willing to make a deal.'

'A deal? You're in no position to be bargaining with me.'

'It doesn't sound that way to me.'

'Back off Armando or I'll... I'll...'

Armando waited while it sank in with his father that he had nothing to bargain or bully with.

'I want my car and my house back,' Armando said and hung up.

He breathed out, shaken by his encounter with his father. Armando had stood up to him before. That was nothing new, but the stakes had never been higher. He was also half expecting his father to call straight back and carry on berating him. But after five minutes and no call, he suspected he'd gone roaring off to speak to his lawyers instead.

Armando was willing to wait. He was good at that. He went to look out of the shop window at the crowds outside. Despite Covid, there were a lot of people. Fans would be live streaming this on social media, the paparazzi would get it into papers and magazines and there was even a television station filming everything. All good.

Helena had no doubt gone rushing in to show his father what Armando was up to. He'd been counting on that. It was rather amusing to use Helena for his own purposes for a change.

He wasn't sure how long he'd been contemplating the view and waiting for a call back from his father when the lab door opened and Céu emerged, supported by her manager and wreathed in smiles.

'Thank you,' she said, beaming down at Diana from her great height. 'It's beautiful. I'll never wear anything else.'

It was exactly what Armando had hoped to hear and it pleased him to see Diana blushing rosily above her mask.

'I'm glad you like it,' she murmured.

'I love it,' Céu said, and gave an exaggerated long distance hug while also blowing kisses at Diana. She stepped outside as her Rolls-Royce came rolling down the street again.

'Thank you, thank you, she said blowing the same exaggerated kisses at her fans. The woman behind me is a genius. You will soon get to share in the most divine perfume known to womankind. I love you all.'

And with that, her manager helped her into her car and they revved away.

'It seems you were a hit,' Armando said as he closed and locked the shop door and then ushered Diana back into the lab for some privacy. 'Tell me all about it.'

'There isn't much to tell.' Diana held out a little square of blotting paper for Armando to sniff. 'This is the perfume.'

'Ah.' Armando took a light sniff, his mouth slightly open to draw in more air. 'It's more churchy than I expected.'

'And me. This is also the most intense perfume I've ever made for anyone. It works well on her, though. She has a flamboyant and overwhelming personality.'

'Many stars do. I think it helps in the music biz.'

'So she needed a larger-than-life perfume, that goes with her whole look and her personality.'

'It will definitely have to be toned down for mass production. Most women wouldn't even wear something that intense for a grand night out to the opera.'

'Exactly,' Diana said as she gave a great sigh and threw herself back onto the sofa.

'You must be tired.'

Armando settled beside her, turned Diana around, and started massaging her shoulders.

'I didn't sleep well last night. There was so much riding on this meeting.'

'Well, you did your part to perfection.'

'How about you? Did your father call?'

'Mmm. He's furious.'

'You expected that.'

'He was angrier even than I expected. My father is a stubborn man. He's been the boss for decades and isn't used to having to listen to anyone. It made him difficult to negotiate with at the best of times. But if he's in a foul mood over an embarrassing divorce, that will make it harder still.'

'Do you think that's what's bothering him?'

'I'm afraid so. He's super susceptible to his surroundings. If he's happy, he's benevolent and genial. If he's unhappy, we all suffer.'

'Wow... it makes me relieved I don't actually know who my father is.'

Armando had some sympathy, especially now, with that view.

'In the meantime, I have to decide what I do next. There's no point just waiting around for my father.'

'So onto plan B?'

It was more reassuring than Armando could express to have Diana on his side. He'd never felt more supported in his life.

'Maybe the best thing to do is build up my own perfume house. After all, if my grandfather could do it, I don't see why I can't do it either.'

'Do you think it's possible? I mean, it's a different era now. The perfume market is highly competitive.'

'I can do it if I have to. I have money and connections. This has to be my starting point and what I must hold on to when my father calls again whenever that is.'

Chapter Twenty-Four

Armando's father didn't ring that day, or the next, or even the rest of the week. Diana could tell it was weighing on Armando. He kept himself busy working on tweaking Céu's perfume for the mass market.

Diana would have loved to have watched him in action and learned something of his skill, but she was kept far too busy herself. She'd never had such a flood of customers before. After Céu's visit, her brand new website nearly broke with all the people clamouring for a personalised perfume.

She was now fully booked till Christmas and pretty full into the new year. It was just as well Armando had set up her booking calendar with breaks over the holidays or she'd have landed up working every remaining day of the year.

There had to be a happy medium where she was bringing in the money she needed for a comfortable life without working so much that she didn't have time to see her friends. She'd only been able to wave to Margarida on her way to and from the Butterfly Cafe for the occasional coffee or breakfast. She was also always with Armando these days, in that loved up state where she wanted to spend every moment with him.

It led her to neglect her friend, which she felt guilty about. Her guilt was slightly reduced when she saw Fernando duck behind a new display of Christmas candles in Margarida's shop one morning as she and Armando swept by. It had been odd behaviour on his part and so surprising that Diana told Armando to go ahead after breakfast and she poked her head inside.

'Are you doing okay?' Diana asked, scanning the shop for Fernando who wasn't visible, but also hadn't been seen leaving.

'I'm fine,' Margarida said, but she looked flustered. 'Thanks to your newfound fame, my sales have gone up. I was ridiculously busy on the day Céu came to visit. How about you?'

'I've never had as much work in my life. I'm not sure how to feel about it.'

'Because you have a Zeller to thank for it?' Margarida said and her voice took on a chill note that surprised Diana.

'My grandmother wouldn't have approved,' Diana said, and the guilt that hung about her over that burrowed a bit deeper into her consciousness making her uncomfortable.

'I always wondered about your grandmother's feelings on the topic,' Margarida said, not moving from behind her counter, which made Diana suspect Fernando was hiding down there. 'It seems excessive. I mean, I know we Portuguese are great at family feuds, but your grandmother's business was fine even if Zeller senior did steal the perfume. She made plenty more.'

'Yeah,' Diana murmured, distracted from thoughts of her grandmother by other things. 'Are you and Fernando seeing each other?'

'What?' Margarida gasped, turned bright red and glanced down involuntarily. 'Why would I do that?'

'I wouldn't mind if you did.'

Diana gave Margarida an encouraging smile and then, mindful that she had an upcoming appointment, she hurried away to yet another busy day.

By the end of it, she was so exhausted that all she wanted was to crawl into bed and go to sleep. Armando, on the other hand, looked perfectly refreshed.

'I don't know where you get the stamina to keep going,' Diana said, watching as Armando held yet another strip of blotting paper up to his nose and gave it a light sniff.

'My work is less emotionally draining than yours,' Armando said and he placed the new paper inside a glass bottle and screwed the lid back on.

'What are you doing now?'

'Preparing samples for our first test panel. I've got a whole lot of young women from our key demographic coming to visit on Monday to do an initial smell test and tell me which of my ten variations on the theme they like best and why.'

'Ah, market testing,' Diana said and gave a wide yawn. 'You'll be doing that out front, will you, in the shop?'

'And I'll be filming the process. Céu seems to enjoy getting all the steps up onto her social media accounts and it's free marketing for us.'

Diana knew Armando was less keen on being on camera, but he was willing to do whatever it took to make the perfume a success. Diana was also certain he was doing this much to attract his father's attention.

'You don't think your dad will just get more annoyed?'

'I'm sure he will. I remember how furious he got when other perfume houses pipped him to the post with new releases, or grabbed somebody prominent before he could get them.'

'I hope this doesn't backfire.'

'Me too.' Armando left the lab bench and took Diana in his arms. 'But tomorrow's Sunday, so let's not worry about it. How do you feel about coming over to the beach house?'

'That sounds lovely.' Diana rested her head against Armando's chest and letting out a deep, relieved sigh. 'But doesn't your friend want his place back?'

'It isn't his only holiday home,' Armando said with a laugh.

The differences in their life experiences struck Diana once again. Up till now, she hardly knew a person who had more than one home, let alone multiple holiday homes. She shrugged that thought away. She would get used to it, probably.

Or maybe she should be careful and not start taking for granted that she'd always be with Armando. After all, she'd thought the same about Fernando. In the meantime, she decided not to worry about it. It was wonderful to have such an elegant and restful place for the weekend.

It was even nicer to lie together with Armando on the sofa the following morning, ostensibly reading, but actually drifting in and out of a light doze. It had got chillier now that they were into November. But the sun that poured into the beach house sitting room through the glass doors made everything so toasty she didn't really need the lightweight fleecy throw she had draped over herself.

'Do you want to go to a party with me next Friday?' Armando murmured into her ear.

'What sort of party?' Diana asked, thankful for the distraction because she'd really been struggling to keep her eyes open as she gazed at her book.

'It's a launch party for a new perfume from the House of Fiorino.'

'Really? You go to rival perfume companies' launches?' Diana said, turning about in Armando's arms to examine his face.

'Sometimes we do. But in this case, it's a partnership. Fiorino is actually a fashion house, not a perfumer. This is their first foray into fragrance making. They're a smaller company than Zeller, but they want this perfume to go big so they approached us to do the production for them. We've got the kind of scale they can currently only dream of.'

'Did they invite you thinking you were still with Zeller?'

'They did, but as I was the one that negotiated the partnership deal with Luca Fiorino I could make a case for being invited to the event.'

'Is it important that you go?'

'It will be useful since there will be a lot of influential connections for me.'

'That doesn't sound like fun.'

'I know. I'm sorry. There is another reason to go though, my father will be there.'

The thought of meeting Armando's father terrified Diana, and she stayed quiet for too long, frantically trying to come up with a non-offensive excuse not to go.

'In the past, these events were strictly business for me,' Armando said after a wait. 'But if you come, it might actually be fun.'

Diana sighed and gave up her internal battle. If she and Armando were going to stay together, she supposed she should meet his family. Maybe a public setting would be best, as they'd be forced to be polite.

'Do you need to confront your father?'

'I want to see his face so I can see what he's thinking. He's being too quiet and I suspect it's because he's up to something.'

'Okay. Do you know anything about the perfume?'

'Of course, I was involved in its creation. It's called Cinderella. Not my style of perfume at all. I find it too complex. But Fiorino liked it and it will have mass appeal. When we launch Céu's perfume, we're going to have to do a launch party for it too.'

'We should do it at a cathedral.'

'That would certainly be different. And I'm surprised you've already considered that.'

'I hadn't, actually. The idea just popped into my head.'

'Well, it's a good one. So what do you say? Will you come on a date with me?'

'Are we even allowed to do something like a launch, what with Covid and all?'

'I assume, as long as everyone takes the necessary precautions, it will be alright.'

'Do you think so?' Diana didn't want to let her nerves show, but the combined risks of Covid and meeting the Zeller family made her jumpy. 'I suppose there will be a lot fewer people than usual.'

Diana wondered whether that was a good thing or not. If there was a crowd, she could hide amongst them. If everyone was keeping exactly two meters apart, it would be pointless to even try.

'I'll buy you a dress,' Armando said as he put his arm around her shoulder and pulled her closer.

'You'll do what?'

'Buy you a designer dress.'

'Why would you do that?' Diana said and leaned back so she could see Armando's face.

'It will be expensive, well over a thousand euros. It wouldn't be fair to expect you to buy an expensive dress like that.'

While a part of Diana felt that Armando owed her, especially after the contract fell through, the modern woman in her couldn't accept the offer.

'I'll buy my own dress, thank you,' she said firmly and, she realised, in rather a frosty tone.

'I didn't mean to offend you,' Armando said, looking appropriately apologetic. 'The thing is, most of the men I know buy the dresses for the women who attend parties with them.'

'Other men? Not you?'

'I have on occasion. Although I rarely take a date.'

'Ah yes... the smell.'

Armando gave her a wry smile and said, 'I really didn't mean to offend you.'

'It's alright. But what about the smell at the launch? Will you be able to cope with it?'

'The one thing I am thankful towards Covid for is the introduction of masks. These events are always pretty damned awful because everyone arrives wearing their favourite perfume, as if to show theirs off. They all ignore the fact that they're there to experience a new fragrance. It's almost as bad as going to the perfume hall in a shopping mall.'

'You don't like that either?' It was a silly question, really. After spending so much time with Armando, she'd come to realise how extremely sensitive he was to smell.

'I'll survive. It isn't my first perfume launch after all.'

Diana turned away so that Armand couldn't see the doubt reflected on her face, but as she lay back in his embrace she asked, 'How are you coping with the smells at my place?'

'Better than I thought I would,' Armando said, leaned forward and kissed her neck.

'I'm glad,' Diana said, but decided against asking about how many pain killers Armando usually used. It seemed to her he was taking them rather frequently when he was in Sintra. Now wasn't the time though, because Armando pushed the fleece she had draped over her away and leaned in for an altogether more passionate kiss.

Chapter Twenty-Five

D iana had never been more nervous about attending a party in her life. She wasn't really a party animal and had given up clubbing a couple of years after she'd left high school. The only reason she'd kept going even for that long was to meet men. Working for her grandmother in her perfume shop wasn't exactly great for finding a boyfriend.

Now she was dressed in a black velvet dress that had cost more than she wanted to think about, with matching black suede wedge heeled peep-toes that, admittedly, were darling but unlikely to be worn very often.

'You look beautiful,' Armando said as he helped her out of the taxi.

'Thank you.'

Diana kept a tight grip on his hand as she took in the Art nouveau style entrance to the hotel that was all swirling carved stonework. Then she allowed herself to be led up the sweeping stairs and through the semi-circular double doors into a foyer that was lit by hundreds of tulip shaped lights providing a golden glow to the gathered assembly.

Diana was grateful for the mask that gave her some anonymity as she checked out the competition. They were giving her a full, indiscreet inspection. She hoped she wasn't frumpy compared to all the exquisite tall thin women in perfect make up.

A woman in a white strappy satin dress and a diminutive snow white fur bolero strolled over to her and her eyes crinkled above her matching satin face mask in apparent pleasure. This surprised Diana, as she wasn't expecting to know anyone. Yet here she was, being approached as if she was a friend.

'Diana Luna, isn't it?'

'Oh!' Diana said as realisation dawned. 'Maria de Gouveia, I do apologise. I didn't recognise you with the mask on.'

'Fortunately for me, your colourful hair is distinctive, otherwise I probably couldn't pick you out from a police lineup either. Allow me to introduce you to Bernardo,' Maria de Gouveia said of a tall, well-built man in a rich brown velvet suit, whose mask barely fitted over his beard and who was, if Diana was any judge of the matter, grinning hugely under his mask at both Diana and Armando.

'Good evening,' he said, bowing slightly.

Diana wished, this one time, that they could go back to giving each other the traditional kiss to each cheek because she was pretty sure that she was meeting the man Armando had created Urso for and she dearly wanted to smell it on him.

'Good evening,' she said, instead with a nod.

'I can't say how happy I am to meet you, Ms Luna. You're the first proper girlfriend Armando's ever had.'

'Come on,' Armando murmured.

'I'm pleased for you, my friend,' Bernardo said, patting Armando's shoulder. 'Now shall we go inside and see what a socially distanced launch party looks like?'

Diana took a deep breath to steady herself before accompanying their enlarged group through the grand entrance of the hotel. At least she now had someone other than Armando she could talk to at the party. The little group crossed the deep emerald green pile carpet with golden art nouveau swirls, following the trickle of guests making their way to a set of double doors that had been roped off with a twisted red velvet cord.

Armando presented his invitation and the suited man at the entrance said, 'Welcome to the Fiorino Launch Party, sir. Please keep your masks on until we start serving the food and remain seated at the tables. They have all been spaced with social distancing in mind. We are asking guests to keep mingling to a minimum.'

'Of course.'

Armando put his arm around Diana's waist and ushered her into a ballroom with an array of spectacular crystal chandeliers. The hotel had done a good job of hiding the empty feel of the hall with large stands of bouquets. They also had centrepieces that subdivided the tables and kept guests separated with trailing flowers that tumbled over the sides.

Armando muttered a swearword under his breath and Diana said, 'What's wrong?' She was expecting him to say something about spotting his father, which made her stomach clench in fright.

Instead he said, 'They've filled the room with lilies.'

'Oh no, is the smell very intense.'

'Mmm,' Armando said with a curt nod. 'Never mind, I'll just keep my mask on. It helps.'

Diana hoped he was right and looked about the ballroom. She estimated the room was at half its usual capacity and she knew from Armando that most of the guests were either fabulously rich or influential, often both. She glanced up at Armando, who was chatting to Bernardo with Maria on his other side as they made their way to their designated table. He looked relaxed while she felt entirely out of her depth.

'This is a disgrace,' Bernardo said as they arrived at a table more or less in the centre of the room. 'How could they put you here, Armando?'

'It's very simple, my friend,' Armando said as he pulled the chair out for Diana, 'I'm no longer the head of the House of Zeller. In fact, I had to pull some strings to be here at all.'

'Should you be sitting somewhere else?' Diana asked, watching Armando closely.

He was a hard man to read and never more so than with a mask on and in a situation where he was being doubly cautious.

'He should be at one of the front tables,' a voice said from behind.

'Mother,' Armando said, and he looked less than thrilled.

Diana leaped back to her feet and turned to take in an imposing woman with pitch black hair piled high on her head and held in place by a diamond tiara. She was wearing a figure hugging black sequined dress that showed off a curvy but slightly portly body and she had a necklace that more aptly exemplified the phrase dripping with diamonds than anything Diana had ever seen before.

'You are the heir to the Zeller empire. They should give you the respect owed to you,' Odemira said crossly. 'I will have a word with your father about it. I'm sure this is all his doing. If not him, then I blame Helena.'

'Don't say anything to either of them.'

Diana had never heard such an implacable tone from Armando, but it suddenly made him feel like a different, far more intimidating person. His mother was apparently also taken aback.

'He probably wouldn't listen to me anyway,' Odemira muttered. 'Although I'm not at all surprised he's behaving in this childish manner. When I think what that dreadful Albina is putting him though. Not that he doesn't deserve it. It's what comes from marrying a socialite.'

Diana wondered what to make of that comment because, from everything Armando had said about his mother, Odemira was also a socialite. Then she wondered what she should do next. Did she wait to be introduced, or just step in.

'Never mind my father,' Armando said. 'Allow me to introduce you to Diana Luna, my girlfriend.'

Odemira was apparently so taken aback by this news that her perfectly plucked, pitch black eyebrows rose considerably as she turned to examine Diana.

'A girlfriend?'

Armando sighed and said, 'Yes, we've been seeing each other for a few weeks now.'

'You have?' Odemira said, and managed to look even more astonished.

'Don't be rude. You're ignoring her.'

Odemira turned to face Diana and gave her the most weighing up look Diana had ever experienced. She wondered if this was typical of all potential mother-in-laws.

'I do beg your pardon,' Odemira said. 'I'm afraid I stopped paying attention to Armando's dates ever since I realised they only ever appeared once. There didn't seem to be any point in getting to know them. Is he... is he really dating you?'

'For the last couple of weeks.'

Diana didn't know how to feel about being so obviously different from every other woman Armando had ever gone out with.

'Wait,' Odemira said, flinging up her hand, 'are you that girl?'

She said "that" with considerable emphasis, and Diana had a bad feeling about what was to come.

Before she could say anything, Armando said, 'What have you heard?'

'She is, isn't she?' Odemira said back to ignoring Diana. 'She's the one from the video, the one that made your father push you out.'

'I did what I thought was right, none of the subsequent fall out is Diana's fault,' Armando said and his voice snapped with impatience.

'Armando, what are you doing? Have you completely lost your mind bringing that woman to a launch party and flaunting her in front of your father?'

Diana wasn't sure whether to be relieved or exasperated that she was being ignored. Armando's mother's outrage, on the other hand, should have angered her. Instead, it left her feeling even more unsure of her place at this party and her right to be by Armando's side.

She was also aware that they were being watched. Bernardo was standing beside his friend. His reddening face seemed to indicate that he was close to erupting in Armando's defence. Maria, who'd sat down at the same time as Diana, had remained seated, but bolt upright and was watching what was close to an argument with an intense expression. Beyond them, in the steadily filling ballroom, those seated closest were also watching and listening. They weren't even bothering to hide their interest.

'Well, well, what a pleasant family reunion,' a slim, elegant, fair-haired woman said as she approached and shook out the wide skirt of her red silk dress.

Diana recognised her despite the mask. This was Helena Zeller, Armando's sister, and the woman he barely said anything about at all. Fortunately, Eddy had told Diana enough to know she was a genuine threat.

'Helena,' Odemira said, turning to glare at her. 'I always knew you'd cause trouble. It's the only thing you're good at.'

'At least I've never tried to give any of my boyfriends a massive payoff,' Helena said sweetly as she waved for a tall man in a black satin suit to join her.

Diana recognised him as the prince from Lichtenstein she'd seen in the society pages. She decided against saying that Helena hardly needed to give her rich boyfriend any money at all. Keeping quiet was the safest way to go with this family and in this situation.

'All your machinations won't work out for you,' Odemira said. 'You think you've got the CEO position in the bag, but you're be mistaken. Armando is the eldest, and that counts for a lot, especially with Homero, who has never been fond of tattle tales.'

Helena's eyes snapped together angrily as she said, 'I'm surprised Armando went running to you with that tale. It's hardly like you've been a supportive mother. Just an ambitious one.'

'Armando is more than capable of looking after himself.'

'He would have to be,' Helena said sweetly.

Then she pointedly turned her back on Odemira and looked Diana up and down. Diana felt at a distinct disadvantage. She was shorter than Helena and most of the society women, who were all so tall and slim they could have become catwalk models.

'I'm amazed that Armando brought you tonight. It's almost as though he wants to provoke our father. All the same, it's fascinating to meet you.'

'I suppose I can say the same,' Diana said, working hard not to lose her temper. 'I'm afraid Armando has barely mentioned you, but I'm learning a lot tonight.'

'You've got some cheek talking to me like that considering the scam you're running trying to extort money from our company.'

'At least I have never broken the law to get what I want,' Diana said, making sure she smiled and kept her voice sweet while at the same time she was shaking in combined rage and fear.

It had been a shot in the dark. Nobody had told her that Helena was behind her shop's break-in, but by the way Helena gasped and her glanced flicked across to Armando, Diana was sure she was right.

'Let's not create a scene here tonight, mmm?' Armando said as he put himself between the two women and his arm protectively around Diana.

Helena glared daggers at him, then hissed, 'You were a fool to bring that woman and I'll make sure you regret it.'

With that, she turned her back on the company and swished her way to the tables at the front of the ballroom. She and her date joined Eddy and his date, another elegant young blonde, and an older man. In build and colouration, the man was remarkably similar to Armando, although his hair had turned iron grey with white at the temples. A quiver of fear passed through Diana to see him. That intensified as he glanced in her direction after Helena said something to him. Fortunately, they were too far apart for Diana to read his expression.

'She's right,' Odemira said. 'Bringing that woman will just provoke your father.'

'I know,' Armando said. 'Now you'd best find your table, too. The launch is about to start.'

His words were accompanied by the dimming of the lights and the music being turned up and Odemira gave him a brief nod, threw another less that pleased look Diana's way and made for her seat. Diana noted she was at a table even further away from the stage than her and Armando.

'I'm starting to feel like your mother and Helena are right too,' Diana said as the two of them sat down.

Armando pushed the row of trailing flowers that separated the two of them into the middle of the table and pulled his chair up beside Diana.

'Don't let them intimidate you,' he whispered into her ear. 'They're two selfish women who are acting up because things aren't going their way.'

'Things appear to be going your sister's way. Isn't she more likely to become the CEO now?'

'That isn't confirmed yet.'

Diana wanted to ask Armando more, but the announcer bounded onto the stage and his voice boomed a welcome over the crowd. Then he started to extoll the virtues of the Fiorino company and go on at length about the perfume, Cinderella. An image of a pumpkin shaped bottle with a trailing vine lid and with wheels and windows like a coach flashed onto the screen behind him. Then young women dressed artistically, either as starving waifs or tulle drowned princesses, paraded down a catwalk, each carrying a bottle and caressing it lovingly. The announcer assured everybody present that this perfume would turn any frumpy working woman into a princess the moment she applied it.

'Thank god they're not spraying that into the air too,' Armando said.

Diana grinned at him.

'Am I right to suspect that it has a strong note of lilies?'

'Good guess.'

'Not really, it explains the lily themed floral arrangements.'

Diana pushed thoughts of Armando's family to the back of her mind as she took in the spectacle. She'd never been to a launch party of anything before, certainly not for a perfume. Once she got over the ridiculous extravagance of the event, she started considering her own process.

Maybe she needed to create little mini events for her customers. Usually she just did what her grandmother had always done, put their scent into a nice bottle inside an elegant box and post it to them. A little celebratory cheer with the first delivery wouldn't go amiss. She was also watching with half an eye to the launch of Céu's perfume. She hoped Armando knew how to pull off something as slick as this because she suspected it took some skill.

Diana was so distracted by the performance that she barely noticed when a waiter slipped a plate of food in front of her. Armando had to give her a dig with his elbow for her to see it. It was filled with elegant, bite sized canapes. Diana assumed this was what happened now in Covid times when waiters could no longer circulate with trays of nibbles for a crowd to help themselves.

A long and rather boring speech from the CEO of Fiorino, extolling the virtues and values of the company and praising his creative team for their wonderful perfume, followed. He spoke Portuguese perfectly, but with a thick Italian accent. He was dressed in a wine red long-tailed velvet suit with a frilly silk shirt. Diana assumed he was supposed to be Prince Charming.

By this time Diana had eaten far too many canapes and drunk too much of the champagne the waiters kept topping up, and she was desperate for the toilet. She waited, trying to decide when it was best to leave, noticed that other people just stood up in the middle of the various speeches and so she decided she could do the same. Murmuring her excuses to the table, she got up and hurried for the door.

She realised as she made her way out of the ballroom and into a quieter corridor that she wasn't altogether steady on her feet. If she wasn't going to have a repeat of her meeting with Armando, she was going to have to switch to water.

Diana emerged from the bathroom feeling relieved. She took a deep breath as she stood in the hallway to gather herself before having to go back to the party. As she did so, someone emerged from the men's toilets. He turned and then stopped to examine her.

Diana froze. She was staring up at Armando's father. He hadn't bothered to replace his mask after the meal and so she could take in his full height and intimidating features. Armando was strikingly similar to him, not only in appearance but also in expression, as he arched an eyebrow in simultaneous recognition.

'Ms Luna, isn't it?' he said in a cool, dry voice.

'Yes,' Diana said, suddenly robbed of breath.

'So, Armando decided to provoke me tonight by bringing you, did he?'

'I don't know.'

Diana really had no idea what Armando was up to when it came to his father. She was starting to think that was a mistake.

'So you haven't got to know him that well yet.'

Homero couldn't have sounded frostier, and his body was tense and ramrod straight, even though he spoke calmly. He also looked a little too pale, which, for some reason, made him even more intimidating.

'I haven't,' Diana said, and frantically tried to think of something else to say.

'Your little con seems to have worked out well for you.'

'It isn't a con!' Now Diana was angry. This was exactly the behaviour she'd been brought up to expect from a Zeller. 'Your father was a thief. Nothing you can say or do will change that. At least Armando had the basic human decency to look into the facts. What have you done?'

'I don't need to do anything. I knew my father. Do you think I haven't come up against frauds like you before? I know your type.'

'You know nothing about me, or my grandmother.' Diana rushed on now, the words tumbling out. 'Do you have any idea how hurt she was? Do you know how she used to go to bed every night praying that your family would get their comeuppance. Do you really think anyone would behave like that for their whole life over nothing? Your father stole her perfume. So you can think what you like of me, but you will never convince me of your father's integrity!'

Homero actually tipped his head backwards as if to get away from her diatribe, but he was the CEO of a vast empire and used to tougher people than Diana.

'You talk a good talk, but let me tell you that as long as you're with Armando, I will never let him back into the family. He will never inherit what was supposed to be his. You remember that when you're getting all worked up over what may or may not have happened to your grandmother,' Homero said in the implacable tone of a man who was used to getting his own way.

He gave Diana a slight nod, turned and walked away as if nothing had happened.

Diana though, was overtaken with the shakes. What a disaster this evening had turned into. Everybody at this damned party was against her. She had no idea what Armando thought he would get from the evening, but she doubted it was this.

⁓

Armando leaned back in his chair, hoping Diana would get back soon. He pressed two fingers against his temple and rubbed in a circular motion. Because he knew what a toll parties usually took on him, he'd taken a couple of painkillers before heading out. Even so, there was a sensation of a too tight hat squeezing his head that he knew would develop into a migraine if he wasn't careful.

It was the damned lilies, along with the profusion of women's scents. Every woman here had come wearing a different perfume, as was expected. Unfortunately, because this was a perfume launch, they seemed to think they needed to apply their own particular scent with a heavier hand than usual.

'Are you alright?' Bernardo asked.

Armando nodded, knowing his friend wouldn't believe him.

'How about you? You're looking cheerful as usual.'

Bernardo grinned, revealing a toothy smile. He too, post food, hadn't bothered to pull his mask back on. It worried Armando, but as he knew his friend was fully vaccinated, he decided against saying anything more, but he sat further back from him than he might otherwise.

'Maria and I are planning a holiday, nothing fancy, no flights involved. We're taking the yacht out to Greece and back again.'

'In winter? Is that wise? The Med can get pretty rough this time of year.'

'I have an experienced captain, don't worry. I just feel Maria could use a break.' Bernardo glanced over his shoulder to make sure Maria wasn't listening. She'd wandered off to chat with friends at another table, but Bernardo lowered his voice and said with a bit more concern, 'she's losing weight.'

Other people's weight was not something Armando paid attention to, although he had to admit that Maria looked thinner than most socialites in the satin dress that clung to her figure.

'Maybe she's depressed.'

He'd spoken without thinking, which Bernardo's suddenly alarmed expression made him regret.

'Did she say something to you?'

'Is that likely?'

'Well, you had an actual meeting alone with her. If it was anybody else, I'd have been jealous. I thought maybe she said something to you.'

Armando was about to turn the remark away with a sardonic, as if. Instead he said, 'How long do you intend to keep her dangling?'

'She did say something.'

'She's not getting any younger. If you don't intend on marrying her, let her go so she can find a man who does want her and maybe wants to start a family.'

'You're sounding like my mother now,' Bernardo said, veering towards petulance.

'The perfume she had made for her, it's supposed to make you propose.'

Armando watched thought after thought flicker across Bernardo's expressive face.

'I don't think I can but... I don't want her to leave.'

Armando had a newfound sympathy for Bernardo's feelings, incoherently as he'd expressed them.

'How long are you going to let your ex rule your future?'

'That hurts.'

'I'm sorry. Especially tonight when I'm grateful you came. This isn't your kind of party.'

'It isn't usual for you to invite me either, so when you did I knew it was important,' Bernardo said, happy to change the subject. 'Am I moral support?'

'Pretty much.'

'Diana Luna's actually holding up better than I thought she would. She's got a feisty spirit.'

'You can say that again,' Armando said and twisted around in his seat to check whether Diana was on her way back.

What had worried him was seeing his father heading in the same direction shortly after Diana had left and now neither of them was back. Eddy, however, was making a beeline to the table.

'Armando,' he said grinning broadly, his mask draped about his neck like a bandit's handkerchief, 'what are you up to?'

'Meaning?'

Eddy nodded a greeting to Bernardo and said, 'We had an agreement. I patch things up between you and Ms Luna, which, clearly, I achieved. And you do, you know what, for me.'

'You know what?' Bernardo asked.

'A trickier you know what than Eddy's task,' Armando said. With so many potential eavesdroppers, this wasn't a good place to explain further. 'Although, if I'm honest, I didn't think you'd manage it, Eddy. Especially not so quickly.'

'And if you keep going the way you are, I'll be the bloody perfume director for life,' Eddy said, and his voice held an edge of desperation.

'Not enjoying it, huh?' Bernardo said.

'You know me. I'm a slacker.'

Armando knew that wasn't true. When it came to surfing, Eddy would put in long hours and work his body to the point of collapse, because that was his passion. Armando felt the same about perfume.

'I am working on it, never fear. How's the divorce going?'

'Badly. You'll note my mother isn't in attendance.'

Armando had, because it was unusual. Albina never missed an opportunity to flaunt herself and her wealthy husband at any society event. Armando wondered whether she regretted shacking up with her tennis coach on an evening like this.

'Ah! Got to go!' Eddy said and launched himself out of the chair like a rocket.

Armando turned around to see what had spooked him, suspecting he knew the answer, and wasn't surprised to see his father making his leisurely but determined way to his table. He felt a quiver of nerves that he suppressed. He was a grown man and perfectly able to look after himself. His father had no hold over him. Armando also remained seated because he refused to jump up and look either anxious or obsequious.

'So you pushed your way into this launch party, did you?' Homero said, looming over him.

'Why shouldn't I come? I designed Cinderella, after all,' Armando said.

'And you thought it was a good idea to bring that con woman with you?'

'She's my girlfriend. Do you want me to leave her at home?'

Armando's main reason for inviting Diana was a personal one. He wanted his family to know he was serious about her. A few weeks spent in close company had confirmed his initial liking, that was deepening into something more. Everyone else had assumed he'd invited Diana as a tactic, but his was a simpler reason.

'I want you to leave Ms Luna. Everything went wrong after she showed up. You're behaving in this strange, unpredictable way. I hardly know you at all.'

His father's words came as a surprise to Armando. Then he thought it was probably true. His father didn't know him well. All he'd ever seen up till now was an obedient son who was good at composing perfumes and running a perfume house.

Armando had grown up going to events like this since. He'd said nothing about how exhausting and sometimes painful they were for him, because it was the only time he got to see his father. Not that they talked much even then. His father was too busy networking to do much more than introduce Armando to a few key people.

'No, I don't think you do know me. I'm sorry about that. As I am about going against you. But on this one thing, I won't budge.'

'Ah, the two senior Zellers together,' a well modulated, slightly feminine voice said from behind them.

The two men turned to greet Luca Fiorino. He was a tall, well-built man with the wavy blond hair and blue eyes of a northern Italian. For some reason that nobody could understand, when Luca inherited the company, he'd moved the entire operation from the fashion powerhouse of Milan to Lisbon.

Gossips fell into two camps as to the reason. One was that he was trying to get away from his father's mafia connections. The other was that he was a cross dresser who'd had to flee because of his predilections. Armando neither knew nor cared about what might be the truth.

'Congratulations on the launch. It's quite a challenge when we've all got to be aware of Covid,' Armando said.

'Yes, indeed.'

Homero spoke in a more brusque tone than Armando was used to hearing from him. It was telling, along with the faint lines of strain on his face, that his father was unaccustomedly uncomfortable.

'Thank you,' Luca said. 'It isn't the best time, but we have a marketing timetable to stick to and I'm hopeful we'll still have plenty of Christmas sales on-line.'

'It's a challenging time to be sure,' Homero said, gave a nod of farewell and walked away.

Armando watched him go with a feeling of unease. His father was going to be more of a challenge than he'd anticipated. Then he turned to discover that Luca Fiorino was watching him with a thoughtful expression.

'I was surprised to hear you'd left the House of Zeller,' Luca said.

Armando wondered how much detail Luca knew about his departure. He'd kept his own disclosure deliberately vague. However much it was, at least Luca was also being discreet about it.

'I've been working all my life. I thought a sabbatical was in order,' Armando said, repeating what he'd told Luca before.

'Will you be going back?'

Armando gave a wry laugh and wondered what Luca was really after. He was familiar enough with being sounded out. He just wasn't sure why Luca was doing it. Either way, it was best to be equally ambiguous.

'I don't know yet.'

'Well, if you decide against returning to Zeller Corp, give me a call. I could use somebody like you.'

'I would never take a cut in responsibility,' Armando said, assuming Luca wanted him as a perfume composer.

'I would never ask you to do so,' Luca said with an enigmatic smile, and wandered off.

Armando blinked after him. What exactly was Luca dangling before him?

'Sorry I took so long,' Diana said as she finally arrived, looking pale and unhappy.

'Did you run into my father?'

For a moment it looked like she was going to say no, her head even tilted halfway to shaking her head.

'I did. It was fine, just intimidating.'

'I'm sorry. I shouldn't have subjected you to that, or to this party.'

'Actually, I learned a lot this evening. I'm glad I came.'

Armando had got to know Diana well enough to realise that she meant what she said. It relieved him that she had found the launch party interesting at least, even with the way his family behaved towards her. Since his head was throbbing and fragments of rainbow flashes scrolled at the corner of his vision, he decided it was time to leave.

'Let's go home. You can tell me everything my father said to you in the taxi,' Armando said, waving a farewell to Bernardo and Maria.

'Sure,' Diana said.

Armando got the distinct impression that she wasn't going to divulge everything, which wasn't a good sign. It looked like his father may have threatened Diana. This filled him with more rage than when his father tried to bully him. He pushed down that strong emotion and tried to keep calm. That was the best when a migraine was coming on.

CHAPTER TWENTY-SIX

B y the time Diana and Armando got to Diana's place,
Armando was pale, sweating and disinclined to talk. She
didn't like the idea of leaving him alone in the taxi for the ride
back to his place. She also worried about him looking after
himself at the beach house.

So she said, 'Come on, you're staying with me tonight.'

Armando barely managed a nod, and Diana had to help him
out of the taxi. It was just as well he was staying. He leaned
against the wall as Diana paid the driver and then allowed
himself to be led upstairs.

Diana felt as if she'd turned invisible as Armando made his
way to the bedroom and reached again for his pain killers.

'Should I get you some water?' Diana asked.

She was hovering like a mother hen over Armando while he
pushed a couple of intimidatingly large pills out of their blister
pack.

'No, it's fine,' he murmured. 'I can get it.'

'But you don't have to,' Diana said, and hurried to the
kitchen.

At least Armando didn't follow her. He was sitting on the edge
of the bed when she got back. Armando said nothing as she placed

the glass in his hand. He didn't even look up, his gaze was fixed on the pills.

Diana got the impression that he wished she wasn't there. He swallowed down his meds, closed his eyes, crawled into bed and curled up on his side, a crease between his eyes.

Diana was too hyped over the party to go to bed immediately and she'd also heard that even the lightest sound or bump could exacerbate a migraine. So she turned off the light, closed the bedroom door as quietly as she could, settled cross-legged on the sofa and turned on the TV. It was past midnight, so there wasn't much on, not that Diana noticed. Now that she was alone, not having to look unconcerned and with no distractions, her encounters with Armando's family played round and round in her head.

The arrogance of the lot of them enraged her. Funny that she'd never felt that from Armando himself, even when he'd first come over, looking all suspicious about her motives. It was a cheek of that family to think she was the fraud; the money grubbing commoner after their wealth. They were the thieves and the liars.

Her grandmother had been adamant about it. The more she considered that, the angrier she got. Her guilt towards her grandmother also increased. Armando might be an exception, but could she accept the rest of his family?

She should just walk away and tell them all to go to hell. That would show them she wasn't what they thought. That would make grandma proud. Would it, though? She was no longer sure, but guilt continued to haunt her.

With so many thoughts tumbling around, it was nearly dawn before Diana finally dozed off. It felt like only seconds later that she was jerked awake by her phone alarm. She pushed off the blanket she'd covered herself with, stood up, and stretched. Sleeping on the sofa always left her with a stiff back.

She crept into the bedroom to find Armando in exactly the same position she'd left him in the night before. His headache pills were lying on the bedside table and a couple more had been taken sometime last night or this morning.

'Armando?' Diana whispered, crouching down so she could see his face.

She got no reaction, so she eased her clothes out of the cupboard as quietly as possible and went to take a shower.

By the time she was done, she only had a couple of minutes before her first customer was due. Sometimes Armando's excellent booking system was rather inconvenient. The two customers she was due to see this morning had booked before she knew she was going to be out last night, and she wished they weren't coming.

In the days before she was fully booked, she would have spent a pleasant morning telling Margarida all about the party and the people and deciding what she thought of everything. Now she didn't even have enough time for breakfast.

Thankfully, the two women who came to get their personalised perfumes developed were interesting and engaged. The first was a kindly, middle-aged, recently divorced woman. She couldn't stop telling Diana about what men were really like and to think twice before getting married.

The second was a Céu fan. She wanted to gossip about her idol and was disappointed when Diana said she couldn't. All the same, they both went away happy.

Her shop door tinkled, indicating another arrival, and Diana groaned. She was sleepy, starving and desperate to get out of the shop if nothing else, so the brisk sharp wind could wake her up.

'Good morning, stranger,' Margarida said, grinning at her when Diana emerged from her lab.

'Margarida, thank God! I didn't want to have to deal with another customer.'

Diana grabbed her bag and hurried her friend to the door before anybody else might decide to come in. She flipped the gone for lunch sign over and locked the shop. Then she took a big, relieved sigh.

'It looks like suddenly becoming a successful businesswoman isn't an unalloyed joy,' Margarida said with a sympathetic smile.

'I have so much to tell you and I've been dying to come over, but I've just not had the time. But before any of that I need to check on something.'

She ran upstairs and found Armando in the exact same position as before. She contemplated calling Mr Rocha but decided to give it a bit more time.

Then she ran back downstairs, slipped her arm through Margarida's and guided her towards the Butterfly Cafe. Although it was chilly and half the leaves that remained on the trees were flapping in a strong breeze, the pair pulled their coats more tightly about themselves and sat outside.

'Well?' Margarida asked once the two of them had ordered ham and cheese toasties, an expresso each and a glass of water for Diana.

'Where to begin?' Diana said as she considered the party. 'I guess with the least important news first. Armando's mother.'

'She's the least important?'

Margarida's surprise was justified. Portuguese men were usually very fond, or at least protective, of their mothers.

'I know. Maybe it's because she left Armando with his dad when he was young, but Armando doesn't seem particularly attached to his mother. Either way, she holds no power over him. So, whether or not she liked me, doesn't matter.'

'She didn't like you?'

'She's self absorbed, and she ignored me at first because... Armando never goes out with the same woman twice.'

'Him and his sensitive nose,' Margarida said, nodding knowingly but with a hint of disapproval.

It wasn't the first time she'd looked less than enthused by Armando. The two of them had talked in detail about his sensitivity to smell though, so no more was needed and Diana wanted to discuss the rest, his family. She could explore Margarida's critique about Armando some other time.

'His sister is a typical bitchy socialite, but I also don't think she really cares one way or the other about me. She's just interested in fighting Armando for the company and she'll use me if it gets her an advantage.'

'What a charming family,' Margarida said and paused as Maria da Conceição brought out their lunch.

Diana nodded agreement and waited till they were alone again before she said, 'The big problem is Armando's father.'

'What did he do?' Margarida leaned in as if joining a conspiracy.

'He threatened to permanently cut Armando off if he carried on seeing me.'

'No! But that's ridiculous. I mean, it isn't the 1800s. Parents can't do that sort of thing, can they?'

'I don't know. He's the CEO of the Zeller Corporation. I guess he can do whatever he wants with that.'

'That's true,' Margarida said and munched thoughtfully on her sandwich.

Despite her hunger, and the cheese oozing seductively from between the golden toasted bread, Diana suddenly didn't feel like eating.

'I don't know what to do, Margarida. I don't want to deprive Armando of something he's expected all his life, and something he's worked really hard for. He might say it's okay now, and to hell with his family. But how will he feel a year from now or ten years from now?'

'So you told him about his father's threat?'

'I need to think about it. I need to do what's best for both of us and I don't want to ruin his life.'

'I'm sure he wouldn't think you were.'

'Not right now, he wouldn't. But I don't want to put this decision on him. I don't want him to reassure me it's alright. I need to work out what's most important without being swayed by him.'

'And there's your grandmother.'

'Yeah.' Diana sighed, just considering her grandmother. 'I don't know how to reconcile the two. I feel like... if she could just have met Armando.'

'Is he really that great?'

Margarida's question surprised Diana again. She was more used to her friend's wholehearted support and approval of the men in her life. Even if, after a breakup, she might have muttered, I didn't really like him. While Diana was in the throes of romance, Margarida would listen and support and try to see the best in the man. For her to be so forthright at the start was unusual.

'We have so much in common.'

'You've only got perfume. What about the rest? You have totally different values and outlooks on life and a massive difference in your incomes. While you at least knew that your grandmother liked Fernando.'

That was also true. Grandma had died a year into her dating Fernando, and the two had got on just fine.

'But what is this? Why are you trying to push me back into Fernando's arms? If you're so keen on him, you go out with him?' Diana snapped and was surprised to see Margarida blush. 'Wait, is he using you as a go between?'

'Don't be silly. But think about it, he's a good man with a steady job and his parents like you, too. You can't say the same for Armando.'

That was certainly true. It also left Diana feeling more uncomfortable than she had so far with the whole situation. Up till now, she'd been luxuriating in the fun of having a new boyfriend. One she thought she had a lot in common with. She regretted bringing it up with Margarida. She suspected if she could talk to Armando about things, she'd have a whole different opinion.

It would be so easy to just give Armando this problem and leave it up to him to solve. She would feel protected and cared for by a man she'd really grown to like. But she was determined to make up her own mind and solve her own problems.

'I'd better go back to work. And then I need to think about it for a while longer.'

Armando lay in bed, staring up at the ceiling. It was ancient, and the paint had yellowed unevenly over the years, giving it a shaded appearance. He felt light-headed, shaky and nauseous, as always after the migraine.

Partly it was because of the headache itself. His muscles were rigidly tense the whole time, and now they could finally relax. The rest probably came from not eating for a while.

He groped for his phone, felt its hard, cool oblong shape, and turned it back on. It was ten o'clock on Sunday morning, so he'd slept all through Saturday. Although slept wasn't quite right. It was more an oblivion where everything faded from significance except the excruciating pain.

Armando tilted his head to examine Diana's side of the bed. It was empty. More than that, it didn't look like she'd slept there at all. The duvet was unruffled. So where was she?

Armando pushed himself upright and looked around. The bedroom door was shut. That wasn't usual. Apparently Diana had decided he needed to be left alone.

Armando was grateful for her consideration, but also felt a twitch of worry and embarrassment. He always shut down with a migraine. As his family had lived with these episodes all his life, they weren't offended when he went into his cocoon.

He hadn't told Diana anything about it, and about how the pain made it impossible to interact or even think about anyone else. Was she feeling pushed out? He hoped not, especially after the launch party.

His phone gave a discreet buzz, and Armando picked it up again and his eyebrow arched in surprise. There were eleven missed calls from his father. A quiver of fright ran through him that something serious must have happened. Why else would he have called so persistently? Armando was about to call him back when the phone rang. His father.

'Yes?'

'Where the devil have you been?' his father snapped.

'What's wrong?'

Armando was more worried about a potential disaster than his father's anger at this point.

'Your brother Eddy has gone and messed up again.'

'Is he alright?'

'Why wouldn't he be alright?' Homero said, and he sounded increasingly impatient.

His attitude exasperated Armando, while at the same time relief crept in. For one horrible moment, he'd thought something dreadful had happened to Eddy.

'Why haven't you been answering your phone?' Homero asked, apparently oblivious to Armando's silence.

'I had a migraine,' Armando said, because he was too spaced out to muster up anything else.

'You haven't had one of those in a while. Is it that woman's fault?'

'It's your fault.' Armando lay back down and covered his eyes with his arm while keeping the phone to his ear. 'You kicked me out of my house, which was how I managed my sensitivity to strong smells.'

'Oh.'

'Are you going to give it back to me?'

'It's company property.'

'You know damn well it isn't.' Armando kept his voice cool and level, even though he was annoyed enough to shout. Firstly, it wouldn't work on his father. Secondly, it might bring on another migraine. 'Do you really want me to take you to court over this and air all our dirty linen in public?'

'There is a simple enough solution to all of this. Leave that woman.'

'Never. I love her. Even if I didn't, I won't allow you to dictate what I do with my private life.'

'Your private life should not involve giving your lover a million euros.'

'It's a smaller settlement than you gave my mother,' Armando said, and regretted it instantly. The last thing he should be doing was reminding his father about divorces. 'Aside from that, she had a strong case which you aren't willing to listen to. So I think it's best you calm down and we talk some other time.'

Armando hung up and grimaced at the now blank phone screen. That hadn't gone well. He was usually better at managing his father. Then again, he was usually better able to focus, but after a migraine, it was harder to do.

Aside from that, until Diana appeared on the scene, he and his father had agreed about most things. They could live with their slight differences of opinion as all of them revolved around the business. Armando had started to wonder whether the only relationship he and his father had was through work.

The phone went off again. Armando wasn't surprised to see that it was his father. He contemplated ignoring the call but decided if it was about Eddy, he should do what he could.

'Yes, what?'

'Don't you hang up on me,' Homero said.

'Don't interfere in my private life then.'

'Alright, we'll talk about that later. I need your help with Eddy's problem now.'

Armando had to admire his father's ability to put aside everything else for the sake of the company, but he wasn't going to make things easy for the old man.

'What happened?'

'He's messed up the contract with Fiorino.'

'Ah.'

'He's messed up the timing of production, so now half the units won't be ready for Christmas. Fiorino is furious and threatening to sue us for breach of contract.'

'That is unfortunate.' It was worse than that and a part of Armando wanted to spring into action and fix the whole damn mess, but he held back. 'It has nothing to do with me, though.'

'Your brother's totally hopeless at the job. I spend my life fixing everything he's messed up.'

'He's new and unsupported. When I took that role, I'd been following you around for years. I also had the previous head give me an orientation for a few months. What have you done for Eddy?'

'What could I do when you–'

Homero stopped abruptly, apparently not wanting to risk Armando cutting him off again.

'Give the job to Helena. She knows the company better than Eddy, and she's good at finding workarounds.'

'Helena?' Homero said blankly.

'You'd do better having her on your side right now, rather than working against you.'

'What are you talking about?'

Armando was astonished by the question.

'You were the one who made us compete over CEO position. Why do you sound so surprised now?'

'Helena?' Homero said again.

'Yes, your daughter, second in line to the Zeller empire, and thirsty for power. She's the one who spread the video with me and Diana around the company, and she's the one who told you about my contract with Diana, isn't she?'

'Impossible.'

'You're too old-fashioned, Dad.'

Armando was not as surprised as he might have been that his father apparently didn't consider Helena as CEO material. The eldest male heir was still the rightful successor. Armando should have known.

He also knew how much his father's attitude would infuriate his sister. Then again, she probably did know how their father felt. That was why she was making such an effort to undermine him.

'Helena's competent and devoted to the company. You ask her to find a solution to Eddy's problem and see what she does.'

Armando hung up again, and this time, he switched off the phone. He had serious reservations about giving his sister the boost he'd just given her. She would find a solution to the contract problem, even if she had to ride roughshod over several others to get it.

That might even win her some favour from his father, but as a solution for the corporation, he didn't like it. He wondered whether he did want to go back or whether he should strike out on his own and create a company he could be proud of. Until he'd met Diana, he would never even have considered the second option. He would at this moment have been fighting Helena for all he was worth.

Now... he still wanted the Zeller corporation. It was what he'd been groomed for and what he felt comfortable with. But he could also see the advantages of going it alone. It was so astonishing it nearly made him laugh.

The sound of the front door distracted Armando from his thoughts. This was followed by more noises from the kitchen and then footsteps coming towards the bedroom.

'Armando?' Diana whispered from outside.

He wondered whether that was what she'd been doing since Friday night.

'I'm up.'

'How do you feel?' Diana asked as she eased the door open with exaggerated care, as if afraid anything might set off another headache.

'I'm fine,' Armando said, embarrassment creeping in. 'I'm sorry I didn't warn you about what the migraines are like.'

'So that's normal, is it?' Diana said, failing to hide her shock. 'I mean, you were curled up and unresponsive all of yesterday. I was getting really worried.'

Armando had never had to tell anyone new about his illness and he felt extremely awkward now.

'Sometimes they last longer, sometimes it's shorter. I can never tell. Don't let it worry you.' Armando wished they could talk about something else and looking around for inspiration. 'Where did you sleep?'

'The sofa. I didn't mind. I sometimes do that when I fall asleep in front of the TV.'

'Mmm,' Armando said and felt at a loss again.

'I bought breakfast. Bread rolls. They're still warm. I thought when you woke up you'd be hungry.'

'I am,' Armando said with a relieved laugh. 'But let me take a shower first. I reek of the launch party and sweat.'

'Ok, I'll make some coffee in the meantime.'

Diana looked perfectly happy as she went back to the kitchen. Armando hoped she wasn't putting on a front. He'd never really considered what a girlfriend would think of his weakness.

Was it burdensome? Was it unfair to expect Diana just to accept it? Even if it wasn't, would she see him in a different light because of it? Would she think him a weaker man and lose her respect for him? He hoped not.

Almira had deliberately used intense smells as a weapon against him, making his life unbearable. She'd also tried to make his father see Armando as a liability who spent more days sick at home than going to school or business events.

Thankfully, it hadn't worked. Mainly because Armando pushed through the pain and went out with his father even on days when all he wanted to do was curl up into a ball of misery in his darkened room.

CHAPTER TWENTY-SEVEN

'Sit,' Diana said as Armando arrived in the kitchen.

He looked fine, if a little pale, but she was still worried about him and determined to look after him.

'It looks like it's going to be a nice sunny day,' Armando said as he looked out of the kitchen window at a cloudless blue sky before going to the table.

'It should be raining by now,' Diana said as she laid a couple of plates and knives on the table along with the basket of bread rolls, butter and jam. 'They say we're going to have a serious drought if it doesn't rain soon.'

'In the meantime, it's Sunday, and the weather is nice. Maybe we should go out?'

Armando's smile made Diana feel much better, as if everything was alright. Only it wasn't. She had made her decision, and it would only be harder to go through with it if Armando was his usual charming self. In fact, she thought, she may have slept less than Armando, what with tossing and turning all night, trying to decide what to do.

'Where do you want to go?' Diana asked as she poured Armando a coffee and then did the same for herself. 'Nothing too strenuous, please. I need a rest.'

Armando paused, his hand halfway to the coffee cup, and gave Diana such a searching gaze she struggled not to squirm.

'Are you alright? You do look a little pale.'

'Oh, yeah, I'm fine. I suppose I'm just used to a lazier life. I don't think I've ever been as busy as I have been since you moved in.'

'Would you rather stay home?'

In a way, Diana would have preferred that, except then they'd probably just be lazing on the sofa and she was sick of that. It would also keep her far too close to Armando, and it would make it difficult to do what she'd decided she had to do.

'What did you have in mind?'

'I just want to get some fresh air and stretch my legs.'

Now Armando was examining her with a cautious, thoughtful expression.

Maybe a day out would be good. A last happy moment to remember before she ended it all.

'Actually, that would be nice. If you won't find it too boring, let's take a walk around the Moorish Castle.'

'Why would I find it boring?' Armando said, looking surprised.

'Because you've been there before? Why else?'

'I've never been.'

'You haven't?' Diana said, staring at him in surprise. 'I mean, I didn't think there's a single local who's not been to the castle. Your parents surely took you as a kid. Or you must at least have been out there on a school trip?'

'Never,' Armando said with a slightly embarrassed smile. 'My father is all about the business so we didn't do trips to cultural places and if my school went, I must have been absent that day.'

'I see, well, then we'll have to rectify that,' Diana said as she finished the last of her bread and jam. 'But we're taking a taxi up and back. It's far too gruelling a walk uphill for me to do on my day off.'

'I'm okay with that.'

Diana was relieved, both that Armando didn't insist on the hike and because he'd accepted a visit to something nearby.

By the time they got up the hill and she climbed out of the taxi and took in the view again, Diana was doubly pleased.

'This was a good idea,' she said, waving her arm to indicate the breathtaking view across the mountains and all the way to a distant, sparkling sea. 'The Moors built this as a lookout, and you can see why. Nobody would be able to sneak up on them for miles around.'

'It's pretty spectacular,' Armando said and started up the grey stone steps that led to the battlements.

They were all that was left of the fortress. The inside of the fort was wild and overgrown with shrubs with great boulders pushing through the ground.

Diana followed Armando up and then leaned her arms on the edge of the crenelated wall, the gap between two taller bits, and took a deep breath of air. The wind was strong and cool, but refreshing rather than cutting.

'Isn't this marvellous? Feel this fresh air.'

Armando came back to her and wrapped an arm around her shoulder so that he could pull her close as he peered through the gap.

'Nice,' he said as he leaned his head against hers and took a deep sniff.

Diana worried immediately about her hair, and the scent of the shampoo, then she shrugged it away. Would it matter today? Not if she had the courage to go through what she had decided she needed to do. In the meantime, it felt so good to have Armando close. She wanted to turn around in his arms and cling to him.

'What do you smell?' Diana asked in a bid to distract herself.

'You,' Armando said, giving her a warm smile that nearly brought tears to her eyes. 'Herbal shampoo and your usual perfume, plus some of the trees around here and a faint whiff of the sea.'

'Really? From way out here?'

'Mmm.'

Armando guided Diana away from the view and onto the broad stone path of the wall that undulated over the highs and lows of the mountain and led them around the perimeter of the fort.

Diana wrapped her arm around Armando's waist and tried to memorise the feeling of his warm body against hers. She was gripping his grey fleece as tightly as a child who was afraid to let go and face the unknown world, even when she knew it was all in vain. Armando's father had given her an ultimatum. Try as she might, she could see only one thing to do.

She couldn't come between Armando and his inheritance. Even more than that, she couldn't come between him and his family. Nor could she come between her and her grandmother, or what her grandmother would have approved of.

'Are you and your father very close?' Diana asked in the vague hope that Armando would give her something to work with, some other way out.

'I used to think we were. If any of my friends had asked, I would have told them we were. I often felt more fortunate than them. Their fathers were also powerful and important men, and they hardly ever got to see them. While I saw my father quite often.'

'So why do you doubt it now?' Diana said, looking up to examine Armando's suddenly far more sombre face.

'This whole episode. I realised that my father and I actually only have one thing in common and that's work.'

'It's a very big thing though, isn't it? I mean, you could say the same about us. We have perfume in common and that's one reason I got to like you.'

'It's one of the reasons I like you too,' Armando said, and leaned down for a quick peck. 'But we have more in common than that. We can talk about other things, about how we're feeling, or about other interests. I think I've told you more about my life than I've ever told my father.'

'You wouldn't have to tell your father. He already knows.'

'I don't think he does.' Armando came to a stop and stared thoughtfully out into space. 'It's why he doesn't understand how important you are to me.'

His words made Diana's heart drop. He was making things harder, even if he didn't realise it.

'And because he doesn't understand that,' Armando continued, 'he's behaving in his usual egotistical way. All he cares about, all he has ever cared about, is the company and my grandfather's bloody legacy.'

The bitterness that crept into Armando's voice surprised Diana. She wondered whether he would go back to his family even if she did break up with him. Then she shook that faint hope away. Armando was hurt, but it would pass.

'I don't think he is completely oblivious. He looked stressed when I spoke to him, and rather pale. Maybe he needs somebody to listen to him too, especially now with the divorce.'

'He brought that upon himself. And it's not exactly like he's been faithful to either of his wives.'

'All the same, I think he's struggling. Maybe you should cut him some slack.'

'Maybe.' Armando went back to strolling along the battlement, stopping to gaze out at the view now and then. 'But he's a businessman. He should know when he has to negotiate, and he hasn't even tried to with me. Even this morning he just called up, demanding I fix a problem for him. No exchange, no quid pro quo, just do it. This after he fired me.'

'That does seem a little unreasonable.'

Diana was going to push Armando away so that he could reclaim his inheritance, but she was now wondering whether it was too late. It seemed that Armando's relationship with his father had suffered a blow. But was it a sufficient one for him to want to walk away from everything that was due to him.

Armando seemed perfectly happy working in her laboratory, tweaking Céu's perfume. Would he be able to strike out on his own and build up a new perfume house? Diana sighed.

There was no sense in asking the same questions she'd asked herself a thousand times since Armando's father had given her his ultimatum.

'What's wrong?' Armando said. 'You seem distracted.'

'Oh, no, nothing,' Diana said and forced herself to smile up at him. 'How's Céu's perfume going?'

'I've finished reformulating it based on the feedback I got from our testers. I plan on giving you the final version to consider on Monday.'

'That was quick,' Diana said, struck by another twinge of guilt. There would be no Monday morning consultation.

'This bit's always the easiest. The next step is to decide who gets to do the mass production.'

'And that I can't help you with.'

It relieved Diana that she'd done all she could for the mass-produced version of Céu's perfume. The next steps needed an industrial system that she didn't have. It was the best time, therefore, to break things off.

'I will always value your opinion,' Armando said, squeezing Diana's hand. 'You know that, don't you?'

'Yes.'

Diana couldn't look at Armando anymore. Her eyes were filling with tears and she hurried away so that he couldn't see her face.

'Diana!'

Armando closed the gap between them too quickly and put his hand on her shoulder, but apparently thought better of pulling her round to face him.

'What's the matter?'

'I think... I think we should break up,' Diana managed to say, although her voice was thick, and it was difficult to speak.

'Break up? I... I don't understand. What's happened? Was it the launch party? Did my father–'

'No, it wasn't him or any of your family.'

Diana couldn't let Armando know what had really happened. He'd blame his father even more, and that would make things even harder to repair.

'Was it the migraine, then? I'm sorry, I should have told you about it. You must have been worried. It isn't so bad, really. Most of the time I manage just fine.'

'Do you?' Diana asked, because she had wondered, but Armando had always brushed away her concerns. 'It seemed to me you took your pain killers pretty regularly.'

'I was fine. I just haven't had to explain to anyone else before. I handled it badly. And I understand if you feel uncomfortable about it but I can explain and I can be more careful.'

Diana shook her head, rubbed her arm across her eyes to dry the tears, took a deep determined breath and turned around. He'd have to see her face to know how serious she was.

'I've been thinking a lot about us, our family history, your health, everything. I shouldn't have got so closely involved with you. It was all too sudden, and this after I just broke up with Fernando. It was probably a rebound thing, and then there was the whole business with the money. I just... it's all too complicated.'

Diana was aware that she was incoherent, rambling and in danger of being persuaded by Armando, who was staring at her with the most appalled expression on his face.

'I should go. Please don't make this difficult. I'd appreciate if you'd move out as soon as possible.'

'Diana?' Armando said at barely a whisper.

Diana pulled herself free from his grip, ran down the stairs and along the well-trodden, eroded path to the drop off point, found a taxi and gave him directions to Margarida's shop. She was sobbing uncontrollably by the time they were halfway down the mountain.

Armando was stunned by what had just happened. Part of the reason he'd wanted to go for a walk was to drive away the detached uneasy feeling the migraines always left him with. He'd been sure if he could spend the day with Diana it would all smooth out and return to normal. Now this.

He leaned his back against the rough stone wall of the fort and slid down till he was seated, his knees pressed against his chest, his gaze fixed unseeing on the well-worn track before him. What had just happened? Was it even real?

The sick feeling in his chest told him it was. He'd never been dumped before, but he'd seen his friends go through it. He thought first of Bernardo, who'd practically collapsed when his wife left him.

Armando had been surprised by how it had changed his easy-go-lucky friend. How his confidence had been shaken. How he'd lost his ability to laugh.

He'd tried to jolly Bernardo out of his depression and taken him out, even when he'd said he just wanted to stay home. Armando suddenly understood how he'd felt. The shock of being fired had come as such a blow that he'd retreated for a week. This was far worse. Armando didn't know what he'd do next.

Time passed, a couple of people walked by now and then, some eyed Armando curiously, most pretended he wasn't there. All the while, he was trying to work out what had gone wrong.

Was it his family? His father had told him to leave Diana. It was more than likely that he'd said the same thing to her. But she'd not blamed his father. Still, it was something to think about.

His sister and mother hadn't been much better. Diana had probably wondered what a nest of vipers she'd fallen into with them. She had no family that he had to worry about, so he'd not had to think about pleasing them. Was Diana afraid of his family? He should have done more to reassure her at the party.

But maybe it had been the party itself. Maybe she'd felt more uncomfortable than she'd let on. Diana was all about people, and making something special for an individual. Maybe this big, showy party full of soulless corporates had been what she'd disliked the most.

Or maybe it was the migraine. That one he'd been trying to avoid as the reason. But this did all happen straight after it had laid him low. So it was possible.

Armando wished he could dismiss the worry that it was his health that had frightened Diana. But he knew some people just couldn't deal with any kind of illness and one that never got better? Would he stick with someone with a chronic condition?

His sensitivity to smell was probably another thing. Diana had been meticulous, changing the bedding every day, washing everything down regularly, throwing the windows open, even when it was cold, to air the place. Going so far as to put a fan in the kitchen so that she could dispel the smells out into the street below. Even getting up early to shower and brush her teeth before she would speak to him in the morning. All of this he'd just accepted. But thinking about it now, he realised how onerous it must have been.

True, he'd helped with the cleaning. Sometimes because she didn't realise what did or didn't offend his overly sensitive nose. That must have been an irritation in itself.

Armando shook his head and realised that having his own sterile, carefully cleaned house had been a mixed blessing. It meant he got fewer migraines, but it had also made him more pernickety about smells. He'd had to put up with them when he was growing up. He should have been more resilient with Diana.

Recrimination was all very well, but it didn't solve his current problem. He didn't want to lose Diana, but what did he do about it? She'd been so adamant she'd even told him to move out.

What was a little reassuring was that she'd also looked heartbroken. She wasn't angry, or desperate, just very unhappy. Was he the cause of the unhappiness or was it the breakup? Was there a way back for him, for them? He hoped so.

Armando finally looked up and realised it was late. It felt like the afternoon already. The wind had picked up, and he was frozen. He was so cold it took some effort to stand, and his fingers ached.

He supposed his first step would have to be moving out. He had no idea where Diana had fled to, but he was pretty sure it wasn't her house. Most likely she was sheltering with Margarida, watching and waiting to see what he would do next.

A part of him wondered whether he should just stay put and force Diana to speak to him. He decided against it. It would be cruel, and she was upset enough as it was.

Armando looked out over the spectacular view. The wind was so sharp now that it brought tears to his eyes. Armando blinked them away, forcing himself not to let them turn into tears of grief. He'd come up with a plan. He always did.

He pulled his phone out of his pocket and called Eddy.

'Armando, I'm sorry,' Eddy said as he answered. 'I'm a screwup. I'm sorry I've dragged you into yet another one of my messes.'

Armando looked blankly at the phone, trying to work out what Eddy was going on about. Then he remembered his conversation with his father. It felt like a lifetime ago and entirely unimportant.

'Forget about that. It isn't why I'm calling.'

'It isn't? I mean, what should I do about Fiorino?'

'Come and fetch me from Diana's house and I'll tell you,' Armando said. 'Tell dad I've broken up with Diana so that he gives you my car keys and house keys.'

'Wait, what? You've broken up with Diana? What happened? You looked perfectly happy on Friday night.'

'Yeah, well, these things happen.'

Armando wanted to ask Eddy about Diana. Even though it was embarrassing that his younger brother knew so much more about dating than he did. But he wasn't willing to discuss it over the phone.

'Now get a move on. I don't want to hang about at Diana's house.'

Fortunately, as he'd expected, Diana wasn't home. He'd not even tried to look into Margarida's shop, but it was coming to dusk now and her lights were still on. Armando took the stairs two at a time, went into the house and looked at it almost like it was the first time again.

It had a forlorn atmosphere now. It was cold and dark and smelled of Diana and a hint of mould. Funny that the mould hadn't really bothered him for the few weeks he'd been visiting. Just being with Diana made everything else tolerable.

Now that was over and a wave of melancholy washed over him. He pushed it back and went to pack his stuff. It wasn't a lot, and just filled the small wheely suitcase Libero had brought so long ago.

Now all that was left to do was wait for Eddy. He hoped he wouldn't take long. Armando dropped all his stuff at the front door and then dug in the drawer of the narrow table beside it for an envelope for the key.

He found an ancient yellowing stack of papers and envelopes plus a selection of plastic pens. None of it looked like it had been used for a while.

Armando smoothed out an envelope and tried to think of something to say. Since he didn't know the reason for the breakup, it was a challenge. In the end, he simply wrote:

Call me if you change your mind. I'll be waiting.

It looked stupid the moment he'd written it, but he shoved the house and shop keys into it, sealed the envelope and put it next to the photo that had remained face down on the table. Armando had never touched it. Now his curiosity got the better of him and he lifted the photo to examine it.

It had been taken on a summer's day and the sun shone brightly down on the two women. Their arms were wrapped about each other, Diana snuggled into her grandmother's embrace. They looked happy and comfortable. Armando doubted he'd ever felt the same way with any of his family. They certainly had no photos like the one he was staring at.

Diana's grandmother seemed to be smiling up at him out of the picture. She was the same height as Diana and very similar to look at, but a thin, wiry woman with her grey hair pulled up into a bun.

'Would you approve of me?' Armando murmured.

He didn't expect a reply, so he practically jumped out of his skin at a sudden fierce knock at the door.

'Armando, Armando, are you in there?'

'Of course I am, you idiot.'

Armando pulled the door open and looked Eddy over. Despite the chilly weather, he was just wearing a ragged t-shirt and an equally ancient pair of jeans.

'What on earth happened?' Eddy said. 'I spotted Diana in her friend's shop bawling her eyes out.'

'In the middle of the shop?' Armando said in surprise.

'No, huddled behind the counter, but I could see their reflection. What did you do?'

'I don't know.'

Armando rolled his suitcase out of the door before turning, giving the flat one last look, and then pulling the door shut. He checked to make sure the latch had caught, then headed down the stairs.

'Oh well, join the club,' Eddy said in philosophical tones.

'What club?'

'The brotherhood of dumped and confused ex's. Every guy has at least one girlfriend who's dumped him for no obvious reason at all.'

'Do the ex-girlfriends all cry about it too?'

Armando made straight for his car without taking the risk of looking into Margarida's shop.

'Women cry at the drop of a hat. One girl was weeping up a tsunami when she dumped me. But the thing is, they go off, cry, and then get over us. It's the guys who feel okay at first and get broody and heartbroken later.'

'That's encouraging,' Armando said as Eddy handed him his car key and he gave it right back. 'You drive, I'm in no mood for it.'

Fortunately, Eddy didn't argue, went to the driver's side and unlocked the car. Armando felt like he should have been more triumphant about getting his car back, but he was distracted as he sat down and his face crinkled in disgust at the smell that wafted up to him.

'Did Pedro Alvares drive this car?'

'Who?'

Eddy gunned the engine and pulled out of his parking space at what Armando considered an imprudent speed. That was younger brothers for you.

'He's one of the security guards at Zeller. He's getting on a bit and is addicted to heavy doses of Old Spice.'

Eddy laughed and said, 'Good God, can you still smell that in the car? Dad did have one of the security men take your car back to your house. I guess it must have been him. But that was weeks ago.'

'Well, the smell's been trapped in here ever since,' Armando said with a sigh, 'I'm going to have to get the interior steam cleaned.'

'Never mind the car. Tell me exactly what happened with Diana.'

So Armando did, every last detail as he remembered it. It was painful to go through it all again, and it left him more confused than ever.

'Do you think the migraine put her off?' he asked as he came to the end of his tale.

'She doesn't seem like the type who would be scared off by something like that, but you never know,' Eddy said. 'I think there's more to it.'

'My overly sensitive nose?' Armando asked with real trepidation.

'She put up with that for quite a long time, didn't she?'

'Mmm, but maybe it was getting on her nerves.'

'Then I'd say she'd be happy to be rid of you and she wouldn't be crying her heart out.'

'It makes no sense.'

'It might never make sense to you,' Eddy said sympathetically. 'That's just women.'

'Mmm.'

Armando had a feeling that was an all too easy cop-out from Eddy who had a tendency not to analyse things, never mind over-analyse.

'So...' Eddy said after they'd driven in silence for some time, 'can I ask you what to do about my fuck up with Fiorino?'

Armando gave a cynical laugh as he turned to examine his younger brother, who was keeping his eyes deliberately pinned to the road.

'I told dad to get Helena to come up with a solution.'

'Helena?' Eddy said, and the car gave a surprised swerve and correction. 'You have got to be kidding me.'

'Not at all,' Armando said as he continued watching his brother to see what he'd do next.

'But that was before you got dumped, right? I mean, now you can fix the problem, can't you? That will be better for you and the company all around, and I can go back to the food flavouring department.'

Armando sighed and considered his brother some more. The problem with Eddy was that he was always too quick to give up.

'Do you know whether Dad has approached Helena about this yet?'

'There is no way. I'm surprised you even suggested it to him. I doubt he'll do it, especially now.'

'Mmm,' Armando murmured and went back to watching the world flashing by as they roared down the highway to Lisbon. It was one of the uglier routes back into the city.

'You know, I feel another migraine coming on. I'll be going straight to bed when I get home and I don't know when I'll reappear. You made this mess. You need to solve it, Eddy. My one piece of advice to you is to discuss it with Helena.'

Chapter Twenty-Eight

It was as if winter rolled in with Armando's departure, Diana thought as she gazed gloomily out of her kitchen window at the heavy fog and dripping trees. The cold and damp seemed to wrap itself around Sintra, squeezing away all warmth.

Fortunately, Diana was kept busy with clients. But every time she met a new lady, she was reminded of Armando because it was his booking system that kept the customers lining up. As Christmas was approaching, quite a few people were making bookings for family and friends. She'd had to send a few away, telling them she couldn't make a bespoke perfume for someone who wasn't present.

Diana wished she could put that additional information onto her website, but she didn't have a clue how to do it. She also couldn't ask Armando. Never again would she be able to speak to him. She had kept his note, though, scrawled on the envelope.

At least he'd left without such rage that he'd said nothing at all or scrawled something nasty as his final words. She didn't think she'd be able to bear it if he had.

'Oh dear,' Margarida said, standing in the kitchen doorway, 'it looks like you're on the verge of tears again.'

'I feel like shit,' Diana said, but made a brave attempt at a smile.

'I brought you some breakfast,' Margarida said, as she put a small white cardboard box down on the table. 'I had a feeling you wouldn't do it for yourself.'

The box could contain only one thing, Diana knew as she lifted off the lid to reveal a quartet of glistening caramel black and golden pastais da nata.

'Now I know I look utterly miserable. This is an emergency breakfast.'

'I couldn't think of anything else that you would eat. They're fresh from the bakery and still warm.'

'What would I do without you?'

Diana reached into her cupboard to get down her little metal cinnamon shaker with the lemon pattern printed on it. She covered all the pastries with a light dusting of the spice. Then she fetched the coffee that had just run through the filter, took the milk coming to the boil off the stove and poured herself and Margarida some coffee. Margarida, in the meantime, got them a couple of saucers and put out the pastries.

'Has he been in touch?'

'Not a word,' Diana said. 'But I don't expect it. His note said he'd wait for me.'

'Poor sod.'

Margarida took a bite of her pastel that caused a puff of cinnamon to take to the air. Diana wondered what Armando would make of that and whether he liked the scent of cinnamon. It was a fairly common component of perfumes. And if not there, then in the food flavouring department, where it was a somewhat overused ingredient.

'Are you actually feeling sorry for him? After being lukewarm about him all the time we were dating?'

Margarida shrugged noncommittally. 'Do you know if he's gone back to work yet?'

Part of Diana would happily talk about Armando all day, every day. Another part of her wanted to never mention his name again because of the pain it caused her. All the same, she'd taken to checking all the on-line perfume social media for news about him every day.

'It's only been a week since he left. Aside from that, the company never formally announced his departure, so they would be unlikely to tell the world when he went back. As far as I know, they're still saying he's on a sabbatical.'

'It was quite a sabbatical,' Margarida said with a cheeky grin.

Diana gave a halfhearted laugh. Thank God Margarida wouldn't go down the, I told you so, route and was doing her best to cheer Diana up.

'You will never believe who got in touch with me,' Margarida continued.

Diana's first crazy, hopeful thought was that it was Armando. But it wouldn't be him. Then she wondered whether it might have been Eddy.

'Fernando!' Margarida said in the tone of one imparting fantastic news.

'Oh,' Diana said, instantly deflated. She couldn't care less about Fernando.

'He wanted to know whether you were still seeing Armando. I didn't tell him anything,' Margarida said, correctly reading Diana's alarmed look. 'But maybe...'

'Never. Even if I never see Armando again, I wouldn't go back to Fernando.'

'He was very contrite. He realises how much he hurt you.'

'No.' Diana put down the pastry she had yet to bite into. She'd lost her appetite again. 'The problem is... I didn't actually want to break up with Armando. That's what makes it all so difficult. I'm still in love with him and–'

'You were in love with Fernando when he broke up with you too.'

'And it really hurt. That's what upsets me the most about breaking up with Armando. He probably thinks I'm a total bitch. I went into our relationship with our entire family history, and his grandfather's betrayal, and then I did that to him...' Diana trailed off as tears welled up. 'And he probably thinks I dumped him because he had no money and couldn't get the contract signed and I don't even care about that.'

'You shouldn't have gone along with his father then. He's the real bastard in all of this. You should have told Armando what he said. Then the two of you could have told his family to go to hell. It would have been you against the world.'

Diana nodded forlornly. It would have been better if Margarida had said the same before the breakup. Or maybe it would have made no difference. After all, she'd told herself the same when she'd been trying to decide what to do.

'I couldn't do it. I kept coming back to the importance of family and comparing Armando's father to my grandmother. If she had given me an ultimatum to stop seeing Armando... I probably would have.'

'But Armando doesn't feel the same way about his family.'

'No, but they are family and when it comes to it, that is a powerful attachment. And I keep remembering how he decided against suing his father to get his house and car back because he didn't want them to become estranged. And that's not even to mention being able to make perfumes for the House of Zeller, the thing Armando really loves.'

'He doesn't have to create perfumes for the Zeller Corporation. He was all set to start up his own company.'

'I'm not sure he was. Why should he anyway when he could just inherit?'

Margarida nodded, but Diana wondered whether she did agree. She just wasn't saying anything out of respect for Diana's decision. It made her doubt herself even more.

'You know... what do you think...' Diana started and then stopped.

'About what?' Margarida asked.

'About you and Fernando,' Diana said, taking it at a rush. 'I got the feeling you were getting on really well.'

'I was trying to help him get back together with you.'

'Do you really think I didn't work that out?' Diana gave Margarida a speculative stare, because her friend was turning pink. 'But you always really liked him, didn't you? As a friend, I know. But maybe, maybe you should think about what else you feel for him. I love you for your loyalty, but really, I will never get back with Fernando, no matter what happens from here on out.'

The rest of Margarida's visit was taken up with Diana trying to persuade her suddenly shy friend to go out with Fernando. It made her feel better to worry about somebody else rather than herself for a while.

But once Margarida left, she felt the all familiar gloom spread through her mind again. She reached for her phone and scrolled through her contacts. She'd learned that sharing really did help ease the pain, and she wondered who else she could call for a chat just as her finger swept past her mother's name.

She was the least maternal woman Diana had ever known, but she only hesitated for a fraction of a second before she pressed the call button.

'Diana, are you alright?' her mother asked without preamble.

'I'm fine, how about you?' Diana said, struck by the thought that her mother sounded older. 'Are you still in Turkey?'

'Turkey? God, no, I left months ago. Istanbul is lovely, but a bit too cold in the winter. I'm in Berlin now.'

'Berlin? I fail to see how that could be warmer.'

'Not outside, but they have decent heating indoors and great nightlife. I'm bar tending at the most amazing place. The Germans really know how to have fun and I don't have to worry about people complaining about me serving alcohol. They're pretty hip in Istanbul but there is a strong religious lobby.'

'I see,' Diana said as she wandered through to her sitting room and curled up on the sofa, pulling a throw over herself.

'I have a feeling you didn't call to hear about me,' her mother said in her usual good humoured way.

Diana had to give her that; she was super easy going.

'I broke up with my boyfriend.'

'The lawyer? I thought he was a bit too boring for you.'

It took Diana a moment to work out when her mother had possibly met Fernando. Then she remembered they had both been at her grandmother's funeral.

'No... I mean, Fernando broke up with me a few months back. After him there was Armando, Armando Zeller.'

She was pleased that she could still shock her mother as the silence on the phone indicated.

'Not from the Zeller corporation, surely?'

'The eldest son.'

'No way!'

Diana wanted to laugh now; her mother sounded like an American.

'Yeah, but it didn't work out. Can you believe that Zeller senior accused me of being a fraud? He said I was just after his son for his money and that there's no way Grandmother could have held a grudge over a perfume.'

Her mother laughed, which surprised Diana.

'How foolish.'

'Foolish? Why's it foolish?' Diana asked, sitting upright on the sofa.

'Do you really think your grandmother went so overboard because of a stolen perfume?'

'She did, didn't she?' Diana was getting more confused by the moment. 'Are you telling me she wasn't furious because of a theft?'

'Think about it, the perfume was called Armour.'

'They were in love?!' Diana shouted and shot to her feet. 'She was broken-hearted?'

'I suppose it isn't surprising that she didn't tell you the whole story. But yes, she and that Zeller chap were deeply in love. Your grandmother was already planning the wedding. Then one day, her beau vanished, taking the formula for Armour with him. The next thing she saw was an announcement in the newspaper of his engagement to a rich girl in Lisbon. That's why she was so furious.

He'd pledged his undying love to her. They'd designed a perfume together and then he'd gone off and married somebody else and taken their lovey-dovey perfume into the bargain.'

A phone call woke Armando. That was unusual, and annoying. He had what would be a potentially life-changing meeting coming up, which had made falling asleep difficult. Even when he dropped off, his brain kept running through scenarios of the upcoming meeting, which left him exhausted.

He groped across crumpled sheets through the dark for the still buzzing phone and noted the time and the caller before he answered.

'For the love of God, Bernardo, it's 5am!'

'You weren't actually asleep, were you?'

'I was, but uncomfortable, which is the only thing that's going to save your life.' Armando set the phone to speaker, left it on the bedside table and flopped back onto his pillow.

'I thought, what with the meeting coming up, there was no way you'd be asleep.'

'Mmm.' Armando closed his eyes. There was no point in having them open in the dark, and he didn't feel like turning on his bedside light yet. 'Why the early morning call? I'm guessing, since you sound calm, it isn't an emergency.'

'Not that. Sorry if you thought it was something like that. I mean, who else would call at this ungodly hour, right? It's just, I honestly thought you'd be awake.'

'And in need of a pep talk?'

'Probably. You have a lot at stake today. Have you made your final decision yet?'

'I haven't. For the first time in my life I can't see what I want clearly.'

'Well, I can.'

Armando was surprised.

'Are you going to tell me what to do? That isn't like you.'

'Good God, no, not your future. I can see mine clearly.'

'So clearly you had to call me at five in the morning?'

'Yeah, sorry. I feel pretty stupid about that, but I've been up all night, pacing.'

'Maria must love you for it.'

'Not in the bedroom. I'm not an idiot. I'm in my study. Listen, Armando—'

Armando waited, but Bernardo had gone so silent that he sat up again and checked that they hadn't been cut off.

'I am listening.'

'I'm going to do it,' Bernardo said. 'I'm going to propose to Maria.'

This was such surprising news that Armando finally switched his light on, as if that would better illuminate what his friend was saying.

'You're going to get married?'

'If she says yes.'

'I don't think that's in doubt.'

'So you say, but I won't be sure until I ask. It's the right thing to do, Armando. I'm feeling better about everything already and I know Maria will be happier. I've been thinking about what you said nonstop since the party and you were right.'

'I'm glad for you,' Armando said and decided that since he was awake he might as well make himself a coffee.

'I'll be hoping for a good outcome for both of us,' Bernardo said. 'Now I'd better go.'

Armando glanced back at his phone, halfway through pulling on a robe, and noted that Bernardo had indeed hung up. Love really did make men do some weird stuff, but he was glad for his friend. At least one of them was getting what they wanted.

A couple of hours later Armando had eaten, showered and dressed and was examining himself in his full length dressing room mirror. He looked fine, very neat in his black suit, just the way he liked it. He wished Diana could see him now. Would she regret her decision then?

He shook that thought away. It was one of many. No matter what he did, it always made him think about Diana. For the hundredth time over the last week, he reached for his phone, determined to speak to her, and then pulled back. He'd said he'd let her make the first move. He had to stick to that.

He did finally check for missed calls. He'd been screening all the calls from his family. Armando noted that Eddy had stopped trying to call him a couple of days ago. His father, on the other hand, had tried half a dozen times overnight.

He wouldn't have much longer to wait, Armando thought as he made his way to his garage. His footsteps sounded loud on the mirror smooth polished concrete floors and he wondered yet again at how astonishingly quiet his house was. He'd been living there for so long that he'd ceased to notice, but the contrast with Diana's home was stark.

Diana again, Armando thought, shaking his head. It was better to look forward. So he ran over his conversation with his father's secretary a few days before.

'Good morning Ms Clarisse,' Armando had said.

'Mr Zeller,' came her cool dry voice, 'the CEO has been trying to reach you.'

Clarisse always referred to his father as the CEO. At first, Armando had found it amusing. Now he knew it was the proper thing to do.

'He's going to have to wait a little while longer. I'd appreciate it if you'd make an appointment for me for Monday.'

'Mr Zeller,' Clarisse said, 'you really should speak to him right away.'

'I appreciate your concern.' Armando wasn't convinced it was concern, but merely a sense of duty. 'And I apologise for getting you involved in something that is more related to the family than the company, but all I want at the moment is to set up a meeting.'

'This isn't like you, Mr Zeller,' Clarisse said, with a strongly disapproving note in her voice.

'I know.' Until now, Armando had been an exemplary and obedient son. He also respected Clarisse for her professionalism and he'd never tried to wheedle or flatter her into doing anything. He had a feeling she respected him for that. 'If I can also ask, as a favour, don't tell him it's me booked in for Monday morning.'

'Mr Zeller! What should I tell him?'

'I'll leave that in your capable hands.'

Now Armando was on his way to the office to finally have that talk with his father. He was determined that this time he wouldn't leave until he'd resolved everything. Thankfully, having a broken heart made confronting his father easier. He was so hurt and upset that he hardly cared about his father's feelings or even whether he'd fly into a rage. He was determined, however, to get his own way this time.

That conviction only strengthened as he arrived at the office and took his usual walk from the underground car park and up in the lift. Then he turned left, to his father's office. It amused him to note that his appearance was causing a commotion.

Managers and directors rushed to their office doors and stared at him in amazement. The rest of the world might not have realised what had happened between him and his father, but the senior executives on the top floor were all clearly in the know. He smiled and nodded a greeting as he passed them, which got even greater astonishment.

'Is he in?' Armando asked as he strolled into reception and noted that even Clarisse Alma looked tense.

'He is. He thinks he's about to have a Zoom call with our German distributors.'

'Ah, I see, thank you.'

'You should take that in with you,' Clarisse said, pointing at a tray with two espressos and a collection of expensive looking biscuits.

Since this wasn't his father's usual fare, Armando realised Clarisse was doing what she could to ensure a successful meeting.

'Thank you,' Armando said with a grin as he hoisted the tray.

Then he knocked and let himself into his father's office.

'Armando!' Homero said, his eyebrows snapping together into a scowl. 'So you've finally decided to show up, have you?'

'I have,' Armando said, working hard not to get swept up by his father's emotions and snap back.

He made his way to the more comfortable sitting area away from his father's desk, put the tray down, settled on the gold striped satin sofa and looked expectantly at his father. He was glaring at him and Armando realised Diana was right. His father looked stressed. The lines about his eyes were deep and tense.

'I can't speak to you now,' Homero said, not budging from his desk. 'I'm expecting a call.'

'The German distributors? That's me,' Armando said and leaned back on the sofa. 'I asked Ms Clarisse to keep it secret.'

'What the devil for?' Homero said, but finally came over to the group of comfortable chairs and threw himself into the single seater at the head of the coffee table.

Armando took his father's cup of coffee and placed it in front of him, along with the biscuits.

'We need to talk, properly.'

'Eddy told me you broke up with that woman.'

'She broke up with me,' Armando said, angry at the way his father refused to say Diana's name.

'She probably decided you were no longer a wealthy catch, so there was no point in staying with you.'

'Unlike your two wives, Diana wasn't interested in me for my money.' Armando's comeback earned him a cold sideways stare from his father as he took a sip of his coffee. 'Diana's more observant and kind than anyone in our family. She was actually worried about you and said you looked pale. I hadn't noticed.'

'What nonsense,' Homero muttered.

Armando shrugged. His father would never admit to any weakness.

'Has Eddy solved the Fiorino problem?'

Talking business would help his father to calm down.

'He and Helena came up with a plan. Helena was all for pulling the production runs of a couple of our smaller perfume producers. Eddy suggested we shouldn't put all the burden on them and reduced the run on some of our brands, too. It will impact our Christmas sales, but not as much as losing Fiorino would.'

'That's good.'

Armando finally took a sip of coffee. At least Clarisse always made an excellent espresso whose taste was equal to the aroma.

'How did you know Helena would have a solution?' Homero said.

'She always does. Don't be fooled by her girly office. She knows everything that's going on in the company.'

'More than you?'

'Probably,' Armando said with a nod, 'And more than you too.'

'Why don't you know as much as she does?'

'I know my part of it, the House of Zeller. The rest of the corporation is your business. Helena, as the marketing director, needs to know about both sectors.'

'It sounds like you think she would make a better CEO than you.'

Homero managed to make it sound like an accusation.

'No, she's too obsessed with the bottom line. She'll cut off valued clients and reduce quality if she thinks it will bring in more money. I believe our relationships with partners and our own products should be treated with more respect than that.'

'Yes,' Homero said and sank into introspection.

Armando watched him and decided that he was tired, worn down by the pressures of the job and the humiliation of his divorce. He regretted adding to that burden, but then again, his father had exacerbated the situation.

He didn't want to add salt to his father's wounds, but he also couldn't let what had happened to Diana slide. Or to just allow his father to think that things could simply go back to the way they were, as if nothing had happened.

'You're right, Helena is as interested in money as her mother. It isn't what I want for Zeller,' Homero said.

'She isn't only interested in money.' Armando was surprised, yet again, that he was standing up for his half-sister. 'She really cares about the Zeller Corporation. Unlike her mother, who you can just pay to go away. Helena would fight to stay. In fact, she's fighting every day because she suspects you don't have any intention of leaving the company to her and she's determined to take it, anyway.'

'That hardly matters now that you're back.'

'Who said I was coming back?' Armando said and looked his father over cooly.

Maybe it was his ambivalence towards the company these days that made him more relaxed about letting Helena take the lead.

'What?' Homero gasped and his coffee cup rattled in its saucer.

'Luca Fiorino called me last week and offered me a role at his company.'

His father stared at Armando as if he'd lost his mind.

'He couldn't possibly offer you a better position than you have here. They are only a fashion house, and he's already the CEO of it.'

'He surprised me by offering a partnership, fashion and perfume. Luca thinks I could catapult Fiorino into the top echelons of the perfume world with my creations. He's particularly eager to see what Diana and I produced for Céu.'

'Armando! You wouldn't... You can't go over to another company and take what we were planning for next year's big Christmas perfume with you.'

'Why not?' Armando said, watching his father even more closely. 'As co-CEO at Fiorino, I would have free rein to do what I like. I can also date whoever I want and write up whichever contracts I feel I need without being summarily dismissed and having all my property seized.'

At least his father had the grace to look embarrassed by that.

'I did what was best for you,' he muttered.

'Really? In what way was it best for me?'

'You were being conned.'

'Do you think me such a fool that I can't see a scam when it's right in front of me? And do you honestly think you resolved the situation in the best way possible?'

'Of course I did.'

'Then you shouldn't have as incompetent a person as me on your staff. And, equally, I don't wish to work for someone who doesn't trust my judgement and acts in such an arbitrary manner. Aside from that, our entire conversation and everything that led up to today has shown me something else.

'I used to think we had a reasonable father and son relationship. At least, a better one than many of my friends. But now, your reaction to me falling in love and the way you went about crushing it has shown me that all I am to you is an employee, and not even one worthy of respect.'

It hurt Armando to be so blunt, but he had to show his father where he drew the line. He stood up and said, 'You have one week to let me know what you want to do about this mess. At that point I will decide who I will work for.'

'You can't be serious about Fiorino,' his father said, gazing up at him, open-mouthed.

'Possibly not, I might set up my own perfume house instead.'

That visibly shook his father, but instead of arguing with him about it, Homero asked, 'What about Ms Luna?'

'What I choose to do with Diana is no business of yours and if you wish to have any sort of family relationship with me at all, you'll stay out of my love life,' Armando said, nodded and left.

CHAPTER TWENTY-NINE

D iana sat at her scent organ with its row upon row of tiny
fragrance bottles with their yellowing labels and gave a
deep sigh. Time was supposed to heal all wounds, but it hadn't
worked for her. She missed Armando more with every day that
passed.

She was tempted beyond what was bearable to call him and
just talk, but the idea also terrified her. She'd broken up with
him after she'd decided it was the right thing to do. Now she
wasn't so certain.

She'd spent days, ever since her phone call with her mother,
trying to work out how she could go back? After all, the
damage was done. Just as she could no longer look at Fernando
in the same way again, she wondered whether Armando could
overcome what she'd said, note or no note.

After all, she would have returned to Fernando in a
heartbeat if he'd walked back into the restaurant where she'd
been drowning her sorrow in expensive wine. But a couple
of weeks later, she'd pulled herself together and found she
felt completely indifferent about him. Partly that was because
of Armando, she realised. He'd arrived in her life as an
unwelcome and persistent distraction and changed everything.

Diana's phone buzzed a discreet alarm notifying her of her next appointment. It had taken quite some doing to set it up, especially as she had to juggle all the appointments coming into her website. She might not have become a millionaire out of Armando, but she no longer had to worry about paying her bills. In fact, her bank balance looked distinctly healthy these days.

Now she took a deep breath to fortify herself and headed to the front of the shop to wait. This was her biggest gamble. After today, she would know whether or not she had a future with Armando.

She'd made the appointment via a woman called Clarisse Alma. Going by the name, she imagined somebody middle-aged but glamorous. Although, she knew better than to guess what somebody looked like by their names. She was unlikely to ever find out. Right now, she didn't care because a black Mercedes had pulled up outside her shop. The driver hopped out to run around the car and open the passenger door.

Homero Zeller, tall, slim, and immaculate in a calf length black woollen coat and cravat-like silver grey scarf, stepped out and looked around. Diana opened her shop door and stepped outside, examining the man.

'Ms Luna,' he said, giving her a slight nod as he peered at her over the top of his mask.

'Mr Zeller?' Diana hoped the tremor in her voice didn't give away how terrified she was about this meeting. 'Thank you for coming.'

Homero Zeller nodded, looked past Diana to the shop, and then back at her. She'd taken extra care with her clothes, opting for something dark and formal. Her grandmother had always told her you needed to dress appropriately to do battle.

'I'm assuming you want to meet in your shop, which gives you the home advantage. Would you be willing to change to a neutral venue instead?'

At any other time Diana would have turned Homero Zeller down, but she needed to negotiate with this stubborn and powerful man, so she felt it best to agree to the compromise.

Then she wondered whether that was her first mistake. Maybe she shouldn't give in to him. Now he'd think she was a pushover.

All the same, she landed up saying, 'We can go to Lawrence's Hotel, it's nearby.'

'Alright,' Homero said and waved his hand as if to say, lead on.

Diana pulled her coat tighter about herself, casting a curious glance at Homero as she did. He didn't look as angry as the first time she'd met him, but he didn't look relaxed, either.

'This way.'

Diana locked her shop and walked along the narrow pavement to the deep yellow facade of a centuries old five-star hotel that was famous because the poet D. H. Lawrence had once made it his home. It didn't look like a particularly large building, but Diana knew that the three stories that were visible from the road were just the tip of a grand old building that descended several stories down the side of the mountain.

Diana led Homero through the entrance hall and downstairs to a landing that harboured a comfortable sitting room like nook. As with much of Sintra, the view outside was spectacular. In summer the terrace would have been ideal with its magnificent view.

But on a chilly day like today, the small space with the fire crackling in the grate was reassuringly cosy. Diana needed that for what she was about to do. She sank down into a red tartan armchair and left the larger solid red Chesterfield for the senior Zeller.

'Now, what can I do for you, Ms Luna?' Homero asked, looking her up and down.

Diana took her time coming up with an answer. She'd played this meeting out so many times in her mind. She'd tested so many opening lines. But now that the moment had arrived, she was floundering.

'I assume Armando told you I broke up with him?'

'He did,' Homero said, and then stopped as they were approached by a waiter. He was immaculately dressed in a white shirt and bowtie, with a black waistcoat.

They each ordered a coffee and Diana waited till the waiter had vanished downstairs again. 'I broke up for two reasons. The first was that I didn't want to come between Armando and his family. He was putting a brave face on things, but what you did hurt him.'

'He'll live,' Homero murmured, then waved a hand at Diana to continue.

'Of course he'll live.' The man's callousness annoyed Diana. 'I know how strong Armando is. My second reason was because of the feud between our families.'

'One I wasn't even aware of,' Homero said in a condescending tone that really did irritate Diana.

'And one you continue to deny.'

'If you are only going to rake up ancient history, then I see no point in this conversation,' Homero said and made to stand up.

'There's more. I don't know why I never realised it, but I was talking to my mother recently and she told me that your father and my grandmother were lovers. My grandmother was apparently more hurt by your grandfather's betrayal of their love, than because of the theft of Armour.'

'Ah,' Homero said, looking for the first time like she had got something right.

'Ah?'

'I had a rather painful conversation with Armando a couple of days ago. It prompted me to look into your allegation.'

Diana tried not to show it, but she was glad to hear that Armando had been talking to his father about her.

'You did? How could you look into it now?'

'I went to speak to a very old friend of my father's,' Homero said. 'She's nearly a hundred and in a nursing home, but still sharp as a tack. I thought if anyone could shed light on the relationship between my father and your grandmother, it would be her.'

'I see.'

Diana didn't want to do anything that stopped Homero from revealing what he knew. He looked like it was quite an effort to go through with the business as it was.

'It turns out that the two of them were quite fond of each other,' Homero said. 'But your grandmother came from a much poorer family and my father had already got engaged to another, wealthier woman. He wanted to break off the engagement but his family wouldn't allow it.'

Diana nodded. It sounded like an all too familiar family tale.

'My father's friend doesn't know how they landed up falling out, but my father left, taking the formula for Armour with him. He claimed it was his right because he played a part in developing it.'

'He would.'

'It might be true,' Homero said as a scowl descended.

'Have you spoken to Armando about it? I think he could show you how it's unlikely as a claim.'

'I don't need to. I'm a perfumer myself. I know the notes in Armour are nothing like the ones used by my father.'

'So why were you so against acknowledging the truth?' Diana said, astonished once again.

'I suppose, because I didn't want to.'

Diana nodded. Every family had a history with bits that they were proud of and other bits they wanted to hide from the world.

'It isn't exactly the same story as I was told, but it sounds similar enough.'

'And because of this your grandmother held a grudge against my family for all those decades even though, I assume, she got married.'

'My grandmother was a very proud woman. I can see how it would have hurt her for such a long time. Although, as you say, she got married eventually and had a happy life with my grandfather.'

'I see,' Homero said. 'But I still don't understand why you wanted to meet with me.'

'Because, if it isn't too late, I want to get back with Armando,' Diana said and her throat constricted in fright, but she pushed on. 'Armando left a note, telling me he'd wait for me. Before I can try to get him back, I need to remove the obstacle that got between us.'

'Me?' Homero said, but this time he didn't look as offended as Diana might have expected.

'I'm sorry, I should have phrased that more politely.'

'I'm a businessman. I prefer direct speaking. As it happens, I also had a reason I wanted to see you today. I came to give you this,' Homero said and placed a fat manilla envelope on the coffee table between them.

Diana feared it was some nasty cease and desist legal threat. This, after she'd tried to explain, felt like the cruelest possible rejection of her attempt to build bridges. So her fingers shook as she eased out the wedge of papers inside.

'Oh, it's the contract,' she said and flicked to the last page and the space for the signatures. Armando's name had been removed and Homero Zeller was typed in its stead.

'You've signed the contract. Why?'

Homero sat back on the sofa with a long, tired sigh. 'I'm being forced to give my wife twenty million euros as part of the divorce settlement.'

'So?' Diana said, because she couldn't see the point of that statement, although she was stunned by the enormous sum of money.

'It's considerably less than Armando offered you.'

'The two are in no way related. One is your private life, the other is strictly business.'

'When it comes to a family business, the boundaries often blur,' Homero said, then paused as the waiter reappeared and placed their coffees on the table. 'I have a feeling Armando wanted you to have some money so that you could enter the family as an equal.'

'I don't think so. I didn't even like him when he first proposed the contract.'

'You might not have liked him yet, but he most certainly already liked you. I've asked Eddy about it.'

'You asked Eddy?' Diana said as she leaned forward to pick up her little cup of coffee.

'I am afraid I don't know Armando very well. I thought I did, but this episode has opened my eyes. I was astonished to hear about him from Eddy. It was as though I was learning about an entirely different person. Armando keeps far more of his thoughts to himself than I realised.'

'But you have taken him back into the company, haven't you?'

Diana wondered how much stranger this conversation might get.

'I would like to, but Armando has yet to agree to come back.'

'What?' Diana said and her hand froze, cup halfway to her mouth.

'You didn't tell him I gave you an ultimatum, did you?'

'I didn't.'

'Why not?'

'Because I was sure he would tell me to ignore you. But I didn't want him to be cut off from his family and his job. I didn't want him to have that regret for the rest of his life.'

'To be human is to regret,' Homero sighed as he took a slow, meditative sip of his coffee and gazed into the fire. 'I have been regretting for a while now.'

'About getting between me and Armando?'

'About behaving like his boss rather than his father. I didn't realise I was doing it till Armando pointed it out.'

'And now? Why are you doing this?' Diana asked, pointing at the contract.

'I suppose I am making amends.'

'I don't really need it anymore.'

'But you want to go back to him?'

'I fear it might be too late,' Diana said and found herself praying it wasn't.

'Ha, I might not know Armando as well as I thought, but you're the first woman we've ever come to blows over. He also left me with the impression, the powerful impression, that he has every intention of getting you back.'

'Does he?' Diana was so overwhelmed by emotion to hear it she barely managed a whisper.

Homero gave a sideways noncommittal nod, then finished the last of his coffee with a gulp and put the cup back down on the table.

'Armando also told me in no uncertain terms never to get involved in his love life again. So I will leave now. I've delivered two copies of the signed contract. Do what you want with them.'

Diana hurried to her feet to make a farewell, but she was too late. Homero Zeller had gone, leaving her to pay the bill. She didn't begrudge him that. He'd given her so much more, including a chink of hope.

Diana sat at a small circular metal table in the Largo do Carmo, absorbing the pleasant winter sun that filtered through the fine spray of bare branched jacaranda trees that were dotted about. It was a remarkably warm day for late November. In fact, the large green digital thermometer of the chemist she'd passed on her way up the hill had proclaimed that it was 21 degrees. It meant that she was overdressed in her long-sleeved t-shirt and light cardigan.

Then a shiver ran through her as she wondered, for the hundredth time, what her meeting with Armando would be like. She'd finally screwed up the courage to message him and ask to meet. What she had to say needed to be said in person.

The message itself had been simple enough. Would he like to meet for coffee? She'd chosen the Largo do Carmo for three main reasons. The first was that it was neutral ground, thus giving neither of them the home advantage. Second, it was within walking distance of Armando's office, had he returned to work. She'd realised when setting up the meeting that she had no idea where he actually lived. The third reason depended on the outcome of their meeting.

Thankfully, Armando had messaged back within seconds that he'd be there. He'd not tried to change the venue, date or time, midmorning on a weekday. Diana chose to see that as encouraging.

Now she gazed across at the ruined remains of the Convento do Carmo, an ancient, medieval cathedral destroyed in the epic earthquake of 1755. They had left it in its ruined state as a monument to that terrible day.

A handful of tourists stood in a well-spaced queue, waiting to go in. In past years, there would have been far more of them. But Covid had cut that to a few brave souls who, judging by the languages being spoken, were Northern Europeans fleeing their harsher winter.

Behind her was an octagonal kiosk where a waiter hovered, ready to serve anybody occupying the tables in the square. He was woefully under occupied as, aside from Diana, there was only an elderly couple sitting at a distant table nursing a couple of espressos while they perused the daily papers, their small fluffy dog idly scratching himself at their feet. Diana wondered whether she'd ever reach that level of comfort. What was it like to have spent decades together in married life and be content to merely be in each other's company, sipping coffee.

That for no reason reminded her about Margarida, who'd been waiting outside Diana's shop as she was leaving.

'Good luck,' she'd said. 'I hope it goes well.'

'Me too.'

'I, um, this isn't the right time to tell you, but I invited Fernando over for coffee. I'm going to tell him to give up on you.'

'I hope you're going to tell him more than that.'

'I'll see how it goes,' Margarida said with an embarrassed smile.

Diana hoped it would turn out well. It had been a while since Margarida had seen anyone. A boyfriend would do her good.

She didn't even mind that it was Fernando. Now that she'd got over being dumped by him, and seen him a couple of times after that, she could even feel benevolent towards him over his future romantic prospects.

'Diana!'

The call shocked her out of her reflections, and she looked around. Armando was threading his way between the tables and chairs towards her. Diana lept to her feet, thrilled and terrified to see him again.

'Armando!'

There he stood, tall and handsome in his black suit. The face mask made it impossible to tell if he was happy to see her, though.

'How are you?' Armando said, tilting his head to examine her.

It was a neutral greeting and Diana still couldn't tell how things would go from there.

'I'm fine,' Diana said, and her face warmed with a blush. 'How are you? Do you want a coffee?' she added in an incoherent rush.

'I'm also fine, and yes, I do want a coffee.'

Armando settled on the chair opposite Diana before giving the waiter a nod. The man barely needed the invitation and hurried over to take their orders.

'Would you like a pastry?' Armando asked.

Diana could hardly face a coffee, but nodded and asked for a croissant. To her surprise, Armando did the same.

'Have you gone back to the House of Zeller?' Diana asked, more for something to say than any other reason. Maybe later she would care, but not yet.

'I haven't decided yet. Much to Eddy's annoyance. He told me he'll kill me if I keep him dangling much longer.'

'Poor Eddy,' Diana said, which got a cynical laugh from Armando.

'How is your work doing?'

'I'm busy. I had to move appointments around to be able to meet with you,' Diana said and regretted it because it meant that now she had to come to the point and she still didn't know how.

'Mmm,' Armando said neutrally.

That was no help at all.

'I... I really missed you.' It took all Diana's courage to say as much.

At this moment, the waiter arrived and placed their orders on the table, interposing his body between the two of them. It couldn't have been timed worse. But at least now that the food was there, Diana had a reason to pull down her mask and Armando did the same.

It felt to Diana, for a second, that Armando looked amused, then that brief expression vanished and he was back to looking neutral. Neither of them made a move towards their coffee. Diana couldn't take her eyes off Armando, waiting to see what he would say next.

He gave a slight smile and said, 'I missed you too.'

While it was reassuring, it didn't give Diana anything to work with. She supposed all she had left was to apologise and throw herself upon Armando's mercy.

'I'm really sorry I broke up with you. It was stupid, but I thought I was doing what was best for you. I've tried to get over you, but all I can do is think of you.' Everything tumbled out in a long, desperate attempt to be understood as tears soaked Diana's eyelashes. 'Can you forgive me?'

Armando reached across the table, took Diana's agitated hands and squeezed her fingers.

'You should have told me my father gave you an ultimatum.'

'I couldn't.'

'I thought you were fed up with me because of my sensitivity to smells, and being sick.'

Diana looked at him in surprise.

'No. I'm sorry if I gave you that impression. It wasn't that at all.'

'Well, I'm sorry about it, anyway. I should have said more and explained. I should have reassured you so that you weren't constantly on edge, cleaning everything in sight and avoiding me in the mornings till you'd brushed your teeth.'

'Oh dear, that does make me sound like I overreacted.' Diana was surprised that this was what Armando thought they'd broken up over. 'I didn't actually explain that day, did I? I just–'

Diana couldn't say more. She was filled with remorse that she'd got things so badly wrong.

Armando drew Diana's hands up to his lips and kissed them.

'You're an idiot, you know that? Adorable, but foolish.'

'I thought I was doing what was best.'

'Next time ask me first.'

'Will there be a next time?' Diana said, looking up hopefully.

'Well... not a breakup. I don't think I'd survive another one of those, but I would like to see more of you. Would you like to start over?'

'I would.' Relief welled up and filled Diana her with happiness. 'But not in the same way. Let's date in the traditional way.'

'The traditional way?' Armando said, giving Diana a quizzical look.

'You know, we meet up for dates and stay over at each other's and get to know each other without being flung together at work as well.'

'I rather enjoyed being flung together,' Armando said, giving Diana such a warm smile she tingled all the way down to her toes.

'So did I. But you have to admit, it was all a bit full on. Let's take our time from now on.'

'If that's what you want.'

Armando broke off the end of his croissant and shoved it into his mouth with a satisfied sigh.

'I needed this. I was so anxious about our meeting I couldn't face anything till now.'

'Me neither,' Diana said and suddenly her mouth was watering too. 'I should probably tell you, although I suppose you already know. I signed the contract your father gave me. I'll be a millionaire soon.'

Armando paused, coffee cup halfway to his lips.

'What contract?'

'The one we drew up for Armour. Didn't he tell you? I'm sorry, I assumed you knew.'

'That cunning so-and-so. He never said a word to me. When did he do that?'

'Last week,' Diana said, and told Armando all about her meeting with his father. 'I was terrified. But in the end, I felt like I got his blessing. Not that I needed it or anything.'

'Not that it's any business of his, anyway. But I suppose, in his own way, he was trying to set things right. I must say, I'm surprised he accepted that my grandfather stole the formula after all, but it does make life easier.'

Diana nodded. None of that mattered as long as she could be with Armando.

'What about Céu's perfume? What will you do with that? Will you let the House of Zeller produce it?'

'I couldn't let the development of that perfume flounder just because I was at a loss, and I didn't think Céu would be entirely happy to have Zeller produce the perfume after she'd fallen out with us, so I did a deal with Fiorino.'

'Really? Fiorino?'

'Luca unexpectedly did me a favour. He offered me a position I could use as leverage against my father. So I felt Fiorino deserved something good in return.

'Now that you and I are back together again, I'll return to the House of Zeller. My father has practically been begging me to do so. At that point, Zeller and Fiorino can work in partnership on that perfume like we did for Cinderella. I'd like to work more closely with Luca Fiorino in the future too.'

'It sounds like everything is falling into place.' Diana was awed that Armando had apparently been waiting to see what happened between the two of them before making a final decision about where his future lay. 'But aren't you making this decision too quickly now?'

'You know I always have a plan A and a plan B,' Armando said as he tore a strip off his croissant, crumpled it between his fingers and flicked it towards a trio of sparrows who had hopped up to the edge of their table and where watching hopefully. 'Plan A was to get back together with you and rejoin my company.'

'And Plan B?'

'Work with Fiorino and try to win you back over time.'

'Over time?' Diana said, her happiness growing to hear Armando had never considered walking away.

'I have learned that Luna women are stubborn and know how to hold a grudge. But, if you put in the effort, they will eventually listen and can sometimes be persuaded.'

'You may be right,' Diana said on a gurgle of laughter.

Armando grinned happily back at her, and the two of them just sat basking in the moment.

'So we're definitely back together then, are we?' Armando said.

'We are, and since that's the case, I have a suggestion.'

Diana put money down on the table to pay for their coffee and dragged Armando towards the Convento do Carmo. He not only allowed himself to be pulled along, he closed the gap and wrapped an arm tightly around Diana's waist. Diana led him through the entrance, paid for admission and stepped out into the extraordinary space.

A long narrow white stoned cathedral with a central nave and two side passageways divided off by towering columns greeted them. What made the place different was the lack of a roof. Diana threw her head back to gaze up at the blue sky dotted with a few puffy white clouds. Then they strolled along the central paved walkway with brilliant green grass to either side all the way to the end of the church and the ruined rose window that centuries before had been filled with stained glass.

'They rent this place out for events,' Diana said as she spun round to encompass the cathedral. 'Imagine this on a summer's night with the open roof and the stars twinkling above. Wouldn't it be perfect for the perfume launch?'

'It would,' Armando said as he drew Diana even closer to him till they were standing chest to chest, their arms linked about them. 'It's a great idea.'

'I'm glad you like it,' Diana said, so overwhelmed to be close to Armando again that even the grandeur of where they were standing paled into insignificance.

'Promise you'll never leave me again,' Armando said as he leaned down for a kiss, his lips brushing hers.

'I can't promise that,' Diana mumbled.

'Then promise you'll forewarn me so I can at least try to make amends before it's too late.'

'You must promise the same, then. I don't want a misunderstanding to ever come between us again.'

Armando wrapped his arms tightly about Diana, squeezing her with all his might and laughed.

'I promise.'

And then they kissed, out in the open at the front of the cathedral, two complex scents blending into a perfect whole.

Enjoyed this book? You can make a huge difference

If you are like me, you use reviews to decide whether you want to buy a book. So if you enjoyed the book please take a moment to let people know why. The review can be as short as you like.

Thank you very much!

Also By

Get all my books here:

MEDIEVAL HISTORICAL FICTION ePub, paperback and hardback

Fraternity of Brothers, *Life of Galen, Book 1* – Cast out for a crime committed against him, his future looks bleak. Until an unexpected visitor gives him hope for justice. A fight for acceptance, absolution and friendship in Anglo-Saxon England.

Comfort of Home, *Life of Galen, Book 2* – Proven innocent, he's returned from exile. Can he recover all that he lost? A tale of friendship and return to a family he thought he'd lost, set in Anglo-Saxon England.

Kindness of Strangers, *Life of Galen, Book 3* – Trapped in a land plagued by vikings, can one small miracle be all they need to survive? A tale of miracles, betrayal and friendship while under viking siege.

The King's Hall, *Life of Galen, Book 4* – As if being commissioned to create a book to turn back the Apocalypse isn't enough, intrigue and romance threaten to destroy everything he's come to rely upon. Friendship, love and intrigue at the court of King Aethelred the Unready.

Restless Sea, *Life of Galen, Book 5* – Just when they thought they could go home, they're thrust into an adventure at sea. A journey that tests the bonds of friendship.

Friend of My Enemy, *Life of Galen, Book 6* – Captured by an implacable enemy, their future looks bleak. Will escape even be possible?

Road to Rome, *Life of Galen, Book 7* — A journey across a turbulent continent. Will Galen find the answers he seeks?

Eternal City, *Life of Galen, Book 8* — Galen and Alcuin delve into the secrets of the corrupt and decaying city of Medieval Rome.

AUDIOBOOKS narrated by Jacob Daniels
Fraternity of Brothers, *Life of Galen, Book 1*
Comfort of Home, *Life of Galen, Book 2*
Kindness of Strangers, *Life of Galen, Book 3*
The King's Hall, *Life of Galen, Book 4*
   Restless Sea, *Life of Galen, Book 5*

HISTORICAL ROMANCE: ePub, paperback, hardback and audiobooks with AI narration
Sanctuary, *a sweet Medieval mystery* – He needs shelter. She wants a way out. Will his brave move to protect risk both their hearts? An optimistic tale of redemption with heart-warming characters and feel-good thrills.

The Duke's Heart, *a sweet Victorian romance* – His body may be weak, but his dreams know no bounds. Will she be the answer to his prayers? A disabled duke, a strong and determined woman and a slow-building relationship.

Duchess in Flight, *a swashbuckling romance* – She's on the run from a deadly enemy. He lives in the shadows of truth. When their lives merge, will their battle for survival lead to love? A reluctant hero, a woman and her children in distress, a chase to the death.

What the Pauper Did, *a body swap mystery romance* – How do you define yourself? Is it through your appearance, your memories or your soul? Intrigue, murder and romance in an alternate Lisbon of 1770.

CONTEMPORARY ROMANCE ePub, paperback, hardback and audiobooks with AI narration

Scent of Love – Can two polar opposite perfumers overcome their differences and create a unique blend all of their own? Love, intrigue and clashing values in the perfume houses of Lisbon.

Sky Therapy — A detective and the son of a serial killer. Is it safest to stay apart, or will they risk everything for love?

Terapia Celeste — My first novel (Sky Therapy) to be translated into Brazilian Portuguese.

SCIENCE FICTION/ FANTASY ePub and paperback

City of Night, *Eternal City, Book 1* – World-threatening danger, a female demonologist, an unwitting apprentice, a city in a single tower, a satisfying ending.

SHORT STORIES: ePub, paperback, and AI narration
Living, Loving, Longing, Lisbon, Vol 1 & Vol 2 – A collection of short stories inspired by the city of Lisbon, written by people from around the world who live in, visited or love Lisbon.
Loves of Lisbon – A Christmas advent calendar of 24 short, sweet romances of the intertwining lives of the residents of Lisbon.

FREEBIES: ePub and AI narration
Shorties – My shortest works: futuristic, contemporary and historical available for free when you sign up to my newsletter.

About Author

Marina Pacheco a binge writer of historical fiction, sweet romance, sci-fi and fantasy novels as well as short stories. She writes easy reading, feel-good novels that are perfect for a commute or to curl up with on a rainy day. She currently lives on the coast just outside Lisbon, after stints in London, Johannesburg, and Bangkok, which all sounds more glamorous than it actually was. Her ambition is to publish 100 books. This is taking considerably longer than she'd anticipated!

You can find out more about Marina Pacheco's work, and download several freebies, on her website: https://marinapacheco.me
Website: https://marinapacheco.me
    Sign up to Marina's newsletter via her website or on Substack to keep up to date on all her writing activities, get early previews of covers and first chapters, short stories and freebies.
Follow me on substack: https://substack.com/@marinapacheco
email: hi@marinapacheco.me

Acknowledgments

Although writing is a solitary exercise, it is enhanced by the support and enthusiasm of friends and family. I may not have got to this point without their encouragement. I owe special thanks to:

My writing friends and my beta readers, who sent back constructive suggestions, and my advance copy team for their early reviews and comments. All of you have taught me so much over the years.

My editor, Katharine D'Souza of Katherine D'Sousa Editorial Services for her thoughtful and kind feedback that significantly improves all my work. http://www.katharinedsouza.co.uk

My meticulous proofreader, Candida Burrows. Any errors that remain in the book are purely my fault. cb0880921@gmail.com

My cover designers, for their fantastic cover. www.100covers

All I can say is thank you, and let's do it all again!

www.ingramcontent.com/pod-product-compliance
Lightning Source LLC
Chambersburg PA
CBHW030933260626
47169CB00002B/463